# Glimpse of *Emerald*

*by*

## Rita M. Reali

Little Elm Press

Copyright 2017, Rita M. Reali.
Cover art by Zach Gagne. Cover by Al Esper Graphic Design.
Author photo by Diane Morey.





Like **Rita M. Reali, Author** on Facebook for news and information about upcoming events and future book releases. Join our Facebook group, **The Sheldon Family Saga**, to connect with other readers and the author.

Reali, Rita M.
Glimpse of Emerald

ISBN: 978-0-9966800-2-8

Printed in the U.S.A.
First American edition, October 2017

*Acknowledgments*

Many thanks to the myriad folks who have made this book possible:

To my dear husband, Frank, who endured countless solo nights (and now Saturday and Monday mornings) as I met with various writers' groups; to cousin Judy, who gamely listened to countless chapters in all stages of completion and offered immediate and valued feedback; and to my family and friends whose support sustained me through 40 years of obsession with Gary & Co....

To Zach Gagne, for his artistry in rendering the cover art I'd envisioned; and to Al Esper for his graphic-design wizardry in making the book cover a reality...

To the Fabulous Fictional Five writers' group, especially George Lillenstein, Connie Muther, Sarah Morin and Elizabeth Cardoso, who offered unwavering encouragement, copious laughter and support – and sometimes overly gleeful assistance in dispatching my "little darlings"...

To Kitty Schooley (whose talk on seeking permission to reprint song lyrics drew me to my first-ever Connecticut Authors & Publishers Association meeting); to my wonderful friend and CAPA shuffleboard partner Richard Moriarty; to the delightful Robin Veronesi for her feedback and encouragement; and to my other CAPA friends & former cohorts, whose support has made this wild ride worthwhile...

To fellow members of the Write Touch and Write Away writers groups, for their valuable input, insights and feedback...

To the Tennessee Mountain Writers, for a sense of belonging in my adopted home state; to the TMW contest judges, for having awarded an excerpt from *Glimpse of Emerald* third place in the Patricia Boatner Award for Fiction in 2016...

And last – but by no means least – to you, dear reader, for your interest in the story I've woven within these pages...

Thank you, thank you, one and all.

For Mrs. Delicious – so named by the librarians at the Thomas Jefferson Library in New Britain, Connecticut, for her perpetual enthusiastic response, "Oh, it was *delicious!*" when asked, "How was that book?" She always loved to "devour" a great story; and she proclaimed this one "absolutely delicious!"

She would phone me periodically while reading an early draft of *Glimpse of Emerald,* to say, "Aww… poor Gary!" and even once exclaimed, "What a *louse* that Gary is!" I knew if I could evoke that kind of reaction from her, I was definitely onto something.

The rest of the world knew "Mrs. Delicious" by many different names, including Mary, Sis, Miss Angelo, Mrs. Lazzaro, Auntie Mary and Grandma. But I knew her as the woman who fostered in me a love of reading… and writing. Thanks, Mom!

For my longtime friend, colleague, cohort and partner in literary crime, John "Jack" (a.k.a. The Feature Creature) Bohuslaw, who encouraged me in my writing, taught me that "violin" absolutely could be used as a verb… and challenged me to me to write the chapters in this book I simply **did not** want to write, but which enhanced the plot and made for a far better overall story. You were right – it made the resolution all the more satisfying!

And for my ol' pal Jim Buchanan – who likely will never quite realize how profoundly he touched my life the past forty years. Without your friendship and gentle presence in my world, Gary might never have emerged from the shadows of my imagination and come to life on these pages.

# Glimpse of *Emerald*

# Prologue

(2 September, 1980 – Tuesday)

The screen door banged. Joey bolted across the tinder-dry lawn. "Gary! Gary!"

"Hey, buddy! I missed you." Gary hugged his kid brother, then ruffled his hair. "What's goin' on?"

The dark-haired child chattered nonstop about everything Gary had missed these past two weeks: the theft of Tommy Wilton's bike; the Devlin twins' new puppy and – the biggest news of all – Katy Monroe cornering Johnny McNamara on the playground and *kissing* him!

Gary grabbed his bags from the trunk. Letting Joey take the lightest one, he made his way to the house. It wasn't dark yet, but the porch light was on. Mom always left it on if she was expecting you.

Diane Sheldon greeted her older son with a hug. "Welcome home, honey. Did you have a nice time?"

"The best!" He decided not to mention the wrong turn that got him lost in New York. "Thanks for letting me take your car. Way cooler than the train."

As he handed back her keys, Gary glanced toward the driveway; his smile decayed. His sister's car was gone. "Where's Marie?"

"Change of plans. She left Saturday."

His jaw tightened. Now he wouldn't see her until Thanksgiving.

"Let me guess: Dad had something to do with it. Sonofabitch," he muttered.

"Language," Diane reminded her son wearily, patting his cheek.

"Sorry."

"Ellen wanted you to call when you got in," she called after him as he went in.

(3 September – Wednesday)

Jeremy grumbled at the TV. "Idiot president… interest rates skyrocketing… unemployment through the roof. Damn country's going to hell!" His ire fueled by a tough loss in the courtroom, he downed his scotch, slammed the empty glass on the table and retreated into his evening newspaper.

Joey had moped practically the whole time his brother was away. And now Gary was spending his last night of vacation with Ellen. Helping Mom serve dinner, Joey acted out, making vomit sounds while plopping mashed potatoes beside the sliced roast beef on his parents' plates.

"Quit making those disgusting noises," Jeremy barked.

Joey obeyed; but before long, he was making walrus tusks out of his string beans.

"Joey… eat," Mom implored, casting an anxious glance at her husband.

The 8-year-old chewed and swallowed his tusks.

"Would you pass me the potatoes, please?"

"Sure, Mom." Eyes agleam, Joey scooped up a glob of potatoes from the bowl and mimed launching them at her. "One helping of mashed potatoes, coming up."

Jeremy glared. "Cut it out!"

The youngster's expression sobered; he hurriedly passed the bowl and resumed eating. When Dad wasn't looking, Joey flicked a pea off his salad plate. The green missile sailed across the table and landed with a little *bloop!* – in Dad's water glass.

Jeremy's fist struck the table. "Joseph Edward!"

Diane's skin prickled. Avoiding her husband's glare, she gestured discreetly for her son to settle down.

Joey shoved a forkful of potatoes into his mouth; they sputtered out amid a burst of nervous laughter.

"Alright, that's *enough*!" Grabbing his son by the shirt, Jeremy brandished a steak knife. "I swear to God, if you don't stop it this instant, I'll—"

Joey burst into tears. Struggling free, he fled the room, screaming.

Diane bolted after her son. She found Joey in Gary's room. She wished again she'd insisted her older son stay home tonight. He'd have grumbled, but he would have obeyed. He *always* obeyed her. Now it was too late; the damage was done – and she didn't know how to repair it. If she even *could*.

Joey lay facedown on Gary's bed, sobbing. Diane sat next to him, tried to act calm. "I'm so sorry he did that to you, honey." Her hands shook as she gathered Joey into her arms. She glanced at the Talking Heads poster on her son's wall. "And I swear: It won't happen again." *Not if I have anything to say about it.*

Over the years, she'd dismissed Jeremy's temper as a result of his stressful job. Or the alcohol he was consuming in more alarming amounts lately. She couldn't continue living in terror. Not when he'd threatened their son. It had to stop. Somehow.

Next morning, she awakened with her answer. It came to her in a dream — as clear as day — a dream of Edward's smiling face. He had always said that she need look no further than him for help. In anything.

As soon as Jeremy left and the boys were off to school, Diane got on the parkway and headed north.


Edward masked astonishment with delight. "Diane! How wonderful to see you!" His welcoming tone turned to alarm as Diane dissolved into sobs. "Sweetheart, what's wrong?"

Hunched on the couch, she clutched her arms around her knees; tears landed in little dark splotches on her jeans. He sat beside her, draping an arm around her shoulders. Producing a handkerchief, he dabbed at her eyes. When she glanced up, Edward marveled at the uncanny resemblance between Diane and Gary. They had the same dark hair, the same fine features, the same expressive grey eyes.

At first, she could do little more than cry. Then she explained why she needed his help.

With a few phone calls, Edward secured a nice rental home in North Madison, enrolled Joey at Our Lady of Mercy School and got her an interview at a major New Haven architecture firm he'd frequently dealt with during his career.

"And what about Gary?" her father-in-law asked, his face gentle, his eyes warm.

Her heart lurched. "I don't *know*. I want to take him with me — I know I *should*; but there's so much I have to consider: school; work; friends. Besides, a teenage boy… he needs his father."

"No boy needs a father that badly," Edward insisted, frowning.

"I can't rip him away from everything familiar. Not now. He's a junior; and St. Joe's is a top school. If he keeps his grades up, every college in America will want him. Then there's Ellen." She smiled. "She's been so good for Gary. If I tear him away from her, he'll be miserable and hate me…"

"And if you leave him there, you'll hate yourself," he interjected softly, patting her hand. "I see your dilemma. Not to mention how he'll feel toward you then."

She swiped at her eyes. "I *know*. But, I think I can deal with Gary being mad at me, at least for a while. Just 'til I can sort things out and explain it to him."

"Tell you what: If things get rough for Gary and he wants out, I'll get him out of there. Okay?"

Diane remained silent a long time. She nodded; then her face seemed to crumple as her determination shattered. "How can I just leave my son?" she shrilled. "Jeremy threatened Joey's life. How can I believe he won't do the same – or worse – to Gary?"

Edward prayed he wasn't leaving his grandson more vulnerable. But right now he had to ensure Diane and Joey's safety. "Gary's a bright boy; he'll stay out of his dad's way. Plus, I've warned Jeremy enough times what would happen if he hurt those kids. Believe me, Diane: I know what drives my son. He's far too concerned about being cut out of my will to try something that stupid."

"But how can you be sure? You can't be there to keep an eye on him" – her voice cracked – "that's my job. And I'm failing at it!"

"You're not failing. You're doing the best you can in a horrible situation – for you and your children."

She crumbled into his arms. "I can't keep my marriage together, can't keep my family intact and – look at me! I can't even control my emotions!"

Edward held Diane close, quieted her. "If you want, I'll speak to Gary. So he knows the truth."

Fear filled her eyes. "No!" The word was a small explosion. "I don't want him to know yet. I'll explain everything when the time's right. I *can't* let him see Jeremy as the bad guy. Not at his age."

"You'd rather Gary believe you abandoned him than know the truth? So he'll hate you both? And maybe even become an abusive husband himself?" Edward had never disagreed more strongly with his daughter-in-law; but it was her family, her decision. He wouldn't defy her wishes. No matter how much it pained him.

Diane arrived home in time to meet Joey's bus. Gary had left a message reminding her he'd be working at the radio station after school today. That night, she made a point of spending extra time with Gary, knowing it would be her last chance… for a while. She reconsidered taking him. She also contemplated telling him she was leaving – and why.

Diane's heart broke as she hugged her older son and told him she loved him one last time, as he left for school Friday morning. She hoped he didn't notice her agitation.

"Love you, too, shorty." Gary gave her a pat on the head; he'd been doing that lately, ever since he'd grown taller than his mother.

Then, with a slanted grin and a wave, he grabbed his books and was off.

She watched Gary climb into his car and drive away. "Goodbye, sweetheart," she whispered to the empty kitchen. "I love you." She hoped he'd remember that.

Edward arrived at 10 and helped her load their belongings into the rental truck he'd driven to their New Jersey home. He'd seen to everything, even the new registration for her car.

Last of all, Diane wrote Gary the note she had agonized over. She wanted to say more, but she couldn't risk Jeremy coming home early and finding it first.

As soon as Joey got off the bus, Diane herded the youngster into her car with its shiny blue-and-white Connecticut plates and left for their new life, with Edward following in the truck.

# *Chapter 1*

(16 April, 1982 – Friday)

When Ellen's pregnancy became evident, the headmaster called her to his office. Equally responsible, Gary went with her. Msgr. Ernst Streng, the silver-haired headmaster with atrophied smile muscles, was big on procedure. An expulsion hearing was set for Monday.

Mornings at the venerable St. Joseph Academy always started with Mass. Gary had been scheduled as one of Fr. Maynard's two altar servers on Monday; now, he wouldn't be permitted to serve.

Fr. Justin Maynard had been named dean of students at the start of Gary's sophomore year; the two enjoyed a comfortable rapport, and talked often; and in the spring of 1980, the priest agreed to be Gary's confirmation sponsor.

Third period on Monday, Msgr. Streng sent a messenger to the senior English classroom, to summon the doomed duo.

Upon seeing his dad in the headmaster's office, Gary's heart lurched. It seeped into his toes as he noticed the young Franciscan priest sitting, crushed and dispirited, at the far end of the room.

Ellen slumped into a seat opposite Msgr. Streng's imposing oak desk, smoothing her uniform skirt over her knees. Her shoulders drooped.

Gary sat beside his girlfriend in the stuffy office. Before Friday, he'd only been in here once: at his pre-admittance interview. Trying to retain a calm façade, he took a deep breath and stole a glance at Ellen. She didn't look back. He tried to take her hand; she yanked it away. Meanwhile, the adults glared. Mostly they glared at him; the looks they reserved for Ellen were more pitying than judgmental.

For Gary, the worst part of the closed-door conference was what he saw in the eyes of the people he loved most. Ellen's folks had always been so kind – more like a family to him than his own. Now their eyes looked so sad, so disappointed. So betrayed.

Ellen, when she dared raise her tear-filled eyes, looked ashamed. She wept into a crumpled tissue during much of the embarrassing ordeal; the rest of the time she sat quietly, with her hands folded in her plaid lap.

Fr. Maynard's expression was the worst. He just looked… well – *wounded.* There was no other word to describe it. Gary couldn't bear that he'd let them all down.

Oh, how quietly Jeremy Sheldon sat! But Gary knew his father was churning with rage. The prominent Manhattan defense attorney sat straight backed and silent during the meeting; only his harsh expression belied his calm exterior. He said nothing to contest the decision; nor did he try to persuade Msgr. Streng to relent.

When the headmaster said Gary was being expelled for "gross moral indiscretion and blatant disregard for the rules of this institution," Jeremy's only response was a gruff, "I see."

The Farricellis pleaded on both teens' behalf: "Let them finish the year; it's only six more weeks," they reasoned. "Surely you can make an exception…"

Fr. Maynard's quiet plea was impassioned. "Monsignor Streng, these are kids who've made a mistake – a big one – but a mistake nonetheless. I've known Gary and Ellen three years; they're good kids. Misguided, yes, but essentially good kids. I can personally vouch for that. To expel them just before graduation" – shaking his head – "would simply be unproductive. Please, Monsignor. *Please* reconsider."

"They know the rules," the headmaster droned in his thick European accent. A deep frown creased his face, drawing his entire countenance sharply downward. "They broke the rules. They will accept the consequences."

As his dad's black Mercedes wended its way off the grounds of St. Joseph Academy for the last time, Gary gazed back at the stately stone structure. In his mind, his future crumbled. Without a high-school diploma, he couldn't even get into community college. And anyway, now he had a family to support. He'd get a full-time job and an apartment. And he and Ellen would get married, naturally.

The 12-minute ride home might as well have taken 40 years. Impenetrable silence rose between father and son. Staring out the window, Gary tried not to dwell on his imminent doom.

As soon as the garage door grumbled shut, Jeremy turned to his son. "Look at me!"

Gary obeyed, terrified by the fury in his father's cold blue eyes.

"You're a disgrace! I have *never* been more embarrassed in all my life."

The teen started to hang his head and got a resounding smack.

"I said, *Look at me!*" Jeremy thundered.

His cheek stinging, Gary obeyed his father's repeated command.

"You get in that house – right now – and you wait!"

Gary slunk inside to await what would surely be his most monumental beating ever. Jaw clenched in defiance, he refused to let Dad see him cry. Once, he'd cried during a beating. Years ago. Just after his thirteenth birthday.

Jeremy abhorred tears, especially from his teenage son.

"Damn crybaby," he'd jeered, hitting all the harder once he heard Gary crying. "You wanna cry, wussy boy? I'll give you something to cry about. You lousy little wimp!"

*Never again*, he'd vowed, steeling himself against the punishment, which seemed to go on and on. All because he and Teddy Faticoni tried to make 5-year-old Joey eat a worm.

"It's your damn mother's fault," Dad criticized. "She coddles you too much. No wonder you're such a fucking sissy! Get outta my sight! Cry somewhere else!"

Gary never again let Dad see him cry; not even during his worst whippings. It took all his strength, because they were always brutal. But that seemed to take Jeremy's sinister delight out of punishing his son. So, for a while, the beatings tapered off. Until Mom left.

Traditionally, Dad's discipline had been meted out with a belt. Against bare skin. Lately, however, fists had become his weapon of choice. Stalking to the bar, Jeremy downed a scotch, then poured another. He yanked Gary to his feet by his tie and shook him fiercely. He unleashed a scathing tirade about his son's "shameful" behavior disgracing the family and ruining the Sheldon name.

Dad emphasized his anger with a clenched fist. "Do you have any idea how it felt to get this call? *Mr. Sheldon, I need you to come in. No, I'm sorry. It can't wait. It's an urgent matter of utmost importance, one that concerns your son's future at St. Joseph Academy.*" Jeremy mimicked with alarming precision the starched tone of the headmaster's "official business" voice – the one that indicated a student was in big trouble. Shoving Gary onto the couch, he leaned forward until they were eye to eye, their faces inches apart. The voice was his own again, as fearsome as his deep scowl. "Then to learn *why* I was called in? You've done some stupid things before, but I've *never* been more ashamed of you!" His fist shot out again.

Gary swore he felt his teeth rattle; he winced.

Dad accompanied his tirade with more punches. Riled by his son's silence, Dad grabbed Gary again and flung him against the wall. Then came a right hook. "You better pray they don't file statutory-rape charges," he boiled as the teen held a hand to his cut lip. "And don't think I'd defend you."

Straightening his tie, Dad reached for the jacket from his $800 suit, folded on the couch. "Expelled for getting a girl pregnant. Just fucking beautiful! Why couldn't you use a fucking condom!"

Finishing his scotch, Jeremy banged the glass on the coffee table. He glared at his watch, then at his son. "You cost me half a day's work! I've got a case going to trial this week and I don't have time to waste on *you*!" He stalked out and slammed the front door.

Gary sat on the couch, willing his breathing to return to normal. It wasn't so bad, as beatings went. There was far less blood than he'd expected; and Dad never even reached to take off his belt. Shaking, he headed up to the bathroom to assess the damage. His lip would stop bleeding soon enough, and that swelling on his jaw would go down eventually; but, man, he'd have a hell of a shiner!

On Thursday, Gary summoned his courage and went to see the ever-compassionate Fr. Maynard. He felt awkward, coming here. It felt like trespassing. Seconds dragged by as he waited.

Finally, the soft-spoken Franciscan priest welcomed the teenager into his office.

"Father, I'm so sorry!" Gary blurted as the door clicked shut. He hadn't intended this to be a confession, but guilt weighed heavy on him. Anguished and ashamed, he explained how alone he felt since his family's disintegration, and how he had turned to Ellen for consolation and belonging in a time of tremendous despair. Gary's voice wavered as he offered the priest tiny glimpses into his world, both before and since the erosion of his family life.

***

Gary had met Ellen the first day of sophomore year. Assigned as biology lab partners, they became fast friends whose laughter rang through the halls of the venerable institution. Before long, it was as common for them to be at each other's home as their own.

9

They were in the kitchen one frosty February afternoon when Gary's mom returned from work. The aroma of beef and herbs caught Diane's nostrils even before she opened the door. The kitchen was warm, the windows fogged. Gary was chopping vegetables; Ellen stood at the stove, tending something that bubbled and smelled wonderful. "Hi Mom," both teens greeted her.

Diane smiled, gave them each a kiss. "Hi." She slipped one arm around her son, the other around Ellen. "What's for dinner?"

"Beef stew in burgundy sauce," the girl replied.

"Over noodles," Gary finished.

"Mmm, smells great. Thanks, you two." She kicked off her boots as she leafed through the mail. "Gary, have you seen your brother?"

"Yeah; he's out back, with Timmy."

"I'm ready for those veggies now."

Gary brought Ellen the bowl of carrots, celery and parsnips. Before emptying the contents into the stew pot, she laid a hand against his cheek and kissed him. He put an arm around her waist and kissed back; his hand slid downward, caressing Ellen's behind.

Looking up from the phone bill, Diane cleared her throat loudly. "Will Dad be home for supper?"

Gary moved his hand away. "I dunno. He called, said he might hafta work late."

Diane frowned. Jeremy was hardly ever home for supper lately; she'd begun to suspect he was seeing someone. Again. "Alright. Ellen, does your mom know you're eating here?"

"I don't think so."

"Better give her a call, then."

Ellen returned a minute later, grinning. "She said she figured as much when she didn't see Gary's car in our driveway."


Christina and Robert Farricelli were delighted their shy eldest daughter had met a nice boy at St. Joe's; the boys at Ellen's public high school in Cleveland last year were uncouth and horrid. The first time Gary went home with her to work on a school project, they were impressed by how polite he was; none of their kids' other friends helped with the dishes or called them sir or ma'am.

Ellen adored Gary's family. His sister, Marie, a sophomore at Siena College, treated her like an equal, not some silly girl mooning over her brother. And Joey's teasing reminded her of Tommy, her own kid brother. But as much as she loved being around them, Ellen dreaded mealtimes with Gary's dad. At home, dinner was a forum for lighthearted discussions and lively chatter. Even with outright silliness. But Mr. Sheldon presided over dinnertime with a fearsome silence no one dared challenge.

Ellen went to all of Gary's basketball games. So did Diane and Joey. But his father deemed it foolishness. Undaunted, the trio sat together in the stands and cheered wildly. When Marie was home, she joined them.

Always close, Gary and his mother could talk about practically anything. He'd even confide some of his deepest feelings about this girl who'd so quickly stolen his heart.

The first time he and Ellen fought, Gary came home well before his 10:30 curfew. Finding Mom in the living room, paging through a magazine, he slumped onto the couch. "You're a girl, right?"

"Last I checked." She slipped an arm around his shoulder.

"Well then, answer me something," he moped. "What *is* it with women?"

Mom stroked his hair. "We're a strange breed, honey. Don't try to understand us. You'll just end up driving yourself mad."

Gary grinned in spite of himself.

"Why do you ask?" she inquired.

He told her about the fight. It was over something stupid – and he said as much. She listened intently, offering suggestions and badly needed insight into the female psyche.

The more they talked, the more questions surfaced.

Mom patted his knee. "Hold that thought, honey. This calls for ice cream."

She padded into the kitchen, son in tow, and unearthed the Rocky Road. This wouldn't be any run-of-the-mill chat over dishes of vanilla. This called for "misery sundaes." Three scoops each. Hot fudge. Whipped cream. Nuts. And a cherry. Sitting at the center island, mother and son dug in.

When Jeremy wandered in late, two pairs of solemn grey eyes watched in wary silence as he stalked through the kitchen. When he was gone, they resumed their conversation.

At last, Gary dropped his spoon into his empty bowl, leaned his elbows against the counter. "I dunno what to *do*," he lamented, resting his chin on his hands.

"Well, you tell her this fighting's gotta stop; I refuse to have permanent circles under my eyes from playing 'Dear Abby' all night." Mom gave him an affectionate one-arm hug.

He hugged back. "I'll tell her. Can't promise anything, though." Gary smiled, grateful for her way of always knowing how to make him feel better.

She glanced at the clock. "C'mon, kiddo, it's after one. Better get some sleep; morning's gonna come mighty early."

Giving him a kiss, she herded her son off to bed.

It took a few days, but the young couple eventually ironed out their differences. Gary apologized for being an insensitive clod – and Ellen agreed he'd been one.

Gary and Ellen were classic high-school sweethearts: When he wasn't at work in the production department at the local rock radio station, they were together. And life was pretty good.

It was the start of junior year when life as he knew it fell to pieces around him.

# Chapter 2

(5 September, 1980 – Friday)

"Well…" A breathy voice drifted from the open door of the production studio. "I don't think we should rush into this all willy-nilly. We should run through it again before going to tape."

Paul Ramsey poked his head in the open doorway. "Lemme guess – Richard Nixon!"

Gary groaned. "Did that sound like a crook to you?" Reagan asked. Next instant, he was the disgraced ex-president. "I tell you, Paul: I am *not* a crook; and I don't know what these bits of tape are doing here. Looks like eighteen minutes' worth. But I don't know anything about that. Honest. I am *not* a liar. I mean, I am *not* a crook. Oh, hell, I'm not *either* of those things!"

The program director laughed. "You're really something, Gary. You've got a real gift there. With talent like yours, you'll be going places. And I mean soon!"

Suddenly the young production assistant was Glinda the Good Witch. "You've always had the power to go any place you want. Talent or no talent. Just click your heels and repeat after me: *There's no place like home – and this is no place like it.*"

Paul's distinctive belly laugh carried through the station. Gary could mimic practically any voice, accent or inflection. Particularly adept at celebrity impersonations, he frequently got pressed into service taping comedy bits as the mayor. Even President Carter. His improvisational tangents left his co-workers stifling snickers – or bursting outright into laughter.

"You're another Rich Little," Dave Stanton marveled, after Gary pulled off a perfect impression of Reagan debating foreign policy with Jimmy Carter.

Gary's lopsided grin told the morning guy he knew exactly what the compliment had meant. "Yeah? Rich little what?"

He always seemed happiest around those who made him laugh; it gratified him to make *them* laugh. It was a major achievement, cracking up the funniest people he knew. And he'd done *that* plenty today!

Gary sang along with a Tom Petty song as he drove home. The school year started off well; classes were interesting, things were great with Ellen… and Paul asked him to fill in on air, week after next, for the nighttime jock. It'd conflict with basketball practice, but he'd work that out with the coach.

Gary's green '72 Nova chugged to a stop out front.

Dad despised oil spots on the driveway; he didn't tolerate what he called "vehicular neglect."

Gary recalled Dad's fury when Marie ran out of gas last summer: "If you can't take care of a car, you don't deserve to have one!" He lectured her about letting it get below half full, then demanded her keys. He sold the car the next day. Marie had to dip into her college savings to replace it.

Gary couldn't afford to let that happen. He made a mental note to get the car serviced that weekend. The house was empty, which wasn't so unusual. What *was* odd was a folded sheet of notebook paper on his bed. He picked it up and opened it.

> *Dear Gary,*
> *I wish we could have been here to tell you in person, but we just couldn't stay any longer. Joey and I had to leave. Can't explain now. I'm sorry, sweetheart. I love you.*
> *Mom*

Gary puzzled over the note. *Had to leave?* He wondered where they'd gone, when they'd be home. *Am I s'posed to start supper?* He stuffed the paper into his jeans pocket.

In the fridge, he found beef and red and green peppers. Two onions sat on the counter. Grabbing a knife and a cutting board, he made quick work of the veggies and sliced the beef into strips for a stir-fry. As he worked, another question nagged at Gary: *Why would she leave a note in my room — why not put it on the message board in here?* For a sickening moment, it occurred to him she might not be coming back. Dismissing the thought, he put a pot of rice on to cook. Then he called Ellen.

Twenty minutes later, Ellen came in the back door. "Where *is* everyone?"

Gary shrugged. "Out." He pulled out the note. "Here."

Ellen blanched. "Oh, Gary! You don't think— She wouldn'ta *left*… would she?"

"No!" Snatching the note back, he jammed it back in his pocket. "She probably had to run out for something and didn't wanna leave Joey alone. Or he coulda fallen off his bike and gotten hurt – and she took him to the hospital and didn't want me to worry…" He shrugged. "I dunno."

They played cribbage to pass the time. It was nearly 8 when they decided to eat. They played while eating – something Dad never would have allowed.

Ellen stayed later than either of them intended.

At 11, when the phone rang, Gary leapt for it. A dozen maybes sped through his head. "Hello?" he fairly shouted.

"Gary, honey, is Ellen still there?"

His hopes plummeted. "Yeah." He held a hand over the mouth-piece. "It's your mom."

After Ellen left, Gary stayed up as late as he could. Slumped on the couch, he watched TV until he couldn't keep his eyes open. It was after 3. Dad wasn't home, but he often worked late on Fridays; sometimes, he even slept on the couch in his office. At least, that's what he said.

Gary left the front-porch light on. Mom did that when anyone was out… said she didn't want her family coming home to a dark house. He knew she wanted them to feel secure in knowing some-one expected them. Gary always felt the warmth of her love when he saw the light's soft welcoming glow.

He woke after noon. The house was too quiet. By now, Mom would be doing laundry or putting away groceries; and Joey would be making noise somewhere. That kid couldn't even tie his shoes quietly! Today, he'd have given anything to hear Joey making noise. The house felt disturbingly silent.

Gary reached for his Rubik's Cube. It usually sat on his dresser, but he had let Joey borrow it while he was away. It was probably still in his room. Intending to retrieve it, he opened Joey's bedroom door.

His gasp echoed in the empty room. His heart clattering crazily, Gary ran to his parents' room. He yanked open the closet. Mom's side was empty. Everything from her dresser was gone – even the family photos. He staggered backward. *They're __not__ coming back.*

All weekend, whenever the phone rang, Gary jumped at it, only to be disappointed by a telemarketer, one of the partners in Dad's firm, or even Ellen; a pang of annoyance struck him when he heard her voice. He added guilt to his heaped-up pile of out-of-control feelings.

Dad finally came home, plastered, late Sunday. Out of some crazy sense of duty, Gary fetched a glass of water and two aspirin, then put him to bed.

Still hopeful, Gary left the porch light on.

Tuesday afternoon, he pulled the note from his dresser drawer. Uncrumpling it, he read it again. No explanation. Just three lousy, stinking lines. His hand shook with fear and rage as he stared at it.

*She took Joey, not you.* He wasn't home when they left; was it as simple as that? Or *was* it that she didn't love him? Darkness crept into his heart as he truly began to suspect the latter. That nagging doubt tore at him endlessly.

He paced. Her leaving went against everything he'd ever known to be true; he *knew* Mom loved him. She'd always told her kids she loved them, and reinforced it with frequent hugs and her own brand of affection. Like their long talks. Or notes tucked into lunch bags with smiley faces in the O of *Mom*. Or even homemade hot chocolate with mini marshmallows on winter afternoons.

A wrenching feeling began in his stomach: What if it *was* all a lie? That possibility hurt too much to consider. Pushing the thought aside, he tried to swallow the golf ball in his throat that was making it hard to breathe.

In an attempt to retain some semblance of normalcy, Gary went downstairs to clean the kitchen. He wiped down all the countertops and the stove. Then he emptied the dishwasher.

He picked up a glass and, with an incensed bellow, hurled it as hard as he could. It smashed into the far wall. Seething, he stared at the spot where it struck. Inexplicably, he felt better; at the same time, his rage flared. He hefted another glass; it met a similar fate, against the cabinet along the side wall. The teen reached into the top rack for another. As a third glass crashed against the range hood, Gary accepted his sickening reality: *Mom doesn't love me; she isn't coming back.*

Smash! Smash! Smash! went three juice glasses in quick succession on the floor at his feet. All the love he'd ever felt, anything he recalled as remotely good about Mom, he knew had been wrong. Those late-night talks, the hugs, the laughter, every holiday and family vacation. All a sham. It didn't mean a thing. And *that* hurt more than her leaving! Rage, pain and longing surged within Gary; with the next thrown glass, his frenzy of unintelligible screams had formed words: "Why did you leave me? Why did you leave me?"

Before long, all the glassware from the dishwasher lay shattered and strewn across the kitchen floor, as did half the dishes. Amid the ruins, the 16-year-old crumpled against the island, pounding it with an ineffectual fist. "Why did you leave me?" he sobbed.

The back door opened. Dad. Unexpectedly early. "What the hell do you think you're doing?!"

Gary turned; in an instant, terror replaced fury in his eyes. In that same instant, Dad tore off his belt and pinned Gary against the island countertop. When the teen struggled, Dad slammed him up against the refrigerator. Then he shoved Gary to the floor, amid the broken glass, and thrashed him with the belt.

Sharp fragments ground into Gary's palms and crunched against his denim-clad knees.

It was a long time before Dad put his belt back on and stalked away, leaving Gary in a gasping heap. "Now clean up this mess!" he ordered.

Too afraid of what would happen to him if he disobeyed, Gary gingerly pulled himself off the floor to clear away all traces of the destruction he'd just been beaten for. His hands reminded him of ground beef, all raw and bloody; and he couldn't stop them from shaking. After picking out all the glass shards, he rinsed his hands under cool water. The pain nauseated him. It was several minutes before the queasiness passed.

Hands wrapped in paper towels to stanch the blood flow, he got out the broom and dustpan and set to work. There was lots of bending and stooping; it hurt like hell to move! It even hurt *not* to move. Just breathing hurt! It took Gary almost an hour to sweep; longer still to clean up the blood. And he still had homework to finish.

*I hate him, I hate him, I hate him,* ran like a mantra through his head as he stared at chemistry equations. It wasn't quite true: Gary hated what Dad had *become.* As kids, he and Marie would run to greet Daddy as he returned from work. They'd clamber onto his back for piggyback rides. It was a nightly ritual: through the kitchen first, for hugs and goodnight kisses from Mommy; then once around the living room and up to their bedrooms. Then toothbrushing, pajamas and prayers. After bedtime stories, Daddy would tuck them in, kiss them goodnight and turn out the lights. Gary loved that ritual. And he loved his father. There was always laughter in those days. Laughter and singing, nursery rhymes and make-believe. And fun. There'd been plenty of fun.

Gary didn't know what had happened to change everything, but it seemed Dad was always angry now. He tried to think back. How old had he been when the anger began overshadowing the love?

Pondering this, he realized the anger had always been there; it just didn't surface as often. But when it did, look out! It didn't take much to spark Dad's rage. It could be something as simple as his kids chattering a bit too loudly during the evening news. And when they'd been naughty, there was a vastly different ritual. Instead of piggyback rides, laughter and kisses goodnight, there'd be harsh punishments, yelling and tears. Much like what had just happened.

Gary shuddered. He recalled Mom's persistent pleas for leniency on their behalf. *Please, Jer, don't be so hard on them. They're only kids!*

Dad's reply still rang in his memory. *They won't always be children,* he'd snarl back. *And I will __not__ have them growing up to be criminals! So they'd better learn to behave properly.*

Gary never understood that: How would fighting with Marie during the TV news turn him into a criminal? Nevertheless, those words always chilled him. Or maybe it was the way Dad wielded that belt.

His bandaged palms throbbed. He forced himself to concentrate on chemistry instead of the pain accompanying every breath.

Gary stayed home Wednesday; he limped badly and his eye throbbed.

After Dad left, he phoned his granddad. "Mom's gone; she took Joey and left."

"Gone?" Grandpa echoed.

Gary explained about the note. He also confided about the beating. He'd never complained about his father's disciplinary tactics before. But this was different.

"Tell me the truth, Gary: Are you alright?"

"I'm fine," Gary assured him, rubbing his swollen ankle. "*Really.* Don't worry about me."

"I *do* worry about you, Gary. I love you. If you need help, I'll get you out of there."

Next morning, at school, Gary's excuse about tripping down the cellar stairs accounted for the limping and the bruises – although not necessarily the swollen eye and the cuts on his hands. During third period, Fr. Maynard called Gary in to his office. Had he really tripped? he asked gently. Did he want to talk?

As respectfully as he could, Gary told the priest to mind his own business, rose gingerly and limped back to study hall. Ashamed to admit what Dad had done, he also steered clear of Ellen. He didn't need her asking questions; it was bad enough the way she looked at him.

Ellen had witnessed one of Mr. Sheldon's eruptions last year; that time, Joey paid the price for his father's fury. Wishing away her headache, Ellen returned her attention to algebra. She finally caught Gary's eye Friday during French class. His bruised face looked less puffy; but his expression was sadder than any she'd ever seen. She knew he wouldn't reach out to her, but perhaps there *was* a way to help.

"There's a kid at school I think is being abused at home," Ellen told her dad after dinner. She danced around pronouns; at the end, she slipped. "I don't wanna butt in, but I don't want him—" she shook her head, realizing her mistake too late – "I mean, *this kid* getting hit. What can I do?"

"Is he" – Robert Farricelli watched his eldest daughter's eyes for a flicker of denial – "someone you could talk to?"

She bit her lower lip and wrinkled her nose. "Not about this."

"I see," he mused. "How *would* you like to help him?"

"Well, it wouldn't be easy, and we – I mean, um…" Ellen glanced at her hands twisting in her lap. Looking up, she blurted, "Could he come live here? Please, Daddy?" Her tormented eyes met his.

"I don't think that's such a good idea, honey," he replied gently. "And not because I don't want your boyfriend living here. That's not it."

Her eyes widened. *How'd he know I meant Gary?*

He hugged her. "We *love* Gary, sweetheart – but I don't think that's the answer. If you're concerned that he's being hurt, we could call Protective Services… but that might just make it worse."

Tears filled Ellen's eyes. "Daddy, you should have seen how he looked! Please, can't we do *something?*"

He stroked her hair. "Talk to him. Let him know he can trust you; he needs a sense of connectedness. If he isn't getting that at home…" his words trailed off to a headshake and a sigh. "And remind him he's always welcome here."

Ellen called Gary Saturday morning, but the wall was already up. He shut out everyone and withdrew into his misery and rage. But she persisted. Gently.

Eventually, he confided in her. And, as often as she assured him she wouldn't, he always prefaced their talks with a distraught, "You can't tell *anybody*…"

While Gary was opening up to Ellen, Dad grew more distant; he left early and seldom returned before 10. When he was home, they said little. A week after Mom left, Dad installed a locking mailbox and kept an almost jealous guard over the only key. The following week, he got an unlisted phone number and warned Gary not to give it to anyone. "If you do, you'll be sorry!" he snarled.

After weeks of begging, Gary finally convinced Dad to let him give the new number to his boss and Edward – and to Ellen.


(18 September – Thursday)

The first time Gary went to Ellen's house after Mom left, he was sure she had blabbed. Her folks didn't stare or call attention to his fading bruises; but he was sure they knew. Mrs. Farricelli always greeted him with a hug. But now, almost two weeks since Mom left, it took all his strength not to run from the house.

During dinner, Ellen's brother and sisters eyed him warily – like a sideshow freak; he could feel their eyes boring into him and he wanted to die. As the evening wore on, Gary seemed almost like his old self: joking, laughing… even teasing the girls.

But while saying his goodbyes, he cringed as Ellen's dad rested a hand on his shoulder. "It was nice to see you, Gary. I've missed having you around."

When Mr. Farricelli hugged him, Gary fought tears again; he couldn't remember the last time Dad hugged him. Sure, he could recount with alarming clarity his last half dozen strappings; but a hug? Not one. Gary pulled free and bolted from the house.

Ellen followed.

At his car, Gary turned on her. "You *told* them!"

"I *didn't*."

His eyes stung. "Then how do they know?"

"Gary, I swear it, I never breathed a word." Ellen reached an imploring hand toward him. "Honey, I'd *never* do that to you!" She touched his cheek. "But when you came in to school that day, all beaten up – I knew I had to do *something*. I told my dad there was someone I thought was being hit at home and asked if that kid could come live here. I *swear* I never mentioned your name – but he knew, Gary. He *knew*."

He could scarcely grasp her words: Ellen wanted her family to take him in. Gary *loved* the Farricellis. They didn't just tolerate each other; they were an honest-to-goodness *family*! He had no words to thank her. Weary of fighting tears all evening, he crumpled into Ellen's arms.

Ellen held him close. She told him she loved him and would never hurt him. At last, she sent him off, with a kiss, to an empty house. Then she went back into her home brimming with love and sobbed in her father's arms.

In the ensuing weeks, the Farricellis' warmth only deepened his isolation and despair, so he eventually stopped visiting. He stopped praying, which left him even more disheartened. Gary had always had a deep faith, and his alienation from that faith quickened his downward spiral into hopelessness.

No longer was Gary the affable, outgoing honors student he'd been his first two years at St. Joe's. His straight-A average slipped to Bs, then to Cs and Ds, as desperation swallowed him whole.

Despondent, he shunned his friends. His teachers worried; the guidance counselor had him in her office almost weekly. He would sit across from Sister Monica Frances and, as often as she asked, stoically deny anything was amiss. He avoided Fr. Maynard's office, even dodging the priest when he heard the muffled swoosh of his brown robes in the hallways.

Edward checked in often, "just to see how things are going." He always reminded his grandson he was only ever a phone call away.

By contrast, long talks with Marie left Gary feeling isolated; she was just another absent woman. Still, they'd always been close and could discuss almost anything; but he told her outright he never wanted to discuss Mom. Ever.

"Please come home," he begged in a late-night call in October. "I miss you so much, Marie; and it's so awful here."

Marie heard a sniffle, then a soft thud – probably Gary's hand bumping the receiver as he wiped away tears.

From the desperation in his voice, she formed an instant mental picture of her brother: sitting on his bed, shoulders hunched, his hand on the phone shaking like a birch in a windstorm. "Okay," she agreed. "My schedule's pretty light," she lied. Midterms were next week. "I'll be home Thursday."

Marie came that weekend; but Dad's overt hostility sealed her decision not to return at Christmas. She came back at Thanksgiving for Gary's sake, but told him she couldn't "handle four weeks under the same roof with that jerk."

After finals ended, she found a job and rented an apartment with friends. The only expense she allowed herself was a 10-minute call to Gary twice a month.

She finally swallowed her pride and turned to Grandpa for help.

His reply was immediate. "Of course! How much do you need? Do you need rent money, too? What about incidentals: groceries, movies, pizza with friends?"

"No, just tuition," she assured him. "And it's just a *loan*."

Grandpa told her to have the bursar send him the bill for next semester. Plus, he said he would pay her senior-year tuition. Marie protested, but he insisted. "There's no need to choose between rent and tuition."

She promised to repay him. But he wouldn't hear of it.

"You just concentrate on your studies. All I want is good grades from you. Not another word about it, Marie. Understand?"

A note arrived a few days later, in his familiar loopy handwriting.

*Put this in your savings account. You never know when it'll come in handy. No arguments. I expect to see this canceled check in my next bank statement. Study hard… and invite me to graduation – that's all the payment I want.*
*Love, Grandpa :)*

Clipped to the note was a $10,000 check.

***

Gary and Ellen began staying out late. With fake IDs, they got into bars; but alcohol held no comfort. So they'd take long drives; only then did he let his guard down. Ellen alone offered relief from his misery. By Thanksgiving, she'd also begun offering herself.

Things grew worse at Christmastime. The stack of untouched Christmas cards grew. Mom had always loved opening them with the kids; one of Gary's favorite things was reading written greetings from family and friends. He opened one card, but it left him joyless and empty. One night, entertaining a glimmer of hope, Gary rifled through the pile, scanning every envelope. *Maybe if she sent a card, it'd mean she doesn't hate me.*

A week before Christmas, Ellen's family drove out to Cleveland to visit her grandparents, Kate and Paul Sweeney. Mrs. Farricelli invited Gary, but Jeremy refused to let him go.

Christmas dawned cold and grey – and Gary faced it alone; Dad hadn't bothered to come home.

Gary looked around the dank, empty living room. No tree, no holly festooned about the mantel; no crèche.

Overwhelmed by misery, he longed to numb the pain. Reaching into the liquor cabinet for scotch at 9 a.m., Gary was horrified that he could resort to any behavior Dad espoused.

Halfway through Ellen's number, he remembered she wasn't home. Emptiness gnawed at him. All he had known and loved was gone. He wondered whether Mom and Joey were having a merry Christmas. Tears stung his eyes. Marie was spending Christmas with friends. Ellen was with her family. He knew *they* were having a wonderful time; even doing the most mundane things, the Farricellis *always* had fun.

Alone in his despair, Gary pulled a pack of razor blades from his desk drawer; every good radio-production person had those. Selecting one, he put the rest back as a strange calm settled over him.

Sucking in his breath, he pressed the blade to his wrist. Someone had said it hurt less if you did it under water. He headed toward the bathroom.

Startled by the telephone's ring, he nicked his finger. Dropping the gleaming blade, Gary watched in dazed curiosity as a bead of blood bubbled from the tiny cut and grew; it dripped onto the carpet. The ringing persisted.

Picking it up to halt the shrill sound, he held the receiver to his ear and mumbled a despondent "Hello," still watching the mesmerizing flow of blood from his finger.

"Hi, hon-eee." Ellen's voice was like a hug. "Merry Christmas. I love you." Her tone was wistful. In typical Ellen fashion, she didn't wait for him to respond before charging on excitedly. Which was okay, really; Gary didn't think he could manage even a "Merry Christmas." He was having a hard enough time breathing.

"It's so beautiful here with all the snow – you should see the farmland!" she gushed. "I forgot how pretty it was. I took lotsa pictures, so you can see 'em when I get home, okay?"

"Alright." The word caught in Gary's throat. A dozen rhinos in cleats thundered across his heart.

"Aww, Gary… you sound so sad! I wish you coulda been here. I'm so sorry you couldn't come. Are you alright, honey?"

"I'm okay," he lied, his hand shaking so badly he could barely hold the phone. Wiping away tears, he smeared blood across his cheek in the process. "It's too quiet here. I miss you." Gary forced himself to ask her what she got.

Ellen told him about the ice skates from her grandparents; she made him promise to take her skating on the pond near her home when she got home. He promised.

When she asked what neat stuff he'd gotten, Gary mumbled, "Oh, nothing," and meant it.

She passed the phone to her parents so they could wish him Merry Christmas, too. Tears stung at his eyes when he heard their voices. Gary longed for an intact family that loved him. They said they couldn't talk too long, because they didn't want to run up the Sweeneys' phone bill.

"I just wanted to say I love you," Christina Farricelli said. The rhinos rumbled back over Gary's heart.

"Love you, too," came out in a choked whisper. He wiped the bloodied finger against his jeans.

"I miss you, sweetie; I'll be home next week," Ellen promised brightly.

Gary could almost hear the smile in her voice. How he missed her smile, her kisses… the incredible softness of her body beneath his! He put the phone down, staring at the blade on the carpet. *I can't do it*, he thought, half frenzied, half relieved. In despair, he sank to his knees. Gary tried to pray; no words came. He tried again. Nothing. He slumped against his bed and wept, his ability to pray – like his resolve – gone. Just like his family and his faith. Gone.

The icy winter plodded on interminably, dragging Gary's spirits with it. In the third marking period, his grades plunged. It was the first time ever he'd gotten an F – let alone three! Sister Monica Frances called Gary to her office again. She was concerned about him, she said. Translating her concern as disappointment, he just nodded, "Mm-hmm"ed, assured her it was just a fluke and slunk miserably back to class.

When Dad saw the little column of Fs, he exploded. "What's the matter with you?" His words hit every bit as hard as his fists. "Don't you know how much this fucking school is costing me? And this is what you bring home: three failures? This better be the last time I see an F on your report card! You're a fucking disgrace!" Eyes downcast, Gary never saw the backhand blow coming.

Again Gary withdrew from everything and virtually everyone. By April, he'd even retreated from Ellen. He struggled through finals and finally managed to pull his algebra and history grades up to a C-minus, but chemistry still vexed him. And at St. Joe's, a D was as bad as an F. Placed on academic probation, he was barred from extracurricular activities.

When finals ended, dreading being his father's punching bag all summer, Gary called Grandpa, hoping to spend a few weeks there.

Relief flooded him at Grandpa's greeting. "Gary! I'm so glad you called! You coming up this summer? Is Tuesday too soon?"

# *Chapter 3*

Ever since he was little, Gary had spent part of the summer with Grandpa. In many ways, Edward was his greatest ally, his best friend. They'd only ever argued once. About food. At its root, it wasn't actually *about* the food; but Gary, then 14, suffered from what Edward termed "chronic teenage attitude."

(August 1978)

Gary had just returned, tracking in the sand that still clung to his bare feet, from an afternoon on the beach with the older kids up the road. Edward stood over the stove, poking at something in a skillet that looked like something people just shouldn't eat. Gary sneered into the skillet. "Don't tell me that *monstrosity* is dinner!"

Grandpa gave him a hasty glance, then looked back at the pan of what was, indeed, dinner. "Okay, I won't tell you, then," he replied, unruffled.

With a *you've-got-to-be-kidding* look, Gary folded his arms across his scrawny adolescent chest. "What is it?" he demanded.

"Eggs and asparagus."

He made an awful retching sound. "I'm not eating it. What else do we have?"

"There's that liver you turned up your nose at the other night."

"Yeech!"

"I'm afraid that's it. I'm going shopping tomorrow. For tonight, this is what we've got."

"I'm not eating that," Gary reiterated, hostility rising in his voice.

"Suit yourself," he said pleasantly enough, grinding black pepper over the burbling yellow-and-green mass. "It's really not that bad. However, it *is* a long time 'til breakfast."

His face showed worry and angry bravado. "You're *not* serious. I mean, there's *gotta* be something else I can eat that isn't" – pointing with a nasty expression – "*that!*"

Edward picked up his spatula. For the first time ever, he considered using it on Gary. He poked at the eggs, moving them around so they'd cook evenly. "No one's forcing you to eat it."

Gary thumped a kitchen chair down in the middle of the floor. Turning it around, he straddled the seat, arms crossed atop its back.

Edward turned off the burner and stepped around Gary to get to the refrigerator. Taking two slices of American cheese, he skirted the pouting obstacle, pulled the cheese into strips and tossed it into the skillet.

"This sucks!" Gary hissed.

"I'm not running a restaurant. We've got this or liver. You want choices?" – Gary brightened, thinking Grandpa was about to give in – "I'll give you two: Take it or leave it."

"Fine!" Gary stalked from the room, leaving the chair where it was. Storming upstairs, he changed out of his wet swim trunks and returned in jeans and a t-shirt.

He was halfway out the door by the time Grandpa, seated at the table with a plate of food, halted him with a no-nonsense, "Get back here."

Gary stopped, his hand on the door. Glowering, he turned.

"What d'you think you're doing?" Grandpa asked.

Gary's answer was short. "Going out."

Edward's was shorter. "No."

"Why?" It was more a challenge than a question.

"Because it's dinner time."

"I don't want that. It looks like puke!" His eyes were wrathful grey, his voice cocky. "Anyway, you told me I could take it or leave it. So I'm *leaving* it."

"You know perfectly well what I meant," Edward countered. "I meant you could eat it or *not* eat it; I wasn't giving you permission to leave."

His calm tone fueled Gary's fury. "Then why'd you say it?"

Acknowledging irrational behavior just encouraged more. And Edward wasn't about to argue with a teenager; he might as well water his garden with a bowl of water and a teaspoon. "Gary, come back and sit down." No *or else*. He knew Gary was fully aware of the consequences of disobedience.

This time his reply was a shout. "No!" But still he didn't move any further out the door.

Edward sighed, again rethinking that spatula's versatility. That troubled him; he'd *never* hit Gary. Never had reason to. But this spate of contentious behavior grated at him. "Gary." His voice held a hint of warning. "You're not leaving this house."

"No? Watch me!" A moment later, the screen door banged shut.

Edward picked up both skillet and plate, slid them into the oven and turned it on low. He sat on the porch to await his grandson's return. It was only a matter of time; it would be dark before long. He knew Gary had gone to the jetty; whenever the boy was angry or troubled, that's where he'd go. Edward pulled a small pouch from his pocket, tamped a bit of cherry tobacco into his pipe and lit it. Soon, bluish swirls of fragrant smoke filled the dusky air.

It was after dark when Gary tromped up the steps; he skulked into the house and toward the stairs.

"Gary," Grandpa called genially, pocketing his pipe. He ambled inside. "Come sit down; I kept supper warm." His voice stopped the teen on the bottom stair.

Jaw set, Gary remained defiant. Sulky. "No."

Yelling would only give the boy the upper hand. "Why not?"

Gary's puzzlement at the question defused his anger. "What?"

Grandpa shrugged. Reason had never been a tool used in Gary's upbringing. At least, not by his father. "Why won't you come back and sit down?" He retrieved the skillet and plate from the oven.

It was Gary's turn to shrug. He had no answers and more of his anger was slipping away every second. Brooding, he eyed Grandpa.

"What're you so angry about?" His gentleness was an invitation. To sit. To talk. Now docile, Gary let his grandfather coax him back to the kitchen. A small jelly jar held the pink beach roses he'd cut that day. Their fragrance filled the cozy room.

Gary sat in the chair Grandpa pulled out for him.

"What's going on with you?" he asked, careful not to sound accusatory. Getting no response, he picked up his fork and began to eat. Gary eyed him in silence; his pride kept him from eating. To give in would be to admit Grandpa had won.

Knowing Gary was awful about breaking down walls, especially those constructed in anger or haste, Edward made it easy for him. He nodded toward the skillet. "Sure you won't have some? It's not bad – certainly not as bad as it *looks*," he offered, voicing his grandson's thoughts.

Gary shrugged and, when Grandpa reached for his plate, handed it to him.

Placing a small greenish-yellow mound onto the dish, Grandpa set it before Gary, who looked like he was about to puke.

Grandpa hefted a big forkful. It smelled all peppery and cheesy. "Your Grandma used to make this all the time. I had pretty much the same reaction as you, first time; now it's one of my favorites." Swallowing it, he shook his head. "Still can't get it quite right." The boy hadn't ventured past pushing it around his plate. Grandpa chuckled. "Don't sit there giving it the hairy eyeball. Try it. It won't hurt you."

Looking down into his plate, Gary poked at the stuff; lifting a tiny forkful, he tasted it. Grandpa watched as the small mountain oozing with cheese slowly disappeared.

After they'd washed the dishes, Edward poured himself a glass of wine, and a soda for the boy. They went to sit on the porch. He gazed out at the sea, knowing Gary wouldn't talk if he was being watched. "Care to tell me what all that anger was about?"

Seated on the floor, his back against the wooden railing, Gary sighed aloud.

"Is it school?"

"I guess." Gary looked questioningly at Grandpa. His eyes narrowed.

Before his grandson's visits, Edward had always talked with his daughter-in-law to learn whether he should be aware of anything upsetting Gary, or behaviors to be on the lookout for. He never revealed anything they discussed, but it didn't hurt to be aware of things. In July, Diane told him Gary was nervous about starting St. Joseph Academy in the fall; she said her normally even-tempered son might be a bit snappish.

"New school; new people…" Grandpa tried his best to sound enthusiastic. "Aren't you excited?"

Gary shook his head. "Not really."

"Maybe a little nervous? It's alright to be apprehensive, Gary. But what is it you're worried about? The teachers? The classes?" He knew Gary had graduated at the top of his middle-school class; he had never lacked for friends, either.

His shoulders hunched, he wouldn't look up. "It's not *that*… What if everyone hates me?"

Grandpa smiled gently. "They won't hate you. Have you *ever* had trouble making friends?"

"This is different. All my friends are going to Jefferson and I'll be stuck at that snotty ol' school."

"So you're afraid you won't fit in?"

"I guess."

Grandpa puffed on his pipe. "I went through that same anxiety myself, once upon a time."

"Really?" Gary sat forward, listening intently.

He nodded. "Fresh out of college, my first draftsman job. I was terrified: What if my calculations were off and the building I was designing wasn't structurally sound? Worse – what if it collapsed?"

"But, Grandpa, they wouldn't have hired you if you didn't know what you were doing."

"Precisely. I just needed to build my confidence. Within a year I was senior draftsman. After getting my architect's license, I took a job in a larger company. Junior architect, brand-new firm. New boss, new coworkers… no idea what to expect. Right back where I started: bottom rung of the corporate ladder, looking up."

Gary listened in silent amazement. Grandpa *did* understand. His distrust dissipated as he recalled long talks they shared every year. Yeah, he decided, deep inside he'd known all along Grandpa *did* understand. He *did* care and, more important: he *did* love him.

Over pancakes the next morning, Gary called that love into question when Grandpa asked what he had planned to do that day.

"I dunno. Probably just hang out with the guys."

"That's too bad. Sounds like it would've been fun."

The distrust was back in an instant. "Whaddaya mean, *'would've been fun'?*"

"I mean you're not going out today."

Sun glinted off the water; waves crashed against the shore. It'd be high tide soon – a perfect beach day! A salty breeze beckoned. "Why not?" Gary demanded, indignant.

"Because, Gary, you need to learn that when I tell you to do something, I expect you to comply."

He slammed down his fork. "This is about those eggs, isn't it? Well, I *ate* the stupid eggs!"

"This isn't about eggs. It's about consequences. And don't you raise your voice to me, young man," he warned, pointing a cautionary finger.

Being reprimanded by Grandpa made Gary uncomfortable. "I *said* I was sorry!"

"You did; and I accepted your apology. But your actions have consequences."

"What actions?" he challenged.

"How about the way you spoke to me last night? Or that tone of voice you just used? Or your walking away after I told you not to? Need more?" Gary just scowled as his grandfather spoke. "You're not a child anymore, Gary. When you make decisions, you accept the repercussions. You chose to defy me. The consequence is lost privileges, like spending the day with your friends."

"That's not *fair!*"

"No, Gary, what's not fair is when you won't obey a simple request." The teen was about to launch an angry protest when a grave look silenced him. "I don't want any arguments, or we can extend it to tomorrow, too," Grandpa warned quietly. "Now, after breakfast, go find your friends and tell them you won't be able to hang out with them today. I'll give you precisely ten minutes. And then I want you back here."

The last vestiges of Gary's defiance surfaced. "Or what?"

He shook his head. "There *is* no '*or what*,' Gary. Be back in ten minutes. Period."

Powerless, Gary began mutilating his pancakes, mooshing them into the plate with his fork.

Edward sipped his coffee as he watched his grandson's hostility play itself out. "I know it's not an easy lesson to learn," he acknowledged, setting his mug down. "But at least you get to learn it here, with me, instead of at the business end of your father's strap. I'm only keeping you in one day; he'd have smacked you clear into next Tuesday."

Gary could hardly argue. He was right. Dad was a big believer in spankings. Hard ones. If for no other reason than that, Gary had ample cause to be grateful he was with Grandpa today instead of at home.

And, to Edward's great relief, Gary proved to be a quick learner. For the rest of his visit, he was more compliant and respectful than ever. And he only challenged his granddad's authority one other time: the following August, just before sophomore year. Caught smoking pot on the beach with those older boys, Gary mouthed off once too often during the resulting lecture. That earned him such a severe talking-to he found himself almost *wishing* his granddad had taken the strap to him instead.

# *Chapter 4*

(16 June, 1981 – Tuesday)

Edward welcomed Gary and promptly solicited his help. He had bought the cottage on the Milford shore in 1950, to enjoy summers with his family. Now, thirty-one summers later, it was time to make it a permanent haven.

Gary savored the invitation.

Too old to do it all himself, Edward was glad of the help and the company. Besides, it would keep Gary's mind off his troubles at home. He afforded his teenage grandson ample time to spend on the beach.

Gary usually declined, saying he preferred to help with the reno-vation project.

For ten weeks, morning to night, grandfather and grandson worked side by side. They measured and cut, hammered, drilled, sanded, rewired and painted. They laid insulation, hung windows and installed new plumbing and heating. Every night, Gary fell into bed exhausted, lulled to sleep by waves lapping at the shore. Each morning, he awakened to the aroma of fresh-brewed coffee – and with a sense of purpose.

After supper, they'd sit on the porch to talk. Anything was open to discussion: the future, the past, work they hoped to accomplish; whatever was on their minds. Edward related stories of his early years with Josie. And occasionally – albeit reluctantly – Gary talked about his troubled home life.

"I don't want to go back," he confided in August, staring out over the water as darkness crept across the shore. His shoulders sagged. "He makes me feel so *insignificant*. Like I'm not even there. Know what I mean?"

"I do." Edward nodded, wondering whether this was his cue to reunite Gary with Diane. "But, Gary, it's only another year 'til you graduate; then you're off to college. And you can spend summers with me. You're always welcome here; this is *your* home, too."

As they watched the last pinks fade to blue-grey, Gary spoke. "I never told anyone. Not even Ellen…" He studied the weathered floorboards. Edward leaned close. "It got so bad" – he sighed with the weight of secrecy – "last Christmas I… almost killed myself."

Edward's eyes widened in alarm and concern. "Gary! Why would you even *consider* that?"

Cries punctuated his words. "Have you ever felt so desperate and so – alone… that suicide seemed like the only escape from the pain? D'you know what that *feels* like? *Do* you?" Edward was silent a moment too long. Fists clenched, elbows gouging into his knees, the teen spat the words. "Well, *I do*. It feels like emptiness – and failure!" He dropped his head against his fists.

"Oh Gary!" Edward pulled Gary to his feet, enveloped him in a mighty hug. "Why didn't you *tell* me it was that bad?" He tried not to sound like he was scolding. Fear took hold as reality seeped in: He'd lost a son too soon, and that had triggered Josie's depression. He couldn't bear to lose his grandson. "Gary, you're seventeen; you've got your whole life ahead of you. What would make you feel like you had no other choice than that?"

Edward's embrace was too much to fight. Sobbing, Gary clung to him; tears soaked his grandfather's shirt.

Finally, Edward spoke again. "Let me get you out of there. I can get you into Milford Academy. You can live here." He wasn't sure Gary had heard, because he didn't answer right away.

Gary shook his head, mumbled something about not wanting to leave Ellen.

Edward figured as much, but he had to offer. Then he posed the question he dreaded asking: "Is your father hitting you?"

"No," Gary insisted. "Of course not! Why would you even ask that?" He crumpled into his chair. His chest ached from crying and his ribs hurt from Grandpa's embrace. And now he'd just lied to him! It felt awful, but he didn't think he had a choice. He couldn't let Grandpa tear him away from Ellen.

Edward fetched him a glass of water. Gary accepted it gratefully, drinking the cool liquid in rushing gulps. It felt refreshing, but it couldn't soothe away the guilt over his lie.

Edward set the empty glass on the floor. "C'mon. Let's walk."

Obediently, Gary followed. The night sand felt cool and soft against his bare feet.

"Tell me about it," Grandpa persuaded, draping a comforting arm around his grandson's shoulders.

For a second, Gary thought he meant, *Tell me why you lied.* Then he realized Grandpa meant, *Tell me why you wanted to kill yourself.* Reluctantly, he told him about his anger at Mom and the insecurity, inadequacy and loss that led up to his thwarted suicide attempt.

"Holidays are rough when you're depressed. Grandma struggled with depression herself, years ago. I understand how overwhelming it can be." Gary turned toward his grandfather in the moonlit semi-darkness, his eyes asking the question he couldn't find the courage to voice. "It was a deep depression that lingered for a long time – back when your father was a little boy," the old man answered the unspoken query.

"What happened?"

"It took a long time, but she eventually came out of it."

"No, I mean: What caused her depression?"

Edward chose his words carefully. "When your dad was little, we learned Grandma was expecting. About six months along, she lost the baby. She couldn't have any more. We'd always wanted a large family and that news was devastating. All our friends were having second and third babies, and she couldn't give me another child."

"I never knew that," Gary said soberly.

"I never meant for you to. But I figured you deserved to know now."

"Because of what I told you?"

"In part," Edward replied. "I wanted to be honest with you. I understand how destructive pain can be."

Gary nodded. His deception twisted in his heart.

"Whatever pain you feel, there's nothing so deep, so awful, you can't share it. There's no reason to suffer alone. *Capisce?*" That was Italian for "Understand?" He ruffled his grandson's hair.

"Yeah." The near-darkness hid a hint of a smile.

***

The Gary who returned to Pine Cove at the end of August was markedly different from the one who left in June; not just because of the auburn highlights in his hair, his deep tan and well-defined muscles. His confidence was buoyed and he carried himself with a certain self-assurance.

Edward phoned weekly and prayed for Gary daily. Within a few weeks, those prayers had begun to bear fruit.

By October, Gary's depression seemed to have lifted. He started attending Mass regularly and paid more attention to his studies. His grades picked up to Bs and a few As. And he and Ellen even talked fleetingly of marriage.

In late December, Gary was accepted at Boston University. He expected to be congratulated when he told Dad.

Instead, he heard, "Great, *another* twelve grand a year I'll have to shell out for you."

Like her mom and grandmother before her, Ellen was accepted at Wellesley a week before Christmas.

When her family went away over New Year's, Ellen invited Gary over. He arrived with a bottle of Asti; she greeted him in a skimpy bathrobe, which she quickly shed. They made love in her parents' bed, using the only condom he brought. A champagne-tinged midnight kiss ended sometime after two. Gary couldn't be sure if it was the bubbly or the absence of a condom that made the resulting sex so intense.

In the morning, they made love again, then quickly made up the bed before her folks came home.


Five weeks later, a weeping Ellen approached Gary in the library with the unsettling news.

His heart pounded crazily. "Are you sure?"

"Gary, I'm *never* this late," she insisted.

"Maybe you counted wrong."

"Or maybe I'm *pregnant*," Ellen hissed.

When her fears were confirmed, they agreed to keep it a secret while they figured out what to do. They did their best to keep up appearances, but soon they stopped sitting together at lunch and study hall. When they had to work on class projects together, they bickered constantly. He stopped going to her house; her parents and sisters wondered why. Even their guidance counselors asked what soured between them; but Ellen and Gary revealed nothing. By the end of March, they'd stopped speaking altogether. And by mid-April, she'd begun showing.

***

In the privacy of his office, Fr. Maynard counseled Gary gently about the sanctity of marriage and the seriousness of his actions. Deeply ashamed, the teen hung his head and said nothing. "I can only imagine what you're going through, Gary. But, it isn't the end of the world; and ohh, our Lord is forgiving! All you have to do is ask Him."

Remorseful, Gary nodded. "Forgive me?" he whispered.

Laying his hands on Gary's bowed head, Fr. Maynard prayed. "Dear heavenly Father, hear our cries for forgiveness. Show us Your mercy and kindness. Send Your Holy Spirit upon Gary, cleanse him from his sin, and grant him Your pardon and peace. We ask this, as we ask all things, through Christ, our loving and compassionate Savior." Giving Gary a mild penance, the priest offered the teen absolution. Then he embraced him. "Your sins are forgiven, Gary. Go in the peace of Christ."

Next day, it seemed the young priest had somehow talked Msgr. Streng into letting them finish their graduation requirements with tutors; they'd get their diplomas, but wouldn't be allowed to attend the graduation ceremony.

To stave off his guilt, Gary put in long hours at the station, filling in on air whenever he could. He also tried to fix things with his dad, who remained angry and aloof. Making things worse, Ellen refused to see him, even threatening a restraining order


Three days before they would have graduated, Gary's boss called him into his office. "I don't want you thinking I don't appreciate your work," Paul Ramsey told him. "We *all* do. You're talented, dependable and we *love* working with you. And I said if anything full time opened up, I'd hire you."

"I remember," Gary said expectantly, nodding.

The program director laid his palms flat on the desktop, fingers splayed. "Unfortunately, I have nothing to offer you."

"Are you letting me go?"

"More like pushing you out of the nest." Paul slid a business card across his desk. "Here; give Steve Reynolds a call. He said he's interested in talking to you. I sent him your 'New Music Monday' demo."

"Not *that!*" Gary groaned, appalled. "Paul – I did that as a *joke.*"

"He liked it enough to want to meet with you."

Gary took the card, smiling for the first time in weeks. "Thanks, Paul." Now he studied it. "Hey, wait a minute – he's in the City!"

"Yes he is." Paul's air of confidence encouraged and terrified Gary. "One kid in a million gets a break like this. And I can't think of anyone I'd rather see it happen to."

Gary called Steve Reynolds that afternoon. They scheduled an interview for Thursday at 10:15.

Steve was amazed that Gary was only 18. "You're really talented. Great on-air presence, quick wit, a terrific voice – and a good ear for music. That's important in this business."

"Thanks," Gary replied, not knowing what else to say. He still couldn't believe Paul had sent that tape. It was just a goof!

At 11:30, Steve stood. "C'mon. I'd like to see you at work. Let's go see what you're made of."

Gary's nervousness got the best of him during his production audition; he criticized himself silently all the way back to Reynolds' office, where Steve handed him a card. "Pete Donovan has an on-air opening; I think you're exactly who he's looking for."

Gary stared at the card. Middlebury, Connecticut? "Thanks." He tried not to sound too defeated. "I'll give him a call."

"Know how many other kids I've referred to my PDs in the last three years?" He waggled two fingers. "Most folks I see aren't good enough. If I had anything here, Gary, I'd snap you up in a second."

# *Chapter 5*

(2:37 p.m., 4 June, 1982 – Friday)

"Listen. I know things have been rough lately; but I know we can work through it. I still love you." Gary gripped the receiver. "Marry me, Ellen."

"You must be joking. Why would I want to marry you?"

"Because I love you – and you're carrying my baby."

"What makes you so sure it's yours?"

Her question ground Gary to a nauseating halt. "Whaddaya mean? Of course it's mine… Isn't it?"

"Maybe."

"At least let me help financially. I don't have much, but I can help you wi—"

"You're too late, Gary," Ellen interrupted. "I didn't want that baby; and I don't want *you*. I never want to see you again. If you come near me, I'll have you arrested. *I mean it.* Now, leave me alone!"


Dizzy and weak, Gary curled into a ball. Ellen loved him; he *knew* that! But she said she didn't. And aborted their baby.

Mom would have known what to say. She'd have sat on his bed, stroking his hair; she would have held him and wept with him over her lost grandchild. But she'd left. And he was left to mourn his baby alone.

That night, Dad confronted Gary. "You'd best be planning to make an honest woman of her. Though I can't see why she'd marry a no-good bum like you!"

"I asked her. She said no." He didn't mention the abortion.

Sneering, Dad refilled his glass. "Well, who could blame her?"

Gary had never openly opposed his father. "I dunno. I can't understand how I turned out so awful… after the terrific example *you* set."

"Why, you lousy little—" Dad slammed his scotch glass down on the coffee table. With a soft hiss of leather through fabric, off came his belt. Doubling it, he lunged at Gary, sputtering.

Gary winced as several blows landed across his back.

Then something snapped. He caught the belt as it lashed toward him. Wrapping it around his hand, he reeled Dad in. "Stop it!" he roared, eye to eye with his father. He hurled the strap across the room. And for the first time, Gary hit back. "I've taken enough of your shit! It stops now!"

Dad stumbled backward against the table, fell onto the couch. The amber liquid sloshed. Scrambling to his feet, he charged, giving Gary a mighty shove. "You ungrateful little fuck!"

Before he could say more, Gary struck again. Dad staggered and fell; by the time he got up again, his son had the upper hand. Gary fought fiercely, retaliating for years of humiliation and beatings. Rage fueled his determination. "You bastard! How's it feel to be on the receiving end?"

A left to the jaw; a right to the midsection; a left jab to the face. Gary felt more than heard the crunch as bone gave way. Shaking off the pain, he watched in smug satisfaction as Dad wiped at the blood streaming from his broken nose.

"You lousy little shit!" he snarled. "I want your worthless ass out of here. Now!" Grabbing for the sticky glass, he gulped his scotch, then poured another.

Dim light still glowed from the study at 52 Field Court. Empty and heartsick, Gary gave a hesitant rap at the door.

"Gary!" The boy had grown since Edward last saw him – he was nearly six feet tall; but the old man still towered over him.

Grandpa had been an imposing figure when his grandkids were young. His great "tallth," as they called it, frightened them. They said he was like an oak tree. And they'd been right. He was tall and sturdy and dependable.

"Dad threw me out," Gary blurted. "I didn't know where else to go."

Edward hugged him. "You came to the right place. Welcome home, Gary."

Gary needed that hug. *Home. What a nice feeling! It feels good to be welcome <u>somewhere</u>.*

***

"What are you going to do?" Grandpa asked on the porch late the next afternoon. "About the girl."

Gary shrugged. "What *can* I do? She won't see me."

"Do you love her?"

He gave a disheartened shrug. "I *did*… but she said she doesn't love me. And now I—"

"So you just turn your feelings on and off like a light switch?"

"*No*," Gary replied, flustered. "I just never thought sex would change things between us so much."

"You should've considered that *before* you went to bed with her." Grandpa shook his head. "I thought you had more sense. Anyway, that baby deser—"

"She got an abortion, alright?"

"She *what?*"

"She aborted our baby," Gary murmured, long pauses between his words.

Edward absorbed the news. "How do you feel about that?" he asked, lost for suitable words.

Before he could apologize for that, and offer his sympathies, Gary bit back. "How d'you *think* I feel? She killed my baby – I'm fucking *delighted!*"

"Gary!" Grandpa stopped in mid-rock. "That has to be the most disrespectful thing I've ever heard you say!"

He slammed a fist against the arm of his chair. "Well, I'm sorry I turned out to be such a fucking *disappointment!* Maybe I shouldn'ta chickened out last Christmas!" The chair fell backward as he leapt up, ready to bolt.

On his feet in an instant, Edward stood between the teen and the steps. "Don't you *ever* talk like that again, ya hear?"

The accompanying slap shocked more than hurt Gary. It startled Edward, too. His hand had shot out as if under its own power. The reference to his grandson's failed suicide attempt was more than he could take. He stammered a hasty apology.

Pushing past his grandfather, a hand to his slapped cheek, Gary stormed away.

Guilt assailed Edward. He'd never struck Gary – not even those times he'd had ample reason, a few years back. "Jesus, forgive me," he mumbled. A small empty place gnawed inside him as he watched Gary disappear amid the tall sawgrass. Edward brushed aside a tear as he righted the toppled chair. He'd have been a great-grandfather. The news dredged up the pain of that long-ago loss.

Gary trudged along the deserted beach, his heart shattered; he'd been wrong last summer; *this* is what failure felt like. Grief bubbled up as he thought of the life he and Ellen created from their love, the innocent life she'd torn from the safety of her body. The sob grew as it tore through him, surfacing as a guttural moan. The baby represented hope of doing better as a parent than the example he had from his own family: a mother who left for – what? He never knew. And an emotionally absent father who never uttered an *I love you.*

Iron bands around Gary's chest forced him to struggle for every breath. He and Ellen were so in love. They could've rented a little place in town; he'd have worked at the station part time and found a full-time job to support his wife and child.

Wearied and bereft, Gary clambered to his feet. Swatting sand from his arms and his jeans, he plodded unsteadily along the beach. He wanted to confront Ellen; but he was in no state to drive. He stared at the water. It was nearing high tide. Coming upon a drift-wood log, he sat. Elbows on his knees, Gary rested his chin in his hands. "If I call, she won't talk to me," he reasoned. "If I go there, she'll call the cops."

Despair settled over him; his aching eyes stung afresh. Not knowing what else to do, he began to pray. "God, help me. Please don't let me screw this up again."

As a child, prayer had meant rote repetition of words long ago memorized. Later, he used different words to express himself. But today, prayer took on a new dimension. Gary talked to God in a dialogue of beseeching and listening, an exchange of pain and comfort. And once, a Monarch butterfly alighted on his knee, beating its wings slowly, as though conducting a miniature orchestra. He watched, transfixed by its silent majesty, wondering whether it was simply a grand coincidence that one of God's magnificent winged creatures had picked that exact moment to call on him.

***

In the study, Edward filled his pipe, reflecting on long-ago times spent here.

The instant the car stopped, the little boy bolted out like a stone from a slingshot. Edward laughed as he bent to hug the youngster

41

hurtling toward him. Lifting him up, he swung the boy around as the rest of the family emerged. He motioned with his free hand toward the reticent 7-year-old beside the station wagon.

"C'mere, Marie. Come give Grandpa a hug." The shy, pig-tailed girl approached her towering oak tree of a grandfather slowly, while her parents looked on.

Moments later, the screen door swung wide and Josie stepped onto the front porch, wiping her hands on her flowered apron. A short, slightly round woman, she wore her hair coiled into a bun at the back of her head. Her smile beamed from beneath deep brown eyes. "Well, look who it is!"

"Grandma!" Little Marie squirmed free of Grandpa's one-arm embrace; she flew up the porch steps and threw herself into her grandmother's waiting arms. Edward stooped again and set his not-quite 4-year-old grandson onto his feet.

"Gamma Jo, Gamma Jo!" the tot yelled as he scrambled up the stairs.

Edward smiled as Gary wriggled his way into the hug with his sister. He still had trouble with his Rs, but the pediatrician assured Diane it was common among kids his age.

A few years later, all the laughter went out of Edward's life.

He and Josie had just returned from a walk. She was pouring iced tea when he heard the terrible thud and the sound of glass shattering. Racing into the kitchen, he found her on the floor in an ocean of tea, amid shards of the broken pitcher. Struggling to speak, she managed only a weak goodbye. In an instant, his wife of more than 37 years was gone, felled by a massive stroke. She was dead before he could call for the ambulance.

Edward had fallen in love with the raven-haired beauty during his first trip to Sicily in April 1931. At 22, Josephine Arena was a secretary in a firm his company did business with. After three days, the 24-year-old draftsman worked up the courage to ask her out.

From the moment she smiled across the table in the restaurant, Edward was in love: in love with that smile; with her lilting voice; with the espresso eyes that peered from beneath thick lashes. In love with Josie. Fortunately, her English far outshone his Italian.

She cried at the dock four days later when Edward left. But he promised to return for her. And he always kept his promises. Three months later, he returned – bearing a bouquet of roses, a steamship ticket and an engagement ring. Josie accepted all three.

Edward remained in Sicily for three weeks. Josie resigned her employment and brought her fiancé to meet her family.

When they arrived in New York, his family was as taken with Josie as hers had been with him. They married the following April.

The days following Josie's death were a blur. He remembered nothing clearly, except his grandkids' bewildered faces. Sounds of weeping filled St. Mary Church that muggy August morning. Marie, in her sailor dress and patent-leather shoes, struggled to understand why Grandma had gone away. Too young to grasp what was happening, Gary was left with neighbors; it would be less traumatic, his dad said.

For Edward, the worst part was coming back to an empty house; the solitude was suddenly lonely. He longed for company. Jeremy, busy growing his law practice, was making the trip more frequently than he wanted. Both children enjoyed spending time with Grandpa; but Gary especially thrived whenever he was with him. This fact was not lost on his parents.

"That kid would live here year-round if we let him," Jeremy remarked the following July.

Gary's head swiveled toward the sound of his dad's voice. "Could I, Dad? Can I stay? I could keep Grandpa company – and maybe he wouldn't be so sad all the time."

In spite of himself, Edward smiled at the 6-year-old's logic.

"But we'd miss you, sweetheart," his mother had reasoned. "Who'd keep *us* company?"

"Tell you what," Grandpa bargained, laying a hand on the boy's head. "If your folks say it's okay, why don't you stay another week, just us. How's that sound?" He glanced at Jeremy and Diane.

Gary whipped around to see what his parents would say. "Can I, Mom – Dad? Please?"

"You'll have to be on your best behavior," Dad cautioned.

"I will," the child promised, nodding seriously.

Their week was idyllic. They took long walks, played checkers, packed picnic lunches and spent lazy afternoons fishing. And one day, they sat beneath the elm tree in the front yard with glasses of lemonade. After that, whenever the family came to visit Grandpa Sheldon, Gary was allowed to stay an extra week.

Before long, there was another baby to be cooed over. Joseph Edward Sheldon arrived in early April of '72.

"Josie would've adored this little fella!" Edward said, cradling his new grandson at the christening. "He has her eyes. Her nose, too — poor little guy!"

They'd all laughed, but tears in the corners of Edward's eyes betrayed him.

Diane laid a compassionate hand on his arm. "We named him after the two of you, Dad."

He looked into the tiny pink face and nodded. If he tried to speak, or meet his daughter-in-law's gaze, he would cry. And he didn't want to spoil their joy.

During the next years, the whole family didn't come up for more than occasional weekends. But Gary was permitted to ride the train alone to spend a week with Grandpa every summer; and eventually, one week stretched into two.

Last year, he'd stayed all summer. That brought them closer than ever. Edward smiled, recalling the gangly teenager who could barely hammer nails. But he was eager to learn — and so grateful for the chance to work alongside his granddad. When he left at the end of August, he wasn't a bit like the sad, awkward boy who'd shown up that June morning.

*There sure have been some rich memories in this place.* Sighing, Edward lit his pipe.

***

The setting sun glanced off the waves in shimmery gold ripples. Mesmerized, Gary watched it sink amid fiery clouds. As he sat, his gaze fixed on the horizon, a flash of brilliant green light gleamed in the distance and shot across the water's surface — like God winking a gigantic emerald eye. Then, as swiftly as it appeared, it vanished. As the gold orb kissed the horizon, Gary watched the sky fade from orange to pink-striped blue-grey to azure.

Darkness had blanketed the shore by the time Gary returned home, aided by the glow of the moon and the rear porch light. *Mom used to leave a light on, too.* A new barrage of tears stung his eyes.

Climbing the steps, Gary heard the drone of a radio; behind the wooden-slat blinds, the golden glow of a lamp shone from the study. The door was open; light spilled into the hallway. Grandpa sat in his armchair, feet on the leather ottoman. In one hand he held a book; in the other, his pipe. A ribbon of smoke wafted from its bowl.

Gary tapped at the door. "Can I come in?"

Taking his feet off the ottoman, Grandpa laid aside his book.

With a slow draw on his pipe, he motioned with his free hand. "Please."

Gary perched on the ottoman. He drew a jagged breath, stared at the deep-brown carpet. "I'm sorry, Grandpa. I shouldn't have sworn at you; or raised my voice. Or walked away." His shoulders drooped. "Guess there's a lotta things I shouldn't have done."

Taking another puff, Edward nodded. "Life's too short to live with regrets." He patted the teen's denim-clad knee. "I owe you an apology as well. I shouldn't have slapped you, Gary. And I am so sorry. Please forgive me."

Gary nodded but did not look up. "Of course," he whispered.

Grandpa squeezed his hand. "If there's anything in your life that needs fixing, best to do that. You've taken the first step by coming back to talk to me. I know it wasn't easy. You need to decide if you can do that kind of fence mending with Ellen."

Gary's shoulders sagged further. "I don't know how. Where do I start?" he implored.

"Go talk to her."

"I tried. She won't even see me now."

Grandpa laid aside his pipe. "I didn't say you didn't try, Gary. What I'm saying is try *again*. And keep trying until she *does* see you."

Gary looked at him glumly. "Or gets a restraining order."

Grandpa held up a finger. "Ah, but at least you'll know you've done all you could. I just don't want to see you torment yourself with what-ifs."

"So how do I get her to talk to me? And how do I get past the fact she killed my baby? *Our* baby. How do I forgive her for that?"

"You're asking some tough questions, Gary – questions I don't have answers to. You'll only find those answers inside. Pray about it. Listen to what your soul's telling you. Or maybe it's time to let go." Edward patted his shoulder. "I know it hurts to consider that; but sometimes accepting is all we *can* do – because, sometimes, other people call the shots. It's just how things are."

Gary nodded, having no reason to suspect Grandpa wasn't only referring to Ellen.

"You must be hungry. I know I am. But I don't feel like cooking. You feel like a pizza?"

"I guess."

Grandpa's eyes twinkled. "Funny, you don't look like one."

***

Edward lay awake, trying not to listen to the muffled cries from across the hall. There was little he could do to ease Gary's pain. He lifted his rosary from the nightstand. *Worry beads,* someone told him once. *That's all they are: worry beads.* But Edward knew better. They offered comfort in desperate times, respite for a troubled soul; and peace for a world sinking ever deeper in turmoil.

As Edward finished the Sorrowful Mysteries, he uttered a prayer for Gary. "Please, God, help him find his way through this pain; let him feel the peace he needs so badly."

*Josie would've known what to do. She always did.*

Like the time Gary had tumbled off the porch… Josie was right there with her gift of comfort. Scooping the toddler into her arms to kiss away the hurt, she sat on the sandy ground and rocked him back and forth until his tears abated. She brushed the sand off his face and kissed his cheek loudly. "All better," she pronounced, picking the little boy up and setting him on his feet. Then, patting his diapered bottom, she'd sent him off to play.

With a sigh, Edward set down his rosary, turned out the light and went to sleep, missing his Josie.

Gary awakened Sunday morning to the aroma of strong coffee. And a tap at his door.

"Good morning," Grandpa boomed, trying to sound cheery.

"'Morning," he mumbled. His eyes hurt and there was a vague ache in his midsection.

The old man handed him a steaming mug. "How'd you sleep?"

He inhaled the brew's rich aroma. "Not real well."

"It's been a rough time; you'll settle in."

They talked for a while, avoiding the topics of Ellen and babies. When Grandpa said it was time to get ready for Mass, Gary shook his head. "I'm not going. I don't want to."

"Whether you want to is not the point. You're going to ge—"

"I'm not going," Gary repeated more firmly. "I have nothing to say to Him!"

"What makes you so sure it's one-sided?" Sitting on his grandson's bed, Edward softened his tone. "Maybe *He's* got something to say. Maybe today *you* just need to listen."

Gary's eyes darkened. "I don't care what He has to say! I'm too pissed off at Him."

"It's okay to be angry," he acknowledged. "Just don't turn away from your faith. Not now." Gary was about to balk when Grandpa continued. "God didn't cause this. He's as upset about your baby's death as you are. Turn to Him, Gary. Don't shut Him out. Not about something this important. If you're angry, bring that to Him, too."

Gary's eyes stung. A single tear found its way down his cheek.

Edward hugged him; tears filled his eyes, too. "Trust me on this, okay?"

***

On Monday morning, Gary called WZBX in Middlebury. "Mr. Donovan, I'm Gary Sheldon. Steve Reynolds suggested I call you."

"Oh, yes – Gary. I'm glad you called. Steve sent me your tape. When can we meet?"

Just after three the next afternoon, a 30ish man in jeans, a blue shirt and silk Daffy Duck tie sauntered out to the lobby. "Brenda, Gary Sheldon's due at three fifteen. Can you let me know when he arrives?"

The receptionist pointed discreetly to the seating area. "About five minutes ago."

The Daffy Duck-tie man approached him. "Hi Gary. I'm Pete Donovan." *God, he's just a kid!*

"Pleased to meet you, Mr. Donovan," Gary said, taking the hand the man extended. "I appreciate your giving me the interview."

"Don't mention it. And don't call me Mr. Donovan." He smiled. "Makes me feel old. Call me Pete."

He brought Gary into his office. Ninety minutes later, the pair emerged, laughing and talking like old friends. Pete showed him around and introduced him to the staff.

Looking up from his flowerbeds, Edward brushed the soil off his hands. The sun's position in the sky told him it was nearly 7. "How'd it go?"

Gary beamed. "I start next Monday – three to seven on air; plus production."

That night, they feasted on lobster at Jimmie's of Savin Rock in West Haven, in a booth overlooking the water.

Edward plunked a lemon wedge into his water glass. "Grandma loved watching the boats out here. Back there" – he pointed – "was an amusement park. But now they've torn it down and slapped up a god-awful housing complex. And a church." He scowled. "Too modern. Immaculate Conception up in Waterbury… now *that's* a church!"

He loved to hear Grandpa discuss architecture, loved hearing the enthusiasm in his voice as he pointed out aspects of buildings he approved of or despised. "That's a mansard roof," he'd explain, indicating the roof line of a great old Victorian. "And look at that gingerbread trim – they don't take time to put in details like that anymore."

Gary figured he'd inherited Grandpa's love of old buildings, like the stately Victorians he passed in Southbury today. The ones he'd see every day now. *I'd love to own one of those someday,* he had mused as he pulled into the station's parking lot.

Next morning, after weeding the garden, Gary began checking the for-rent ads. That afternoon, he looked at four apartments, including a third-floor walkup in a three-family building in Middle-bury.

"It's a terrific apartment," he told Edward that evening. "It's got four rooms, wainscoting in the kitchen, front and back porches, a garden, grape arbor and this old chicken coop in the backyard – and great views! Plus, there's a garage. *And* I can afford it."

"*That's* always a plus," Grandpa teased.

"But I gotta come up with the first and last months' rent. *And* a security deposit."

"Let me help you out."

"Grandpa," Gary objected. "I can't ask you to do that."

"Who said you're asking?"

"There's no sense arguing; I'm not gonna win, am I?"

The old man winked. "You catch on fast."

"I'm gonna pay you back, soon as I can."

Edward smiled as though guarding a secret. "If you insist."

"It's not available until August. Okay if I stay here 'til then?"

"This is your home, Gary. Always has been. One other thing: It's an older apartment, right?"

"Yeah."

"Then you'll need authentic pieces to furnish it." He grinned.

"Grandpa…" A warning tone rose in Gary's voice.

"Hey, you need furniture. I just happen to know a few places to look."

"Okay," he agreed reluctantly. "But no funny stuff" – he did his best to sound stern – "like trying to pay for it."

The white-haired gentleman feigned shock. "Would I do that?"

"I wouldn't put it past you. But, Grandpa, *don't* – you've done more than enough already."

During the week, Edward took Gary prowling through antique shops. In one, they found a porcelain-top kitchen table with four chairs. In another, a handsome art-deco bedroom suite.

Running a hand over the dresser's veneer surface, Gary bent to admire the Bakelite drawer pulls. He'd helped Grandpa refinish a similar piece years earlier. *Like I really helped! I just held the steel wool.* Years of grime came off with oil soap and steel wool; Grandpa removed layers of varnish and lovingly cleaned the dresser again. It now gleamed with a warm golden luster in Gary's room at the cottage.

Gary checked the price tag: $650 was an awful lot of money he didn't have. Maybe he could pay some each week 'til August. *It's… just over $80 a week.* Between that and repaying Grandpa, he'd be eating peanut-butter sandwiches and boxed macaroni and cheese for years. But he could afford the set.

Meanwhile, Edward considered a black-walnut liquor cabinet at one end of the shop. He called Gary over. "What do you think?" he asked, stepping back to inspect it. "Belongs in the study, doesn't it?"

"Yeah," Gary agreed. "Over in that corner, by the bookcase."

"Well then, it's settled," Grandpa said. "I'll just need to get it." He went to talk to the owner of the shop.

As Edward wrote out a check, Gary carried his granddad's latest find out to the car. On the way home, the teen remarked that the bedroom set was perfect, even if he really had no use for the vanity.

"Oh, you should never break up a set," Grandpa cautioned. "Someday, your wife will absolutely fall in love with it – and you'll be glad you kept it."

Gary smiled. Grandpa had this way of talking about the future – a knowing kind of way – that made Gary believe he might just be right.

# *Chapter 6*

On his first day at WZBX, Gary bungled the call letters, forgot the phone number and botched a live read of a commercial for a major sponsor. "I can't do *anything* right," he exclaimed when Pete ventured in just past 4. "Are you *sure* you really want me here?"

"Don't be so hard on yourself. Relax. You'll be fine," he assured Gary. "It took me ages to get the call letters right. I had to post a sign with the request line – right up there. It stayed up for weeks."

Just before 7, a young man in jeans and a Danbury Y Lifeguard t-shirt burst in. "Hey," he said by way of greeting as he pulled off his sunglasses. "I'm Marc Lindsay; I do nights. Welcome aboard."

Gary forced a smile and shook the hand Marc offered. "Thanks, man. It's great to be here." He hoped he didn't sound too desperate. Or phony. If he did, Marc didn't seem to notice; if he did, he didn't let on.

"Hope you don't mind me saying, but I think you'll settle in nicely before long."

"Why would I mind?"

Marc shrugged. He spoke at a dizzying speed. "Oh, you know; radio people can be so weird: like they think, *What? Don't I fit in here already?* Don't get me wrong: I don't mean it as a putdown. It's just, you sound a little bit nervous." He smiled. "I like your style. I think you'll do well here."

He paused as Gary read the weather, adding that Marc would be in at 7.

As Gary pulled off his headphones, Marc nodded. "See? You're startin' to sound more comfortable already. Lemme know if you need anything, 'kay?"

Gary nodded; he was just now catching up to what Marc had said before his last break. He never in his life heard anyone talk so fast! *I bet he can do a five-hour show in two hours flat!*

Mired in thought, he didn't see Marc bolt from the studio; of course, he left so fast Gary might not have noticed anyway.

***

On Saturday, Gary and Edward tinkered with the old Chevrolet convertible in his garage. They replaced belts and hoses, changed the oil, then backed it out to wash and wax it.

Finally, Gary stepped back. "Look how the sun glints off that chrome," he said eyeing the white '67 Camaro longingly. "She's a beauty."

"Glad you approve," Grandpa told him. "She's yours. I planned to leave it to you in my will, but I figured you might as well have 'er now. Especially with how that Nova of yours has been coughing and sputtering. But don't try using her to impress girls." Edward's eyes shone. "*That* you've got to do yourself." At Gary's silence, he continued. "There's more important things than having a kick-ass car. You need something besides flash and good looks. You need to have substance, Gary. And integrity. Whatever else you may accumulate in your lifetime, *nothing* is worth more than your good name. Never forget that. And when you screw up – and you will, because we all do – be man enough to admit it… and do whatever it takes to fix it."

***

The next weekend was Father's Day. Gary arose early, his heart wracked with sorrow. In a fog, he didn't notice the beige envelope that had been slid beneath his door in the night. He started a pot of coffee and went for a long, solitary run on the beach.

Edward expected to find Gary on the porch enjoying a mug of coffee; what he found was an envelope on the kitchen counter, with *Grandpa* in Gary's neat blue script. The front of the card depicted an old man and a little boy walking, hand in hand, along a beach. The inside was filled with the same careful writing.

Edward smiled; he fixed his coffee and sat on the porch to read.

*Grandpa,*

*How can I begin to thank you for all you've meant to me these past 18 years? As long as I can remember – and certainly years before that – you've always been there to love and support me, in a way no one else ever could.*

*Some of my earliest memories are of times spent here… and it's no coincidence my <u>fondest</u> memories are of time spent with you. It doesn't matter whether we're weeding the flowerbeds or* *just sharing a glass of lemonade; I treasure every moment I get to share with you.*

The words swam through his tears. Grabbing his handkerchief, Edward mopped at his cheeks and blew his nose. He continued reading, keeping his handkerchief handy.

*I'm so grateful for the chance to get to know you - especially these past few years. Your love, encouragement and faith have sustained me through some of the worst times of my life. I honestly don't know what I would've done without you.*

*Even the stinging memories of my lowest and most miserable times here (last summer and my first few days here this year, in particular) far outshine any memory of my life back home. As far as I'm concerned, disowning me was the best thing Dad could have done. I've come to realize that, all along, you've been a better father to me than he ever was.*

*I thank God every day for having blessed me with such a tremendous example of fatherhood. If I'm ever fortunate enough to have kids of my own, I only hope I can imitate your example. If I can be half as good a father to my own children as you've been to me, I'll know I was a success - at the most important job in the world.*

*Grandpa, thank you for being the most giving and loving man I've ever known. Thank you for loving me enough to take me in when I had nowhere else to go; for being compassionate when my spirit was battered and my faith shaken... and for caring enough to be tough with me when you knew I needed it most.*

*You've taught me some great lessons. First, not to cheat at checkers. But more importantly, you taught me to believe in myself - but always to trust God - and not be afraid to accept the hand of another reached out in friendship, because it just might be the hand of God extended in human form.*

*Grandpa, I love you more deeply than I could ever begin to put into words, and I hope you understand how much I appreciate everything you've done for me all my life - even things I may not be aware of.*

*In love and gratitude - on Father's Day and always,*
*Gary*

This boy he loved so deeply — and had walked the beach with so many times — needed to acknowledge Father's Day, but his own dad had disowned him; so he reached out to the next-nearest father figure. He studied the front of the card, recalling their walks. Young Gary would chatter endlessly, about one thing or another. Longing for quiet, Edward would smile fondly at the child whose tiny hand was tucked into his own enormous one. As Gary grew, he became more autonomous, opting against holding Grandpa's hand; instead, he ran ahead, hurling stones into the choppy waters of Long Island Sound. More recently they trod the beach yet again, now nearly equal in height. His little-boy stature and fiercely independent spirit both gone, Gary was content to walk with his granddad's arm draped about his shoulder.

Today Gary chose to focus on more innocent times, when walks on the beach with Grandpa were one of life's greatest joys. Edward smiled; the talks they shared gave him a glimpse into Gary's soul, a chance to touch the hurt that lurked there – even if he could do nothing to heal it.

Edward caught sight of Gary up the beach, running. Running hard. *That pain can't be escaped by running. No matter how hard or how fast you go, it's still there. Waiting. Wherever you stop.*

After finishing his coffee, Edward went inside. In his study, he re-read the card.

Gary returned – exhausted and panting – his cheeks flushed, his t-shirt soaked. He ran up to shower. As he dressed, he spied the beige envelope.

Inside was the same card he had selected: the old man and the boy on the beach. The inside was filled with Grandpa's small, loopy handwriting. Gary sat in the chair where Grandma Jo used to rock him to sleep.

Through the words, Grandpa's voice nudged at Gary's heart; his words mended the shattered bits, soothing the teen's wounds like a healing balm.

> *My dearest Gary,*
> *I knew this would be a difficult day for you, and I want you to know you're not alone. I share the pain you must certainly be feeling. My first Father's Day without my child was the most brutal silent suffering I ever endured. I understand the depth of your pain – and I ache, knowing I can't do anything to ease it.*
> *I only hope time will lessen the sting of this cruel reality and you'll find in God the peace you seek, the strength you need to someday trust and love again and – within the precious bond of marital love – give life and love to the children you so richly*

*deserve to have sharing your life.*

Lately, the tears were always ready to spill over at the slightest provocation – or none at all. Cursing his weakness, Gary read on.

*Gary, I know the loss of your child isn't the only grief you are bearing today. As hard as you try to hide it, I know the heartache you feel over your father's abandonment weighs heavily on you. I wish things had turned out differently. Perhaps in time you can heal those wounds and repair your relationship.*

*I've seen how sad you've been these past years; it's difficult to watch someone you love suffer so terribly. But I must tell you - even through that pain - your presence has brought such joy to my life, along with a kind of peace I never thought possible.*

*It has truly been a blessing, watching you grow into such a fine young man. In you I gained what I lost out on when my son died: a second chance for the love, laughter and pure delight a child brings into both heart and home. Through you, I witnessed the sense of wonder in your discovery of the world around you - and the gentle unfolding and blossoming of your faith.*

*When your grandmother died, I thought all the brightness had gone from my life for good. But you helped restore that sense of love and laughter, Gary - to both my heart and our home; and for that, I will be ever thankful.*

*Perhaps we have been called to help each other. If so, I'm more than happy to give back some measure of the comfort and peace you've brought me over the years. I couldn't have loved you any more if you'd been my own son. There'll always be a place in my heart - a special place, where there used to be hurt and longing - that you've helped to heal.*

*Time will bring happier Father's Days for you; I feel certain of it. In the meantime, I wish you all the healing you need and the sense of belonging you seek in this world.*

*Gary, please know that my love is with you wherever you go - and for however long we may be apart. And know that nothing can ever diminish that love. Not careless words spoken in anger; neither fear nor lost faith. Not even death.*

*Grandpa*

Edward looked up when Gary appeared in the doorway. He crossed the room to meet his grandson halfway, the card still in his hand. "This is, by far, the nicest Father's Day gift I've ever gotten."

"How do you always know just exactly the perfect thing to say?"

Gary asked at the same time.

Understanding the emotional waver in his grandson's voice, Edward hugged him. "That pain doesn't go away easily. But trust me, one day it won't seem quite so bad."

Embarrassed, Gary drew away, swiping at his eyes. "I feel so foolish."

"Nothing foolish about grief," Edward reassured him. "You've suffered a terrible loss. And it's a *real* loss. One that no one talks about. And it hurts."

"I guess you're right," he mumbled at last, sniffling.

Edward steered Gary toward the kitchen. "C'mon, let's go have breakfast." He gave a hearty laugh. "You do realize I'm turning into your grandmother. She was Italian – food fixed everything."

He was gratified to see a smile light Gary's face as they ambled into the kitchen.

# *Chapter 7*

A week later, Edward and Gary returned to the shop where they'd found the bedroom set. Gary, full of eagerness on the drive to the little shop that smelled pleasantly of old wood and furniture polish, even had his $100 first payment. His happy anticipation crashed as he noticed the red tags. "It's just been a week," he lamented. "How could it have sold so quickly?"

Grandpa patted his shoulder. "It's a risk you take with antiques. You never know if a piece you saw a week ago, or even yesterday, will be there when you go back. Why didn't you ask him to hold it?"

"I didn't know I could."

"That's alright; we'll find you something else. Maybe something you'll like even better."

The shopkeeper noticed Gary's expression. "That set was a real find. That same afternoon, a young woman came in, said it was like her grandparents' set. If I knew you were interested, I'd have held it for you," the man said apologetically. "I'll probably get another; but it could take a while. You need it right away?"

"Not 'til August."

"Plenty of time. I'll call you if something comes in I think you'd like."

They had better luck at the other shop. The kitchen set was still there; and now Gary could pay for it. And the owner didn't mind holding it until August; that gave him time to use it as a showpiece for the gaily colored Fiestaware arranged atop it.

At work, Gary developed an easy rapport with traffic reporter Steve Fugacy; they would engage in lively non traffic-related banter, much to the dismay of the sales staff, who hoped to lure sponsors.

Same with meteorologist Jack Dennison. Gary found an album

of sitar music to use as background music for "a visit with the weather guru." And because he and Steve often talked about the weather, it was only fitting for Gary to discuss traffic with Jack.

That didn't sit well with the sales team, either. But as much as they complained, calls in favor of "that new guy" poured in faster; and he was given carte blanche.

When he introduced New Music Monday, it was an instant hit. From 3 to 4, Gary played music from artists otherwise relegated to college radio: the Cure, Modern English, the Smiths. Within weeks, they'd expanded the show to two hours. Listeners responded as positively to the music as to Gary's infectious personality. He was gregarious and mildly irreverent, much to the consternation of sales manager Charlie Burns.

Pete frequently prodded Gary into his antics. And it was he who gave Gary the nickname that would come to spell trouble for him later that summer. In good weather, Gary would drive to work with the top down in the Camaro. One afternoon, he bolted into the studio late, looking like a windblown porcupine.

"Sorry, Chief," he blurted as Pete turned on the microphone.

The program director's annoyance evaporated. "Hey, *Spike* – so glad you could join us."

Perplexed at his boss' greeting, he put a hand up to his hair and immediately smoothed it down.

Pete was undeterred. "I guess that'll wrap things up for me, Pete Donovan; I'll be back tomorrow at ten. *Spike* Sheldon finally blew in… literally. He was out gettin' his hair done. Too bad this isn't television. He'll be here to steer you through the rest of your afternoon on Z97-3. See ya tomorrow. Bye."

Soon nearly everyone at work was calling him Spike. Everyone but Charlie.

One Tuesday in August, Pete prodded Gary on-air to show up at the next afternoon's remote at Moroni's Chevy Emporium with his hair spiked. "So people can see the *real* Spike."

Gary took it one step further.

The next night, Charlie demanded a meeting with Gary and Jim Burdell, the operations manager; Jim called Pete in on the meeting.

Gary appeared in Jim's office, straight faced and earnest – three-inch spiky green hair and all – for the 7:30 meeting. Pete laughed so hard he had to leave the room. On his return, it was all he could do to keep his composure while the sales manager ranted.

"He looks like a damn Muppet!" Charlie fumed, waving his cigar. "*Look* at him! He's an escapee from Sesame Street! And you let him go to a remote looking like this? Like a – a – a *parakeet?*"

Pete bit his lip and looked at Charlie Burns' raging face. He glanced at Jim before trying to placate the sales manager. "Charlie, I can understand your concern—"

"What're you gonna do about it? I want him fired!"

"I'm sure you do," he replied. "But that's a bit extreme; besides, hundreds of folks have called over the last few months, saying they love him. Any of them are potential car buyers, Charlie. Check your sales figures for last quarter. They're up twenty-two percent over last year. Why d'you suppose that is?"

Infuriated, the red-faced sales manager pointed his cigar at Gary. "You! Get outta here. I want to talk to them alone."

Jim cast Charlie an angry look. "Sit down, Gary," the boss said softly, not even glancing in the teen's direction. "Now, listen here, Charlie," he rebuked, "this may be your meeting, but this is *my* office. And you don't dismiss *anyone* from my office."

Charlie glared vipers at Gary, who didn't dare look at him.

Jim turned to Gary. "Gary? Anything you'd like to say?"

"Yeah. We burned through every giveaway and promo item. We had a hundred t-shirts, a gazillion bumper stickers and about five dozen car-wash certificates. Add it up. Even disregarding bumper stickers, that's still a hundred fifty people. At a little car dealership. Midweek. I'm thinking if I used *red* Jell-O instead of green, folks might have mistaken me for a stop sign and come to a screeching halt."

Charlie leapt up, gesturing with his cigar hand. "You see? This is what I mean! That's what you get for hiring a stupid, irresponsible kid – he doesn't take anything seriously."

Jim was poised to reply when Pete defended his afternoon DJ. "Charlie, sit down. It's obvious to me that Gary takes his work seriously. Even if he *does* have a quirky definition of 'serious.' And what he said about those promo items speaks for itself. When's the last time we ran out of giveaways?"

Disgustedly chomping at his cigar, Charlie stared at the program director and shrugged.

Pete glanced in the other direction. "Gary?"

Gary shook his head. "Not since I've been here."

"Exactly. Not once." Pete looked from one of them to the other. "But I have a feeling things are going to start turning around."

"Y-you – you're not going to put a stop to this foolishness?" Charlie stammered, outraged.

"I don't see why. If it ain't broke, don't fix it."

"You can't be serious."

Pete remained calm. "Oh, I am. It's all a matter of marketing. Gary's highly marketable – and I intend to capitalize on that as much as possible."

"Capitalize on what? He's a fucking disgrace!"

Gary felt like he'd been kicked; but the derision didn't end there.

"He's a fucking embarrassment to this station – and the whole broadcast industry!" Charlie spewed, pounding the desk with a fist.

Jim bristled. "Charlie, that's enough. I understand you're upset, but just remember who you're talking to." He addressed Gary now, *sotto voce*. "You can go, Spike; I'd like a word with Pete and Charlie. Nice job today. I thought that bit with the cat on the windshield was hilarious."

"Thanks." Gary stood and headed toward the door. "See you in the morning, Pete. G'night, Charlie."

The sales manager ignored him.

"I resent this," Charlie snarled after the door closed. He pointed a finger at Pete. "I call that punk in for you to reprimand him – and you encourage him! You're as bad as he is!"

Pete rubbed his temples. "Charlie, you've worked in radio a long time; you know it's important to keep the talent happy. Gary's clever; he's personable and funny. Plus, he's funny without being rude. If he goes overboard sometimes" – throwing his hands in the air, he glanced at Jim – "where's the harm? Cut him some slack."

Jim nodded. "I agree. Spike's having a bit of harmless fun. So *what?* Pete's right. Give the kid a break. Listeners *love* him!"

"Well, we'll just see what David has to say about this," Charlie grumbled.

David Guilmartin was the station manager.

Pete's head pounded. "Fine. Do what you've got to do. But just remember this: *He* gave the okay to hire Gary."

***

After Charlie's black Mercedes tore out of the parking lot, Pete appeared at the production-studio window. He opened the door. "It's safe to come out now."

Gary pulled off his headphones. "Thanks." He poked at the

slimy goo on the cushioned headpiece, then wiped his fingers on his jeans. "Blech! I didn't have gel, so I used Vaseline. Can't wait to wash this crap outta my hair!"

The program director laughed. "I'll bet. What'cha working on?"

"Just a traffic 'non-sponsorship' spoof. I'm sure Charlie'll have something to say about *that*, too."

"Don't worry about him; he's harmless. And Jim told him to get off your back. Can I hear it?"

"Sure." Gary hit the rewind button. "Not quite ready, but it's close." He adored piecing together elaborate bits for the morning team or his own show. It was a luxury he'd never had at WTRR; anyone who needed the production studio could displace him from whatever project he was working on. But here he had unrestricted access to two state-of-the-art studios. And unlimited time to play.

Noticing bits of discarded tape strewn about, Pete marveled at the quality of Gary's project, especially in view of the number of splices it apparently contained – none of which he could detect.

When Gary pressed 'Stop,' Pete nodded in approval. "Like I told Charlie: Style, humor and talent: You got the whole package. Steve Reynolds was right: We've only seen the tip of your 'talent iceberg.' I expect great things from you."

So did Edward.

"You were supposed to go to BU this fall, weren't you?" the old man asked Sunday night.

"Yeah. But that didn't work out."

"There are some fine colleges around here." Edward held up a hand to stave off the forthcoming protest. "I know what you're going to say, Gary; but I wish you'd let me help you."

Gary's response was immediate. And adamant. "No. Absolutely not. I don't want to be a burden on you."

"You'd hardly be a burden. Besides, I *want* to help."

"You already *are!* You gave me a car – and you paid my security deposit. Grandpa, that's more than enough."

Edward shook his head. "I wish you would reconsider. A college education is so important. Anyway, you need to be around people your own age. And just because your dad won't pay, doesn't mean you should have to go without. I know how much you want to be independent, but let me do this. It'd mean a lot to me."

"Let me think about it, okay?"

Edward smiled, knowing he'd prevail in the end. "Okay."

Next day Gary went to the University of Connecticut Waterbury campus to get an application and course-selection guide. He did the same at two other area colleges. UConn had the widest range of courses and the greatest scheduling flexibility; however, it was also the most expensive.

Before he could apply at either school, one last thing stood in Gary's way.

He tapped on the boss' door early the following morning. "Pete? Got a sec?"

"Sure, c'mon in, Spike." He laid aside a report he was writing. "You're here early. What's up?"

"Would you mind if I did my production work after my show instead of before?"

"Do it at midnight if you want. Why?"

Gary perched at the edge of a chair. "I was thinking about taking some courses; but I wanted to check with you before I signed up for any early-afternoon classes."

"That's great, Gary. Where?"

He hedged. "I was thinking UConn or Briarwood; but I dunno. It's kinda late…"

"Maybe not." Pete reached for his phone. "I used to date someone in admissions at UConn. Let me make a call."

Gary listened awkwardly as his boss made small talk; then he came to the point.

"Listen, Cory, one of my jocks wants to apply this semester. Any chance you can help me out?" In the silence, Gary wondered what she was saying. "Uh-huh. Yeah, freshman." Pete jotted something. "Got it." He scribbled something else. "Great. Thanks, Cory. I owe ya one." He put down the phone.

"You're in luck." Pete handed over the name of the admissions counselor fielding late applications. "Her name's Gretchen Salanna. Her assistant Tanya can help you. She's there two to five today; tell her Corinne sent you."

"But even if I get there right at two, I won't have time to meet with her and still get back befo—"

Pete waved away Gary's objection. "Tell you what; you do ten to two today; I'll cover your shift." He nodded toward the course guide the teen held. "What're you taking?"

Gary laid the booklet on his boss' desk. "Basic stuff: Intro to Broadcasting; Intro to Production; Interpersonal Communication; Current Trends. Plus some core classes: Poli-Sci and Psych 101."

Pete frowned as he read the course descriptions. "Spike, you've been in radio, what, four years? You could probably *teach* half these classes. Take a test to prove you know the material and they'll give you the credits. How many credits you taking?"

He totaled them up. "Eighteen."

Pete whistled. "You'll be swamped. Something's gotta give. And as your boss, I'm telling you: Your work better not suffer." He eyed Gary. "You really think you can handle such a heavy course load – plus a full-time job?"

Gary recalled the academic and athletic schedule he'd maintained at St. Joe's. Plus working at WTRR. He nodded. "Positive. Besides, it's only three months."

"True. And if you test out of those Intro courses, that'll cut it back to twelve. When are your classes?"

"This term they all end by noon. Except one." He waited for Pete's reaction. Getting none, Gary's words gathered speed on their own. "Interpersonal Comm. meets Tuesday evenings, seven to ten; that's the only time it fit into my schedule. It's co-requisite to Intro to Broadcasting; and it's a *pre*requisite to almost everything. I'd have to leave at six thirty – but it's only for this semester." Fidgety, Gary glanced at his boss' face.

Pete handed back the worksheet. "Well, sounds like you got this all pretty much worked out." The pause that followed made Gary anxious. "Be sure you get there today, so you don't get shut out of anything... especially that night class."


Gary met with Tanya Jackson, a sweet, self-conscious junior who worked in admissions part time. She had cornflower-blue eyes and a river of glossy auburn hair cascading almost to her waist. She introduced him to Gretchen, who reviewed his application. After a call to St. Joseph Academy to request his transcripts, she approved Gary's application. Tanya registered him for his classes and directed him to the bursar's office.

"That tuition bill will make your head swim," she cautioned. In an endearing Midwestern twang, Tanya told Gary he would need to meet with the department head about testing out of classes. "Don't let 'im scare you," she advised. "He'll try to come across as gruff to intimidate you. But he's really a pussycat."

***

Gary aced both exams. Before the semester started, his college transcript indicated six earned credits. And a 4.0 average.

On the 15th, Edward and Gary drove to Middlebury to move him into his apartment. He didn't have much and Grandpa convinced him to leave some things at the cottage. Aside from clothes, he had tapes, an AM/FM-cassette player, three boxes of books and a handful of personal items. He insisted Edward not carry anything, except a bottle of champagne.

"It's got character," Grandpa said, after touring the apartment. "Lots of windows, plenty of light." But because it was on the third floor, it'd also get beastly hot, he noted. And the heat that day was stifling.

As his grandson bounded up and down the stairs, Edward stepped onto the porch; the view was great. The landlord puttering in his garden reminded him of his father-in-law – a little old Italian fellow with a fringe of white hair around the equator of his head. The man wore old shoes, a shabby t-shirt and bagging work pants. Edward smiled. He looked content in his garden. *Content is good. And it's good for Gary to be on his own; gives him a chance to get back on his feet.* Maybe things were starting to turn around for the boy.

When they went to arrange delivery of the kitchen set, the shopkeeper said his crew did afternoon deliveries. Grandpa told Gary there was no need for him to take time off; he would let them in.

Next day, as the tail lights of his grandson's car disappeared up Oakland Avenue, Edward called his friend to tell him Wednesday afternoon was perfect.

The kitchen set arrived first. It took less than thirty minutes to get everything inside and fifteen more to get everything situated – including setting up the furniture. Edward thanked everyone and tipped them all handsomely for hauling everything up to a third-floor walkup in the August heat.

Arriving home, Gary took the stairs two at a time, eager to see how his new kitchen set looked. It suited the space perfectly, as if it had been meant to be there all along.

"See? I told you: you need authentic stuff." A smile played about Grandpa's lips. "Now, if we could just find a nice Victrola for your living room… and something that'd look just as good in here," he added wistfully, meandering into the bedroom. He waited for his grandson to follow.

"Where'd you *find* this? It's just like that oth…" Gary's voice decayed uncertainly. "Did you talk that lady out of buying this set?"

"Of course not. It was nothing that underhanded," he admitted. "While you carried the cabinet out to the car that day, I settled up with the owner on it, and the bedroom set; he gave me a deal. I asked him to make up something to explain the sold signs and stall you on finding another." Grandpa's eyes twinkled.

Torn between gratitude and anger, the teen scowled. "I thought you agreed, no funny stuff. That was part of our bargain."

Edward grinned. "I remember: No funny stuff." A playful tone crept into his voice. "But you didn't specify no sneaky stuff."

A bit miffed because his granddad had steamrollered over him, Gary shook his head. "Grandpa… I *know* you want to help – and I appreciate it; but how am I gonna learn to do things myself if you keep swooping in and saving me? I know it sounds ungrateful, and I don't mean to be; but how'll I know what it's like to succeed if I'm not allowed to try – and fail – once in a while?"

The next day, Gary drove around Middlebury, familiarizing himself with the town. The library, church and town hall were grouped around the green. The grocery store was in a plaza with a drugstore at one end and a bank at the other. It had that old New England feel, and it already felt like home. He stopped at the church office and said he wanted to join the parish.

The only person there was the director of religious education, who welcomed Gary and introduced himself as Greg Andrews.

After they'd talked a bit, Greg half-jokingly asked if he wanted to teach first-grade religion. "The lady who was going to do it backed out an hour ago. Classes start in two weeks and I'm stuck."

Something about the prospect intrigued Gary.

"It's ninety minutes for class on Saturdays and time to prepare lessons," Greg went on. "It's pretty easy. You'll get a million hugs from the kids; they're great at this age! And it really is rewarding. I'd highly recommend it. Even if I *wasn't* desperate."

Gary nodded. "Ya know what? You sold me. I'll give it a try – but just for this year."

Greg clapped him on the shoulder. "Great. You'll need to fill out this sheet, and a parish census form for Lucy."

Greg put the filled-out census form on Lucy's desk and gave the other sheet a cursory look. "Gary Sheldon. You're that New Music guy. I *thought* your voice sounded familiar."

"Yeah." He was still getting used to being recognized in public. It was a definite ego boost – but, at the same time he was finding it could be a bit disconcerting.

"Welcome to the parish. Glad to have you join us. St. John's is a nice community. I'll get you a bulletin so you can see what goes on around here. Anything else I can help you with?"

"Actually, I'm looking for a place to go running. Is there a park or something in town? Or do I just take my chances on the roads?"

Greg gave him a quick overview of three area parks. "They're all within" – he glanced at the form – "ten minutes of your place. If you want, I'd be happy to show you some of the routes I take."

They began running together a few times a week. Despite Greg's being 10 years Gary's senior, they had enough in common to forge a dynamic friendship.

Greg appreciated Gary's enthusiasm and fresh perspective; and Gary benefited from the wisdom of Greg's years.

On the first day of CCD class, Gary arrived early, with name tags for each of his students. Before they arrived, he printed on the classroom blackboard the rules he expected his class to follow. It would be their first lesson. They weren't quite the Ten Commandments, but they were close:

1. Remember that God loves you.
2. Remember that God loves everybody else, too.
3. Be nice to everybody.
4. Obey Mommy and Daddy.
5. Always say "Please" and "Thank you."
6. Be happy with what you have.
7. No bad words.
8. No cheating.
9. No stealing.
10. No lying.

As kids straggled in, they took seats. Standing at the front, Gary felt awkward towering over them. So he sat on the carpeted floor and asked them to join him.

At first, they were reluctant: Teachers usually hollered if you got out of your seat. But with his soothing voice and ready smile, a few brave souls came forward; others followed. The most confident ones filled in spaces up front. Gary's charges ran the gamut from painfully shy to nonstop chatterbox.

He asked them to introduce themselves and say something they wanted him to know. He listened as each child talked about their siblings, pets, parents or teachers. The last child to speak, a little boy sitting beside him, said he was sad because his new puppy died the day before. Gary hugged him.

One dark-haired girl raised her hand. "Um… teacher – what about you? What d'you wanna tell us?"

Gary smiled. "Thanks for asking, Miranda. I'm Gary. And I want you to know" – he scrambled for something to say – "I'm new in town, so I don't know a lot of people yet. But I'm glad to know you all. And I'm looking forward to teaching you."

A little blond boy raised his hand. "Um – Gary? Do you have any kids?"

Gary hadn't expected that tug at his heart. "No, Justin," he said. "No kids."

"Any pets?" someone else asked – the boy whose puppy had died.

He shook his head. "No, Ryan; I don't have a pet."

"What about a wife?" a little girl wanted to know.

"No, Sara; no wife either."

Jessica's blue eyes were wide. "Why not?"

Before he could answer, a boy at the back piped up, "'Cause girls are icky!"

"Stephen, that's not nice," Gary corrected gently. He glanced around at their little faces. "I just haven't met the right lady yet. Now, let's take a look at the blackboard. These are The Rules."

Gary stood; fifteen pairs of eyes followed. He read each rule aloud, explaining the behaviors he expected. He said they needed to obey the rules both in class and at home, because it wasn't just what he wanted, but what God expected, too.

"Do you know about the Ten Commandments?" he asked. A few wide-eyed children nodded. He explained those were the rules God gave people to follow. "These are like that. *Kind of.* Some of 'em are the same: 'No lying,' 'No stealing' – and the one about obeying your parents."

"God never said to obey your parents."

"Sure he did, Elizabeth. 'Honor thy father and mother' is a fancy way of saying *Obey your parents.*"

"What about saying please and thank you?" she challenged.

"Well, no," he admitted, taking his place again amid the cluster of children. "God never said that; but *I'm* saying it. Because it's polite."

He sent them home with two copies of The Rules: one to post on the refrigerator; the other to keep inside their religion books, so they'd always know what was expected of them.


Testing out of classes freed Gary up to take Shakespearean Comedy and the sophomore-level Creative Marketing. That brought him back up to 18 credits.

After work on Fridays, he would get a loaf of crusty bread from Luigi's and drive to Grandpa's for supper. Sometimes it was pasta and meatballs with homemade sauce; other times, Grandpa spent hours cooking up a stew, pork roast with apples, or veal Florentine. Whatever he made always smelled great. They'd chat animatedly over dinner; their conversations often spilled out onto the porch afterward, to be finished by moonlight. And when he didn't have to teach, Gary stayed all weekend, helping Grandpa in the garden or doing home repairs.

"Don't you have homework?" Grandpa asked one Saturday.

"I'll do it later," he promised as he headed out the door to mow the lawn.

"No. You'll do it now. The lawn can wait. Better yet, I'll do it." Plucking the worn leather gloves from Gary's hand, Edward used them to shoo his grandson away. "Go to your room."

Gary grinned. "Look at you, trying to be so stern." He shook his head. "This is the first time I can remember you *ever* sending me to my room."

"It won't be the last," the old man promised, brandishing the gloves menacingly. "Now scoot."


(2:37 p.m., 8 October – Tuesday)

The phone seldom rang these days. And hardly ever mid-week. Despite the day's warmth, Edward felt a sudden chill. "Gary's not here," he told the caller.

"When he gets home, tell him to give me a call."

"He doesn't live here anymore."

"I need to talk to him."

Anger surged through Edward's veins; he kept his tone cordial. "When I see him, I'll be sure to tell him you called."

"That's not good enough, Dad," Jeremy insisted. "What's his number?"

"He's asked me not to give it out."

"You have no right to keep that information from me!"

"That's where you're wrong, Jeremy. Gary has a right to privacy. And I respect that. If he wanted to talk to you, he'd have called you himself."

"I'm his *father* for God's sake!"

"In name only. You were never there for him. *I* was the one who listened, who cared for Gary and looked out for him all these years."

"How *dare* you!"

"No, Jeremy, how dare *you!*" Edward spat out. "Where were you when your son needed you? You couldn't be bothered. Then, when he needed support and compassion the *most*, you kicked him out! I don't call that being much of a father. You were so wrapped up with work and your other women, you couldn't see what *really* mattered!"

Jeremy sputtered unintelligibly in his fury. Finally, he blurted, "What other women?"

"Whom do you think you're kidding, Jeremy? Do you think I never knew about your womanizing? That tore your family apart. That, and your drinking – and abuse. Diane was a *saint*, staying as long as she did. Only thing I can fault her for is *how* she left. Gary always thought *he* was to blame. I did my best to convince him otherwise, but Diane didn't want me telling him the truth." Edward paused to steady himself. "She knew it was only a matter of time before he found out what a miserable louse you are. But she didn't think he needed to know that when he was sixteen!"

"You're a damn liar!"

"For Gary's sake, I wish you were right. But we both know better. I'm hanging up now."

Jeremy sputtered. "Don't you dare—"

Edward set the receiver in its cradle, halting the ugly stream of venom. He rubbed his throbbing temples; talking to Jeremy always left him jittery and anxious. To calm himself, he went for a walk.

Walking by the shore soothed Edward; so did praying the rosary.

Whether it was the repetition of prayers, the smooth onyx beads between his fingers or the peace the devotion offered didn't matter. All that mattered was when he got home, he felt a sense of restored serenity.

"Talked to your dad lately?" A warm breeze stirred the air. They had just finished cleaning up after supper and were sitting out on the porch. It was Columbus Day weekend, so Gary didn't have to teach.

He made a face. "Why would I wanna do a thing like that?"

"Just asking."

"Grandpa, I'd think by now you'd know *not* to."

"He called here the other day; wanted you to call. Sounded like it might've been important."

"I have no desire to talk to that man." Challenge prickled in his voice. "You should know that. You don't like him either."

Edward shot his grandson a warning look. "That's not true."

Gary rolled his eyes and exhaled audibly. "Oh, come off it! You hate him as much as I do."

"I don't think *anyone* hates him as much as you do," Grandpa countered evenly, not admitting anything. "I'm just keeping lines of communication open."

"Well, one of us doing that is plenty" – he took a swig of milk – "and, frankly, if someone has to do it, I'm glad it's you."

Edward bit into one of the chocolate-chip cookies they'd made that day – with extra nuts. Just how they liked them. They were two of a kind, in many ways – even in their stubbornness. "There may come a day, Gary, you'll regret feeling that way. He won't always be around, you know – and he *is* your father."

"The day he's not around anymore… *that* day can't come soon enough," Gary grumbled. He reached for a cookie. "And as for his being my father" – he took a bite – "he was highly over-rated. And I'd appreciate it if you'd stop calling him that."

# *Chapter 8*

Monday before Thanksgiving, Gary proclaimed a "Week of No Turkeys." On the studio door he hung a poster of a turkey holding a cigar in a red circle with a slash through it and "THIS MEANS YOU" in block letters. Atop the turkey's neck, Gary pasted a caricature of Charlie's glowering face.

When Charlie roared into the studio on Tuesday, Gary indicated the poster. "Hey, Chuckles! This is a 'No Turkeys' zone. Hit the road!"

The sales manager thundered into the program director's office, slamming the door. "That's it, Peter. I've had it! I want that little punk outta here!"

Pete looked up tolerantly. "What'd he do now?" Thinking better of it – he had enough on his mind without Charlie's disgruntled ravings – he held up his hands in surrender. "Never mind. I'll have a talk with him."

Leaving Charlie staring after him, he strode down the hall. As soon as the on-air light went out, Pete pushed open the door to the studio. "We need to talk. *Right now.*"

"Sure, chief. What's up?" Gary glanced up from checking off ads on the program log. "The 'Poultry Prohibition' zone?" When Pete nodded, he threw up his hands, exasperated. "Whaddaya want from me, Peter? He's on me all the time. Over *nothing!* You want me to make nice? Fine. I'll take it down. I'll apologize for tossing him outta here – hell, I'll polish his damn shoes if you want!"

Pete shut the door. "Spike, please, could you call a truce? Just for the holidays? They're hard enough without you two at each other's throats." He hated to rehash this, but Gary deserved an explanation. "A few years back, over Thanksgiving, two of Charlie's kids died in a car crash. Charlie was driving. Janice nearly died, too; she was hospitalized for weeks. Since then, this time of year…" Pete paused. "Look, don't make it any harder on him than it already is, alright?"

"Come in," Charlie grumbled when he heard the knock on his door during the 4-o'clock news.

The door creaked open a smidgen. "Can I see you for a sec?"

"What do *you* want?"

The remorseful teen who stepped into the sales manager's office was nothing like the brash, cocky brat who had mocked him not 10 minutes earlier. "Charlie, I—" Fumbling for words, Gary twisted a paper tube in his hands. "Here…" In a conciliatory gesture, he held it out. "I'm sorry. I was way outta line."

Charlie unrolled the offending turkey poster. *Must've been Pete's idea.* "Yeah, you were." He dropped the poster onto his desk, dug a handkerchief out of his pants pocket and blew his nose mightily.

Gary shifted from foot to foot. "I know we kinda got off on the wrong foot, Charlie; and I know you don't approve of the crazy stuff I do. Look, Pete just now told me abou—" Slumping into a chair, he gestured pleadingly. "Charlie, I'm so sorry. I swear, I never meant to be malicious."

Charlie eyed him, trying to determine if Gary was yanking his chain. He wasn't sure, but it looked like the kid's eyes were misty. Gary caught Charlie's gaze, then looked away, unable to maintain eye contact.

Charlie exhaled slowly. "I give you a lot of credit for coming here, young fella." His eyes were watery, his words measured. "I admit, I didn't like you at first; but you've shown me a new side of yourself today, and I appreciate that. There's no way you could've known about… the accident. I don't blame you for that; and I *have* been riding you pretty hard, so I guess I deserved the 'No turkeys' comment. In fact" – he unrolled the poster – "that's a darn good likeness." He smiled at the caricature. "And if you don't mind, I think I'll put this up, right here, as a reminder." He taped the poster to the wall, then stood. "Don't you have a radio show to finish?"

Swiping at the tears that blurred his vision, Gary nodded. "Yeah. I guess I do." The onetime adversaries smiled. "I really am sorry, Charlie. I never meant to hurt you. Honest."

Charlie patted the teenager's shoulder. "I know. Now get outta here… you turkey." He grinned.

The following day, a "Gary-free Zone" sign – a promotional

headshot in a red circle with a slash through it and "THIS MEANS YOU, SPIKE!" – appeared on the studio door.

Gary scrawled a mustache, goatee and horns on it. And an arrow through the head. It signaled the end of the hostilities and the start of the practical jokes.

Pete began to wonder which was worse: Gary and Charlie hating each other or getting along. Gary sneaked into Charlie's office and filled the sales manager's desk with packing peanuts. Charlie put a live mouse in Gary's desk; in payback, he found Vaseline smeared on the underside of his doorknob. So he yanked the pages for the 7th, 15th and 23rd of each month out of Gary's desk calendar. Gary glued Charlie's letter opener to his blotter.

Before things escalated further, Pete called them into his office and declared a moratorium. "Next thing you know, there'd be slugs in headphones and snakes in trash cans," he said, chuckling. "Now please, go to neutral corners – and behave yourselves."

As they left, Pete heard Gary tell Charlie, "Snakes in trash cans. Why didn't *I* think of that?"

***

For Christmas, Gary worked with the promotions staff to implement the idea he'd developed for his Creative Marketing project. He organized a "stump the Z97-3 traffic guy" contest – to collect toys for a local shelter. In his final report, he outlined a plan for the contest period, culminating with a fundraising party. He estimated they could collect a thousand toys for the kids and $5,000 for the food pantry.

Professor Philip Stollman was impressed with Gary's ingenuity; so was Jim Burdell. Gary got an A on the project – and kudos from the operations manager for pulling it off.

The contest ran from Monday after Thanksgiving until Friday before Christmas Eve. Four times an hour, Gary invited listeners to call in with trivia questions for Steve Fugacy, "ace traffic reporter and master of minutia." If he answered correctly, the player agreed to bring in a new, unwrapped toy to the station; if the question stumped him, the station donated $10 for "Z97-3 Zanta's elves" to buy extra toys and items for holiday food baskets. Many successful contestants brought toys anyway.

Each contestant received two invitations to the Z97-3 "Holiday Bash" December 18 at Pomperaug High School. The event was open to the public; tickets were $10, plus a non-perishable item

Listeners also donated toys. Lots of them. Even people who didn't get on air brought in donations.

By the end of the first week, the reception area was piled with boxes of toys and paper grocery sacks. Soon they lined both sides of the corridor to the AM studio and filled an empty sales office. And Gary persuaded Charlie to solicit advertisers for raffle prizes.

Gary's adviser was apprehensive about approving his 18-credit schedule for the spring semester; but Professor Hilliard, head of the English department, taught the Shakespearean Comedy class, so he knew the quality of Gary's work. After consulting with his advisee's other professors, he relented and okayed the schedule.

Because classes didn't start 'til mid-January, Grandpa asked Gary to stay until after New Year's. Gary relished the invitation; it didn't feel like Christmas at his apartment.

Thursday, before he signed off, Pete issued an on-air challenge for Gary, host of the Holiday Bash, to show up dressed as Zanta's head elf – spiked green hair and all.

Gary raced to Charlie's office. "I need your help. I know it's short notice – and a real long shot – but can you call Moroni's and see if they'll donate a car for Zanta's head elf to arrive in?"

Charlie balked; Gary persisted. His mind sped. "I'm not looking for anything fancy; just something basic. See if you can get us a car. Red. No, green. Little enough to drive into the gym. We'll raffle it off at the end of the night. Since it's a donation, it's a tax write-off for Moroni's. C'mon, Charlie, they might be willing to do it."

The sales manager shook his head. "Gary, I don't know about this…" But Gary badgered him so insistently, Charlie relented. Shooing the kid out of the office, he picked up the phone.

He waved Gary back in a few minutes later, grinning. "I don't know how I let you talk me into these things, kiddo, but I've got you a car."

Gary flew into the on-air studio, dancing so gleefully he made Lauren Fisher, his normally unruffled newscaster lose her place. As she introduced Gary, he poked at the button to start his jingle-bell music bed, grinning.

"Thanks, Lauren; it's 3:05, I'm Gary Sheldon; thanks for joining me on Z97-3. In case you missed it: Minutes ago, Pete Donovan dared yours truly to show up at our Holiday Bash Saturday dressed as an elf. Now, I've never been one to turn down a dare. So you get the costume, pal, and I'll wear it — right down to the pointy little shoes. Oh, and at the end of the night, we're gonna be raffling off Zanta's Z97-3 Elfmobile!"

Pete suddenly appeared at the large studio window, mouthing a disbelieving, "What?"

Gary waved him in as he turned off the mic and told him about the car. "Hey, Santa's got his sleigh, so Zanta's head elf *has* to have an Elfmobile, right?"

Pete shook his head. "I don't know where you get these ideas, Gary; I'm just glad you don't work for the competition."

Marc Lindsay was already at Pomperaug High, setting up sound equipment, when Gary arrived at the station Saturday evening. Pete had procured an elf costume, complete with pointy-toed green felt shoes, green tunic, felt neckpiece with jingle bells at each tip… even green tights.

Gary wore a pointy cap adorned with a huge silver jingle bell. He sported the requisite festive red-and-green hair. Properly spiked this time, with real hair gel. "No more of that Vaseline crap," he told Pete as he headed into the production room to change.

Charlie was waiting outside when Gary arrived at the school. "I got your car, Elf-boy," he called, grinning. He tossed a set of keys to Gary, who whooped and jingled to the would-be Elfmobile. Gary circled the bright-green Camaro. "It just stands to reason the Z97-3 elf should drive a Z28," Charlie observed, smiling.

More than 700 revelers filled the gym to capacity. Thrilled at the turnout, Gary was amazed to see one person in particular.

Professor Stollman chuckled at Gary's elf garb. "I couldn't miss *this*. I had to see how your project would turn out. You've outdone your original plan — especially in that getup. And raffling off a car? Good thinking, Gary! You've really earned that A."

All night, it seemed everyone wanted to dance with the elf. He always obliged.

Kids asked him to bring their Christmas wish lists to Zanta; he stuffed dozens of lists into the pockets of his tunic, promising them next-day delivery.

Young women asked for his phone number; older women did, too. He said Zanta frowned on that kind of thing.

Monday, Gary called the food pantry and shelter to give what he expected to be a final tally: more than 1,500 toys, 900 bags of food and, due in large part to the car raffle, in excess of $18,000.

The Z97-3 van made dozens of runs to the shelter, with toys and bags of food. And Tuesday morning, Gary, in full elf regalia, presented the food pantry with a check for $15,000.

He also announced that the station would match the more than $3,000 in remaining funds to buy other items for the shelter kids.

*** 

These days, Charlie no longer hid behind his closed door.

Returning from the food pantry, Gary slouched into the chair across from Charlie's desk. "Hey."

"What's up, Elf-boy?"

The sales manager's greeting made Gary smile. "Thanks again for all your help. You came through in a *big* way." He shifted, not quite sure how to say what was on his mind. "I know it's a hard time of year for you. If there's anything I can do to make it less awful, I hope you'll let me know."

"That really means a lot to me; you're a good kid." After a brief silence, he asked, "How old are you, Gary?"

"I'll be nineteen, middle of next month. Why?"

Charlie pasted on a smile. "My Robbie would have been your age. You really remind me of him sometimes. God, I miss him so much!" His mustache twitched as he blinked back tears.

Quietly, Gary shut the door. "I'm sorry, Charlie. I didn't mean to upset you."

The older man waved away the apology. "It's not you. It's just, like you said… a bad time." He paused, wiped his eyes. "Hey, why don't we do lunch. There's this new Chinese place that just opened; you got a *yen* for Oriental?"

Gary groaned. "Sure. Just give me ten minutes to change. I doubt they'll let me in looking like this."

An hour and a half and a few Zombies later, Gary and Charlie returned, laughing like old chums. Charlie still couldn't figure out how to use chopsticks, but he'd had an uproarious time learning. And, by the time they left Wong Lee's, Gary had a new sponsor for New Music Monday.

Before starting his production work, Gary called Moroni's Chevy Emporium, to thank the owner for his generous donation.

"What donation?" Dominic Moroni wanted to know.

"The green Z28. For the party Saturday night."

"There must be some mistake, Gary; we didn't donate a car. But your sales manager did come in on Saturday morning to *buy* a green Camaro… said it was for his kid."

# Chapter 9

(23 December – Thursday)

A heady Christmas-tree scent roused Gary from his sleep. After he made coffee, he stood in the festive room and inhaled the piney tang that carried through the cottage. Marie was due tonight and Grandpa wanted everything just right. And, Gary had to admit, this was about as close to perfect as Christmas could get!

Marie arrived just after 9, laden with grocery sacks and gaily wrapped parcels bulging from New York City department-store shopping bags. While Gary carried his sister's things upstairs, Grandpa ushered her into the living room.

There stood quite possibly the most beautiful Christmas tree she'd ever seen. It was only about six feet tall, but it was full and round as Santa himself and it looked simply magical!

Tiny lights gleamed amid the boughs. Tinsel fluttered on the slightest air currents. From each branch hung stunning ornaments. Some were the delicate European glass ornaments Grandpa and Grandma had collected over the years; others were purchased more recently or given as gifts. And affixed on glittery silver wires were the seashells Gary had helped Grandpa gather at low tide on the still-mild mornings.

"Grandpa! It's gorgeous! It's just what Christmas should look like!"

Three stockings hung over the hearth; evergreen garlands wound down the staircase and around the newel post; the crèche was set up across the wide stone mantel. A smattering of gifts waited beneath the tree: big, tempting squashy parcels; medium-sized boxes; and several small flat packages – all tied with enticing, crinkly bows – and without name tags. Edward chuckled, amused at his grandkids' attempts to guess what was inside, and what was for whom.

Grandpa built a fire and declared it time for cider and cookies. The cider was fragrant, the cookies luscious and buttery. The trio sat up late, talking, drinking and munching.

After a restorative salt-air sleep, Marie awakened early. The aroma of pancakes and bacon woke the others. After a leisurely breakfast, they mapped out their day. Marie and Edward went to the fish market; Gary did the dishes, then headed to Middlebury.

Stopping at the apartment, he checked his mail. Slitting open the envelope containing his grades, he saw a long string of As in one column, and a second column with 4.0s. At the very bottom, the total credits read 24.

When Gary got home, Sam and Martha – who lived four houses up – had arrived. Edward and Sam Johnson had been business partners; Martha and Josephine were best friends. The Johnsons were like family to Edward and they'd always spent Christmas Eve together. Greeting them warmly, Gary went into the kitchen, from which scrumptious aromas emanated. Shedding his coat, he tended to last-minute salad prep.

Using Grandma's cookbooks, Marie had prepared a traditional Italian seafood feast of baked scrod, *baccala* (dried, salted cod) in tomato sauce, fried shrimp, scampi, fried calamari, smelts, and baked calamari over linguine in anchovy-infused olive oil. Grandma always prepared seven dishes, a tradition handed down from her mother, and her mother's mother before her.

As Marie busied herself at the stove, Grandpa poked his head in. "Anything I can do in here?"

She looked up from stirring a burbling pot of linguine. "Nope; all set. Thanks, Grandpa."

"No. Thank *you*." He kissed her forehead. "You two have made it Christmas in this house. That's the best Christmas gift ever."

Everyone joined hands at the table as Edward offered grace. He gave thanks for the delicious array of food and those who prepared it, and for the gathering of friends and family; the love present in the room; loved ones absent that night – whatever the reason; the cozy home in which they gathered, the freedom to so gather and the Savior whose birth they celebrated.

After supper, Gary cleared away the dishes while Marie washed. Martha offered to help; she said it'd been way too long since she'd made herself useful in this kitchen. Sam and Edward wisely retired to the living room; Marie brought them snifters of brandy to enjoy by the fire.

Before they opened gifts, Edward set up his camera and tripod and had everyone gather at the tree. He positioned Gary and Marie in front, with Sam and Martha behind them. He stood beside Sam, one hand on Gary's shoulder. Using the remote shutter release, he snapped a dozen shots while they all laughed and mugged for the camera.

Amid the sound of carols (and paper wrappings being torn from simple gifts), laughter and chatter filled the room. Edward looked around. *This is what Christmas is about. Not rushing around malls to buy, buy, buy — but spending time with family and friends.*

Many of his gifts to loved ones were framed photographs. One present to Sam and Martha was a gilt-framed photo of them at their 50th-anniversary party earlier that year. His gifts for Marie included two framed photos. The first showed her at the Holiday Bash, dancing with her elfin brother; the second captured them a few minutes later. Gary, in profile, had his head thrown back in laughter; Marie grinned from beneath the pointy cap as she tried to pat his spiky hair.

Marie leapt up to hug Grandpa. "Thank you! They're perfect!" She handed them to Gary, seated on the floor. Giddy from a little too much wine, he snickered gleefully and passed the photos along to Sam, who looked them over with a perplexed expression, then tilted them for Martha to see.

"Interesting getup you've got there, Gary. Working part time for Santa?" Sam's blue eyes danced amid the crinkled laugh lines in his weathered face.

"He did it on a dare," Edward said by way of explanation.

Sam chuckled. "Say no more." He was well acquainted with Gary's penchant for outlandish dares.

Smiling, Martha returned the photos to Marie. "Sure looks like you two enjoyed yourselves. But Gary, sweetheart… what ever possessed you to dress like that?"

Grinning sheepishly, he briefly explained about the fundraiser and Pete's dare.

"I heard about that," Sam said, "on TV the other night. They said you raised quite a bit of money."

"Yeah, I guess." Eager to change the subject, he nodded toward the small package Martha held. "Aren't you gonna open that?"

It was a pair of pearl earrings. Delighted, she put them on, then hugged Marie. "Thank you, dear! They're beautiful."

"And they look beautiful on you."

For Edward, there was a pair of cozy red woolen mittens Martha had knitted; a book from his longtime partner that combined his two passions – photography and architecture: a photo retrospective of classic art-deco buildings; a zoom lens and high-speed film from Marie; and, from Gary, *Building the Perfect Feast*, a cookbook that featured recipes from notable restaurants located in architecturally significant structures.

The Johnsons watched in delight as Gary opened his college-survival basket, including a book called *How to Survive College… or Die Trying*, a ream of typing paper, a typewriter ribbon and a bottle of correction fluid; a case of Kraft Macaroni & Cheese; the Cliff's Notes to *Macbeth* and three other Shakespearean tragedies; a roll of quarters for the Laundromat; and a dozen hand-printed coupons, each redeemable for four dozen homemade cookies of his choice made with love by Martha.

Gary hugged them both. "Thank you! This'll all really come in handy. Especially *these!*" He indicated the cookie coupons.

Marie had Gary open only one of his gifts from her. "Save the rest for tomorrow," she said, handing him a small parcel clad in green paper and tied with gold tulle: a book of quotes by famous people about their siblings – compiled and edited by someone she knew from New York.

Grinning, he read the inscription aloud. "Merry Christmas, little brother! When *you're* famous, I expect you to say nice things about *your* sister, too." Gary hugged her. "Okay, how about this: 'She sure could dance well for an old lady.'" His eyes twinkled with mischief. "Ouch!" he exclaimed as she jabbed him in the ribs.

From Grandpa, there was a rectangular box far too heavy to be a sweater. When he pushed aside the tissue paper, Gary found a pair of sturdy leather work gloves. And a hammer. "Are you trying to tell me something?" he asked with a laugh.

The old man smiled. *I love that sound! And I hear it far too seldom these days.* "Yeah; you've got work to do," he quipped. "So quit lolly-gagging!"

Something else lay nestled among the folds of tissue paper. Gary lifted out a long rectangle; his laughter built to a crescendo. The triad of photos, taken two summers ago, caught him in the process of smashing his thumb with a hammer. The first photo showed him setting a nail and lining up the hammer; the second captured the precise moment it landed squarely on his unsuspecting thumb. The third picture depicted the hammer going flying – and a look of surprised pain on Gary's face.

"You were *waiting* for that, weren't you?"

"It was only a matter of time. But it took plenty of patience. You didn't do it all that often. I used up a lot of film to get those last two shots."

Gary's smile lit his face like sunlight emerging from a bank of clouds. "Great; so while *I'm* slaving away in the sun, *you're* playing with your camera."

"*Someone* had to document the moment for posterity," Grandpa kidded, tousling Gary's hair.

While the two hugged, Sam reached for the camera, to capture yet another moment for posterity.

***

Edward awakened just before 9; he ambled downstairs to make coffee. Seated at the kitchen table, he watched the snow fall over the choppy water. Hard to tell where sky ended and water began; they were the same grey. Reflecting on last night, he didn't think he could be happier. *Then again…* In the quiet moments, that niggling uneasiness reminded him the peace he craved eluded him still. He wished he'd had all his grandkids here. And their mom. It would be awkward, with Gary still so angry. His brow furrowed. *That* wound needed serious healing; but some things were best left alone for now. Last time they'd spoken, Edward had told Diane how upset Gary still was and asked, again, when she was going to talk to him.

"Oh, Dad… I don't even know how to begin! If he's that angry, he won't be receptive, no matter *what* my reasons were."

He knew his daughter-in-law was right about that. He also knew he'd been wrong – and wished more than ever he could take back his promise of silence. He wondered whether telling Gary now still constituted breaking it, now that Gary's relationship with Jeremy was severed. Edward sighed. *Damn that promise!* He worried, too, about the harm he was inflicting on their own relationship. Gary would be livid when he learned his grandfather had deliberately deceived him.

Edward hated keeping secrets from him; they'd been too close for too long. If only there were a way to broach the subject without making Gary feel like he was forcing it on him. Deep in thought, he sipped his coffee. He would have chosen Diane over Jeremy any day! But it wasn't his decision. She had been adamant about that: Gary wasn't to know. Not yet. And he certainly made adhering to those wishes easy. Whenever Edward spoke of Diane – even saying her name – Gary's eyes turned stormy. *Like the sea looks now.* And he would shut down. Finally, Edward stopped mentioning her. And Gary seemed happier for it.

Diane and Joey lived 40 minutes away. Joey, who looked much like Gary had at 10, was fine without Jeremy; but he'd *adored* Gary, and life without him caused the child anguish. Edward remained cautious about what information he doled out to Joey about his big brother. He felt deceitful, hiding from Gary that he was in regular contact with Diane and Joey.

His biggest lie was how surprised he had acted when Gary called that day – devastated – to say Mom had left. Edward suspected Gary secretly longed for a reunion, but pride wouldn't let him tear down the barriers around his heart. He *could* orchestrate a meeting; but Gary would see it as an act of deepest betrayal. The nagging feeling remained, an irksome uneasiness surrounding his deception.

Edward was startled back to reality from the demons pestering him by the sounds of Marie and Gary racing downstairs.

"Merry Christmas, Grandpa!"

Edward stood and embraced them. "Merry Christmas!"

Gary poured coffee for himself and Marie. Standing over by the window, he watched the snow, nodding toward the porch, where it had already begun to accumulate. "It's pretty."

"Mmm," Grandpa agreed.

Marie went to the fridge. "What d'you guys want for breakfast?"

Looking at each other, they shrugged. "Whatever you feel like," Grandpa said.

She turned back to him with a playful grin. "What if I feel like *baccala* pancakes?"

Grandpa laughed. "You make *that*, Marie, and I'm going out for breakfast. How 'bout you, Gar'?"

"I'd pay to see her eat them," Gary teased.

"Lucky for me, *you're* the one who can't resist a dare. Now, what's that nickname? Elf-boy?"

"Hey, that's *Mister* Elf-boy to you!"

Amid their banter, the phone rang. Excusing himself, Edward went to the study and shut the door.

Gary stared after their grandfather. "Hmm," he said half-aloud, his brow furrowed.

"What's wrong?" Marie's voice startled him.

"Huh?" He shook his head absently, still staring at the closed door. "Nothing."

"Then what's with the look?"

"What look?"

"That… I dunno – *disapproving* look."

"Don't be silly. I haven't got any *look*."

"Gary, don't give me that. I always could read you." She shook a finger at him. "And you're lying, kiddo. Now what's that look for?"

"He's never done this."

"What? Answered the phone?"

"No." His tone was impatient.

"Then what're you talking about?"

Shaking his head, he looked intently at the closed door. "He's hiding something."

Marie's expression told him she thought he was nuts. "Leaving the room to take a phone call doesn't mean he's hiding something. Maybe," she baited him, "he's got a girlfriend."

Gary snorted. "It's not some… *paramour*, Marie. I'm telling you, something's not right. He's hiding something."

"What, like a terminal illness? You think that's his doctor telling him he's got three weeks to live?"

His eyes clouded. "No. And anyway, why would a doctor call on Christmas?" He looked from Marie to the closed door and back again. "This isn't like him."

Marie made a disgusted face. "Just drop it, Gary. Let him have his privacy, alright?"

Irked, Gary let the porch door bang shut behind him. Leaning against the rail, he stared at the snow, despite the chill wind that sliced through his sweater and the frigid feel of the wet floorboards. Drawing his elbows in close to his sides, he shivered, cupping his hands around his coffee mug.

When Edward returned to the kitchen he refilled his mug. Marie was poking irritably at scrambled eggs on the stove. Something moved beyond the curtains. Peering outside, he asked her, "What's he doing out there?"

Marie smirked. "Sulking." She tried to sound conversational. "Who was on the phone?"

"A friend."

He stepped outside for what he hoped would be only a moment. "Want some company?"

Gary glanced up. "Huh? Sure." He made room along the icicled porch rail.

Grandpa draped an arm around Gary's shoulder. "Pretty out here, huh?"

He nodded, looking straight ahead. "Mm-hmm."

"What did you two fight about?"

Gary turned to look at his granddad. "She told you that?" he asked testily.

"Didn't have to." Grandpa stared him down and won. "What's got you so upset?"

Agitated, Gary returned his gaze to the sea.

Edward waited.

Not a word from Gary.

The silence continued.

At last, Edward shattered it. "I'm waiting."

Gary's voice spewed icy disrespect. "For what?"

"An answer. What's bothering you?" If Edward noted the tears in Gary's eyes, he didn't let on.

He stared at the sand. "I dunno." Absently, he drank his coffee, reveling in its warmth against his palms. "I'm just angry."

"Oh." Grandpa settled against the rail. "At *me?*"

He shook his head.

"Marie?"

"I dunno. Maybe." Gary pushed back from the rail. "Maybe it's just… Christmas."

"Ah." Now the silence felt less hostile. When Grandpa spoke again, his voice seemed nearly apologetic. "It was your mom."

"What?" The one word might as well have been a slap.

"On the phone. Your mom."

A cold hand gripped Gary's insides, squeezed hard. So hard it hurt. "I don't care," he seethed.

Edward went on, as if Gary hadn't responded. "She wanted to talk to you; but I didn't think it was a good idea just now. She said to tell you she loves you. And misses you. So does Joey."

At the mention of his brother, Gary's heart lurched. "Didn't you hear me? I don't wanna hear it!" he hissed, reminding Edward of a cornered cat.

"I hate to see you upset, and I thought it might help if you knew how much she loves you."

"It *doesn't* help! So do me a favor and don't talk to me about her. Ever!" He turned to go.

Grandpa laid a hand on his arm. "Gary, wait," he said softly – so softly the teen almost didn't hear.

He didn't want to hear more; but out of respect, he stopped.

"Alright," Grandpa agreed. "I'll honor that. As long as you don't walk away now."

Gary folded his arms – partly in grudging resignation, but mostly because he was so cold.

"Just answer me this, Gary, and I promise, I'll never mention her again. Okay?" Edward waited for his nod, then asked the question that would plague Gary for weeks: "If she means as little to you as you want me to *believe*, why do you still get so upset at the mention of her?" He held up a hand as Gary balked. "Please. You wouldn't be so hostile if there wasn't still some love there."

Inadvertently, Gary shivered. Not from the wind that buffeted them, though. Grandpa was right. But it hurt too much to admit it, even to himself. Ashamed, he slumped against the rail, grinding away tears with the heel of his hand.

Edward draped an arm around Gary, who felt his frozen insides begin to thaw. "I just wanted you to admit your real feelings. She really does love you; I thought you should know." Now he pulled his grandson into a comforting hug.

"So why did she *leave?*" His voice sounded small and plaintive, muffled against Grandpa's shoulder.

Edward hugged him tighter. "I can't answer that for you, Gary."

Gary's heart had throbbed with anguish at her leaving. But now, to hear Grandpa say she still loved him – it just didn't make sense.

Even if he wanted to let Mom back into his life and his heart, he didn't know how. The pain was too much a part of him. It would take far more than a few gentle words of reassurance to repair the more than two years of damage – damage that had worsened daily since they left.

# *Chapter 10*

"I feel like I can do so much good here," Greg confided one April morning. "But lately, I've had this… *urge* toward something deeper, spiritually."

"You mean, like the priesthood?" Gary asked.

"See, I don't know. Sometimes I feel that way; but other times I think I'm just bored."

For a while, the only sound was the thud of feet on pavement.

Gary recalled the men who served as permanent deacons in his granddad's parish. "What about becoming a deacon?"

"Funny you should mention that. I've thought about it." Greg stopped, retied his laces. "I guess I should give that some more thought. Maybe pursue it."

Meanwhile, beguiled by the freshman's humor and ready smile, Tanya was busy pursuing Gary. However, for the most part, he was oblivious. Lately, he was always dashing to or from class, or poring over books in the library. One April Monday, she invited him to sit with her on the quad to talk. "Why do you keep avoiding me?"

Gary piled his books on the grass. "I'm not avoiding you, Tanya. I mean, I'm here, aren't I?"

She swung a curtain of hair over her shoulder. "You hardly ever stop to talk; you're always running off." She fidgeted. "Gosh, I'm beginning to think you don't like me…"

He gave her a cockeyed grin. "Of course I do; but I'm taking eighteen credits again – and doing production work at the station here; plus I work at Z97-3."

"Oh yeah? You interning there or something?"

"I do afternoon drive – that's why I only take morning classes."

Realization struck Tanya like a mosquito hitting a windshield in July. "Omigod! *You're* Gary Sheldon? I just thought it was a neat coincidence, you having the same name. You're really him? I mean, he's you?" Shaking her head in frustration, Tanya tried to get her words to come out right. "I mean, you're *you*?" Her hand flew to her mouth. "I didn't know you were *famous*!"

There it was again. Gary hated being fussed over. "I'm hardly famous."

Awkward silence enveloped them. She gathered her courage. "Umm… you wanna go out sometime?"

A slow smile crossed his face. No one had ever asked him out before. "Sure."

"Friday okay?"

"Can't." He sounded apologetic. "I have dinner with my grandfather on Fridays."

Tanya's smile was sad. She ran a hand through her auburn mane. "That's nice. Lots of kids break ties with family when they go off to school." She paused, a moment too long. "When I started here, I couldn't be bothered to visit my Nana. Said I was busy, too much homework; any excuse would do. She wrote me letters all the time; I never wrote back. I said I'd visit over summer break. But by then it was too late," she whispered hoarsely. "I couldn't even go to her funeral, 'cause I had three exams that day."

Without thinking, Gary hugged her. "Must've been awful."

Tanya nodded, enjoying his sudden nearness. "It was. And I felt so guilty."

She smelled wonderful. It felt inappropriate, but Gary wanted to kiss her. She tasted like springtime. He kissed her again. His fingers caressed her face. She kissed back, hungry, melting into his arms.

Reluctantly, Tanya pulled away from him. "So what do you and your grandfather do on Fridays?"

"Mainly, talk. I do most of the listening. He's far wiser than me. Plus, he's a terrific cook. After dinner, we usually go for a walk or hang out on the porch… watch the sun set over the water."

"Sounds like you have a great relationship. And your Friday-night tradition sounds fun." Tanya noticed Gary was holding her hand. Another silence crouched between them.

Gary wanted badly to kiss her again. "So… you free Thursday?"

"Yeah."

He gathered his books. "Great. Think of something fun. I'll see you tomorrow; we'll talk then." He gave her a kiss; when she kissed back, Gary's insides fluttered. He hadn't felt that quivery feeling in ages.

Next day, after class, Tanya sank into a seat at the student center. "Man, that Professor Hilliard's a killer!"

Gary nudged her shoulder with his. "Aww, he's not so bad."

"You're just saying that 'cause you're acing his class," she told him with a laugh. She had a musical laugh.

"What's your point?" He grinned, sliding an arm around her. "So, what about Thursday?"

She turned to find his face inches from hers. "I thought *I* was s'posed to ask that."

Taking advantage of her nearness, he tweaked her nose.

She smiled. "So, what about Thursday?"

"Funny you should ask." He kissed Tanya's upturned, laughing mouth; as she drew away, Gary's eyes flickered with his unspoken *Why?*

Tanya touched his face tentatively. "Mmm. You kiss nice. Like an angel." They kissed again. "I really like the way you kiss."

"Good. 'Cause I really like kissing you." He leaned in, kissed her lips, her throat. "So, Thursday. What did you have in mind?"

***

After work, Gary raced home to shower and change. He'd never been on an actual date; by the time he and Ellen started going out, they were so at ease it never seemed like dating. His heart twitched. Even after all this time, he still felt it. Damn it! Damn those old feelings! Damn Ellen! And damn him! He couldn't escape her… or these feelings.

When Gary picked Tanya up at her dorm room, she slipped into his arms. "Hi," she cooed.

She wore a shimmery dress in shades of cream, purple and green that looked like a Monet watercolor and felt like silk beneath his hands.

"You look great." He handed her a bouquet of daffodils, purple freesias and white tulips.

Tanya took a deep whiff. "Mmm. These are gorgeous. Thank you." She arranged the blooms in a vase and locked up the room.

"If you're chilly, I can put the top up," Gary offered when they reached the car.

"I'm fine," she insisted, pulling her sweater more closely around her.

After dinner, Gary took Tanya dancing. As he returned from the bar with their drinks, he caught her staring at him; with a slow wink that said, *I see you watching me*, he watched her blush.

Too soon it was past midnight, and they both had early classes.

"Guess we better get back before the ol' chariot turns back into a pumpkin," Gary kidded.

At the door to her room, Tanya said, "I had a really nice time."

"I'm glad." Still holding her hand, Gary kissed her, slow and sweet.

Her lips parted readily; her arms slid around his waist. "Are you sure you have to go?" she asked. He lifted his head long enough to say he really did have to go, then continued kissing her. She kissed back, pressing against him.

"Are you sure?" Tanya asked breathlessly five minutes later.

His kisses were becoming more intense. "I really should go."

"Are you *sure*?" she asked a third time, running her hands along his arms and back.

"No. Not sure at all."

Arching her back, she stretched against him; her mouth found his and kissed it hotly. Gary groaned, shifted position; he pulled her closer, their bodies fully against each other.

Up the hall, a door opened; a sleepy student passed on her way to the bathroom.

"I'd better go," Gary whispered. Leaving was the last thing he wanted to do.

"Yeah. It's late." Tanya wrapped her arms around his neck and kissed him again. "Thank you for a wonderful time."

He kissed her on the nose. "I'm glad you had fun. Can I see you again?"

Tanya raked her fingers through his hair. "I wouldn't have it any other way."

***

Gary took two classes during each of the two summer sessions. By August, he had 54 credits, just two classes shy of full junior status. In the first session, he and Tanya took a poetry-writing class together. They'd sit on the quad before class and read one another's writing.

Gary loved how Tanya's words flowed; he could hear her lilting cadence as he read.

She, in turn, was grateful for the introspective glimpse into the tender poet who emerged from his protective inner walls. But other than letting Tanya read his poetry, Gary never spoke of his years of abuse.

On Saturdays, they'd go out. To dinner, a movie or the beach. He even brought her to meet Grandpa. Tanya was enchanted by Edward, who was lively and engaging and seemed as interested in her as she was fascinated by him. For Gary, it was like meshing the best parts of his two worlds.

The evening quickly grew late. Tanya laid a hand on Gary's knee and said they ought to head back.

Edward insisted they stay. He showed Tanya to the room at the end of the upstairs hall and left Gary with a glance that warned him against any nocturnal visits.

After a leisurely breakfast and a walk along the shore the next morning, they headed back home, after promising Edward they'd be back soon… and often.

***

In mid-August, during an early-morning run, Greg confided to Gary he'd scrapped his aspirations of priesthood and was staying on as DRE at St. John's.

"What changed your mind?"

A faint smile flickered across his lips. "Well… you know Kim Watson?"

"That blonde lady who works in the parish office? What about her?"

"Well" – Greg's smile broadened – "I think *Kim Andrews* has a nice ring to it, don't you?"

# *Chapter 11*

In the fall of 1983, the start of his second year at UConn, Gary again carried 18 credits. His efforts paid off in the form of straight As; but those grades hadn't come easy. That semester was a killer; and spring '84 was harder still.

By April, he was spending far more time studying, keeping later hours and getting less accomplished. He wasn't eating right and he was haggard, bordering on gaunt. He hardly slept. And it showed. The day he showed up to work barely on time – on too little sleep, wired from too much caffeine – Pete hauled him into his office for a talking-to during the news.

"Sit down," the program director ordered. He paced for a few seconds, then perched on his desk. In the harsh silence, indefinite dread gnawed at Gary's insides.

"I told you when you started school, it better not interfere with work. Maybe you didn't think I was serious; maybe you thought you could handle it. Either way, you were wrong, Gary. And I'm *very* disappointed." Frowning, he ran a hand through his hair. "This is a first warning; the next one will be in writing. Understand?"

Staring at the floor, he nodded. "Yes, sir," he barely whispered.

Pete's tone softened. "Have you looked in a mirror, Spike? You look like hell! When's the last time you had a decent meal? Or got eight hours' sleep? I normally don't do this, and I *won't* do it again; but I don't have a choice right now, 'cause *someone's* gotta be in there in two minutes – and you're no good to me like this, Gary. Go home. And go to sleep. I don't want to see you here tomorrow, either. But when you come back Thursday, I want you *rested.* Have I made myself clear?"

Gary shook his head in protest and gestured futilely. "Pete…" he implored.

Pete silenced whatever else he was going to say with a grim look.

"We shouldn't even be having this talk. But since we are, let me say this: I hate like hell having to be the heavy; but *dammit*, Gary! I need you to make your job your top priority. And if you can't do that" – sighing, he nodded toward the door. "Now, go on, get outta here. But I want to see you – *in here* – Thursday at two. Got it?"

"Yes, sir." Gary felt as small as his voice sounded. He slunk from Pete's office, berating himself all the way to his car. He'd been called on the carpet for something he *swore* he'd never let happen.

*Pulled off the air for two days – ouch!* He winced. Pete was right: He *had* warned him about this.

Pete stalked into the on-air studio, scowling. Lauren finished her newscast and introduced Gary. Too late, she glanced up to see Pete donning his headphones.

"Thanks Lauren." He sounded far cheerier than he looked. Or felt. Especially since he had a whole pile of work to finish. "It's 3:05 on Z97-3 and no, I'm not Gary Sheldon. It's me, Pete Donovan, back for another go-round. I can't seem to get enough of this place today. Gary's takin' a little bit of time off. It's nice to see you again. Thanks for letting me keep you company this Tuesday afternoon."

As the day wore on, Pete began to regret the dressing-down he'd given Gary: Maybe he was too harsh; it was the kid's first slip-up… and he was a good employee. Dependable, enthusiastic and full of promise. *But he has to learn some things just aren't acceptable; and coming in a virtual zombie is one of them!*

*Still, did you have to come down so hard on him?* Pete chided himself.

The following afternoon, Pete phoned Gary. He knew Gary had morning classes… but if he was out now, he'd *really* let him have it!

Gary finally answered on the sixth ring.

"Hey Spike; it's Pete. Did I wake you?"

Gary rubbed his eyes. "Mm-hmm."

"Sorry. Call me when you're awake. We need to talk."

Hours later, a hungry nudge awakened Gary. He rubbed his eyes and tried to blink away the sleep. Raising himself on one elbow, he glanced at the red glow emanating from his clock radio: 9:39. Was it daytime or night? Disoriented, he had a vague memory of someone calling.

Reaching for the phone, he punched in the number and waited. There was a click and a "Hello?"

"Chief?"

"Spike? Is that you?"

"Yeah. You said to call… I hope it's not too late…"

"No. You just woke up now?"

Gary realized Pete hadn't seen him nod; he stifled a yawn. "Yeah. I'm still so tired."

"I'm not surprised. You've been running yourself ragged! Look, I know I said to come in at two tomorrow, but can you get here a little earlier? We have to talk."

"You said to take tomorrow off…"

"No, I said to take *today* off."

"Yeah; you said to take tomorrow off, too," he insisted sleepily, resisting the urge to lie down again.

Pete sounded frustrated. "No…!" Then he asked, "What'd you do after you left my office?"

Gary's brain felt like it had ants crawling in it. "I came home and went to sleep." *After I finished writing my Ethics paper.*

"And you just woke up now?"

It felt like interrogation. "Yes, I just woke up."

"Gary, what day is it?"

*Stupid question.* Gary sighed aloud and slumped against his pillow. "It's *Tuesday.*"

"Spike, you slept through Tuesday. And most of Wednesday."

Gary felt sick. "Oh geez. Tell me you're joking, Pete."

"Nope. It's Wednesday night."

*No wonder I'm hungry!* His last substantial meal had been dinner at Grandpa's on Sunday. Then something else hit him. "*Shit!*" he spat as he sat upright.

"What's the matter?"

"I had a paper due today. *Shit!*"

"So hand it in tomorrow."

"It's *late.* They take off points for lateness." He gritted his teeth. Still distracted, he exhaled loudly. "I'm sorry, what'd you want?"

"I wanted to talk to you. Can you come in at one fifteen tomorrow?"

Gary scratched at his two-days' growth of stubble, tried to think. "I – uh, yeah – I guess so." He raked a hand through his hair. His brain raced. *I gotta get that paper turned in! I can't believe I slept through all my classes today. Damn!* He pounded a fist against his head. His mind sped ahead to tomorrow. First, he had to turn in that paper and explain why he missed class. Attendance was mandatory. Between classes, he'd have to see his other professors, find out what they covered – plus borrow someone's notes. *I'll hafta do twice as much homework tomorrow just to keep up.* Gary sighed in despair, feeling like he was drowning. Then he realized Pete was still talking.

"… work to catch up on." He didn't catch all of it; and while he was trying to piece together the first part of Pete's last sentence, he missed the start of the next one. "… keep 'til Friday, you know."

Gary rubbed his eyes. "Chief? Can we talk about this tomorrow? I'm just *really* tired."

Mercifully, Pete agreed. He said goodnight and hung up.

"Geez! How could I possibly have slept for so long and still be so tired?" Gary asked aloud. More than that, he was ravenous.

On the way to the kitchen, he spied his reflection in the mirror. His eyes were dull and sunken, with dark circles around them. *I look like a freakin' raccoon!*

He found cereal, a quart of milk, three ribs of celery, an onion, two carrots, seven slices of moldy bread and an egg. He tossed the bread, poured himself some cereal, added milk and ate it. Trying to decide if he had the energy to eat anything else, he scrounged through the cabinets until he found some tuna. Was there mayo? He could make a sandwich. No – wait, the bread was bad. He put the tuna back and went to stare into the fridge again; this search yielded a small cube of cheese, some sad-looking parsley and a Dr Pepper.

If Grandpa was here, he'd chop and cook the onion, then whisk the egg with some milk. *First he'd give me a good talking-to for getting so run down; then he'd cook the onion and whisk the egg with the milk.* He'd shred the cheese, chop the parsley and make a perfectly respectable omelet.

Gary sat at the table, head in his hands. *Too much work.*

Besides, he was exhausted. He glanced at the calendar. Spring break was a few days away. Maybe he'd survive 'til then. *On an egg, some veggies and a can of tuna?* Pulling himself to his feet, he made that omelet. He felt better after eating; but he still felt so exhausted! *I just wanna crawl in bed for 10 more hours.* Instead, he opted for a shower. It made him feel almost human again.

Setting his alarm, he put the volume on high. He opened the windows and put new sheets on the bed. It always felt so good, climbing into a bed with fresh linens, especially with the cool night air refreshing the room. Gary imagined the *whoosh* of waves against the shore. Seconds after his head hit the pillow, he was asleep.

Awakening before the alarm sounded, Gary felt better than he had in weeks! He yawned hugely, filling his lungs with restorative air. He frowned at his reflection in the mirror; it frowned back. He'd need a machete to get through that stubble. *Maybe I'll just let it grow. Grow a beard? You can barely grow a houseplant!* He laughed aloud at the absurdity of that notion, then grabbed his shaver.

He gathered his books and the report he should have turned in yesterday. Professor Godreaux would knock off a half grade for each day it was late. He did the math; the best he could get was a B-plus. *There goes the ol' 4-0.* He couldn't afford to do badly in her class; it was in his major… one of them, anyway.

Partway through this semester, Professor Hilliard commented that with Gary's "propensity for English classes" and "gift for written expression," he might want to consider majoring in English. Gary had balked; a communications degree was more useful than one in English. Looking over his advisee's transcript, the professor made what Gary felt was a radical suggestion: "Why not double major? You just need six more credits in each area. And you can minor in marketing." He paused. "You're taking an awful lot of classes this semester. How're you holding up?"

Gary shrugged. "So far? Fine."

But that was two weeks ago.

***

Sixth period. Math stymied Michaela. Slumping low, she glared at the clock, willing the hands to move. No use. It was still 12:52. She gnawed at her thumbnail, hoping Mr. Stanley wouldn't call on her. All those Xs and Ys baffled her! And even after all this time, she was afraid the other kids would make fun of her.

At 16, she wasn't just the eldest in her class; she was the oldest at Memorial Middle School. Probably the oldest eighth grader ever! She wasn't dumb; she'd just missed so much school. Ten and a half years earlier, in October 1973, she'd complained of feeling tired all the time.

Her parents had dragged the first grader from doctor to doctor, never getting any real answers. What was worse than constant visits was all the waiting: sitting in waiting rooms with all those people staring at her; sitting on the cold metal table in the doctor's office – waiting for yet another doctor; trying to be patient while he jabbed and poked at her… waiting for someone to say what was wrong.

She'd undergone dozens of tests before a specialist finally provided an answer.

She didn't understand what leukemia was, but she watched the sound of it turn Daddy's face grey. And watched her mother cry.

All she knew was that silly-sounding word made her feel worse than she ever thought she could. But that wasn't the worst part of being sick. It wasn't having to always go to doctors. Or all those blood tests. Or chemo. The worst part was how the kids at school made her feel. They teased her when her hair fell out; they laughed and called her Softball Head. And when their cruel taunts made her cry, they teased her even more, calling her Wimp and Crybaby.

Truth was, she was neither of those. She'd endured months of chemo with scarcely a whimper. "Pretty remarkable for a six-year-old," Daddy would say. He stayed with her during every treatment, holding her hand and reminding her what a brave little girl she was. "You're a trouper, Kayla. A real trouper."

She faced her illness like a stoic little warrior, never letting on to Daddy how ill she felt. When nausea overwhelmed her, she never let him see her cry as she hunched over the toilet; she didn't want him to be disappointed, or think she was weak. Not that he ever would have thought that. She was his princess; she didn't have to be strong or brave. Michael Conwaye loved his little girl exactly as she was. Michaela just wished Mommy felt the same way.

Susan Conwaye made no secret that her daughter's illness was a burden. She had to cart the girl to doctor's visits, to the pharmacy, to the library for books. On each successive trip, her patience wore thinner. And when her irritation flared and Michaela responded in a way her mother deemed "childish and inappropriate," Susan lost all control and screamed at Michaela until the little girl cried.

She got a clean bill of health in August 1976. But when she got the go-ahead to return to school in September, she was horrified at being put back into first grade. As brave as she'd been throughout her illness, she couldn't bear this final cruel blow.

She sobbed when she learned she had to stay back, begging to be allowed to join the rest of her class in fourth grade. "I can catch up," Michaela insisted. "I just *know* I can!"

But all her pleading and wide-eyed assurances were of no use. She would have to repeat the grade, the school administrators told her parents; she'd missed practically the whole year.

Michaela felt as humiliated as a 9-year-old with no hair could feel. She went from being the same age as her classmates to being the class freak! She was an oddball, the bald kid *and* the oldest in first grade. Worse still, some of the kids in her class wouldn't be six 'til October! And she'd been nine since May. So she felt old and awkward *and* stupid. And their teasing didn't help.

But one little girl, Patricia Deming – Trish for short – befriended her. Trish, whose big brother also survived a bout with cancer, stuck up for Kayla when the others picked on her. She stood up to them at recess, ordering them to stop laughing at her friend. Trish even talked her mother into letting her cut her long red hair short. Really, *really* short! And she took to wearing baseball caps to school, so Michaela wouldn't feel quite so different.

Over time, most of the kids tired of harassing Michaela. But the meanest ones – like that awful Jennie Falmouth – still made her feel like a big gawky idiot. Even now. But, she figured, she should be used to it. Jennie and her evil brood had taunted her all through elementary and middle school.

For the most part, running had become Michaela's escape – the safety valve when her pressure-cooker life built up too much steam. But Jennie was on the team, too; so even *that* offered little peace.

Michaela was slight of stature as a child – a little wisp of a thing. But she'd been the tallest kid in class since second grade; and when she got her period in third grade, that was the worst!

During a math test one spring morning, she had felt a strange, drippy sensation and ran from the classroom, only to discover her clothes were bloody. Terrified, she locked herself in a bathroom stall and cried. Years earlier, she'd lain in a hospital bed with tubes in her arms; bags of blood and clear liquids hung from IV poles. She recalled thinking she was dying. And now there was all this blood! She didn't know where it was coming from – or why. She'd sobbed in the bathroom stall, terrified she was going to die.

When Michaela didn't return, Mrs. Moss asked the next-door teacher to mind her class while she went to check something out. She hurried down the hall to the girls' lavatory. Stepping inside, the teacher heard muffled sobs. Little matchstick legs showed beneath the door of the second stall from the end. Mrs. Moss' heels made little click-clicking noises as she crossed the tile floor. She tapped at the door with a fingernail. "Michaela? Is everything okay?"

She began to hyperventilate and cry even harder.

Her teacher remained calm. "Michaela, honey, are you in pain?"

"N-n-no," she stammered, sobbing and hiccupping.

Mrs. Moss, whose own daughter was about that age, followed her Mommy instinct. "Sweetie, listen." Her voice was reassuring. "Don't be afraid, but is there blood in your panties?" The child's wails gave the teacher her answer. "It's okay, sweetie. Nothing to worry about."

Mrs. Moss helped Michaela clean up, then walked her to the nurse's office for a sanitary pad while they waited for her mom. She decided – right then – if *she* ever had children, she wanted to be as good a mommy as Mrs. Moss must be to her own kids. She spoke softly and made her feel like everything would be okay.

***

Michaela looked at the clock: 12:56. Class would end soon; only English class remained. Just then she gave a start. Mr. Stanley was calling her name. She sat up. "Huh?"

Students around her snickered.

"Go to the board and solve problem number two on page two twelve."

*Why can't the bell just ring?* If she took her time writing, she might get out of actually having to solve it. She picked up a piece of chalk and began copying down the equation. Dizzy and hot, she prayed she wouldn't collapse. As she wrote the last bit, the bell rang. She replaced the chalk on its ledge; still facing the board, she heard 22 chairs scraping backward as the exodus began.

As she went to collect her books, Mr. Stanley's voice turned her blood to clumps of ice. "Miss Conwaye, finish that problem."

"Okay." She bobbed her head in assent as she turned to go. "I'll have it for you tomorrow."

He leaned back in his chair and stared at her. "Finish it now."

"But, Mr. Stanley" – she gestured with her chalk-dusted hand – "I have to get to English class."

"I'll write a note for Miss Pritchard. Please finish the problem."

The lump in her throat felt like a potato. "I – I can't," Michaela whispered. "Don't make me do it up there; let me figure it out at home and hand it in tomorrow. Please?"

"So someone else can do the work and you can just hand in the answer, pretty as you please?" He shook his head. "I don't think so, Miss Conwaye. Go back and finish the problem."

She kept her face turned toward the board so he wouldn't see the hot tears pricking at her eyes. Brushing them away, Michaela ended up with an eyeful of chalk dust. Wiping her sleeve across her face, she took a deep breath and a fresh look at the problem. She threw her hands up in resignation. "I don't know where to start!"

"If you were paying attention, you'd know how to solve the problem."

"But I" – her cheeks burned – "I don't *understand* it!" Her voice grew shrill.

"Well then, you'll just miss English class, because you're not leaving until you finish it. Correctly."

Despising Mr. Stanley, she blinked back chalky tears. "Fine." She willed herself to comprehend the tangle of variables looming there.

"Just staring at it won't help," he derided. "You actually have to *think*."

She didn't have to turn around to know what his expression looked like; she heard the mocking sneer in his voice.

"Your badgering me doesn't help either!" Turning abruptly, she sent the chalk whizzing past his balding head.

Grabbing her books, Michaela ran for the girls' room; the chalk dust in her eye was driving her crazy!

***

"Hey, Spike," the pretty blonde receptionist greeted Gary. "Pete's looking for you."

"I know." He checked the clock: 1:39. "Shit," he muttered.

"I think I should warn you." Brenda's words froze the young DJ in place. "Don't do anything to tick him off. He's grouchy today."

"Great." Gary forced a smile. "Thanks for the heads-up, Bren."

He opened the studio door. "Sorry. Got tied up at school." At seeing Pete's expression, he floundered. "I know: You didn't want to hear that." Before Pete could reply, words spewed from Gary's mouth like water from an open fire hydrant. "About the other day: You're right. This is my primary obligation; and I let you down. It was *totally* unprofessional. You were completely justified, pulling me off the air. And I want you to know, Pete: I am *so* sorry. It'll never happen again." His heart pounding, Gary stopped, expecting the program director to tell him he'd got *that* right and if he wanted to keep his job, he better start showing up on time for meetings with his boss, dammit – and just who the hell did he think he was, anyway?

For the longest time, Pete said nothing; when he did speak, it was to the listeners. "Twenty minutes 'til two on Z97-3; I'm Pete

99

Donovan; thanks for having me along on your Thursday. We've got Phil Collins up next; Cyndi Lauper's on the way and at three: the return of Gary Sheldon." Starting a commercial, he jotted the time on the log. "I appreciate your candor, Gary; but I'm afraid your thinking's a little off base."

Gary crumbled. This was it: He was gonna be fired. But then why would Pete have mentioned on air he'd be back? He waited for clarification.

But, maddeningly silent, Pete pressed another button. Another commercial; another notation. And a third. *Then* he addressed Gary as he cued up a record. "I was dead serious when I said I was angry about your work slipping. Yes, I meant to reprimand you. But I didn't take you off the air as punishment. That was *never* my intent, Gary. I think you know that's not how I operate."

"Then why…?" Gary's words trailed away amid his uncertainty.

Pete took a swig of Coke. "Maybe, on some level, I meant to rattle you. If it frightened you into taking your job seriously, that's a good thing. But— hang on. Eighteen minutes 'til two, Z97-3. Pete Donovan and you: We sure make a great team, don't we? We'll be together another hour or so, then Gary's back to take you through 'til seven." He poked a button to engage a turntable, sliding the volume up so the music came up under his voice. "Here's the latest from Phil Collins on Z97-3 WZBX."

Pete put the just-played ads in the revolving rack to his left, then tapped his pen on the counter. "Now where was I? Oh, yeah: why I took you off the air." His expression grew serious. "Like I said, Spike: It wasn't to punish you; this isn't the amateur hour. I was worried about you. You were a zombie. And you're no good to me like that."

The door opened; Lauren handed Pete a new weather forecast, then slipped out. He propped it on the copy stand.

"I'm disappointed you'd come in so worn out. Especially after I warned you" – his edgy tone made Gary cringe – "but I sent you home for your own good. You do understand that. Right?"

Gary nodded solemnly. "Yeah. And Pete, I really feel bad about this."

"Don't feel bad about it," Pete replied kindly. "Just don't do it again." He motioned to the door. "Now go; you've got a world of production to catch up on."

Pete wasn't kidding! Gary had at least a dozen spots – four of them for today! Two were straight reads, with music beds; but the others would require some creativity. Gary started with the easiest ones. He did the first spot in one take; the second took longer, but it was still pretty straightforward. The third would be a challenge! A Christmas-in-April promotion for Moroni's. With elf voices. On the "talent" line, indicating who was to record the spot, was scrawled "EB" – with a pointy-eared smiley face next to it. Gary grinned. Charlie was such a goofball. EB stood for Elf-boy.

He set the reel-to-reel machine's recording speed to 3.75 inches per second and read over his copy to familiarize himself with the wording. He put on his headphones, rolled tape and opened the mic. He'd have to speak distinctly, so his words wouldn't sound garbled at 7.5ips. Gary taped the first elf voice, then disguised his voice for the second. The third posed a problem. It was supposed to be female. He frowned; no amount of disguising his voice would yield a believable female elf.

He opened the studio door. "Bren? Can I borrow you? I need a girl elf. Can you read three lines for me?"

"I'll try."

"Sit here" – Gary settled her behind the mic, his hands on her shoulders – "and put these on." He adjusted his headphones over her ears. Turning as he leaned to readjust the mic, the shy blonde found herself nose to nose with Gary.

He didn't seem to notice. "Okay, I need a volume level. Just say something. You should hear yourself through the phones."

"What do you want me to say?" She jumped when she heard her voice in her ears.

Busy watching the needle on the control board, Gary patted her shoulder. "That's great, Bren. Keep talking. Here's what I need you to read – slowly and clearly." He reached for the copy. "Might as well get familiar with it while I set the recording levels."

Upon returning to her desk, she found a terse note from Pete: *Brenda: See me. Immediately!*

Twenty minutes later, Gary perched on a corner of Brenda's desk. "Wanna hear your spot?"

She avoided making eye contact. "Umm, that's okay. I'll hear it on the air."

"C'mon, it'll only take a minute. It's great! You make an adorable elf."

"Gary, I *can't.*" Brenda's hair swung as she shook her head and returned to her work.

"Okay." Gary flipped to the scheduling sheet clipped to the production order. "It's on at three fifty. I think you'll like how it came out." He headed toward the studio, his stack of commercials in one hand, headphones in the other. He kept looking back, wondering what caused her abrupt shift in demeanor.

"What the hell were you thinking, letting Brenda hang out in the production studio while you're working?" Pete assailed him.

Now Gary understood Brenda's unusual behavior.

"You've got your job; she's got hers. In case you hadn't noticed, they don't intersect, unless she has messages for you. She doesn't belong in production – especially while you're recording. What's the matter with you?" Pete fumed.

Gary couldn't resist. "Well" – he leaned against the doorjamb – "it was kind of a testosterone thing."

"Well, that makes it even *more* inappropriate! It's not enough she moons after you like a lovesick puppy; must you encourage her? You wanna date her, do it on your own time. Just keep your damn hormones in check during office hours. Geez! I can't believe you actually said that!" Seeing the grin dancing across Gary's face, Pete glared at him in exasperation. "*What* are you smirking about?"

"For one thing, your record's ending," Gary said.

Pete jammed the legal ID into the cart deck and started it.

"When I said it was a testosterone thing, I meant there's no way I coulda voiced the female elf in that Moroni's spot. Some things just cry out for a real woman." Gary grinned. "Me, for instance."

"You pain in the ass! You should know better than to pull that kind of crap when I'm pissed at you. I nearly took your head right off!"

"Yeah. But that look on your face was priceless!" Then, turning serious, Gary said he didn't realize Brenda would get in trouble; he apologized, conceding he should have sought permission. "From now on, I'll know better. Vicki and Jen are out and I needed it today, so I had to improvise."

It was a less contentious Pete who stopped in the lobby after his shift. "Brenda, I owe you an apology. I didn't realize Spike asked you to do that spot – which sounds terrific, by the way. But in the future, have someone cover the phones when you're recording, okay?"

# Chapter 12

Michaela sighed. Math variables swam before her. She'd stared at number two forever and it *still* made no sense. Dreading her classmates' snickers didn't help. But that wasn't her only distraction. The commotion downstairs made it impossible to concentrate. She shut her door; no use. She turned up the radio, but the chatter between the DJ and the traffic guy was less conducive to math than her parents' bickering. This battle seemed to be over work. Susan, a realtor, and Michael, district attorney for Waterbury, didn't agree on anything lately. Money and alcohol were frequent topics for these top-of-their-lungs discussions.

"I'm not the one who fixes martinis the moment I get home!"

"Of course not, Susan; you keep a bottle in your desk drawer!"

"Do you have any idea what kind of pressure I'm under?"

"I had no idea house showings and real-estate contracts were so taxing. Maybe you'd like to juggle six criminal cases at once. That's *much* less stressful!"

"Oh Michael – come off it. No one said your work's not—"

*I wish they'd get divorced already!* Michaela laced up her running shoes. "Going for a run. Back in a bit," she shouted, tearing down the stairs and out the front door. Lately, running seemed the only release for her pent-up anger. There was plenty of *that* now, with her parents' constant fighting. Their hostility was rubbing off on her. Anger by association. She ran hard, her feet pounding on the road. At Wickham Park, she gazed up at the trees along both sides of the path, just starting to bud. *They look like great big stalks of broccoli.* Michaela smiled at the notion of running through all that broccoli.

Running felt like freedom. Except, while she could outpace most of her teammates, she couldn't outrun her troubles. Whenever she stopped, they always seemed to be gaining on her. Her folks' voices clamored in her head, even out amid the broccoli trees. She double knotted her laces and did a half-mile sprint to the end of the track. She loved feeling the wind rush past her face. Her chestnut hair streamed behind her. After four laps, Michaela pulled to a stop, her cheeks flushed. Wiping her face against her shoulder, she headed home at a trot.

"I'm back!" she yelled as she burst through the door.

The house was quiet. *Make-up sex?* Nope; as loudly as her folks argued, there was never any question as to when they were making love. Michaela stood in the hall, listening, then moved through the house, expecting to find Mom banging things in the kitchen and Dad on the porch with a cigar. Not only was Dad *not* on the porch, his Audi was gone. She checked the basement. Mom, snuffling, slumped against the dryer, clutching an open vodka bottle.

"Mom?" Michaela approached uncertainly as Susan tried to hide her tears and the bottle. "C'mon, Mom. Let's get you upstairs."

After guiding the swaying blonde up the stairs, the girl sat her at the kitchen table. She poured the vodka down the drain, then sat facing her mother. "What happened?"

Susan forced a smile and waved her hand. "Oh, it was nothing, sweetie. Everything's fine," she slurred.

"Everything's *not* fine. I heard you arguing. Now, why were you in the basement crying – and drinking? And where's Daddy?"

Susan eyed her daughter for a long numb moment, her lower lip trembling. "He's gone."

"I can *see that*. But where?"

"I don't know. Gone. Packed his things and left."

"Left!" Michaela squawked. "Why? What'd you fight about?"

Her tears started again. "We were *not* fighting."

"Noo, of course not." Her voice oozed sarcasm. "You just have *really* loud discussions."

"Stop it!" Susan pounded the table. "Just stop! I don't need you judging me. You always take his side! You two are just alike. And I'm sick of you both!" She flounced away.

The gnawing in Michaela's stomach resumed. It was always like this after a fight: the screaming, the increased drinking, the palpable tension. *No wonder he left.*

Half an hour later, the phone rang.

"Hi Kayla."

"Daddy, where are you?"

"At a hotel. I'm looking for an apartment this weekend. Wanna help?"

*No. I want normal parents with a normal marriage.* "Maybe. I dunno. Daddy, what's going on?"

"It's complicated, honey. Your mom and I – sometimes we just don't see eye to eye."

"Lately it seems like a lot of the time," she observed. Her insides twisted; the knots tightened when Dad didn't respond. "Are you getting a divorce?"

"No!"

*He answered too fast. They're getting a divorce.* Her heart pounded. "Can I live with you?"

"We'll talk about it later, sweetie, alright?"

She ignored this. "You left before I got back. You didn't even say goodbye."

"Michaela, please, this is hard enough." He sighed. "I'm sorry, princess; I should have stayed 'til you got home. But things don't always work out how we want them. I know it's not fair, but this is how it's got to be – at least for now."

"But *why*, Daddy?"

"Sweetheart, it's grown-up stuff and you're only—"

"I know: I'm only sixteen; but I'll be seventeen next month. And whatever you and Mom do affects me, too!"

"True. But I'm still not going to discuss it with you now. We'll talk later. Will I see you this weekend?"

"Guess that's your call, isn't it?"

Her frosty tone put Michael on the defensive. "Why are you snapping at me?"

"'Cause *you're* the one who left; and you left me with *her*!"

"Kayla, I already explained to you—"

"You explained *nothing*. I gotta go."

***

After Tanya graduated, Gary spent nearly every waking moment at the station – except for weekends at Grandpa's and summer classes. Pete and operations manager Jim Burdell both realized the young DJ was full of ideas about the station's musical direction and wasn't shy about expressing them.

***

The last snow hit at the end of May. By then, Michael had rented an apartment in Waterbury. Michaela spent every other weekend there, after doing her chores. She didn't mind the housework, but she despised cleaning up after Mom and making excuses for her last-minute cancellations.

At least grocery shopping got her out of the house for a while every Saturday. Meandering amid the aisles, she watched the other shoppers: that frizzy-haired blonde whose two kids always seemed to have runny noses; the guy with the jean jacket and ponytail, who loaded his cart with canned cat food and boxes of mac & cheese. And the cute guy in the UConn sweatshirt with the Walkman. Oh, and that old lady who wears that red wool hat all the time, even in summer. She mumbles to herself – *sings, sometimes*, Michaela noted.

One stormy July Saturday, the old lady in the red hat didn't have enough money for all her groceries. She started to cry when a sour-faced man near the back of the line yelled at her.

"Chrissakes, lady, hurry up and pay already. Or put something back and get outta here," shouted the crab, readjusting his straw hat on his nearly bald head.

Next in line behind the frail woman, Michaela seethed over how the grouch had made her cry. As the lady wiped her eyes with a tissue, fretting over what to put back, the teen slipped the cashier a twenty. She patted the lady's shoulder. "It's okay, ma'am. Your bills got stuck together. See? There's plenty of money."

The old woman stared in disbelief as the cashier confirmed the teen's fib. "Sometimes the humidity makes 'em stick. Here's your change." The cashier laid $12.53 in her open and trembling palm.

Michaela quickly sorted through her cart, selecting several items she could forgo. She had to be sure she had enough for bus fare; she'd hate to walk home in this rain!

Right behind her, Gary considered doing what the girl had done for that sweet old woman – after all, the old lady could easily have been his grandmother; but he didn't want to embarrass her.

The next week, Gary spotted the girl again. She counted peppers into a plastic bag, crossed them off her list and moved on to stare at the tomatoes.

Week after week, he would watch her trudge down the aisles, a careworn look on her face. *She always seems so sad; wonder what's wrong?* Shrugging, Gary would remind himself everyone had worries. He'd also invariably wish he could cheer her up.

∗∗∗

In the fall of '84, Gary began his last semester at UConn. He got a letter from Tanya in August, saying she'd been hired at a public-relations firm in Philly and found an apartment in a neighborhood overlooking a city park. They traded occasional calls, but went their separate ways.

With a lighter class schedule and a virtually nonexistent social life, Gary began clubbing in New Haven or Hartford. Or, when he felt adventurous, New York. It was entertainment *and* research. At night, he'd watch dancers' frenzied gyrations; by day, he prowled record stores for music. His record collection grew weekly, as did his music-scene savvy. Both enhanced New Music Monday.

One Monday in mid-September, Pete called Gary in for a meeting with Jim Burdell.

Getting pulled into a meeting with the big boss meant one thing: He was gonna catch hell for something. Maybe even get fired. Gary struggled to recall what he might've said or done to put his job in jeopardy. He couldn't think of anything that would land him in the operations manager's office.

Seated in a black leather chair in Jim's office, Gary looked from his boss to his boss' boss, his heart clattering crazily. Awaiting the inevitable, he flashed back to the expulsion proceedings two and a half years earlier in Msgr. Streng's office. His mouth went dry and his throat closed up.

Jim wasted no time: Jenna Glesson, the music director, needed to care for her ailing son. He wanted to appoint an assistant to help run the department. "You've got the broadest musical knowledge base of anyone here. And, with some of the promotions you've pulled off, you've proven you can handle record-company execs. We figured you were the logical choice."

Stammering his astonishment, Gary said that was the last thing he'd expected.

"Well?" the program director prompted. "What'll it take for you to accept?"

"I don't understand," he admitted.

Pete smiled. "This is the salary-negotiation part."

Jim scratched two sets of numbers on a pad and slid it across the desk. "Here's what you make now. And this" – he pointed to the bottom number – "is what we're prepared to offer."

Gary gulped at the second figure; it was larger than the first. Obscenely larger.

But before he could respond, Pete sweetened the deal. "We're willing to work around your schedule 'til the end of the semester. I'll basically do whatever you need to ease the transition: lighten your production load, cover an air shift a week 'til exams end. You let us know what you need. We want you for this position; it's extra work, but you can handle it. It's a real opportunity to advance; and there's no one we think is better suited to it than you."

Gary looked from Pete to Jim and back. He wished his heart would quit pounding so loudly, so he could at least think. "How soon do I have to let you know?"

***

Gary cued up his last song and glanced at his updated weather. Madonna throbbed in his headphones; he flipped the mic switch and pressed the remote-start button for the left turntable. Turning up the mic, he leaned in close to it on its jointed metal arm. "It's forty-two degrees in Middlebury under partly cloudy skies. Expect clearing skies and chilly temps tonight, lows in the thirties; mostly sunny, cooler tomorrow, high around forty-five. Again, forty-two right now outside our studios. Four minutes to seven, I'm Gary Sheldon; that'll do it for me. Thanks for letting me keep you company this afternoon on Z97-3. It's been fun, but I gotta pick up my toys and head on out of here. Marc Lindsay's up next to take you through 'til midnight. I'll leave you with Giorgio Moroder and Philip Oakey, 'Together in Electric Dreams.' I'll see you in *your* electric dreams, and I'll see you back here tomorrow at three, right after Pete Donovan. Make it a good night now. Bye." Turning up the monitor, Gary danced around the studio while he filed records. As the song faded, he played the legal ID and started Marc's first song.

A few minutes later, he leaned in the doorway of his boss' office. "You're here late."

"Yeah. Catching up on some work. Hey, I like that last song you played; sounds like Human League."

"That's 'cause Phil Oakey's their front man. It's off the 'Electric Dreams' soundtrack; terrific track, but it's not moving, chart-wise. What I'd *really* like to do is use it as a closing theme." Perching on the arm of a chair, he grinned. "It's catchy and hip – and it basically says what I try to relate through the music I feed these nice people: Even though we have only a short time together, we can connect in a meaningful way on other levels."

Pete repressed a grin. "Go ahead, commandeer the new music for your own selfish purposes."

"Are you agreeing or just making fun of me?"

Walking to the door, Pete patted Gary on the shoulder. "A little of both, I'm afraid. But mostly agreeing."

(11 December – Saturday)

_This is my family_. Gary glanced around his kitchen at everyone Marie had invited. _So what if we're not related? These are the folks who care about me_. A knock at the door sent his thoughts scurrying.

With a conspiratorial wink at Marie, Edward watched as Gary went to answer it.

On the porch shivered Tanya. "Congratulations, graduate!" She was in his arms in an instant.

After a spirited kiss, he drew the new arrival into the little group. "Are you my present?" He draped an arm around her. "Can I keep you?"

"You couldn't afford me," she teased, kissing Gary again before rushing to give Edward a hug. "Oh, it's so good to see you," she exclaimed from within the old man's embrace. "I've missed you so much!"

"As have I, my dear." He smiled. "And to answer your question, Gary: I flew her in just for the party. _This_" – reaching for a large cube-shaped box under the table, he handed it to Gary – "is your gift." Unexpectedly light, it bore a huge bow. Whatever was inside wobbled. "Go on, open it."

Something about Grandpa's eyes reminded Gary of Santa. Lifting the lid, he peered inside. He was greeted by a tiny "Me-you?"

On a round flannel cushion sat a tabby kitten with enormous green eyes, bright-white whiskers and a tiny pink nose. And a green bow on its collar. "Me-you?" it asked again.

"Hi there, little guy," Gary greeted the creature. He looked at his granddad, delighted. "He's adorable!" Dropping to his knees, he lifted the kitten and held it close. It sniffed at his shirt, then nestled beneath his chin and began to purr.

After everybody left, Gary decided the kitten must feel foolish wearing that great big bow. He noticed something wrapped around its collar. Unhooking it, he found a strip of paper. A note. Written in squiggly kittenish print: _Look under my cushion_.

Lifting the cushion, he found an envelope taped to its underside. Inside was a check. He figured Grandpa would give him money; he just didn't know how he'd manage it. Grandpa was forever hiding $20 bills in Gary's apartment and in his room at the beach house. Gary would collect the money and stuff it into the ceramic pig in the kitchen that held Grandpa's grocery coupons. As often as he returned them, he found new ones. The War of the 20s became a kind of game. Gary had to admit they came in handy, especially early on. But this was different. Gary stared at the check. *Twenty grand!*

With his new pet perched on his shoulder, he went to the phone. "Grandpa, this is *way* too much!"

The old man's voice reflected his smile. "I wondered when you would find that."

"Thank you. But I can't accept this!"

"It wasn't my idea; that cat wanted to be sure you can keep him living the life he's used to. He was one pampered pussycat. If he hasn't got a cadre of mice feeding him kippers, he'll come looking for me." His voice turned serious. "Besides, you want to live in that apartment forever? That can be a down payment on a house some-day. Maybe even one of those old Victorians. Put it in the bank and forget about it."

"But..." Gary's protest was halfhearted.

"Or splurge a little: travel; buy something you really want. Stock up on cat toys and save the rest. Have some fun, but be practical. You worked hard these last few years, Gary. I'm proud of you; this is my way of expressing that."

Gary scritched the kitten under the chin. "You *coulda* just sent a card."

"I wanted to be a little extravagant. Don't argue with an old man."


(10 March, 1985 – Sunday)

Since his first attempt to contact Gary in October of '82, Jeremy tried repeatedly to reach his son via his father. Each time, Edward's response was the same.

"I've given him your messages, Jeremy. Every one. If he wants to talk to you, he'll call." Edward recalled the fire in Gary's eyes the time he commented the teen was a lot like his dad. "But the pain runs deep with that one; he's still hurting over the way you left things. Can't say I blame him. You disowned your son, Jeremy. That's no easy hurt to overcome."

"I'm trying to reach out to him. Damn it, Dad, can't you make him see that?"

When Jeremy explained why he was calling, Edward blanched.

"I'll make sure he calls you," the elder Sheldon promised. "Or, better yet: Let me tell him. I think he'll take it better coming from me."

He decided to drive up to see his grandson the next evening, to tell him in person; his presence could help soften the blow. *No sense alarming him by calling him now.* He would see Gary tomorrow night. They'd talk then.

***

"I feel like a human ping-pong ball," Michaela grumbled to the four walls of her other bedroom. It didn't seem fair that Mom got the house. *He pays the mortgage; why should she get to live there?*

"Kayla, ready to go?" Dad called through the door. "C'mon, hon, it's nearly five. You know how Mom gets if you're late."

When she emerged, he took her satchel, pretending to stagger under its weight. "Oof! What do you keep in here?"

Her reply was as icy as her stare. "Everything I need to live in two places."

He set down the bag, turned and laid his hands on his daughter's shoulders. "I know it's hard on you. I'm sorry. But Mom and I… we can't seem to agree on things these days." Scowling, she looked away. "Kayla, talk to me. How can I help if you won't talk to me?"

"I don't *want* help," she exploded. "I want a normal family, with normal parents in a normal home. It's no use *asking* me if you aren't willing to do anything about it!" Flying down both sets of stairs, Michaela burst out into the unusually mild March sunshine.

# *Chapter 13*

Attila greeted Gary at the door Monday evening with a little "Mrrew?" As Gary crossed the kitchen, the kitten leapt onto a chair and mewed insistently. Smiling, Gary patted Attila's head. "Okay. Be with you in a second." Leaving him standing with his front paws on the table, Gary disappeared into the bedroom. It felt good to kick off his sneakers and relax. He fed Attila, then put some left-over pasta in the microwave; he opened a Dr Pepper and watched Attila devour his food.

"How 'bout some dinner music?" Gary ambled into the living room to put on the stereo. Attila followed him. The answering machine's incoming-message light flashed.

"Gary, it's just after two. Please call me when you hear this."

Absently Gary scratched Attila's head as he dialed the number Sam repeated twice. Purring wildly, Attila rubbed his head against Gary's hand.

Gary's heart lurched as Martha answered. Her voice sounded strained.

"Martha, it's Gary. I just got Sam's message. What's the matter?"

"Perhaps you'd better come down here," she replied vaguely.

Gary had no recollection of the 40-minute drive. He went right to the Johnsons' home; the front door was ajar, the porch light cast a welcoming glow. Taking the steps two at a time, he knocked at the screen door's wooden frame.

"C'mon in," Martha called from somewhere inside.

He found her in the kitchen, fussing over a pot of coffee. The instant he saw her face, pale and weary, he knew something was wrong.

Martha, who'd been a surrogate grandmother to the Sheldon kids since Gamma Jo died, wiped her hands on her apron. She took Gary's jacket, steered him to a chair. "Sit down, honey." Draping his coat over her chair, she sat beside him. Her hands shook. "Sam and your granddad were out walking this morning. Your granddad collapsed. They think it was his heart."

Stricken with fear, Gary inundated her with questions. "Where is he – what hospital? How is he? When can I go see him?"

"I'm sorry, sweetheart." Martha patted Gary's hand. "It was so sudden," she finished in a whisper.

He shook his head as the enormity of her words sank in. "No… *No!*" He couldn't feel the words tumbling from his mouth. "I was here with him yesterday. He's *fine*. We sat on the porch and talked and said it didn't seem like March at all, it was too warm! We're gonna pick out seeds for the garden this weekend." He gestured helplessly as Martha drew him to her considerable bosom.

"I'm sorry, honey. I know how much he meant to you… he loved you so much."

Gary didn't hug back, just sat in disbelief. His stomach turned over and he was glad he hadn't eaten.

Sam came in. "I'm so sorry, son," he said kindly, patting Gary's shoulder. "Your grandfather was a good man." Sam took Gary's hands. "He was proud of you, Gary. So proud." He forced a smile. "You made him very happy."

Sam's eyes were red; he'd been crying. Gary took a deep breath, released it slowly. His voice was shaky. "What do I do now?"

Sam gave Gary's hand a gentle squeeze. "We'll help you with the funeral arrangements, if you want."

That wasn't what he meant. But he nodded. "Okay. What else do I have to do?"

At the stove, Martha poured a mug of coffee. She stirred milk into it and set it before Gary. "You'll want to call your family, of course, dear. And pick out a suit for him to be buried in."

Gary stifled a cry at the word 'buried.' "I can't do this," he whispered, shaking his head. "I can't." The mug felt warm against his ice-cold fingers. His hands shook as he sipped the soothing liquid.

Martha suggested he use the living-room phone to call Marie.

To Gary's relief, she offered to call Dad. "What about Mom? Did you call her?"

"I don't have the number." His rigid tone warned her he didn't want it, either.

"Gary," Marie began sharply. Then she sighed and her tone softened. "I'll call them."

After Gary hung up, Sam came to sit beside him, cupping something in his hand. "Your grandfather wanted you to have these."

Grandpa's rosary beads, the ones Grandma had given him on their wedding day. The sterling medal and crucifix glinted in the floor lamp's glow; the black onyx beads felt cool against Gary's palm. He looked into Sam's face, his eyes silently questioning.

"He was holding them when he had the attack," Sam said, as if he had heard Gary's question. "He often prayed the rosary as he walked the beach. Kept 'em in his pocket. Didn't want to seem unapproachable – or make anyone uncomfortable."

Gary's hand closed around the beads, his final link to Grandpa; he clutched them to his heart as a cry swirled within him. *He was holding these when he died. They must've been such a source of comfort...* Wrapping his other arm about himself, he lowered his head, yearning for some of that comfort; the tears flowed again.

Martha came in and sat beside Gary. "It's okay, honey." She held him close. "Let it out."

When they eventually returned to the kitchen, the Johnsons took turns relating stories, which proved a soothing balm to Gary's troubled soul. Sam spoke about his early years with Edward and their fledgling architecture firm... and how Martha and Josephine helped out "in the lean years."

The men had thrived as partners; their wives had grown closer than sisters. Friendship blossomed as they worked together; it flourished when each had an infant to care for. Two years later, they rejoiced in each other's second pregnancies, announced weeks apart.

When Josephine miscarried her little son at 26 weeks, Martha grieved the loss alongside her best friend. She even understood when Josie begged off as godmother to her baby, due right after Christmas. At the devastating news that Josie could bear no more children, her grief deepened into a depression that lasted over a year, worsened by the sight of Martha cuddling her infant son. Josie's depression intensified, evolving into resentment; the fissure threatened to unravel years of friendship, especially when Martha became pregnant a third time.

After an agonizing six-month silence, which also strained the partners' working relationship, Edward suggested to his despondent wife that perhaps her arms might not ache with such terrible emptiness if she were to try holding her friend's new baby. At first,

Josephine resisted. But finally, sunk so low in her desperation she could see no other way out, she decided to give it a try. Shame made her unable to bring herself even to pick up the telephone to call her dearest friend; she implored Edward to arrange for them to call on Sam and Martha.

The Sheldons went to visit a few weeks after the birth of the Johnsons' little girl. Martha greeted her estranged friend as warmly as ever. Her hug conveyed what words between them could not. It begged a healing of the rift and offered a promise: While Martha couldn't shield Josie from her pain, she would do whatever she could to ease it, and restore the friendship to its former closeness.

Josie had cried – over the relationship damaged and the time lost. She clung to her friend and let her tears wash away all the hurt and bitterness. Then she had asked to see the baby. Both women wept as the introductions were made. But Josie's tears were tears of release, of healing and of longing. She'd ached to hold that little baby, to feel her sweet breath against her cheek, the softness of her skin, her wisps of fair hair tickling her chin.

The moment Martha placed little Josephine in her namesake's arms, she knew her months of prayers had been answered.

Martha looked up from relating this last piece of the story to find Gary's eyes welling with tears. She pulled a tissue from her apron pocket and pressed it into his hand. He looked at her with grateful eyes; she couldn't have known his tears were as much for his own lost baby as his grandmother's.

As the young man swiped at his eyes, Sam filled in the final puzzle piece. The son Edward and Josie had lost would have been named after his paternal grandfather, Gary Sheldon.

Grandpa had turned to *him* as a surrogate for his lost child – just as he had done with his CCD students. *That's not such a bad thing, though,* Gary consoled himself. *Not such a bad thing.*

When Gary finally left the comfort of the Johnsons' home, the cottage felt far too quiet. He wandered room to room, expecting – *longing* – to see Grandpa in any one of them. But even the study was empty. Now his death was undeniable. Gary felt as though he was encased in plastic, sealed off from reality. He sank into Grandpa's armchair, trying to connect with whatever emotion would let him mourn the loss. As freely as his tears had flowed earlier, now he couldn't summon one. Gary reached for the phone.

With no concept of time, all he was aware of was the ache that wouldn't leave him.

"Hi, it's Gary," he told his boss' machine. "I don't know if I'll be in tomorrow; my grandfather died. I don't know how long the funeral arrangements will take." His voice wavered. "Could you call me when you get in?" Gary's hand shook as he hung up.

Pouring himself a scotch from the black-walnut cabinet in the corner, he went out onto the porch and leaned against the railing. The amber liquid burned his throat. In his mind he heard bits of every conversation he ever had with Grandpa, from their earliest ones, to their discussion about tomato seeds. *Was that just yesterday?* Gary took another sip. Suddenly, he felt cold. So cold. His reverie was shattered by the ringing of the phone.

"Gary, I'm so sorry." Pete's voice sounded familiar, comforting. "It must've been such a shock."

"Yeah," he heard himself mumble.

"Don't even think about work," his boss advised gently. "Take the week. And if there's anything you need, let me know, huh?"

***

Gary sat with Marie on one side and Joey on the other. Jeremy sat, stoic and silent, on his daughter's other side. Three additional armchairs at the front of the parlor remained empty. Father and son sat less than four feet apart, but Gary wouldn't acknowledge his presence. His eyes were fixed on the still figure in the polished mahogany casket. Grandpa couldn't be dead. *But you don't go lying in caskets if you're alive, right?* Tears stung at his eyes.

Marie patted Gary's knee. "We sure had some good times with Grandpa, huh?" All he could do was nod. She squeezed his hand. "Hang in there, kiddo."

Streams of mourners filed in throughout the afternoon: business associates, employees, neighbors, clients, friends. Each with a fond memory to share. A brief lull followed… then more people, greeting the family, offering condolences.

The quiet moments in between afforded Gary and Joey time to reconnect; after nearly five years apart, they were virtually strangers. Joey told his brother he was in seventh grade now and would be 13 soon; he was awed to learn Gary had his own radio show. "You're *famous?*"

Gary tugged at the sleeve of his suit jacket. "Nah; but I get to meet some famous people." He decided he'd send Joey something neat for his birthday… maybe something autographed by someone famous.

"I miss you," Joey admitted, wistful. "Can I call you?"

"Of course." Taking a business card from his wallet, Gary wrote his home number on the back. "If you need me – for *anything* – you call. Okay?"

The boy nodded. Turning the card over, Joey read it. "Assistant Music Director? Cool!" After a long, companionable silence, Joey spoke. "Mom really wanted to be here" – he faltered as his brother scowled, then continued in a blur of words – "she knew how much it'd upset you… and she didn't want to hurt you." The youngest Sheldon fidgeted. "She loves you, Gary. I do, too. Please, can't you fix things? *Please?*"

"I don't want to talk about her. Not now, not ever!"

Joey shoved his brother's arm away. "Jerk!" he muttered.

Looking over as Joey hurtled toward the door, Marie tugged at Gary's arm. "What'd you say to him?"

"Get offa me!" he hissed, yanking away. Stalking to the back of the room, he slumped into a chair. His insides knotted with grief, rage and pain. He refused to cry. Not here. The overpowering smell of chrysanthemums and lilies sickened him. People continued to swarm in, but he felt so alone. Mom was gone; and now, so was Grandpa. He was abandoned all over again. He had no idea how to get past missing her, or reconnect after all this time. It had been so long! And now his brother and sister were mad at him. He couldn't blame Joey, really; but Marie… He sighed in frustration. *Grandpa, why'd you have to go and die?*

Marie followed Joey, stopping beside Gary as she went. "Nice going, ace!" she jeered in an undertone, pinching his arm. One of those horrid, big-sister twisting pinches that really hurt. Even through his suit jacket. "Why don'cha just alienate the *whole family*, ya little shit!"

Seconds, then minutes, ticked by.

"Want to take a walk?" Sam put an arm around Gary and led him outside. They walked out behind the funeral home, away from the ushers wearing their black trench coats and solemn faces.

Gary had sworn he wouldn't cry. That resolve vanished the instant the cool air hit his face. He crumbled against Sam's shoulder. "I miss him so much! I can't make it stop. And now I'm driving away everyone I love."

Sam patted Gary's arm. "The thing is," he explained, "folks who love us usually understand when we say hurtful things in times of distress."

Accepting the tissues Sam offered, Gary wiped his eyes and blew his nose. He shoved the tissues in his pocket. "Thanks, Sam. I don't know what I'da done without you these past few days."

Sam patted his shoulder. "Your grandfather was a wonderful man, in so many ways. He'd have done the same for *my* grandkids."

Back inside, Gary returned to the front. Dad still sat at one end. Gary sank into the seat at the other end. Marie returned with Joey. Gary felt a twinge of regret, another of jealousy. They sat, Marie beside Dad and Joey next to her. Gripping the arms of his chair, Joey looked around: at the lamps, at the floral arrangements at both ends of the casket, at the casket itself – anywhere but at his brother.

Swallowing his pride, Gary got up and went to sit beside Joey; he laid a hand on his brother's arm. The boy flinched. He didn't pull away; yet, he wouldn't look at Gary.

"Joey, look, I didn't mean to snap at you. I just lashed out 'cause it hurts so bad. I'm really sorry." Gary paused uncomfortably. "Tell her I said *Thanks*, okay?"

"Yeah." Turning his palm upward, Joey entwined his fingers with his brother's; they sat quietly for a while. Sniffling occasionally, Joey turned. "Can I have a hug?"

Suddenly, he looked so much younger than 12. Gary opened his arms. Wrapping his arms around his big brother, Joey held on tight.

A little past 4, the funeral-home henchmen herded everyone out. Sam and Martha, whom the funeral director knew from the previous day, were permitted to stay.

The three grandchildren and the Johnsons grouped together at the rear of the room. Visibly uncomfortable, Jeremy approached; as he did, Gary left to kneel at the casket. He reached out to touch Grandpa's hand; bereft, he leaned his head against the old man's grey-suited arm. A hand touched his shoulder. He expected it to be one of the funeral-home folks, cautioning him against getting tear stains on the casket's satin lining. Gary knelt there for a long time.

Martha stood beside him and stroked his hair. At last, he stood; towering over her, Gary buried his face in the sturdy, dependable comfort of her dark-blue shoulder.

Lots more people came in the evening. For a while, nonstop streams of mourners flocked past the casket, hugging the family and murmuring sympathies. Gary almost didn't recognize Pete; the suit threw him. David Guilmartin, the station manager, and Jim Burdell were right behind Pete. All the jocks were there, too – even Marc, who should have been on the air.

Pete hugged him. "I'm so sorry, kid." Gary's eyes were filled with tears. So were Pete's. Brushing away his tears, Gary introduced Pete to his kid brother.

On the other side of the littlest Sheldon, Marie gave Gary's boss a mighty hug. "Thanks so much for coming, Pete. I know it means a lot to Gary. Me, too."

She introduced him, and the others, to Jeremy.

"Mr. Sheldon, I'm so sorry for your loss," Pete said. "Your dad was quite a guy. I didn't know him well, but I'd met him at station events and at Gary's graduation party last December."

Jeremy, who knew nothing of station events or graduation parties, just nodded.

Gary sat to collect himself before facing the swarm of DJs and office staff. One by one, his coworkers offered hugs and pats on the back.

Last in line was Charlie. "I'm so sorry," he said, his mustache twitching sadly. "I know how close you two were." There was something distinctly soothing – fatherly, perhaps? – about his hug. Knees and defenses failing, Gary crumbled against him, but did not cry.

Greg and Kim Andrews came in next. Murmuring condolences, Greg clasped his friend's hands, then embraced him. "I know how special he was to you. Just know a part of him will always be with you."

Kim hugged Gary for a long time. "I'm so sorry, honey. I know how hard this is." She stroked his cheek, then took his hands. "We love you… and we'll be praying for you."

Later, during a lull, Pete found Gary slumped low in his chair. Crouching alongside him, Pete reached into his jacket and slipped something to Gary. "Charlie thought it would help to see this in print. He was afraid it might upset you, but he said he thought it fit your relationship with your grandfather perfectly."

Curiosity overtaking grief, Gary unfolded the paper.

His hand flew to his mouth to stifle the cry that caught him by surprise. "Thank you." Gary looked away so Pete wouldn't see the tears as he read the lyrics to the closing theme he used each day:

Rita M. Reali

*"I only knew you for a while,*
*I never saw your smile*
*'Til it was time to go;*
*Time to go away (Time to go away)*
*Sometimes it's hard to recognise,*
*Love comes as a surprise*
*And it's too late,*
*It's just too late to stay, Too late to stay.*

*We'll always be together,*
*However far it seems (Love never ends)*
*We'll always be together,*
*Together in Electric Dreams.*

*Because the friendship that you gave*
*Has taught me to be brave*
*No matter where I go*
*I'll never find a better prize (Find a better prize)*
*Though you're miles and miles away,*
*I see you every day.*
*I don't have to try,*
*I just close my eyes. I close my eyes."*

# Chapter 14

Kim taught Gary's class that Saturday; she let the kids make cards for him. With their teachers' approval, the students he'd taught the previous years did likewise.

Gary returned to work Monday. By 7, he was exhausted from a long, fruitless day of trying to reach record-company execs about a station promotion and four excruciating hours of fake cheerfulness. To make things worse, it was sleeting. The nasty weather started unexpectedly, about noon. He wasn't prepared to contend with clearing the nearly five inches of wet snow from his car. Before he finished, Gary's gloveless fingers were chilled to immobility, his canvas-clad feet sopping. Plus, the Camaro was lousy in winter! He'd almost run off the road twice.

When he pulled into his garage bay, Gary pried his hands off the wheel, shook them, then stretched and flexed his fingers. His knuckles were white from the death grip he'd had on the wheel the whole way. *If I can get upstairs without slipping and breaking my neck, I'll be happy.* Breaking his neck on the wooden stairs. Not a pleasant thought. More unpleasant was the notion that his landlord, a sweet old man who came up for coffee sometimes, could meet precisely that fate on the ice-slicked steps. Retrieving the old aluminum snow shovel he found hanging from a nail in the garage, he set to work.

Snow-packed clouds shrouded the moon and stars. The ankle-deep snow was wetly heavy; the dented shovel felt clunky in Gary's frozen hands. It took an hour to clear the slush from the front and back walks, both sets of stairs and the driveway. His hands were raw; sleet seeped through his jacket. Even his hair was caked with ice, which wouldn't have been so bad if it weren't slowly melting and dripping down his neck. His lower back ached as he returned the shovel to its makeshift hook. All he wanted was to take a hot shower, scrounge up something to eat and go to bed! Shivering and bone weary, Gary climbed the stairs, rubbing his hands together vigorously and blowing warm air into them.

A large brown envelope leaned against the door. He reached for it with numbed hands.

Attila greeted him at the door. "Me-you?"

"Hey, you!" Tucking the bulging envelope under one arm, Gary lifted the critter and swung him onto his shoulder. Asking the kitten about his day, Gary kicked off his sneakers and set them by the heater to dry. Then he turned his attention to the peculiar package. Squishing it couldn't reveal what might be inside. But even curiosity couldn't overtake his longing for a shower.

He tossed the enticing parcel onto the couch. "Here, guard this. If anyone tries to get it away from you, swallow it."

Attila gave him a perplexed look and sniffed at it.

Later, dressed cozily in sweats and the thick, warm slipper-socks Martha had knitted last Christmas, Gary joined Attila on the sofa. One by one, he studied the crayon drawings, contemplating the sentiments each child had written; their expressions of compassion, sympathy and true affection brought tears to his eyes.

Some of the cards depicted the children giving him hugs. Some had hearts and flowers. Others had drawings of Gary with his cat. "Don't cry, we love you," read one of the hugging cards. A second one said, "I'm sorry your Grandpa died. I was sad when my Grandpa died, too. So it's okay to cry." Another said, "I'm sorry you feel so sad. I hope you feel better soon." One even said, "Two rules: 1. Remember that God loves you. 2. Remember that we love you, too."

Kim had made a card for the teachers to sign. On the front she'd drawn two hands clasping a third. In calligraphy beneath the illustration read, *He grieves deeply who has loved much.* There was also a card from the staff. Gary wiped away tears as he read his pastor's deeply spiritual and comforting words. He looked at the pile of cards in his lap. The day they met, Greg had likened the parish to a big family. Seldom had Gary felt such a sense of belonging, except with Grandpa and the Johnsons. And the Farricellis.

He shoved that last thought away. Before he could start feeling sorry for himself, Attila marched across Gary's lap and announced loudly that it was supper time. He sat with his front paws together, tail curled around them. Stretching one paw upward, he touched Gary's face. "Mrrew?"

"Yeah, that sounds like a good idea." He swept the kitten up and ambled out to the kitchen. After they'd eaten – fisherman's platter for Attila and a can of soup for Gary – they returned to the living room. They played 'get the mouse,' but Gary's heart wasn't in it; so Attila curled up in his lap, purring. He stroked Attila's fur absently for a while. Then, feeling a powerful need for a human voice, Gary reached for the phone.

"I'm so sorry, sweetie!" Tanya gasped. "Is there anything I can do?"

"Not really," he replied flatly. Gripping the receiver, he glanced about the room. "I feel so… *alone*. I mean, I knew this day would come; but now that it *has*…"

"I know what you mean. It must've been awful. I wish I'd known. You want me to come out?"

Gary begged off, saying he appreciated the offer, but it wasn't necessary. She made him promise to call if he changed his mind or if he felt like talking. He promised, thankful for her insistence and grateful for her friendship.


Gary slogged through his days in a haze of sadness. He reserved all his energy to create an illusion of enthusiasm on air; but, deep grief lurking in his heart, he struggled daily to adjust to the void in his life. On weekends, he'd drive to the shore and wander, lost and empty, through the cottage. Part of him felt like he was trespassing, like he didn't belong there anymore.

All that seemed to ease his emptiness was the multitude of hugs from his students. Gradually, the reality of Edward's death settled over Gary; with acceptance came a certain calm. Not peace. More like resignation.

Three weeks after Grandpa's funeral, the siblings sat around the polished-mahogany conference table in his lawyer's office, eyeing one another and Jeremy stoically. The table's rich color and glossy surface reminded Gary too much of Grandpa's casket. He tried not to think about it – just as he tried not to think about Dad seated beside him. Or the reason they were all there.

The door opened and Derek Loughton entered; a slight, balding man in a dark suit, he carried a thick file folder with sticky notes jutting out at odd intervals. Sitting in one of the red-leather chairs, he opened the folder and watched four sets of eyes watching him. "Since we're all here, we can begin."

"This is it? Just the four of us?" Jeremy asked.

Gary glanced at his father. His eyes were red, but he didn't smell like scotch.

Attorney Loughton nodded. He eyed them intently, as if trying to memorize their faces. "Your dad – your granddad" – he nodded toward the grandchildren – "was an astute man. He worked hard all his life and he invested wisely. He left a portion of his estate to charity and to other individuals not here today. And he set up trust funds for the three of you, accessible once you reach the age of twenty-five."

Marie caught Gary's gaze over Joey's head. *Did you know about this?* her arched brow queried. "Excuse me, Attorney Loughton. What does this all mean?"

"What it means, dear," he replied kindly, glancing at her over his glasses, "is, in addition to assets already disposed, your grandfather left you and your brothers" – he glanced down at the file in front of him – "in excess of six-point-seven million dollars each."

"He what?" Gary blurted. "Wait. That can't be right. He didn't have that kind of…"

Jeremy nodded. "Yes he did. It's true, son. Your granddad was extremely wealthy."

The look Gary fired at him said, as clearly as if he'd uttered the words, *Don't ever call me 'son' again.* He addressed the attorney. "But – he never…" he trailed off, shaking his head.

"No, he never flaunted it. That was never his style," Dad said quietly.

Gary whipped about to face him. "Was I talking to you?"

Joey and Marie stared, astonished, at their brother.

Attorney Loughton ignored the outburst. "There's a provision for disposition of his personal effects." He flipped ahead a few pages. "Here we are: 'All my beloved Josie's jewelry, including her engagement and wedding rings, I leave to my only granddaughter, Marie. My home in Milford, all its contents and furnishings shall become the sole property of my grandson Gary, who shared my love for the solitude and comfort it offers.'" The others nodded.

Only Gary couldn't believe what he'd just heard. "I-I'm sorry; what was that last part again?"

The lawyer removed his glasses. "He left you his home – and everything in it. He also set up an account in your name, to cover property taxes through 1990."

Gary looked from the attorney to Dad, then his siblings. He pressed his hands against the table to stop their shaking. "He left me the beach house?" His lips felt thick; they moved sluggishly. *This is your home,* he heard Grandpa's voice in his head. He could see the old man's smile. *Your home.*

Dad laid a hand atop his. "He knew how much you loved him, Gary; he also knew you loved that house. This is his way of acknowledging that, and thanking you for everything you did there."

An unaccustomed thought made Gary shudder: For the first time in ages, physical contact with Dad wasn't violent. He took deep breaths to retain his composure as he tried to focus on the lawyer's words.

"There's also a provision for Joseph's high-school education: Payment has been made in full for four years' expenses at Milford Academy. Another account, in Joseph's name, accessible upon his graduation, funds all anticipated expenses at a private university or college." He gathered the papers into his folder. "A few other small matters need attention; but, basically, that's it. I'll be in touch soon to finalize everything."

"Wait." Jeremy still held his son's hand. The lawyer stopped his gathering. "You said the will specified I be here; but you never mentioned me."

The attorney sat. "Correct." Pulling an envelope from the folder, he handed it to Jeremy, then patted the file. "A notarized copy's in here. It's all legal. And binding. This is what he stipulated be given to you."

As soon as the lawyer left the room, Gary tugged his hand away and stood.

Jeremy blocked Gary, laid a hand on his arm. "Son. Wait."

Gary faced Dad for the first time in three years. "*Don't* call me that," he warned, his eyes murky. "Just don't." Moving away, he gave Marie a kiss, hugged Joey and slipped out the door.


After everyone left, Jeremy slit open the envelope. Inside was a sheet of ivory stationery and a check drawn on Edward's account. *His grandkids, the damn church — and God-knows-who else — get left millions… and I get a lousy five grand?*

He looked inside the envelope. It was empty. The letter was dated 18 January, 1985.

*Dear Jeremy,*

*I have been writing these letters every year, starting the January after Diane left. I'll remind you now that, before she left, I warned you repeatedly if you abused my grandchildren as you abused her, you'd be cut out of my will. My attorney has advised me against this, as you would doubtless be crafty enough to get my wishes overturned and somehow wangle a share of their inheritance. I have no intention of allowing that, Jeremy; hence, this token monetary bequest.*

*You probably didn't realize this letter was written on Gary's birthday. I wrote all these letters to you on his birthday - I felt it was only fitting, because he's the unfortunate one who bore the brunt of your abuse after Diane left.*

*Gary kept me well apprised of the situation at home. But he knows nothing of these letters - so I advise you not to take out your hostilities toward me on him. After learning about the verbal, physical and emotional abuses you heaped on him - and in light of your having disowned him over the debacle with Ellen - I intended that you <u>never</u> see a cent of my money.*

*But I know redemption is always possible and I have been willing to accept that likelihood. In fact, I have prayed for it constantly. As devastated as I am over these abuses, I sincerely hope this is <u>not</u> the letter you end up seeing. I don't wish to be remembered as "the bastard who cut you out of his will." I'd prefer you recall me as the father who welcomed you back when you repaired your broken relationships. I hope at some point you'll recognize your error and take the necessary steps to mend these rifts. And I sincerely hope - more than you can realize, Jeremy - that I get to write a more positive letter on 18 January, 1986. I do love you and I have been praying for healing within this sorely broken family.*

*In closing, I feel I must say you were wrong when you called Gary a failure and a disgrace. Your son is a fine young man who has done remarkably well in the face of adversity. And you should be proud of him - as you should be of all your children.*

*I wish you peace and healing.*
*Dad*


"Sonofabitch!" Jeremy crumpled the letter in his fist. "Miserable, lousy sonofabitch!" Finding nothing suitable to fling, he slammed the door behind him.

***

Right after class on Saturday, Gary drove to the cottage. His cottage. It didn't look any different... sure didn't feel different. It was nearly four weeks since Grandpa died. Monday would be four weeks. He glanced wistfully at the calendar in the study. It was still March in there.

Gary sagged into Grandpa's chair, his heart filled with an empty and indefinite ache. Mired in self-pity, he fell into a troubled sleep. Awakening late that night, he stifled a yawn, hauled himself to his feet and trudged up to bed.

Gary awakened, exhausted, to daylight. Reluctantly, he climbed out of bed to face the day. He'd just stepped out of the shower when the phone rang, startling him nearly out of his skin.

"I thought I'd find you'd there. Why don't you come over for breakfast?"

Gary's voice snagged in his throat as he heard himself accept Martha's offer.

When he arrived, Martha greeted Gary with a hug, then fed him scrambled eggs, bacon and coffee. "Didn't know whether you had anything to eat over there… I didn't want you going hungry."

In the ensuing weeks, Gary began a brief, albeit intense, flirtation with alcohol. When Jack Daniel's failed to blot out his pain, Brenda proved a willing and far more effective distraction.

She reveled in being Gary's lover. He wooed; he brought flowers and held doors. And once, he spent an entire evening holding her after Charlie tore her to pieces for bungling a message from a major client. But Brenda craved more than sweetness and remarkable sex; if she was going to get involved with Gary, she wanted it to be for keeps.

"I'm not what you need, Gary," she lamented, guilt-ridden, as they lay entwined after their best sex yet. "You need something to dull the pain you're feeling. And I'm sorry, but I can't be that. I've been crazy about you for years; and this has been the most amazing two months of my life. But it just isn't right – for either of us."

"I know," Gary acknowledged. "I'm sorry. You deserve better, Bren. Any other time, we could've been good together – *real* good. Maybe even forever." He caressed her face and dressed hurriedly.

"I'm sorry," he murmured, his lips barely brushing hers. Then he was gone.

# *Chapter 15*

(1 June – Saturday)

"A buck twenty-nine? That's absurd! Would you pay one twenty-nine a pound for *this?*"

Michaela looked across the produce bin. UConn-sweatshirt Guy held aloft a small bunch of broccoli. "Not likely," she replied with a trace of a smile. "I'm a teenager; we don't eat broccoli."

He raised an eyebrow. "But if you did: Would you pay that much for this… clump?"

"Bunch," she corrected with a smile. "Depends who I'm trying to impress." She turned to inspect the zucchini, then looked back. "See, I've got this killer chicken Divan recipe. If I wanna knock someone's socks off, it's worth it. Otherwise, I'd use frozen. All depends on your motivation."

Leaving him still hefting the broccoli, the girl disappeared amid shoppers and seven varieties of onions. Frowning, he put the vegetable back and he threw a bag of spinach into his cart.

Comparison shopping for applesauce, Michaela examined jars for weight and price, then put them down. Backing away to get an overall view, she bumped into someone perusing canned peaches. "Oh! Excuse me—" She turned to find herself face to face with the broccoli man. "S-sorry," she stammered. Blushing, she scuttled away, her applesauce forgotten.

Their paths crossed a third time in detergents.

"Are you following me?" He sounded amused.

Michaela met his gaze. *That voice! I know that voice.* "No. Are you preceding me?"

Caught off guard, he smiled. "Guess I must be."

She returned the smile. "Well, cut it out."

"We gotta quit meeting like this, Michaela," he told her by the kitty treats. "People are gonna talk."

*That's Gary Sheldon!* It was her turn to be taken by surprise. "How d'you know my name?"

He gave a mysterious shrug. "I know lotsa things."

She scanned his cart quickly. "Yeah, well, there's one thing you *don't* know."

"That's not your jacket?"

"Oh, it's mine," she replied vaguely, fingering its golden script embroidery above her left breast.

"Then what?"

"You haven't got a clue how to make chicken Divan."

"Maybe not; but my veal Florentine is *out of this world.*" Gary winked.

Michaela's heart oozed into her sneakers. "I'll bet it *is,*" she said, maneuvering her cart around his.


Michaela scrounged for bus fare. A search of her pockets turned up lint and seven dingy pennies. "Damn it!" she muttered.

It was a 40-minute walk in optimal conditions; this wasn't even close. The skies, partly sunny earlier, had darkened; a brutal wind kicked up. Turning her collar up, she pressed onward, shifting the sacks occasionally so her arms wouldn't tire too badly. Her wrists ached where the plastic bags' loops cut into them. Cars zoomed by. *Wish I'd gotten frozen-concentrate juice instead of cans. And why didn't I have them put <u>everything</u> in plastic?*

As she jostled the heaviest paper bag from one arm to the other, it tore. Groceries tumbled to the ground; the jar of dill pickles smashed on the sidewalk. Kneeling beside the torn bag, Michaela salvaged the rest of her things and packed them into the other bags. She picked up the broken glass and the pickles, wrapping them in the remnants of the bag; this she stuffed down the sewer grate up the road before struggling to lift her too-heavy paper sacks. Traffic continued to whiz by.

One car stopped, backed up to where Michaela crouched on the sidewalk. The driver approached and effortlessly lifted one of the overstuffed grocery bags. "Let me help you."

She looked up at Broccoli Guy. "N-no, really, I'm okay. Thanks anyway."

"Where're you headed?"

Blowing a wisp of hair out of her eyes, Michaela struggled to pick up another bag. "Home."

"Great; I'm going home, too. Hop in." He took her second bag.

"Thanks." Grateful, Michaela shook out her aching arms.

"Where's home?"

She reached for two more bags. "Mapleside. But you don't have to. I can manage."

He eyed the bulging bags, then the threatening skies. "It's gonna storm any second. I'm going by there; let me drive you." He took the bags from her as she sized up the car, a vintage Camaro ragtop. "I'm not a kidnapper, if that's what you're worried about. I'm not a rapist or a psycho; heck, I'm not even the guy your mom warned you about."

Michaela tried to look intimidating. "Then what are you?"

"Basically a lousy cook who needs a killer recipe for chicken Divan."

"Touché."

The first raindrops darkened little circles on the paper bags.

"C'mon." Unlocking the trunk, he began loading her groceries into it.

"Not so fast." Michaela held back. "I never accept rides from strangers."

Gary half grinned. "Sounds like a line to me."

Her return smile was coy. "Maybe it is. I'm Michaela. Michaela Conwaye. But you knew that."

"Pleased to meet you, Michaela. I'm Gary. Gary Sheldon."

"I know. I listen to you all the time. I *love* you!" she gushed. *Oh, Jesus!* Madly blushing, she stammered, "I–I – I mean, I– I love your *show*."

The skies opened up. Gary helped her into the low-slung car and put the rest of her bags in the trunk. Getting back in, he turned down the music blaring from the tape deck. Michaela recognized it from New Music Monday. The rain beat against the roof.

She fidgeted. "I really appreciate this. You didn't have to…"

"Don't be silly; I couldn't let you walk home in this mess." Gary squinted; the rain slashed down so hard the wipers were powerless. "I've seen you before," he observed. "You're there every Saturday."

"Yeah," she replied. "I love a good run-in with old ladies out for bargain oatmeal."

"You're funny."

She enjoyed the sound of his laugh. "I wasn't trying to be. But since you mentioned it, you were pretty funny yourself, making a scene in the produce aisle."

"Yeah, well…" His voice sounded like an admission. "I had to get you to smile *somehow*."

Michaela stared out the window at the rain. "Did I look like I needed to smile?"

"Truthfully? Yeah."

She didn't know what to say. They drove for a while without talking. Absently, he sang along quietly with a song from The The.

Stopping at a traffic light, Gary turned to the girl. "You got quiet. Trying to tune out my singing?"

She watched him watching her. "Nah; it's fine. Don't go quitting your day job or anything," she teased, "but it doesn't suck."

He chuckled. "There's a ringing endorsement."

Michaela grinned. "Ya know, you coulda just come up and said hello," she ventured.

Gary made no effort to hide his surprise. "Just like that: Hello? And what would I have said next? I notice we use the same dish detergent?" He shook his head. "Not my style."

A brief silence intervened. "You actually noticed what kind of dish soap I buy?" Michaela whistled, shaking her head. "You have *way* too much free time, mister."

"Yeah, I've been meaning to enroll in a cooking class; always wanted to learn how to make chicken Divan."

Laughing and chatting easily, they hauled her soggy bags inside. As Gary lifted one onto the counter, the wet paper gave way. His attempt to intercept the eggs failed; they landed with a thud. "Shit," he muttered, stooping to pick up the oozing carton.

Sodden hair clinging to her rain-soaked jacket, Michaela grinned as they retrieved her fallen goods. "So *that's* why they don't let you play on the station softball team."

Gary tried to stifle a laugh. "Sorry." *She's beautiful when she smiles.*

"It wasn't your fault." Crawling beneath the table after a renegade cat-food can, she found herself eye to eye with the intriguing young man on her kitchen floor lamenting her eggs.

Gary set the damaged carton on the counter and helped her up.

"Let's get the rest of the stuff; we can worry about that later," she said.

They dashed back out. Gary handed her one bag and followed her in with the last two. Plus something from his own groceries.

"Here…"

She pushed them back. "I can't take your eggs."

"Please. You shouldn't have to do without them because I can't catch."

"Who are *you?*" Susan Conwaye's voice prickled with suspicion.

"Hi, Mom," Michaela said with forced enthusiasm. "This is Gary; he's the afternoon guy at Z97-3. I was short bus fare and he was nice enough to stop for me. Just before it started pouring."

"She's home; you can leave now." She sneered. "And take your eggs. We don't need your *charity.*"

"Ma-aah! He's only being nice; don't act so nasty." Then, to Gary: "I'll get you that recipe."

Susan's eyes darkened. "How dare you use that tone with me!" A sharp slap resounded through the room. As Michaela cried out, her mother seized the carton and thrust it at Gary. "We don't want them." She opened the door and stood with a hand on the knob, tapping her foot. "Goodbye!"

Gary looked from mother to daughter. Tears shone in the girl's eyes; she avoided making eye contact.

"And don't you be calling here," Mrs. Conwaye warned.

The door slammed. Over the downpour, Gary heard shouting. Another slap. Another muffled cry. He wished he could have done something to protect the girl. He'd smelled alcohol on her mother's breath; booze and a nasty temper added up to abuse. *I shouldn't let her just beat the poor kid up like that. But who am I to impose?*

Now he understood how torn Mr. Farricelli must have been when Ellen asked him to intervene; he recalled the warmth he'd felt when she told him she'd asked her father to let him live with them.

That night, Gary's troubled past bombarded his memory. He remembered Dad berating him over the most insignificant things; and he cringed at the recollection of beatings endured at his hands. Heart pounding, Gary lay awake, wondering why such long-ago events still evoked such terror.

Unable to sleep, he heard Mrs. Conwaye's vicious slap over and over, and Michaela's surprised and humiliated cry. Dozing at last, Gary got no peace; the shrew haunted his dreams. She brandished empty scotch bottles and screeched, "Get out! We don't want your filthy eggs!" Awakening with a jolt, he flipped on the bedside light.

Gary rolled down the car window; the cool night air blew across his face. The long drive helped clear his head. Unlocking the door, he stepped into the living room. *Home.*

*That kid would live here year-round if we let him,* Dad had said.

It was true. Gary paced aimlessly, seeking the calm he'd always known here. But tonight, his mind and heart sorely troubled over Michaela, peace eluded him.

He stepped onto the back porch. Breathing deeply of the salt air, Gary began to calm down. Approaching the water, he skirted driftwood and rocks, aided by moonlight and the kitchen light's glow behind him. Waves lapped at the rocks as he reached the end of the jetty.

Dangling his feet over the edge, he shivered. Leaning back on both elbows, Gary gazed at the stars and the half moon. His smile was reflexive at the thought of Michaela.

*But she's what, 16? What could you possibly have in common, anyway, aside from detergent?* He couldn't put aside the image of her smile, lit by china-blue eyes. She'd set him at ease with her cool confidence, intrigued him with spitfire assertiveness, yet stirred his compassion with her vulnerability. Gary conjured an image of Michaela, hand to her cheek, eyes filled with tears. A sudden gust chilled him. *How can she endure that abuse and still be so… perky?* He knew the answer; he'd done it himself. Suddenly, his eyelids felt heavy.

Squelching a yawn, he headed inside and opened the bedroom windows. The sound of waves lapping at the shore lulled him into a deep, dreamless sleep. Just like always.

Tangy salt air, sunshine and the screech of seagulls wheeling overhead greeted Gary Sunday morning. Invigorated, he flung back the covers, shivering in the early morning chill as he dressed.

Barefoot, he stepped outside, gazing at the ocean. It was low tide. Venturing to the water, he picked up an angel's-slipper shell, surf-tossed onto the sand, soft orange and glistening in the sunlight.

Now he could reflect on yesterday without last night's confusing jumble of emotions. He scratched absently at the rough growth of stubble on his chin. Walking into the gentle surf to test its coldness, he quickly retreated from the foamy water whooshing at his ankles. Cool sand clung to his feet. Above him, seagulls scolded no one in particular in high-pitched screams.

An old man appeared, with a golden retriever pup out for an early frolic. Even from a distance, Gary recognized Sam. He raised a hand in greeting.

"'Morning, Gary. Beautiful day, huh?"

"Sure is." The puppy ran over to sniff at Gary's feet. He stooped to pet the wriggly pooch, fondling its silken ears. "Gorgeous dog. How old?"

"Three months."

"Uh oh; I hear that's when they start causing the most trouble."

"Alas, you're a week late," Sam confided with amusement. "And Martha's furious. She's already chewed the coffee table, shredded a sofa cushion and piddled on the living room rug. The dog, that is, not Martha."

Gary laughed, envisioning Martha gnawing at sofa cushions. "Good luck. Sounds like you'll need it," he called as the pup tugged Sam along the sand.

Ambling toward the cottage, he checked his watch; time to get back for Mass. He snapped his fingers. "That's where I know her from."


As Gary waited for Michaela after Mass, a little girl shouted his name. He turned to see Tess O'Rourke galloping up the sidewalk. "Gary! Gary! I'm so glad to see you!" she squealed, hugging him tight.

Megan O'Rourke hurried to catch up. "I told Tess she'd see you in class next week, but she couldn't wait 'til then. I'm sorry; I told her not to bother you."

Beaming, arms wrapped around the girl, Gary looked up into the woman's face. "That's alright, Meggy. I've missed this little lamb."

With gentle fingers, he smoothed away the wisps of red hair that had fallen across his young charge's cherubic face. "I'm glad you're feeling better, Tess. We've missed you the last few weeks." He stood again to speak with the girl's mother. He loved his kids, but her timing was awful!


Spotting Gary, Michaela's heart danced. Until she noticed the strawberry blonde. And the child gazing at him in a way she could only describe as adoringly.

The following Saturday, she tucked a few extra dollars into her jeans pocket, for bus fare. Michaela's stomach back-flipped as she pretended not to notice Gary in the meat department. She ducked into the canned-goods aisle before he spotted her.

"I was hoping I'd see you again," he hailed her cheerily in health and beauty aids.

Scowling, Michaela maneuvered silently past him. In the bread aisle, he tried again; again she ignored him.

He stopped her in the parking lot as she tromped toward the bus stop. "Is something wrong?"

Michaela's jaw tightened. "Does your *wife* know you come here to pick up girls?" Gary stared at the girl in stunned silence as she continued. "And your daughter – does she have any idea what kind of scum you are?" Accusation and tears stung her eyes. "And don't try to deny it, either. I saw you. You're disgusting!" she hissed. "How could you *do* this to them?"

Gary pointed a finger in Michaela's face. "You don't know what you're talking about."

She slapped his hand away, trying to channel her fury into words. "I saw you after Mass with your wife and daughter! And I think it was" – she scrambled for the right word, then spat it out – "*wrong* for you to be flirting with me when—"

"*Flirting* with you!" Gary seized her arm. Sudden fear in her eyes made him loosen his grip. Holding her gaze, he spoke firmly, his voice low. "I was trying to be nice. As for my *wife and daughter,* as you keep calling them: Megan is not my wife and Tess is not my daughter. Not that it's any of your business, but she's one of my CCD students."

It was Michaela's turn to gape. "You're a *religion* teacher? I didn't know that."

"There's plenty you don't know," Gary grumbled, releasing her arm. "And I resent your accusation."

Deflated, she stared at the ground. "I'm sorry," she muttered, kicking the wheel of her grocery cart.

"What? I didn't hear you. You weren't as loud just then as you were a minute ago, when you accused me of being unfaithful to a wife I don't even have."

Now Michaela looked him in the eye. "I'm sorry. I was wrong. I shouldn't have jumped to conclusions about you; and I apologize."

He watched her fidget for several seconds. "We did look pretty cozy, huh?" he said at last. She nodded grudgingly. "And I can kinda see how you'd get the wrong idea," he conceded.

Michaela rubbed the hurt out of her arm where he'd grabbed it. "So, am I forgiven?"

"This time," Gary intoned with a hint of a smile; he tweaked her nose. "C'mon, I'll drive you home."

She considered this. "Is it gonna rain?"

"If it doesn't, I can do a dance." He took her bags and placed them into his cart.

Michaela snickered. "I'd pay to see that."

"Maybe next time." He nodded to the far end of the lot. "I'm over here." His smile melted the last icy traces of her ill temper. She followed him, rubbing at her arm. "I'm sorry I hurt your arm." His remorseful tone stopped her cold. "I'll never do that to you again."

On the way home, Michaela confided that her mom's drinking was intruding on all areas of their lives. "I'm afraid she'll get fi—" She stopped. "*Why* am I telling you this? I hardly know you."

"Maybe I'm just easy to talk to."

"I guess. It kinda feels like I could tell you almost anything." She settled against the seat as Gary turned down the music. "But you've got more important things to think about than silly teenage drivel."

"Micki." The way he spoke her name made her spine tingle. "It's not drivel. It's hard to adjust when your home life falls apart." Gary looked at her. "Believe me. I know."

*Micki.* She liked that he called her that. Looking at him, her eyes widened.

"Doesn't matter how commonplace it is; it's devastating when it happens to you. Everyone else's parents could be divorced and it *still*" – he thumped the steering wheel – "doesn't make it any easier. You've only got one set of parents; if they break up, it throws your whole world into a tailspin. My mom left when I was sixteen," he blurted before he could stop himself. "Don't let anyone tell you teenage guys don't need their moms. It's like saying you don't need your dad. It's a lie! Kids need *both* their parents. I could never do that to *my* kids, leave their mother."

Michaela wondered what specific memory he'd conjured up that felt so awful. "Must've been hard," she murmured, forgetting her own troubles.

"Mm," Gary mumbled. "So, when's school get out?"

She understood he wanted to drop the subject. "Thursday after next. And I can't wait…"

Soon, they were meeting at the store every week. They shared coupons and two-for-one offers; and the ride home gave them private time to talk.

"You don't have anything frozen back there, do you?" he asked one afternoon, motioning toward the trunk instead of answering one of Michaela's difficult questions.

"No. Why?"

"I thought we'd take the 'scenic route' – through Woodbury – so we can talk; sometimes it's easier talking to someone who's not looking right at you, so you don't feel like you're in a fishbowl."

Her brow furrowed; she studied Gary's face. "That's *exactly* how I feel! How'd you know?"

His voice sounded wistful. "That's how I always felt."

"Did you have someone to ride around and talk with?"

Gary nodded – sadly, she noted, and wondered why.

Michaela wanted to know more about him. She hoped he'd talk some. "Did it help?"

He gave a long, slow sigh. "While it lasted, yeah. After my mom left, my girlfriend and I would go out and drive – just anywhere. And we'd talk." He shrugged. "Well, *I* talked. Ellen had the greatest home life, said she had no complaints. Her parents were together; they loved her – and her brother and sisters. And me." Coasting to a stop at a light, he looked at Michaela.

"Did that bother you? That she had it so good?"

He revved the engine absently. "Nah. It was kind of an ideal – how I wanted my life to be when I had a family. Her parents were so in love. I could hear it in their voices." He paused. "I must've spent more time there than with my own family. Everything I know about love and compassion came from Ellen's family. Or my grandfather. *He* was a great guy!"

Despite the bitterness when he mentioned his parents, she loved how Gary's eyes lit up when he spoke about his grandfather. "Tell me about him," she urged.

He shook his head. "I wanna hear what's going on with *you*."

Michaela smirked. "Mom's a drunk. I hate living with her. Dad has room for me…" She gave a sigh of frustration. "What good is talking? It won't change anything."

"Sometimes it helps," he said so softly she had to strain to hear, "just to say the words… so they're not bottled up inside. What bothers you most about your situation?"

"Having to be the grownup. Not having my dad around. No, ya know what I hate most? Feeling like I can't even breathe" – she thumped her chest – "like there's a cement truck parked right here!"

***

It was mid August before Gary mustered the courage to invite Micki to join him for coffee before grocery shopping. By October, they were regulars at the diner. At 12, Paula would set mugs of steaming coffee at their usual booth. Occasionally they'd linger over refills and a slice of warm apple pie à la mode. With two forks.

"My best friend's brother wants to ask me out," Micki confided on Columbus Day weekend. "He's a junior – in college; I'm still in high school. I don't think it'd work."

"Because of the age difference, you mean?"

She waved a forkful of pie. "It's not even that; he's only just a few years older than me. I was kept back as a kid. I was out almost three years."

"What happened?"

She didn't want to get into it. Not now. "I was sick."

Gary nodded. In his head he did math. *If she's three years older than I thought, that means she's… 18? That changes things. And if he's a junior… hell, he's gotta be __my__ age.* Picking up his mug, he watched her over its rim as he took a sip. *She's got beautiful eyes!*

"The school decided I should repeat the first grade, even though I'd gotten nearly halfway through the year before I had to leave. I was nine by the time I went back."

"That had to be hard; kids can be so cruel."

She set her mug down, nodding. The silence grew awkward. Finally, she spoke, just to have something to say. "So… what d'you think I should do about Regan?"

"Your friend's brother? Other than the age thing, d'you like him?"

"I suppose." Michaela shifted uncomfortably. "But dating's so *awkward!* There's never anything to talk about – and you just end up sitting there, *gawping* at each other."

Gary shrugged. "Well, we always find stuff to talk about; and we haven't gawped at each other yet."

She waved her now-empty fork at him. "True, but we're just friends."

In the ensuing weeks, each broached the subject of dating once more. Both times, the other danced around the subject… until they returned safely to, "Yeah, but we're just friends."

138

# *Chapter 16*

(2 November – Saturday)

"I suppose you're going to see *him*."

Mom sneered as Michaela tugged her Dartmouth sweatshirt over her head, the one Dad got her at alumni weekend years ago. It was fading, blotched with paint and the ribbing at the cuffs was beginning to fray.

"Matter of fact, I am."

"Like *that*? What will he think when you show up dressed all raggedy?"

Flipping her hair from beneath the collar of her sweatshirt, she secured her chestnut ponytail with an elastic. "Mother, Gary and I are just friends."

"You fancy yourself in love with him. Does he tell you he loves you while he's *fucking* you?" She spat out the word.

Michaela's cheeks burned. "You're disgusting!"

"Don't tell me you're not doing it, either, you stupid slut. You're not even smart enough to do it for money. You just do it because you're *in love* with him," she mocked. "Why else would he waste his time on you?"

"That's not true!" Michaela shouted back. "I'm not sleeping with Gary! Why are you saying these horrible things?" Tears pricking her eyes, she fled.

Michaela sprinted to the diner. No sign of Gary's Camaro yet. She slid into their booth, her cheeks streaked with wind-dried tears. Her lungs ached from the cold; her fingers felt numb and stiff.

Paula came over with a coffeepot. "Hi, hon; flyin' solo toda—whoa, what's wrong?" The waitress pulled tissues from her pocket. "Here, honey; now, you just tell me all about it."

Gratefully accepting the proffered tissues, the girl dabbed at her eyes.

Paula poured Michaela's coffee and set a handful of creamers on the table. "Is it him?"

She shook her head. "My mom doesn't like me spending time with Gary." She blew her nose. "Said I *fancy myself in love* with him. Have you ever heard anything so ridiculous?"

Paula smiled gently. "Sweetie, I been here twenty-nine years and I seen a lotta couples come through these doors. I gotta tell ya, I know *in love* when I see it; and honey, you're in love."

Michaela's head drooped. "I guess you're right; 'cept he doesn't know it."

The waitress repressed a knowing smile. "Here, you wanna look pretty for him, don'cha?" Paula slipped her a moist towelette and went to see about an order. Michaela discreetly cleaned her face with the lemony-fresh wipe, then dabbed at her eyes with a napkin. Returning with Gary's coffee, Paula patted Michaela's hand and pronounced her beautiful. "Cheer up, sweetie; your mom'll come around."

A minute later, the door opened, admitting Gary and a blast of cold air. He tugged Michaela's ponytail in playful greeting. "Hey, you. Been waitin' long?"

She managed a feeble smile as he sat. "Hours. What kept you?"

Gary stirred cream into his coffee. "So many girls to flirt with in the produce aisle today." Seeing the puffiness around her eyes, his smile vanished. He took her hand. "Micki? What happened?"

She looked away, shook her head. "It's nothing."

"Nothing made you cry? You just spontaneously burst into tears now?"

"Gary, just leave it, okay?" Micki's lower lip trembled; she still didn't look at him.

His voice was a verbal caress. "How can I help?"

"There's nothing you can do!" She jerked her head around to face him, then lowered her eyes and her voice. "So I don't see what difference it makes." She glanced at Gary, then into her coffee and reached for his hand; a tear glided down her cheek, landing on her mug's handle. "I didn't mean to snap at you."

"That's okay." Gary's hand closed around hers. "Tell me what's wrong. It might help to talk."

"I dunno." She bit her lip, blinking back new tears.

"Alright. If you want to talk about it, that's fine; if not, that's okay, too."

Settling back, Michaela rested her feet on the seat beside Gary.

Paula brought several more creamers and a ramekin of ground cinnamon. "Can I bring you anything else? I've got a doozy of a lemon-meringue pie."

Michaela shook her head.

"Just coffee today, Paula," Gary said, dropping a pinch of cinnamon into each mug.

"All-rightie." She flashed her brightest smile. "I'll be back with refills in a jiffy. Just holler if you need anything else."

Gary grabbed and wiggled one of Michaela's sneakered feet. "So, what's up for the weekend?"

She scrunched up her face and thought. "Not a whole lot." She lifted her mug, inhaling the aroma of cinnamon. "Going to my dad's tomorrow; I can't wait."

"Mom's really gettin' to ya?"

She snorted. "Like you wouldn't believe! I mean, if she were just a bitch, I could handle that; but she's drinking all the time now. And when she drinks, she gets *mean*." She paused. "I can't stand it there."

"You're eighteen; can't you choose where to live?"

"If I lived with my dad, I'd have to change schools." Michaela built a pyramid with the unused creamers; not looking up from her construction project, she said, "My mom doesn't like me seeing you. She's said all along she doesn't like you."

"At least she's consistent." Seeing her grim expression, Gary quit joking. "Sorry."

"She really outdid herself today. It was *horrible!*" Tears filled her eyes. "I won't even repeat what she said." She tugged out the elastic holding her ponytail.

"How bad could it be?"

Her hair swung loose as she shook her head.

"Hey." Gary reached across the table, wiped at Michaela's tears. "There's nothing you can't tell me."

She liked the touch of his fingers against her cheek. "She called me these awful names and said we're – *you know…*" Micki gestured feebly and mumbled, "sleeping together." Her ears burned. "And that's the only reason you have anything to do with me."

He laid a hand atop hers. "You know that's not—" Just then, Paula sailed by, refilled their mugs and left the check. Gary folded his hands on the Formica tabletop. "I think it's time your mom and

I had a talk." He removed the topmost piece from the creamer pyramid.

Michaela shook her head. "That'd only make things worse."

He stirred in more cinnamon; after a long, slow sip, he set down his mug. "How? How can it be worse? She's reduced you to tears. And for what? We need to sit down and talk. Like adults. And soon."

She exhaled in audible desperation. "Do we *have* to? Couldn't I just move in with you?" Little crinkles formed around her eyes; her freckled nose wrinkled as she squinted at him.

Gary squeezed her hand. "Then they'd *really* have reason to hate me."

"My dad likes you just fine; it's my mom you gotta worry about."


In the grocery checkout line, Michaela mused aloud about going to her dad's that night instead of the next morning. "She'd never go for that. Anyway, she's in no condition to drive."

Gary slipped an arm around her. "I could drive you." Without thinking, he kissed her on the temple.

Her insides fluttered at his kiss. "I don't want you going out of your way for me," she protested.

"It's not out of the way. In fact, there's a payphone over there; give him a call."


Susan stepped onto the porch, arms folded. "I wondered when you'd get around to coming home."

From Mom's argumentative tone and pronounced slurring, Micki could tell she'd pounded back a few in the past two hours. "Mother, don't start." An icy fist tightened around her insides; she pushed a wisp of hair off her forehead and took a deep breath. Taking a bag from the trunk, she headed up the walk. Gary carried the other two.

"I didn't expect you so soon." The diminutive blonde advanced, hands on her hips. "I thought for sure you'd be out slutting around with Mister Sports Car 'til well after dark."

Michaela turned toward the protective comfort of Gary's arm; a whimper caught in her throat.

"Let it go," he cautioned. "She's just trying to get a rise out of you."

"And you!" Susan hurled an accusatory barb at Gary. "Must you prey on teenagers? Can't you get anyone your own age to sleep with you?"

Gary ignored the taunt. "I'm glad you're home, ma'am. I was hoping we could talk."

Above her refolded arms, her chin jutted out stubbornly. "Okay. Talk."

"Maybe we should take this inside. You'll catch cold" – lowering his voice, he glanced left; a door had opened and the next-door busybody stood on the porch – "and the neighbors don't need to hear this."

"Fine." Turning on her heel, Mrs. Conwaye stalked back inside.

Michaela tugged at his sleeve. "Not now," she implored. "*Please*. She's been drinking."

He squeezed her hand. "I'll be careful."

Inside, Susan sat stiffly in a high-backed wing chair.

Gary sat on the couch, facing her. Michaela hovered beside him.

"Would you like something to drink?" the girl asked, suddenly timid. "Coke or something?"

He looked up; his smile melted her insides. "That'd be great. Thanks."

Noting the whiskey smell enveloping her mother, she tried to sound carefree; her voice came out high-pitched and strained, like a throttled mouse. "Mom? Something to drink?" *Something non-alcoholic?*

As Michaela headed to the kitchen, Gary got right to the point. "Micki tells me you don't approve of our friendship. But I assure you, ma'am, I mean your daughter no harm."

"Is that so?" Challenge flooded Susan Conwaye's voice. "Are your so-called assurances supposed to make me feel better about something I don't approve of?"

Her tone made his skin prickle. Curious, he cocked his head. "Such as?"

"I don't approve of *you*, Gary Sheldon." She spat out his name distastefully. "I don't like you."

Gary chose his words guardedly. "You don't know me, Mrs. Conwaye. But I hope this can be a step toward changing that. Still, doesn't Micki's opinion count?"

"Not about *you*." Susan's temper threatened to erupt.

"Have I done something to offend you?" he asked serenely. "If I have, please tell me so I—"

"I've seen your kind before: smooth talkers in fast cars. You're all alike. And you're just bad news. My daughter doesn't need to get mixed up with that."

"I'm sorry you feel that way, ma'am. But eventually you'll have to accept Micki's choices – even if you don't approve – because they're hers to make."

Returning with three glasses of Coke, Michaela handed one to her mom and one to Gary. When he smiled, her insides seeped into her sneakers. She set coasters on the table, then sat beside Gary; her eyes darted between them, as if watching a tennis match. Then Mom spoke and she wished she could vanish.

"I don't appreciate being told how to raise my daughter," she said icily. "And I certainly don't approve of her being in love with you."

Gary nearly choked on his soda.

"*Mother!*"

Susan faced her daughter, her eyes coldly determined. "Well, aren't you?"

When Micki's eyes met his, Gary suddenly took a prolonged and avid interest in the ice in his glass.

Michaela didn't reply, so Susan taunted her. "You're in love with him. *Aren't* you?"

"You *bitch!*" she hissed. Covering her face with her hands, she hunched forward.

For several uneasy seconds, the only sounds were Michaela's sobs and the mantel clock ticking. "If that *is* how she feels" – Gary sidestepped the verbal grenade – "maybe you should accept that." Setting his glass down, he gave Michaela's shoulder a comforting squeeze.

Susan's mouth formed a grim line. "Are you trying to tell me how to raise my daughter?"

He held up a hand in protest. "Certainly not, ma'am. I wouldn't presum—"

"Good! I can do without another man meddling in my life."

"I'm sorry you feel my concern for Micki is meddlesome."

"Well, it is. And I'm not about to watch her throw her life away, chasing after some two-bit nobody. It's a silly waste of her time."

"Maybe she's not the only one walking around with stars in her eyes."

Michaela hoped Gary hadn't heard her gasp – or the crazy way her heart was pounding.

Susan's face was a mask of disgust. "Why, you're just as silly as she is! A real modern Romeo and Juliet, that's what you two are."

"Actually, we're not quite what the Bard had in mind, ma'am; he was thinking more along the lines of—"

"Oh, shut up!"

At last, Michaela dared to glance at Gary.

"I respect that you're Micki's mom; but that doesn't permit you to tell hurtful lies about her. Plus, who are you to accuse me of – what was it? *Preying on teenagers?* I should be deeply offended. But considering your obvious alcohol intake, I'm not surprised."

"How dare you!" Susan stood, pointing at the door. "Get out of here!" she commanded.

Gary drew back the hair hiding Michaela's tear-streaked face; he kissed her on the forehead. He wiped the tears from her eyes, then whispered something. She smiled.

Susan stamped her foot. "I said, *Get out!*"

Gary stood.

When Micki accompanied him to the door, Susan demanded, "Where do you think *you're* going?"

Hands on hips, the girl raised her chin defiantly. "I'm staying at Dad's; Gary's driving me. Dad likes him just fine."

Outside, as the car idled, Micki twisted her hands in her lap. "Gary? Wh-what you said in there – about me not being…"

"The only one with stars in your eyes?" Gary finished. "What about it?"

"Did you mean that?" she squeaked.

"Of course I meant it."

Michaela faced forward. "Oh."

"Is that okay?"

She looked at him again, her eyes wide. "Yeah, it's okay. In fact, it's… perfect."

"Oh," Gary mumbled before an awkward silence intervened. Then, "What your mom said—"

"She said an awful lot." Glancing down, she found their fingers entwined and realized she had no recollection of that happening.

"About you being—" he stopped abruptly.

Michaela looked into his eyes. "In love with you?" Her words seemed to come from somewhere distant.

Gary looked away – at the stick shift, the mirror, the steering wheel. Anywhere but at her. "Y-yeah."

*I've never seen him look nervous.* She fidgeted. "Guilty as charged."

"Then I guess you won't mind terribly if I do this?" He leaned in, one hand on her shoulder and – oh so gently – kissed her.

Her pulse quickened. His lips felt warm, soft. Her first real kiss. And it felt wonderful! As Gary pulled back, Micki – quivering – licked her lower lip and laid her head against the headrest. She nodded toward the house. "Uh-oh."

Susan glared at them from the front window.

"Well, she's seen us," Gary conceded. "Only one thing to do about that." Taking Michaela in his arms, he kissed her again. Long and slow. And wonderful.

Her lips parted at the slight pressure of his mouth. She gave a little moan; her cheeks flushed as she realized he must've heard it. Her heart thumping, Michaela squirmed as she felt stirrings deep inside – new feelings that excited, overwhelmed and frightened her.

"I think she's seen enough," Gary murmured at last, drawing away. "We should get you to your dad's."

"Yeah." Glancing away, she wiped the back of her hand across her mouth, then fastened her seatbelt as Gary backed out of the driveway.

While waiting at a red light, he broke the tense silence. "I didn't kiss you just to give your mom fits," he admitted, gripping the wheel. "I've wanted to for – well, awhile."

An impatient honk made Gary return his attention to the road. They rode the rest of the way in silence.

Michael Conwaye greeted them warmly. "Gary! Good to see you again. How've you been?"

"Never better, sir. And you?"

"Can't complain," he replied as he bear-hugged his daughter. "Oh, am I glad to see you!" Michael led them into the living room. "I had an interesting conversation with your mother. She was going on about 'your impertinent snip of a daughter and that rude man she's sleeping with.' Now, Gary," he added with a straight face, "I suppose you're the rude man who's sleeping with this impertinent snip? I apologize for the phrasing; my wife's never been one to sugarcoat things. She kept going on about how 'She's denying she loves him, but he said he's in love with her; and all I know is they were sucking face in my driveway.'"

As Michael looked at them, Micki stifled a snort. Gary squeezed her hand to make her stop.

"I told her, that doesn't sound like *my* Kayla; but she assured me it was," he went on. "I assume there's a kernel of truth here, albeit a really twisted one. Am I right?"

"Yes, sir," Gary replied. "And Mr. Conwaye – or is it *Attorney* Conwaye?"

"Just Michael."

Gary winced, uncomfortable with that level of familiarity. "How 'bout Mr. Conwaye?"

Michael nodded. "Fine. You were saying?"

"She's right. Sort of. It was just a couple of kisses. A couple of really *nice* kisses; but that's all. We weren't—" His explanation was interrupted by the pizza-delivery guy's arrival.

Over dinner, they related the afternoon's events. "Daddy, it was awful!" Michaela exclaimed. "She kept saying these terrible things! She called me a whore and said Gary only wants me for – for *sex.*"

"I know it's none of my business," Gary picked up, "but I had to speak up. I may have been totally wrong, sir; and if you think I was, I'll apologize to her. But my intention was to defend Micki."

"She did call you rude and insulting. But she made no mention of how she spoke to you; although, knowing her flair for words, I can just imagine."

"She's lying! Gary was really polite to her, right up 'til she started accusing us of – you know…"

"I believe you, honey," Michael told her with a nod. "And Gary, I commend you for keeping your cool as long as you did. I know how difficult Susan can be." He looked from one of them to the other. "I don't get it, Kayla: All along you've insisted you're just friends, nothing's going on." A teasing smile crossed his lips. "Now all of a sudden, you're making out in parked cars and sleeping with this rude man. What changed?"

The pair smiled reticently. "It wasn't anything we planned," she said, glancing at Gary's hand holding hers. "It just happened."

"I think your wife knew Micki would be mortified if she accused her of being in love with me. What she didn't know is I've been wrestling with my own feelings for her. Honestly, if she hadn't said anything, or if Micki had denied it, I wouldn't have kissed her."

Later, over coffee, Michael said he had something he wanted to discuss with them. A solemn Michaela sat beside an equally serious Gary, their unobtrusive hand-holding the only indicator of any sort of fondness between them.

Gary seemed surprised by Michael's opening question. "I'll be twenty-two in January."

Micki stared; she'd never exactly thought of Gary as having an age. They eyed each other nervously, waiting for her dad to go on.

His tone commanded their full attention. "I know we joked about this earlier, but I'm dead serious. Make no mistake, Gary: I'm trusting you with my daughter; you are not to mistreat or take advantage of her. In any way. Is that clear?"

"Yes, sir."

"And I'm telling you now, young man: If I ever find out that you have, you *will* regret it."

Gary nodded. "I understand."

"And Kayla, I know you're levelheaded and I can trust you; but at this point, three years is a significant age difference." She started to protest, but he stopped her. "Hear me out: Ordinarily I'd say no. But Gary seems responsible. I have no problem with your seeing him." The two smiled at each other. "But – and I won't say this again – to either of you." He looked from Gary to Kayla and back, tacitly commanding eye contact. "I know all about being young and in love. I also know about facing an unexpected pregnancy. Don't rush into anything you aren't fully prepared for." He looked from his daughter's wide-eyed expression to Gary's contemplative one. "Is that understood?"

"Yes," they responded with one voice, nodding soberly.

"Good." He reached for the coffee pot. "Now that that's out of the way, I'll pour."

When Michael offered a refill, Gary declined. "You two have things to catch up on; and I've got to get home and feed Attila."

"Attila?" Michaela asked. "As in Attila the Hun?"

"Attila the *Hungry*," he clarified. "My cat."

As Gary carried his mug into the kitchen and rinsed it, Michael commented to Michaela, "A man who cleans up after himself, eh? Looks like you've got a good one here, princess."

"I really like him, Daddy," she confided. "He's so sweet. And I like that we were friends first, 'cause we know there's a real connec-tion between us."

Michael hugged his daughter. "It's good to see you smile, honey. You look happier than I've seen you in ages."

"Mr. Conwaye, it's been a pleasure," Gary said. "Thanks again for dinner, and for being so welcoming. I really appreciate it, sir."

Michael took the hand Gary offered. "You make Kayla happy and that's good enough for me. You're welcome here anytime. But would you *please* quit calling me sir?"

Michaela waited by the door. "I'll walk him down, Daddy."

Downstairs, she hugged Gary. "Thank you. For spending time with us… and making me laugh. And caring enough to stand up to my mother." She looked into his eyes with affection.

Gary shook his head. "No, thank *you*. This was nice." *Like being part of a family.* He leaned in to kiss her, then caressed her cheek. "Sweet dreams, baby."

# *Chapter 17*

"I want Kay to stay here awhile. You need some time apart and I think you need to get into rehab."

"Well, I don't care what you think! I don't take orders from you anymore. And you better bring my daughter back here by five."

*My daughter?* Michael gripped the phone. "Sorry, Suz; you're in no condition to care for yourself, let alone Kayla. Now, either you get into detox, or – "

"Or what?"

"Or," he went on, unruffled, "I drag you into court to overturn the custody agreement."

"You can't do that."

"I can, Susan. And I will if you don't cooperate. And this time, Julia will rip your lawyer to ribbons. Now, will you do as I ask or do I make that call?"

"You wouldn't."

"I mean it, Suz. Don't force my hand. Either you get into treatment, pronto, or Julia files my motion to keep Michaela for good."

"She's not a piece of property, for Pete's sake. Michael, she's our daughter."

"And the best you're willing to offer our daughter is drunk and irresponsible behavior?" he bit back. "That's not acceptable, Susan. I want Kayla to have a decent home."

"She had one! But you ruined that when you left," she screamed, then hung up.

Driving back from lunch, Michaela's talk with her dad turned to Thanksgiving. "Can I spend it with you? I really don't want to deal with Mom and her drinking."

"Kayla, don't be so negative. She needs help. I spoke to her this morning about getting into rehab."

"Yeah? What'd she say?"

He hedged. "She wasn't really clear on that."

"Slurring her speech already?"

"Kayla, come on; this is what I'm talking about. Cut her some slack. She's doing the best she can."

"Really? I don't know anymore who's the kid and who's the grownup. All I do is make excuses and clean up after she ruins everything. I *refuse* to spend another holiday that way."

"I was actually thinking of having it at my place. Sort of a conciliatory gesture."

*I can think of a more fitting gesture.* She wrinkled her nose. "You think that's a good idea?"

"What could it hurt? At the very least, you don't have to cook; at best, we get to share some quality time, like a real family."

"It does sound nice," she admitted wistfully. An easy silence fell as father and daughter enjoyed the Litchfield hills by the dwindling early-November daylight. A wet snow began falling.

"I told your mother I want you to stay with me for a while," Michael said at last. "She's fine with it."

Micki arched an eyebrow. "Right. What'd she *really* say?" Silence was her answer. "Hmmph – I figured. She didn't agree to anything. She's probably already leaving rude messages on your machine."

Sinking low in her seat, she stared out her window. *I hate being a pawn in their marital bullshit!* "Can we go home?"

"I thought you wanted to go for a drive."

"I'm really tired, Daddy; I just want to take a hot bath and make it an early night."

He looked at his watch. "More like a late afternoon. You sure you're alright?"

"I'm sick of being caught in the middle of your fights. I'm like a cheap little end table neither of you really wants, but you don't want the other to have, either."

"Kayla, honey, that's not true."

"That's how I feel!" she shrilled, clasping her hands to stop their trembling. "Now please, can we just go home?"

Kayla tensed at her mother's sharp tone and slurred words on the machine. "Michael, if she's not back here by five, I'm calling the cops."

Dad erased the message. "Don't worry, sweetie. She hasn't got a legal leg to stand on." His tone softened when he saw Michaela's about-to-cry expression. "It's been a rough weekend. You go take that bath. I'll call Mom and get everything straightened out." Then, noting her cynical look, he added, "I'll be nice."

As soon as he heard the bathwater running, Michael called Susan. Kayla's voice on the machine told him no one was available.

"Susan, I know you're there," he said at the beep. "Pick up. We need to talk." He waited a few seconds. "I know you're there, Suz. Pick up the phone."

There was a click, then his wife's voice. "When do I get my daughter back?"

He exhaled slowly. "Before you say anything, Suz, I know about your fight yesterday, and the incident with Gary. You two need to go to neutral corners and cool off for awhile."

"I don't need to cool off!" Her shrill hostility made the hairs at the back of his neck stand up.

"Yeah, Suz, you do," he said, not unkindly. "You also need help. Please. I'm begging you: Get some help before it's too late."

She was uncharacteristically silent.

"I've given this a lot of thought, Suz, and I'd like to propose an arrangement."

Still no reply.

"There's a facility near here, Cloverdale, that has a three-week treatment program. You'd be home by Thanksgiving. If you won't do it for you, do it for Kayla. Give *her* something to be thankful for this year."

Susan fingered the brochure on the table, the one her boss gave her last week: The Cloverdale Rehabilitative Treatment Center.

"What's something like that cost, Michael? Do you think I'm made of money?" Her voice wavered. "I can't afford—"

"Susan, A, you can't afford *not* to; and B, I'll pay for it. *Whatever* it costs."

"I can't let you do that, Mike. You're not responsible for me anymore."

*Mike.* She hadn't called him that in ages. Not since things went bad. "Honey, this isn't just for you. Or Kayla. *I* want to see you get well, too." He paused. "Sweetheart, I still love you."

Blinking back tears, Susan touched her gold Claddagh wedding band. "I love you, too, Mike."

When Michaela emerged, snuggled in a blue terrycloth robe, hair turbaned in a towel, her dad greeted her with, "I know you wanted to turn in early, but how d'you feel about coming for a ride?"

"Where?"

"Cloverdale; Mom's going into rehab. She's hoping you'll come with me to see her off."

As Dad's green Audi pulled up to 45 Mapleside at 5:05, Michaela braced for confrontation.

Susan waited inside, suitcase at her side. She hugged her daughter. "Thanks for coming, honey. I'm so sorry about how I acted yesterday; please forgive me."

Michaela squirmed free of her mom's whiskey-scented embrace. "You also owe Gary an apology."

"Would you tell him for me?"

"It'll keep 'til you get back, but you need to do it yourself."

"Okay," she agreed. "Maybe he can come for supper one night."

Susan greeted her estranged husband with a smile, then hugged him. "Darling, how can I ever thank you?" They kissed. Not just a brief peck, either. Michaela pretended not to notice.

Brief bursts of conversation punctuated the ride to Cloverdale.

"Kay and I were talking earlier. About Thanksgiving. I'm thinking about having you over to my place." Michael took his wife's hand, looking at her expectantly. "How's that sound?"

She smiled; her fingers closed around his. "I think it sounds nice. How about you, Kayla?"

"I think we should keep the poison-control number handy."

Michaela couldn't recall the last time she'd heard them laughing. The knot in her insides loosened, letting her relax a little.

***

Next day, Trish stopped Michaela in the hall. "I tried to get you over the weekend, KayCee. I musta called a dozen times, but there was never any answer. Where were you?"

"I'm staying at my dad's. What's up?"

"Well," Trish began in a singsong voice. "Guess who's finally decided to ask you out?"

"Who?"

When Trish blurted the name, Michaela did a double-take. A junior at Southern Connecticut State, Regan Deming had taken quite a shine to his sister's best friend. He was awfully nice and he had a terrific sense of humor. Plus, he was easy on the eyes: auburn

153

hair, hazel eyes, quirky smile and the cutest dimples! And freckles everywhere.

"You'll say yes, right?"

Apprehensive, Michaela hesitated. "I can't."

Trish sounded affronted. "Why? Oh, I know; it'd be too weird, you dating my brother. We could never discuss anything personal 'cause, well… I totally understand. Besides, I don't think I'd wanna know the intimate details of his love life."

"Trish – that's not why."

The other girl looked hurt. "Then what?"

Michaela savored her secret. "I'm seeing someone." *I like how that sounds.*

It took her a moment to register this information. "No you're not. Who?"

She couldn't keep the smile out of her voice as she told her friend.

"*Gary!*" Trish screeched. "You're dating Gary Sheldon?" Everyone in the corridor turned. It felt like an EF Hutton ad. Michaela nodded as Trish went on. "But – I thought you were just—"

The bell rang.

A smile flickered at Michaela's lips. "So did I. Gotta get to class; talk to ya later, 'kay?"

"You can't leave me hanging like this. KayCee!" Trish stood in the middle of the hall. "I want details!"

At lunch, Trish cornered her in the cafeteria line. "So, when did he ask you out?"

"He didn't, really. It was kinda sudden. One minute we're just friends, and the next, we're" – she blushed and stared at her lunch, all fidgety – "out in his car… kissing."

Trish grabbed Michaela's arm, nearly toppling her tray. "What! When? Why didn't you tell me?"

"I *told* you, I'm staying at my dad's; I hadn't seen him in a while. I was gonna tell you today."

"So, what happened?" she persisted as they found seats.

"It's complicated."

"Whaddaya mean, *complicated?* We've got half an hour; spill it."

Sticking a straw in her milk carton, Michaela summarized the confrontation on Saturday; and Gary's 'starry-eyed' admission. "Isn't that the sweetest thing?"

Trish's eyes bulged. "So… Is he a good kisser?"

Michaela sighed dreamily. "Like you wouldn't believe!"

***

Susan phoned Michael twice a week; their conversations grew progressively affectionate and tender. By the time she came home, he felt confident in the foundation they'd laid for a renewed and lasting bond. Meanwhile, he and Michaela planned Thanksgiving at his apartment.

"Can I invite Gary?" she asked two weeks before Thanksgiving. "He doesn't have family nearby; I'd hate for him to be alone."

"You'll bring Attila with you tomorrow, won't you?" Michaela asked, mincing celery and onions. "I hate to think of the poor thing all alone with a can of Fish Surprise and a bowl of water while we feast on turkey. He'll be sitting amid the shredded remains of your couch, all morose. Probably won't speak to you for weeks."

*She sure paints a dismal picture.* "I'm not going to bring my cat to dinner at—"

"It's okay, honest. My dad said he doesn't want to be responsible for your furniture."

Gary chuckled as he cued his closing theme. "I'll mention it to him. If he hasn't got plans, I'm sure he'd love to come. Can he bring a mouse casserole or something?"

***

Micki ran outside. "I'm so glad yo– *What?*" she asked, startled, as Gary abruptly withdrew from her embrace. "What's wrong?"

"Don't! You'll squish him."

A furry head poked out from the front of Gary's partly zipped jacket. "Me-you?"

Micki squealed at the appearance of the legendary Attila, looking decidedly adorable. "Ohh! He's so cute!" She scritched the little cat behind its ears.

Purring, Attila rubbed against her hand. Emerging, he draped his front paws around Gary's neck.

Carrying towel-clad bowls upstairs, Gary and Michaela chattered nonstop. Suddenly, the words froze on his lips. He steeled himself for confrontation.

"Hello, Gary." Susan eyed the tenaciously clinging cat.

"Hi, Mrs. Conwaye. Happy Thanksgiving. You're looking well."

She wore tailored beige slacks and a green sweater. Her blue eyes were clear, her hair held in place with a slim headband. Her once-sallow skin had a ruddy glow. "Thank you." Her smile broadened; she met his gaze. "Happy Thanksgiving to you."

She turned to her daughter. "Will you excuse us for a moment, honey? I'd like a word with Gary alone."

"Um… sure, Mom. I uh – I'll be out there." Michaela thumbed backward, glancing nervously at Gary. "I'll get Attila some water and treats. Then he and Ginger can get acquainted."

Plucking the protesting cat from his sweater, Gary deposited Attila in Micki's arms.

They sat on the couch. "I'm glad you came," Susan began as her daughter left. Gary's expression must have been one of surprise, because she continued quickly. "*Really.* Kayla's quite fond of you. I was happy when she said you'd be here today, Gary. I owe you an apology. For last time."

He started to protest, but she was adamant. "I've done a lot of thinking these past few weeks. I was just awful to you. I hope you'll accept my apology."

Gary's tone was as gentle as the hand he rested on her arm. "Of course" – he glanced away for a moment – "if you'll accept mine."

"You got a deal." Smiling, Susan gave his knee a maternal pat. "And I want you to know: You were right. It *is* time for me to accept Kayla's decisions."

Shoving aside the memory of long-ago talks with Mom, Gary shook his head. "No. Please, forget I ever said that, ma'am. I was out of line."

"She's not a kid anymore. She wants you in her life, Gary. I'm fine with that." Susan smiled with quiet grace. "And I hope we can be friends."

Smiling back, he squeezed her hand. "So do I," he said, meaning it.


By the time they sat down to dinner, the dreaded tension was a fading memory. Susan was warm and outgoing; and if his smile was any indication, Michael was falling in love with her all over again.

Susan reached for the onions. "Gary, Kayla says you're in radio. How long have you done that?"

"Almost seven years; but I've been at 'ZBX just over three."

She passed the creamed onions to her husband. "How'd you get interested in that?"

"I worked at a station back home in high school; this job kind of came up from that. I also did some college radio."

"You don't say. Did you go to Pomperaug?"

"No, ma'am. I grew up in Jersey. Little town called Pine Cove. I went to a small Catholic school there."

"So, that would've been… what, '80 or '81 that you graduated?" Michael asked.

"Eighty-two."

While Michael considered this, Susan spoke. "Where do you go to college?"

He took a sip from his water glass. "I graduated last December. From UConn-Waterbury."

"I didn't know they offered associate degrees."

"No, ma'am. I've got my B.A."

Susan looked skeptical. "In two years? Is their communications program that easy?"

Annoyance flickered in Gary's eyes, but he kept his voice gentle. "Actually, I double-majored: Communications and Shakespearean Lit. Minored in marketing. And I did it in two-and-a-half years."

"My goodness! You *are* ambitious," Michael remarked. "How'd you fit it all in?"

"Creative scheduling and a *really* understanding boss. It wasn't easy: working full time and teaching on weekends. But I took extra courses each term, lots of summer classes. And tested out of a few things early on."

Susan's skepticism persisted. "How were your grades?"

Gary glanced away, a gesture she misread as an admission of defeat or, at least, embarrassment. "My GPA was 3.97. I graduated summa cum laude."

"*Summa!*" Michael whistled. "I'm impressed."

Michaela smiled. Inside, she was bursting with pride at Gary's achievement – not to mention, secretly glad his reply had taken her mom down a peg or two.

"You mentioned teaching," Susan intoned coolly. "What do you teach?"

"First-grade CCD. Here at St. John's."

"Where do you find the time?" Michael asked.

"I don't. I make the time; 'cause it's that important. Kids need a solid background in their faith." Gary smiled hugely. "And I love it! The kids want to know absolutely everything. I've got thirteen this year; they really keep me on my toes."

Michael remembered what Kayla had been like as a first grader; he thought about having a dozen more like her all at once. "They must be a handful."

"It's not bad. I've got 'em an hour and a half a week. I guess it's like having nieces and nephews: Play with 'em while they're fun and ship 'em back when they work your nerves."

"You sound like the voice of experience. How many do you have?"

"Nieces and nephews? None yet, sir. Probably none any time soon, either."

"How many in your family?" This was Susan.

"There's three of us: Marie's twenty-five; Joey's" – he subtracted eight from his age – "thirteen and" – anticipating her next query – "I'll be twenty-two in a couple months."

"What do your parents do?"

Michaela glanced at Gary, then grasped his hand under the table.

"My father's a lawyer; my mom" – he shook his head – "I don't know." His hand shook as he reached for his water glass. "I haven't seen her in years."

"Well, how can you *not know* what your own mother does for a living?" Susan blurted.

Gary looked stricken. Mr. Conwaye stared at Michaela in horror.

Thick silence filled the room. No one could think of anything to say. The awkwardness lingered. It felt to Micki like the entire room was stuffed with cotton, the four of them set in slow motion.

At last came the sound of a chair being pushed back.

"Suz, could you give me a hand, please? I forgot to bring in the pies from my car."

As her parents left, Michaela touched Gary's hand. When he looked her way, she wanted to cry. There was no way she could fix the pain in his eyes. She wanted to apologize for her mother's insensitive comment. Her fingers closed around his; her voice was timid. "Are you okay?"

Gary forced himself to meet her gaze. Not trusting his voice, he just nodded.

By the time her folks returned, pie-less, Michaela and Gary were talking quietly, as though nothing had happened.

# Chapter 18

The holidays loomed and Gary dreaded them. It wouldn't seem like Christmas without Grandpa. At least Holiday Bash prep kept him so busy he didn't have time to give holidays, past or impending, more than a passing thought. Which was good. Last thing he needed was time to brood.

Marie drove up the weekend before Christmas. Admitting he wasn't up to decorating the cottage, Gary enlisted her help. Friday, they cut a tree and set it up in the living room. Next morning, he hauled boxes of ornaments down from the attic. Marie handled the actual decorating. When she finished, she took a look around; the little cottage looked cheery and Christmas-y.

"I'm glad you asked me to help, Gary. I needed something to conjure up Grandpa. What d'you think?"

The blue spruce was as lovely as it was fragrant, but it might as well have been an umbrella stand strung with colored lights. Gary manufactured enthusiasm. "It looks great; smells terrific, too!" He hugged her. "Thanks for doing this, Marie. I couldn'ta done it."

That night, in full elf regalia, he leapt about the Pomperaug High gym as if he hadn't a care in the world.


(11:30 a.m., Christmas Eve – Tuesday)

"I dunno whether it's easier to be here, like you, immersed in memories, or removed from him, in the City," Marie mused as they prepared the seafood. "I almost envy you, able to surround yourself with everything Grandpa loved, anytime you want."

"I guess in a way, it *is* easier, being here." Shelling shrimp, Gary looked back to see his sister perusing a page in one of Gamma Jo's well-worn cookbooks. "We sure had some great times here. But sometimes that makes it hurt all the more."

"I know we never talked about it, but we inherited a lot of money, Gar'. A *lot* of money. I still can't believe it. You lived with him; did you have any idea he was so rich?"

"Not a clue. I was as surprised as you — as all of us! And I guess I must've hoped he'd keep this place in the family; but I never dreamed he'd leave it to me outright." He turned back to the bowl of shrimp.

The mantel clock in the living room ticked away minutes.

"Hey, Gar'? When are you gonna patch things up with Mom? You haven't spoken in years."

Gary felt like she'd hit him in the back of the head with a board. His shoulders stiffened; he gripped the edge of the sink. "How many times do I have to say it, Marie?" he intoned. "I don't want to discuss it."

She persisted. "But Gary, if you only *knew* why she—"

He whirled to face her. "That's just it: I don't *wanna* know! I don't want to *talk* about her. I don't want to *know* about her! I don't fucking care about her! Is that clear enough for you?"

"Plenty! And what's clearest of all is that you're a self-centered, childish brat!" Marie banged her knife down on the cutting board, sending onion flying everywhere. "She *loves* you, you asshole! But you're just like Daddy: so damn stubborn!" She stomped off.

Gary worked in furious silence until a heap of raw shrimp and an equally impressive pile of shells lay in large Pyrex bowls. He tossed the shells into a pot of water, threw in a fistful of parsley and set it to boil for stock. Retrieving the onion skins strewn about the table, he tossed those in, too.


Arriving home after work, Gary found Marie poking at a baking sheet loaded with fragrant calamari; he waited until she straightened up and shut the oven door. "Hi."

She jumped. "Jesus, Gary! You scared the shit outta me!"

"Sorry. I thought you heard me come in." He hesitated. "Can we talk?"

Ignoring his question, Marie thrust a bowl of cornmeal at him. "Here, coat the scallops and shrimp and start cooking. Sam and Martha'll be here soon."

Glad to have something to busy his hands, Gary dredged the succulent morsels in the coarse yellow granules, then plunked them into the boiling oil.

"Careful, Gar'. Don't burn yourself," Marie cautioned, preparing anchovy-infused olive oil for the calamari.

As he fed the fryer cornmeal-encrusted seafood, Gary swallowed his pride in the interest of salvaging the holiday. "I'm sorry about before. I don't want to ruin Christmas by fighting."

Marie slipped an arm around her brother. "Neither do I." She stood on tiptoe, gave him a peck on the cheek. "I love you, kiddo."

Abandoning his deep fryer, Gary wrapped his sister in a hug. "Love you, too."

They finished cooking just before the Johnsons arrived. At Marie's suggestion, Gary set out the group photo from Christmas Eve '82 – the one Edward had framed for each of them – hoping it might help lift everyone's spirits. But, perhaps because they were all trying so hard, the celebration held little of the warmth that was so abundant while Edward was alive.

Dinner was the longest hour Gary ever endured.

Insisting on tackling cleanup alone, he sent the others into the living room. After stowing the last pot in its cupboard, he slipped out to the porch. Huddled in a quilt taken from the study, Gary sat in Grandpa's rocking chair, listening to the lonely sound of the sea. And missing him terribly.

The screen door creaked.

"Mind if I join you?" When Gary shook his head, Sam sat and rocked in the same rhythm as Gary.

It was a while before Sam intruded on the quiet again. "I know you're missing him out here, son. We're missing him in there, too. Sure would help if we could all be together." Gary rocked harder. Sam patted his shoulder. "You want to talk about it?"

Gary's bones ached from the weight of grief. His back and shoulders hurt from being hunched up out here in the cold. His eyes felt so sore he wanted to rip them out. When he opened his mouth, what came out sounded like an animal caught in a trap. It frightened him. He stopped rocking, slumped forward and wept. He clutched at Sam's hand, craving human contact to ease the hurt. When he could speak, Gary admitted how empty and lost he felt.

"I can understand that," Sam told him. "We'd been neighbors thirty-five years. Friends even longer. Some days I still expect to see him ambling across the sand. I can only imagine how you must be feeling his loss."

Next morning, at breakfast, Gary said he was going to close up the cottage and not come back. Not for a while; maybe not ever.

"It just hurts too much, being here. Too many memories." He shook his head. "I dunno. Maybe I'll just sell it." He desperately wished someone would talk him out of it.

Martha laid her hand atop his. "Honey, memories are what makes this place *home*. Sure, it hurts now. But in time, the memories that are so painful now will be the ones that'll give you the greatest comfort."

Sam took Gary's other hand. "She's right, son. Don't make rash decisions you'll regret later." The old man's hand was warm. Like his smile. "Sure, it's hard to be here now, with the ghosts of the past. Someday – maybe even someday soon – you'll be glad you stuck around. Count on it."

Marie hugged her brother. "They're right, Gar'. But *you're* right, too: There *are* lots of memories here. But, sweetie, aren't they *good* ones? Look around: So much of you has gone into this place, I think you'd regret it if you sold it. I know the decision's yours to make; but think it through before you do anything."

After everyone left, Gary began rethinking his anger toward Ellen: Maybe he'd been wrong to cling to it all this time. They'd survived rough times before, they'd get past this. They weren't kids anymore; they could talk out their differences like adults. Right?

His insides knotted as he reached for the black rotary-dial phone. He remembered playing with it as a child. Sitting under the desk, he'd pretend to call people. Of course, Grandpa had taped the hang-up buttons down, "so you don't go calling Peru," he'd chortled, mussing the child's hair. Gary dialed the area code and Ellen's exchange. Atop the recliner, Attila purred.

Gary's hand stopped; he'd dialed her number hundreds of times; but suddenly he couldn't recall if it was -3296 or -2396. He thought hard. It *had* to be 32. His heart raced. The phone rang once, twice. A third time. What would he say? "I forgive you?" "I still love you?" He had no idea. On the fourth ring, there was a click.

A young male voice answered. "Merry Christmas!" Startled as much by the greeting as the unfamiliar voice, Gary was silent. "Hello?" the voice said. "Is someone there?"

*Could that be Tommy? He'd be what – 12 now? Maybe 13?* His hand holding the receiver shook. "Y-yes," he stammered. "Is – um – is Ellen there?"

It seemed forever before the voice spoke again. "I'm sorry. You've got a wrong number."

How could he have gotten it wrong? He'd dialed it so many times! Did he remember it wrong? Maybe he wasn't meant to talk to her. Gary plucked Attila from the back of the old brown chair. With the little cat rumbling contentedly in his lap, he picked up the phone again. Dialing the number, he waited for the ring.

At last he heard a familiar, "Hello."

"Merry Christmas, sweetheart."

"Hi," she purred. "Merry Christmas! I thought you'd forgotten me."

"How could I forget my Michaela Divan? It's been a real busy day. Besides, I wanted to call when there weren't a zillion other things distracting me."

"Why? 'Cause I'm enough of a distraction, Jersey Boy?"

"Exactly." She'd begun calling him that after his accent surfaced a few weeks ago; it did that at unguarded moments. He guessed it showed how comfortable he felt around her.

"You at home?"

"Yeah – no. Well…" He decided not to get into it now. "No."

"Can't decide, eh?" she teased. "You been drinking?"

Her playful query rattled Gary until he realized how confusing his vague reply must have sounded. "Not yet – but that's not a half-bad idea. And no, I'm not at my apartment."

"So, where *are* you? Are you okay? You sound kinda down."

*You sound so sad.* Ellen's words from Christmases ago tore through him. "Yeah, I'm fine."

"Gar'?" She sounded unconvinced. "You *sure* you're okay? You don't sound so good."

He sighed, grateful for Michaela's concern, yet just the slightest bit irked. "Mick, I'm fine. *Really.* Don't worry about me, huh? It's just – well, Christmas is just kinda rough…"

"D'you wanna talk about it?"

He'd done nothing *but* talk lately. Gary touched the wrist he'd nearly slit five years earlier. *It woulda been so easy,* he thought ruefully. He shut his eyes against the memory. Desperate tears squeezed from beneath tightly closed lids as empty sadness filled him. "Not really."

He did anyway; he confided about this first Christmas without Grandpa. But he couldn't bring himself to say why Christmas was so difficult, overall. Before they said goodnight, he thanked her for listening.

"You've done that for me plenty enough. It's time I returned the favor."

Gary ached for one of her hugs. "Thanks." He stopped short of whispering, "I love you."

As his relationship with Micki blossomed, Gary and Michael also grew close; the three often went to breakfast after Mass. Sometimes Gary would call if he found himself in need of guidance or a listening ear. When Gary phoned one evening in May, Michael invited him to drop by to talk.

Michael ushered Gary into the living room and offered him a beer. "What's on your mind?" he asked.

"I've given a lot of thought lately to something you said, back when Micki and I first started seeing each other… what you said about us not sleeping toge—"

"That's *not* up for discussion."

"No!" Gary replied hastily, misunderstood. "Of course not, sir. That's not what I meant. I just – well, I want you to know you have nothing to worry about."

The older man took a sip of his beer. "I *always* worry about my daughter."

"Granted" – he hesitated – "but I want to assure you, sir: She'll *always* be safe with me."

"I'm glad to hear that." Michael sounded amused. "And why would that be?"

Gary sat forward, elbows on his knees. "Mr. Conwaye, umm… can I level with you, sir?"

"Of course, Gary. What's on your mind?"

He took a steadying breath, eyes fixed on the bottle he rolled back and forth between his palms. "I appreciate how supportive you've been. And I hope what I'm going to say won't make you change your mind about me."

"Have you left a trail of bodies in fifteen states?"

"No, sir," he murmured, eyes downcast. "Years ago – a *few* years ago," he corrected himself, "I got my high-school girlfriend pregnant. It was April of senior year. Catholic school. I said if they were gonna kick her out, they'd have to expel me, too."

Michael's lips were a tight line. "They threw you out just before graduation?"

*I may as well leave. No way in hell he'll let me keep seeing Micki now!*
"Yes, sir."

"And what happened with this girlfriend?"

Gary fidgeted. "I wanted to marry her, wanted us to be a family. But she didn't want anything more to do with me."

"And now that's changed? Is *that* what you're telling me?"

"No, sir! Absolutely not. We haven't talked in years. Not si—"

"And the baby?" Michael interrupted. There was no masking the disapproval in his voice.

"She had an abortion," Gary whispered around the lump in his throat. "I've never forgiven myself for not…" his words decayed to regretful silence.

Michael laid a hand on Gary's shoulder. "I'm so sorry, Gary. I can't imagine how awful that must have been for you. I appreciate your confiding in me. And I admire your courage in coming to me about this."

"I swear to you: I am *never* gonna put your daughter into that predicament. And I wanted you to know about this before I told Mic—"

"Hold on. Is that really something you want her to know?"

"Not really. But here's the thing: I don't want there to be any secrets between us. I'm in love with her an—"

"You're what?"

Gary held up a hand to stave off what he was sure would be a storm of protest. "I know what you're thinking, sir: She's only nineteen. But – I can't explain it. She's sweet and funny and caring. I like how her eyes light up when she smiles; I love how I feel when I'm with her an—" His voice had grown wistful. "And I shouldn't be going on like this."

Michael watched Gary for several moments. "You're in love, alright."

He tried not to cringe. "Is that a problem?"

"No. I like you, Gary. Plus, I like the changes I've seen in Kayla: She's more confident, less vulnerable." Draining his beer, Michael nodded. "I think you've had a lot to do with that."

Relief flooded him. "So you're still okay with me seeing her? I mean, even after… this?"

"Of course. Nothing's changed, except now I know one detail about your past. And that's what it is, Gary: your *past*. I don't mean to sound callous – especially about the baby, because that really is tragic; but don't let it come between you two. Kayla's fond of you; and frankly, so am I."

***

The last Saturday in May, when Gary met Michaela at the diner, she'd been crying. A classmate dating one of the senior boys was killed the night before in an alcohol-related crash after the prom.

Attending a 16-year-old's wake was one of the saddest things he ever had to do, but Gary couldn't let her face it alone. The line of mourners, mostly teens, snaked around the block. Every face in the line reflected anguish. The family's faces were masks of torment – especially Vincent, the teen whose drunk driving caused his sister's death.

A chill ran through Gary as he and Michaela knelt at the casket. *She's just a little older than Joey! There's gotta be a way to keep this from happening again. But what?*

When he awoke on Monday, he had an answer. He spent most of an hour scribbling ideas. As soon as he got to work, Gary went to promotion director Laira Penfield's office. She was new – on the job just a few weeks. He doubted she even knew who he was.

Laira listened to his proposal. "Great idea, Gary; but it's a lot to coordinate in three weeks." His eyes, full of enthusiasm moments earlier, displayed dejection. "Still," she added, "you outlined it well. It's got great community-involvement potential. It just might work. And I hear your ability to pull things off on short notice is *amazing!*"

They pitched the idea to Pete. When they finished, he smiled. "Great idea, Gary. Run with it."

Gary called Jackie DeMay, a counselor at Pomperaug, his point of contact for the Holiday Bash; the school was closed so students and faculty could attend the funeral. He reached her the next day.

Jackie was thankful for his wanting to help "turn tragedy into hope" and grateful for his condolences on behalf of the station, which she promised to extend to Felicia's family.

Gary was overwhelmed by local businesses' generosity. Markets donated dozens of cases of sodas; pizzerias promised food; a print shop run by the family of two students printed flyers. Other companies wanted to help, but either didn't know what to do or didn't make a product to donate, so they gave money. Plenty of it. The project evolved from solely an alcohol-free party into a scholarship fundraiser in the girl's name. The all-night party would be open to

166

graduating seniors, friends and family; once you went in, you stayed 'til morning.

Between ticket sales and donations, the Felicia Jane Dandrow Memorial All-Night Post-Grad Alcohol-Free Dance Party was a wild success. Everyone got a Z97-3 t-shirt emblazoned with the name of the event and the date: June 20-21, 1986. Marc DJ'd; Gary served as host. Rob Tyler, filling in on the air, did live cutaways to them all night.

Just before 9, Marc challenged Gary to dance, nonstop, 'til the party ended at 10 the next morning, "*If* you're up to it," he added. Marc knew that expressing doubt was the best way to get Gary to accept a dare.

During one cutaway, Jim Burdell upped the ante: The station would donate $500 for each hour Gary danced; if he lasted 'til 10, the operations manager would personally add $3,500.

Marc conveyed that news to the roomful of revelers. "Hey, no pressure or anything, Gar', but the boss just called. He's gonna put his money where his mouth is – or rather, where your dancin' shoes are. If you survive 'til ten tomorrow, he's gonna give a nice chunk o' change to the scholarship fund. How's another ten grand sound to you?"

Thirteen hours later, Gary wore a smile of weary satisfaction. He'd helped bring the total raised to nearly $20,000. He went home and slept for 18 hours straight.

***

The Conwayes invited Gary for Christmas; knowing his sister was in town, Michaela invited her, too.

It was the nicest holiday Gary could remember since before Grandpa died.

"I like her," Marie told her brother on the way home. "I totally see why you're gaga over her. And her parents really seem to like you."

"I'm not so sure about *that*. Most of the time I think her mom still hates me."

"If she doesn't like you, she's putting on a really good act. Didn't you notice how she'd touch your arm when she talked to you? Or keep eye contact so long?"

Gary considered this; he supposed he had to give his sister's observations credence. After all, Marie *was* doing her psychiatric residency at Bellevue.

"I love the lapis earrings Michaela gave me." She pulled out the porcelain trinket box in which Micki presented the earrings. "And this box is just precious!"

"You made quite a hit yourself. Micki loved that journal you gave her, with those quotes by famous authors. And that fountain pen you got her is beautiful!"

They rode in silence for a bit. "She really is a sweet kid." At a frosty glare from Gary, Marie clarified, "I meant *kid* in that she's younger than me." She gave a conciliatory smile. "I really like her."

"Good, 'cause you'll be seeing a lot of her." He said she was the first girl he'd been serious about since Ellen. He mentioned again he didn't think her mom liked him much. "But Michael's terrific; I feel like I can really talk to him."

"Interesting that you should mention your relationship with her father."

Gary sighed with disdain as the car crunched to a stop. "Spare me the psych workup, huh?"

Marie held up a hand to fend off his accusation. "I just think it's interesting, that's all, that you form such strong relational bonds with the fathers of your girlfriends."

He yanked the emergency brake. *Plural?* He didn't need to say it aloud.

"First there was Ellen, now Micki," Marie ticked them off on her fingers, "and God-knows-how-many in between."

"I was never *friends* with Bob Farricelli." Attila mewed in protest as Gary grabbed him more roughly than he intended. "Michael treats me like an equal. I mean, I'm seeing his daughter, sure; but we can talk about stuff – stuff I'd *never* have said to Mr. Farricelli."

"So you feel like you can confide in him," she baited.

He retrieved the bag of gifts. "In a sense, yeah."

"So he *is* a father figure to you!"

"No!" Gary slammed the trunk. "Whatever you're getting at, drop it; it's getting old real fast." Stalking inside, he let the storm door bang shut behind him.

Marie stared after him, shaking her head. "Denial ain't just a river in Egypt," she muttered.

# *Chapter 19*

In February, Susan relapsed. She resisted Michael's efforts to get her back into rehab, denying she needed help. So Michael, who'd contemplated coming home since her first anniversary of sobriety, renewed the lease on his apartment.

To minimize her time in proximity to her mother's alcohol-fueled toxicity, Michaela began spending more and more time with Gary. One Saturday in April, after grocery shopping, he asked what her college plans were.

"Haven't really given it much thought." She gave a disinterested shrug and picked at her nail polish.

"Shouldn't you start applying to schools soon?"

"Geez, Gary, you sound like my mother!"

"It was just a question. I was making conversation."

They drove in murky silence. Pink flecks accumulated on the floor mat. "I like working with kids," she offered, her anger seeping away. She shrugged, eyes still fixed on her hands. "Maybe I could – I dunno. Something with kids?"

"Hmm." He recalled her enthusiasm over her summer-camp job last year. *She's got such patience with kids. With* me, *I'm not so sure.* Lately she seemed angry a lot.

Finally Micki spoke again. "I wasn't gonna say anything, 'cause I didn't want you to say I was crazy."

Instead of downshifting to turn onto her street, Gary shifted into fourth, heading toward Woodbury. "I wouldn't do that. When I told my folks what I wanted to do, my dad laughed at me. It sucks when people criticize your dreams."

"What I *really* want to—" Michaela shook her head. "I can't tell you. You'll think I'm nuts. Even if you don't say it, I know you'll be thinking it." It took more prodding, and he promised he wouldn't laugh or criticize. "When I said I want to do something with kids, I didn't mean teaching. What I really want to do, I don't have to go to college for. I—" She paused. "I wanna be a wife. And a mom. T-to your kids."

Approaching a light, his hand flew off the stick shift. The jarring metal-against-moving-metal grinding noise sent a jolt up his spine.

"*What?*" Gary pulled to a stop behind a VW Beetle.

"I told you you'd think I was nuts."

"No." He took Michaela's hand. "I *don't*. If you're serious, let's talk about it."

"Don't tell me you don't want kids…?"

"Of course I do! And I'd love more than anything for you to be their mom. And my wife." He smiled. "But we both need to grow up before we think about getting married and starting a family."

***

(22 May, 1987 – Friday)

"I'll spare you the singing, but I wanted to be the first to wish you a happy birthday."

Michaela grinned. "I appreciate that; but my dad beat you by ten minutes. It was *awful*. I almost didn't pick up just now, in case it was him, going for the second verse. I'm glad it wasn't."

Gary chuckled. "Ah, I see. So you're not necessarily glad it's me; you're just relieved it wasn't him."


Micki packed a bag to take to her dad's. She slung it over her shoulder and ran downstairs. Not even a card from Mom.

After school, she emerged, engrossed in conversation with Trish and the Jamieson twins, Brian and Linda, comparing plans for the Memorial Day weekend.

"Regan gets home today," Trish bubbled. "We're going to my grandparents' place in the City."

Linda sighed. "Sounds like fun. Wish we had somewhere to go. We're just gonna do the backyard-barbecue thing. What about you, KayCee?"

"Seeing Gary tonight; spending the weekend at my dad's." She shifted her bag to her left shoulder. "He'll probably wan—" Spying Gary headed toward her, she stopped. "Oh!"

"Happy birthday."

She hugged him, nearly crushing the bouquet of roses he held. "Thank you!" Burying her face in the bouquet, she inhaled their intoxicating aroma. She noticed a single red rose amid the copious white blooms. "They're beautiful!"

"They're just flowers." He lifted Micki's chin and met her gaze. "*You're* beautiful." He kissed her, then greeted her friends as he took her bags.

"Don't you have to be at work soon?" she asked as they pulled out into traffic.

Gary reached for her hand. "I took the day off."

"Oh." Michaela enjoyed the warmth of his hand around hers. "Can we drop this stuff at my dad's? And get these in some water?"

"We *could*... but there's been a slight change in plans."

Disappointment began to gnaw at her. "How slight?"

"Well, Mick, I dunno if you're gonna like this..." Gary hedged. "Instead of your dad's, how'd you feel about... oh, say, spending the weekend at the beach?"

"It sounds *great*! But, Gary, what about my parents?"

"I didn't invite them."

"No... I mean, they're gonna have a fit!"

"I gave your dad the number; he promised not to call unless it's an emergency."

"He's actually going to let me go away with you – for a long weekend?"

"Provided we 'behave responsibly' and you're home by nine Monday night. But, yeah, he's given us his blessing." He paused. "Hope you packed something cozy; nights are still kinda chilly."

"Only some jeans and t-shirts. And this jacket. Nothing really warm."

Gary shrugged. "So we'll buy you something. You should have pretty things for your birthday."

"Gary..."

"*Michaela*," he mimicked. "You'll need appropriate clothing."

"We can go back to my mom's to *get* something appropriate."

"What kind of fun would *that* be?" He released her hand just long enough to shift gears. "You'd deny me the chance to spoil you rotten on your birthday?"

Without suitable reply, Micki slipped her hand away; she studied his face. His tone was stern, but his face remained stoic, revealing nothing. *Is he angry?* As if in response to her unspoken query, the corners of his mouth turned upward in an elfin grin. She conceded defeat. "Fine. You win."

"I had every intention of winning," Gary assured her, upshifting into fifth.

Pulling up to a little shop outside West Haven half an hour later, he cautioned, "I don't want to catch you peeking at price tags. Pick out whatever you like."

Michaela found a cream and blue hand-knit pullover with roses embroidered all over it. Self-conscious, she awaited his approval, trying to ignore the price tag she couldn't help noticing.

Gary looked it over. "It's… *nice*. But what about something for tonight?"

She wrung her hands. "I don't think so; besides, I brought a dress with me."

It was as if she hadn't spoken. "How 'bout this?" He held up an emerald-and-black dress with a full skirt. "This would look *stunning* on you."

She gazed longingly at it. It *was* lovely. He certainly had an eye for style. She shied away, shaking her head.

Gary held out a sleeve. "Don't you like it?"

Michaela fingered the material. *Silk.* "Of course I do," she stammered, aware of the clerk's gaze on her. Catching a glimpse of the price tag, she gulped. "I just wish you wouldn't insist on buying me things."

"Alright," he conceded. "Just this, then," he told the saleslady.

Fifteen minutes later, Gary pulled into the driveway at 52 Field Court. Helping Micki out of the car, he shouldered her duffel bag.

"Here we are," he announced with a broad sweep with his hand. "My favorite place on earth."

She surveyed the wood-shake house with its dark-green window boxes spilling red geraniums and wide, welcoming porch. As Gary unlocked the door, she cupped her hands to her eyes, pressing her face to the windowpane. Peering inside, she could just make out soft, shadowy images beyond the curtains.

He motioned her ahead of him. Inside, it smelled of surf, sand and salt air. Gary set the duffel down.

She looked around the living room. Lace curtains hung in the windows along the front and right side. Tall bookshelves and old, framed family photographs lined the walls. Comfortable-looking furniture in neutral tones hugged the corners. A stone fireplace ready to be lit took up much of the rear wall. Candles of all sizes filled every space: the massive stone mantel, end tables and shelves.

In another part of the house, a tinny radio played '40s music. "This is *fabulous*!" she exclaimed, slipping her arms around him.

He smiled and kissed her nose. "If it wasn't such a long drive to work, I'd live here all year." Enjoying having her in his arms, Gary held her awhile longer. "C'mon, I'll give you the grand tour."

Taking Micki's hand, he led her into the kitchen. It was cheery and homey, in white and shades of blue, ranging from sky-hued swirls in the tan floor tiles to cobalt jars set along the windows to catch the light. Micki found the source of the music: a small art-deco radio.

The south-facing windows let in an enormous amount of light and afforded an exquisite view of the shore. The adjacent half bath reflected the same color scheme: white walls with pale-blue trim, the same seashore-inspired floor tiles and crisp white curtains. Miniature gilt-framed seascapes graced two walls.

Gary took a blue-and-white speckled pitcher from a high shelf; filling it with water, he arranged the roses, set the makeshift vase on the table and ushered Michaela onto the porch. Leaning against the rails, he inhaled deeply and stared out across the Sound.

Micki leaned her forearms on the rails and looked out over the water. An unexpected gust made her shiver.

Gary slid an arm around her to stave off her chills.

She rested her head against his shoulder. "This is really nice."

They watched a sailboat scud across the choppy water. Seagulls wheeled overhead, crying raucously. A few houses further up, three children with shovels and buckets sat by the water, digging a moat around their sandcastle.

When they tired of watching the children's excavation project, Gary resumed the tour.

The study was also filled with comfy, well-worn furniture. The nut-brown couch was lumpy but full of character; anything else would be out of place. The recliner also could be at home nowhere else. Shelves filled with architecture books and old leather-bound editions lined the walls. The empty fireplace looked like the larger one in the living room; the study also lacked the aroma of recently burnt wood.

Gary led Micki up the narrow staircase. A full bath in sea-green and ecru was at one end of the hall; next to it, a small room. "Here we have the blue room." To one side stood a double bed, its azure spread drawn over the pillows. Afternoon sun streamed in through parted curtains; salty ocean air wafted in from the open windows.

The walls reminded Micki of the early-evening sky. An '30s-style bureau sat against one wall. In the corner, a stately spindle-backed rocker waited silently.

"Gary, this is gorgeous!" She ran her hand over the bureau's lustrous finish, then examined a framed black-and-white snapshot at the edge of the crocheted doily. A tanned, 60ish woman sat on the porch, arms encircling a wriggling little boy eating a Popsicle. "Is this your grandmother?"

"Yep. We'd just come back from swimming. I told her I wanted to spend all my summers here with her. She said my Grandpa had told her the same thing years earlier; and someday I would spend summers here with *my* wife. I told her that'd never happen, 'cause girls were yucky. She started laughing and tried to kiss me. Of course, I had to get away." He paused. "Grandpa was always Johnny-on-the-spot with a camera. He snapped that just after she planted a big wet kiss" – he poked at his left cheek – "right here."

Michaela smiled. "That's a great story."

A wistful smile crossed Gary's face. "She was a great lady."

"Did you always spend summers here?"

"We spent a lot of time here. When I was a baby, she'd rock me to sleep in that chair. Always left the windows open, so I'd get used to the sound of the ocean; she'd sit there and rock me to sleep."

"You remember that?"

"No." Gary shook his head – sadly, Micki noticed. "But that's what my grandfather always told me. In fact, there's a picture here somewhere he took of us in that chair, with sunlight coming in through that window. The light was shining from behind her; she looked like an angel, smiling at me. I asked her once who that baby was." He paused. "She just smiled and said he was the apple of her eye."

Michaela loved hearing Gary tell stories; his eyes had a particular warmth whenever he talked about his grandparents. Yet now they looked so faraway, so sad. She wondered why.

"That's what she used to call *me*; I figured someone she loved more had taken my place. I didn't realize it *was* me. I remember it like it was yesterday: I said I hated her and ran out of the room, crying. Nobody knew why I was so upset. And I never told anyone. 'Til now." He smirked. "Silly, huh?"

"Not at all," Michaela cooed, taking his hand.

Gary's eyes misted; he didn't want to finish the story, but he felt impelled. "Three weeks later, she died. I was five; I didn't know what a stroke was. I thought she left 'cause I said I hated her. They wouldn't let me go to the funeral; I never got a chance to tell her I was sorry and I loved her. Or say goodbye."

Tears pricking at her eyes, Micki gathered Gary in her arms. *So much sadness in this house. So much pain.* "I'm sure she knew you didn't mean it," she murmured, not knowing what else to say.

A breeze stirred the curtains, carrying in a rush of salt air. "I'm sorry," he mumbled, pulling away. "This was s'posed to be a nice weekend. I didn't mean to spoil it."

"You didn't spoil anything," she insisted. "C'mon, show me the rest of the place." Tugging at his arm, she moved toward the door.

"Wait." His tone was as soft as the hand stroking her cheek. "Thanks, Mick. For being here."

She gave his hand a little squeeze. "I love you, Gary; I'll always be here for you."

"You don't know how I needed to hear that."

She slid her arms around him again. "Why do you come here if it makes you so sad?"

"It's not like this all the time; there are plenty of good memories here, too – memories of happy times. Back then, and recently. Guess I must've been missing her more than usual," Gary mused. "I love you, Micki; I'm so glad you're here." He drew back. "Hey, want some iced tea? It's raspberry lemon."

Michaela smiled, relieved to see his demeanor brighten. "Mmm. Sounds good."

Back in the kitchen, Gary took an old-fashioned glass pitcher of pinkish liquid from the fridge and poured a generous glassful for each of them. Rinsing two peaches, he handed her one in a napkin. They headed out to the porch.

Having abandoned their sandcastle, the trio of children splashed in the surf. Their laughter made Gary smile. "What a great sound, huh?"

"Mmm." Micki bit into her peach; juice dribbled from a corner of her mouth.

Gary leaned in, licked away the sticky juice; then he kissed her. "Mmm – tasty."

Blushing, she kissed back. After a few more kisses, they went back to looking out over the water, watching the screaming gulls scatter as the children raced toward them.

A few minutes later, Gary hailed an old gentleman walking a golden retriever. "Hi, Sam."

"Hello there!" Walking a little way up the sand, Sam whistled. "Amber… c'mon girl." The dog bounded after her master. Sitting at his feet, she scratched an ear, her tags jangling. "Wasn't sure you'd be down. Martha wanted me to ask you to supper tomorrow if you're around. She's making barbecued chicken and a green salad. Of course, you're welcome to bring a guest." He nodded toward Michaela. "Hello."

She smiled shyly. "Hi."

Gary introduced them, adding, "Sam and Martha have lived four houses up, long as I can remember. Longer, actually. He's kind of a fixture 'round here."

"No kidding?" Leaning over the rail, Michaela took the hand Sam extended toward her. "Pleased to meet you, Mr. Johnson."

"The pleasure is all mine, miss," he replied. "Please, call me Sam. And I'm afraid your young man here is just being polite, calling me a fixture. What he should have called me is an old fool." His mustache twitched and his blue eyes sparkled like the sun off the ocean.

"That's not true," Gary protested. "You're nothing of the sort."

The old fellow patted her hand. "I am, too," he said, as though imparting confidential information.

Micki enjoyed his spunkiness. "How long *have* you been here?" she asked, hoping to settle the matter.

"It'll be thirty-five years in July. Seen every kind of weather come through you can imagine. Floods. Hurricanes. Blizzards. You name it; we've lived through it."

"*Blizzards!* You mean you live here in wintertime, too? Right here at the shore?"

"Yep. Now, if that doesn't qualify me as an old fool, I sure don't know what does."

"But aren't these just beach houses?"

"They were meant as beach houses. Folks winterized 'em, put in insulation, furnaces," Gary explained, "so they could live here year-round."

"That's right. I remember, Gary, when you and Edward fixed up this place. That was a project."

"Sure was." Leaning on the rail, he smiled with satisfaction. "It was worth every aching muscle, every splinter and hammered thumb. I wouldn'ta traded that summer for anything."

Michaela's eyes widened at the promise of another story. "Why's that?"

Gary brushed back a wisp of her hair. "It's the summer I really got to know my grandfather. We'd always been close, but that built a special bond between us," he reflected. "I grew up that summer."

"That you did; when you showed up, you could barely swing a hammer. And, as I recall, there's photos to prove it," Sam said with a grin. "But by the end of August, you had a kind of peace about you; no matter what went on around you, you were unshakable. You hit it right when you said you grew up that summer." He gave a glance at the dog shifting restlessly at his feet, then squinted at the sky. "I'd best be getting along. I hope you'll come tomorrow; six o'clock. Michaela, I'm sure Martha'll just love you!"

She looked at Gary in eager anticipation; he squeezed her hand. "Tell her we'd be delighted," Gary replied. "Can we bring dessert? Micki makes a wicked lemon-icebox pie," he enticed.

"Sounds great; we'll look forward to it." Sam clipped the leash on the dog's collar. "C'mon, girl." Amber shook sand from herself and followed him back home.

Michaela watched as Sam disappeared behind the sea grasses. "What a sweet man!"

"Wait 'til you meet Martha; she's a hot ticket," Gary said. "Care to take a walk on the beach?"

Michaela smiled. "Sure." A sudden breeze made her shiver; she clutched at her bare forearms.

Gary took the glasses and peach pits inside; he returned with a sweatshirt for himself and a thick cable-knit pullover for Michaela. "Here, put this on." The sleeves were too long, but it was cozy. She followed him down the steps; he held her hand as she stepped onto the sand, which gave way beneath their feet at every step. "C'mon, it's easier walking down near the water."

Their sneakered feet made little squinching noises in the wet sand. They walked the entire east length of the shore. Engrossed in conversation, they scarcely noticed the gathering storm clouds.

"Tell me more about the Johnsons."

"They're good people. Sam and Grandpa were partners. Martha and Gram were like sisters. They're the closest I've got to grandparents since" – he flinched – "since Grandpa died."

Partway home, they sat on a driftwood log and watched the haze encroaching on the shore. "How long 'til sundown?"

"Couple hours. Why?"

"I've never seen sunset over the ocean."

"It's quite a sight. And, if conditions are right, there's a flash of emerald-green right there" – Gary extended an arm and pointed – "almost where sky meets water. Just as the sun sets."

Michaela rested against him. "Have you ever seen it?"

He was silent for a time. "Once. Years ago."

She snuggled closer and tilted her head to look at him. "What's it like?"

"It's a vibrant flash right above the horizon. Turns the surface of the water green" – he snapped his fingers – "for that long. But it's only there for a second. Blink and you miss it."

"Sounds neat. I'd love to see it sometime."

"You won't tonight." He pointed at the menacing thunderheads. "See? It'll be storming before long." Michaela shivered suddenly. "Cold?" Gary asked. When she shook her head, he lifted her chin with one hand. "Then why're your lips blue?"

"'Cause no one's been kissing 'em."

As Gary leaned to remedy the situation, large raindrops plonked onto them; he looked skyward as the rain started to fall in earnest. "Maybe we should head back."

"Why?" she asked between kisses. "Afraid you'll melt?"

His South Jersey drawl surfaced with his grin. "It's not me I'm worried about."

Leaving their driftwood settee, they chased one another across the beach as the rain fell faster. Micki lost her footing in the soft sand near the cottage. Gary dropped to his knees beside the girl and embraced her.

A sizzle of lightning sent them scurrying. Reaching the safety of the porch, they kicked off their sneakers. Micki peeled off the now-drenched, sandy sweater and gave it a vigorous shake as a jagged slash slit the sky. Shedding his sweatshirt, Gary ushered her inside as the accompanying thunder crashed overhead.

Crackling with lightning static, the kitchen radio played an old Frank Sinatra tune. Safely out of the storm, they continued where they left off. Soon, they were slow dancing around the room, their bodies swaying to "Summer Wind."

"I never finished showing you the house," Gary murmured against her hair. He danced Micki into the living room.

Their bare feet padded against the worn wooden risers and past the blue room. Marie's room, he told her. The walls were a pleasing canary yellow; white lace curtains framed both still-open windows overlooking the sea. And the deco furniture's warm finish lent an inviting glow. There was a maple rocker in here, too, like the one in the blue room.

As Gary lowered the windows, Michaela ran a hand over the waterfall-style dresser's swooping front. "This is lovely!"

Picking up a framed photo, she studied it. Gary identified everyone. "You met Marie and Sam; this is Martha" – his finger paused for an instant over the other man – "that's my grandfather. And in case you hadn't guessed, this shady-looking character's me."

The smile in his voice spread across his face as he replayed some clearly wonderful memory. Michaela was relieved to see this place did hold good memories for Gary. "You looked so happy."

"Why wouldn't I? It was the best time I ever spent here. My first Christmas here. In 82."

"What made it so good?" Micki was filled with a sudden desire to know everything about this man. Starting with that.

"Everything. It'd been a horrible year, but – well, I was *home*. With family. And friends. It was nice to belong." A particularly close thunderclap chased his daydream.

Michaela watched Gary's smile drift away as the memory faded. Doubling back down the hall, they stopped across from the blue room.

"This," he said as the rain beat overhead, "is the rose room. Last stop."

Turning the knob, Micki was met by the scent of roses and rain. The curtains billowed inward, carrying the heady aroma on the rain-soaked breeze. She gasped. Roses everywhere! Barely open red buds on the nightstand; huge white blooms on the dresser; full-blown, pink-tinged cabbage roses on the writing desk. A double bed with a carved rosewood headboard stood in the center of the room.

Moving closer, Micki ran a hand over its luxurious wood as Gary shut the windows. "Gary, this is gorgeous!" She slid into his arms, drawing in her breath as he scooped her up and lowered her onto the bed. The scent of roses filled her nostrils. Her pulse raced. *Given us his blessing… provided we behave responsibly.*

His lips caressed Micki's face, her throat, her fingertips as he lay beside her. His hands were unhooking her bra, smoothing her hair, cupping her small, firm breasts, unfastening the snap on her jeans.

She reached to unbutton Gary's shirt, yanking its tails free of his jeans. Pushing it aside, Micki ran her hands along his chest, her fingers playing lightly over his nipples; he quivered in response.

Outside, the storm raged. Rain slashed at the windows; thunder rumbled, brilliant lightning illuminated the storm-darkened room, where a different sort of storm raged.

Michaela loved the feel of Gary's mouth kissing her, his body beside hers. She recalled the first time he'd touched her like this. Dad was out and they were watching a movie. She'd begun kissing him, then slid his hand beneath her shirt. Leaning closer, she lifted her shirt, arching sensuously. Gary kneaded one breast; swirling his tongue around the other nipple, he sucked at it, sending little shock waves through her. When she reached to undo his jeans, he moved her hand away.

"No," he'd told her firmly.

"But I want to."

"So do I." That was evident. "But that doesn't make it okay."

Michaela had pouted but, in the end, had to admit he was right. Gary pulled her shirt back in place and kissed her. "We'll know when it's the right time for us."

She watched him now, taking his pleasure at her breast. She stroked his hair. "I think it's time."

He looked up. "For what?"

"What it wasn't time for at my dad's a few months back." She reached down and unfastened his jeans.

"Oh?" He wore a trace of a smile. "In that case, I'll be right back." He kissed her, slid off his jeans and dashed to the bathroom.

*I'm not happy about this!* a familiar voice chided as he reached for a condom.

Gary whipped around, reddening slightly. *This is silly.* He must've imagined the voice. Still, Grandpa wouldn't have approved of this birthday celebration. He dropped the packet back in the box and drew his hand away. *I'm sorry,* he thought, suddenly contrite. *I'll try not to let it happen again.*

*Try not to!* He envisioned Grandpa shaking his head, annoyed, frowning deeply. *Is that how I raised you, Gary? I'm ashamed of you!*

Ashamed? His cheeks burned. Grandpa had *never* uttered those words to Gary in his life. *Well, it's not his life, is it?* he mused crossly.

But he was right. This wasn't how Grandpa had raised him.

The scolding continued. *You should have more respect for that young lady. Especially since you're going to marry her.*

*Marry her!* he nearly blurted aloud. *Wait just a minute–* Grandpa had always had this way of knowing things before they happened. Raking a hand through his hair, Gary struggled to regroup; he hoped Micki wouldn't notice the beet-red flush of his cheeks. Or that he was trembling. *Alright, Grandpa. Message received, loud and clear. No sex 'til _after_ we're married. I promise.*

*Good,* Grandpa replied gruffly. *Now go put on some clothes.*

The only thoughts remaining in Gary's head were his own. Had he imagined the exchange? He stole a glance in the bathroom mirror. If he *had,* he wouldn't be blushing. Sufficiently chastised, he returned to the bedroom and hastily dressed. Embarrassed, he hoped Michaela didn't notice what he was doing.

*Putting _on_ your clothes isn't what you should feel embarrassed about!* the voice rebuked again.

"Here" – Gary retrieved Michaela's bra – "we need to talk."

Looking fretful, she took the lacy garment he held out to her. "Gary, what's wrong?"

"Nothing. Come sit." He patted the bed.

Prickly silence filled the room, broken only by the pounding rain and heart-stoppingly close thunder.

"Wh-what's the matter?" she stammered, hooking her bra. "Did I, uh… do something wrong?"

Gary tried to gather his thoughts.

"What?" Michaela looked at him, worried.

"Michaela, I love you. And because I love you, I can't do this."

Tears filled her eyes. Her hands shook. "Are you breaking up with me? Gary, if you are, just say it."

"No!" he said vehemently; then, more gently, "No." He laid his hands on her shoulders to soothe her.

"Then what? You can't do what?"

A strange calm settled over Gary. He took Michaela's hands in his. "We shouldn't be doing this. Not yet. Not 'til we're married." He paused. "I'm not breaking up with you."

Michaela pulled her hands free and slid her arms around him, laying her head against his chest.

Reassured by her embrace, he stroked her hair, delighting in its smooth ripples. As she rested there, his words – the words he knew

Grandpa expected him to say – came easier. "I should've never seduced you; it was wrong and I'm sorry. We shouldn't be doing something we're not ready for."

Michaela was silent. Motionless.

"Did you hear me?"

"Mm-hmm." She gave a small nod and nestled closer.

"Do you agree?"

"I think it's probably not a bad idea to cool it for awhile." She noticed Gary shaking his head. "What?"

"No good."

Michaela wrinkled her nose. "What's no good?"

"You said we should cool it *for awhile*. That's not good enough. I want us to wait 'til we're married." He took her hands. "Micki, what I'm trying to say is: I love you and I realize sex is a *gift* – meant to be shared by two people committed to each other. Our first time together should be special. And it *will* be. On our wedding night. I don't want to spoil that. You're worth waiting for, Michaela. And I want to wait. With all my heart. I *promise* to wait for you."

Her mouth quivered. "I wanna wait for you, too," she squeaked. "I promise."

They sat in silence for a long time. Gary kissed her on the forehead. Lifting her chin, he met her gaze. "I love you." She looked so sweet! He would have hated to steal that innocence! No amount of passion was worth that. *Thank you, Grandpa. Thanks for making me do the right thing.*

A smile tugged the corners of his mouth upward.

Michaela gave him a questioning look. "What?"

Eyes gleaming, Gary nodded toward a door at one side of the room.

# Chapter 20

Michaela loved Gary's playful grin. She loved everything about this man. Especially that he'd promised to wait 'til their wedding night to make love to her! She loved surprises and he always seemed to know how to tickle her fancy. In the closet hung the green-and-black silk dress. She stared at it, then back toward Gary.

"You knew I wouldn't let you buy this for me."

"I also knew it'd look fabulous on you; I just had to make you think about wanting it."

Michaela hugged him. "You're sneaky."

Gary settled into her arms. "Sneaky is such a negative word. I prefer clever."

"Okay then; you're clever," she agreed. "But whatever you call it, you're wonderful, Gary! Thank you."

After the storm passed, Gary shooed Micki off to take a shower. "Towels are in the cabinet," he called after her. "You'll find a new toothbrush in a drawer under the sink. You can keep that here if you want. Toothpaste's in the medicine chest."

When she emerged, all clean and smelling of lilac, he suggested she put on her new dress. She protested, saying she didn't have the proper shoes.

Gary inclined his head toward the closet. "Go look."

"What is this, the magic closet?" She approached cautiously, as if expecting something to leap out.

He gave a mischievous grin. "You didn't look down before."

Now she did. And she found a pair of black-satin pumps. Size 7½ medium. Slipping her arms around him, she rested her cheek against his flannel-robed chest. "Thank you!" She kissed him. "I love you."

"I love you too." He patted her behind. "Now get dressed. We gotta leave in half an hour."

Precisely at 8:15, they arrived at one of New York City's most fashionable, upscale French restaurants.

Other than knowing how to ask whether Sylvia was at the pool (and she seriously doubted *that* would come in handy) Michaela couldn't recall any of her French vocabulary. She felt intimidated by the maître d', the waiters and the menu, which was entirely in French. Gary set her at ease with a squeeze of her hand and the assurance he wouldn't let her eat goat intestines. He ordered for them, in French, discussing with the tuxedoed waiter which wine best complemented each entrée.

After dinner, he took her dancing uptown.

They got home well after 3, ready to fall into bed.

Micki rooted through her bag for a nightshirt, then trudged wearily off to the bathroom.

By the time Gary finished straightening the bedclothes, Michaela was back. His keen awareness of their clothing disparity – her in a sleep-shirt, him in his suit – was, in itself, arousing. He broke from Micki's embrace before his arousal became common knowledge.

He blurted a plausible excuse: "I *really* gotta pee!" Which was, in fact, true… but not as urgent as he'd made it seem.

Gary leaned against the bathroom door. At this rate, he'd *never* make it 'til the wedding night! Stripping off his clothes, he turned on the shower as cold as he could stand it. He reeked of cigarette smoke. At least he could use that as an excuse.

Teeth chattering, he toweled off and hurried back to the bedroom. Never had the prospect of a warm bed seemed so appealing, until he remembered Micki was in that same bed. He soon realized she wasn't as asleep as he thought.

Turning toward him, she instantly undid all the good that cold shower had done. "Hi," Micki purred sleepily. "Where'd you go?" She no longer smelled of lilac, but rather, of tobacco.

"To take a shower," he whispered back. "I hate smelling like cigarettes."

"Mmm. Why didn't I think of that?" She slid out of bed and padded toward the bathroom.

Where she'd lain, the sheets smelled faintly of smoke. He turned them back to let it dissipate. Fresh air would help. He opened a window; a soft breeze blew tangy salt air into the room.

Gary was asleep before Michaela returned. She climbed into bed, cuddled close and drifted off, lulled to sleep by the incoming tide.

Saturday night, the Johnsons welcomed Michaela like family. Martha adored her (she told Gary as much); and Micki's lemon icebox pie was the hit of the evening. They ate supper on the deck, watching the sun set. As it grew dark, they trooped inside. At Sam's urging, they stayed far later than they'd anticipated. By the time Gary and Micki made their way back across the sand, it was nearly 11.

***

"Good morning, sleepyhead," Gary greeted Michaela on Sunday morning. "Here, this'll wake you up." He handed her a mug of steaming coffee. With milk and a pinch of cinnamon. He steadied her hand on the mug as she sat up. "Sleep okay?"

"Really well." She smiled. "Must be the salt air. How 'bout you?"

"Fine," he murmured. "Hungry?"

"Famished."

"Good. 'Cause breakfast is ready."

Breakfast was pancakes, scrambled eggs and sausage, orange juice and coffee. "I forgot to give you this the other day," he said, directing her attention to a package on the table.

"But Gary, you got me that dress; and those shoes. And you took me to dinner. And dancing. Plus the sweater you bought me."

"Oh, this isn't from me."

"Then, who?"

"Open it," he suggested mysteriously.

Michaela opened the envelope; the card had flowers and *For a delightful young woman* on the front. Inside was a sweet verse. But the signature left her looking perplexed:

*Happy 20th birthday, sweetie!*
*See you soon,*
*XOXO, Cyn*

"Love and hugs – *who?*"

"You gonna ask questions or open your gift?" He handed her the package. Inside was a pretty frame with an envelope taped to its glass. It didn't seem to be a photo. "What is it?" he asked.

"I dunno. Lemme get this off." Tugging off the envelope, Michaela saw what was in the frame. She held it up for a closer look. And gasped. "Is this – is this real?"

He looked over her shoulder. "Who would give you a fake glove?"

185

"No! I mean, is it really her? Did Cyndi Lauper really sign this?"

Gary checked the signature. "Yep." He smiled. "So, what's in *there?*"

As he'd hoped, Michaela had forgotten about how the card was signed. She set the frame down to open the envelope and found tickets to a concert that night at Toad's Place in New Haven.

Micki looked at the tickets, then at Gary. Squealing with delight, she threw her arms around his neck. "Thank you!"

"Don't thank *me*. They're from her."

Her jaw dropped. "You're kidding…"

"Last time she was in town, I got to interview her. I mentioned how upset you were at having to miss the show; so she promised us tickets next time she toured. When I said this concert was right after your birthday, she insisted on doing this. But there's more."

He pulled something out of his pocket: photo ID badges. His read, "Media: Full Access"; and hers, "Guest: Full Access."

Across both badges – in huge red letters – was stamped a single word: "BACKSTAGE."

# *Chapter 21*

In late November of 1987, WZBX was sold to a media group from New York City. The staff anxiously awaited sweeping changes; there were murmurings about who'd be let go and when the ax would fall, but management remained tightlipped. The longer the uncertainty dragged on, the edgier everyone became.

In January, longtime radio funnyman Ken Coffey showed up and a new morning-drive team took over: "Barbie and Ken, with your morning Coffey and 'right-to-the-point' news with Barb Dwyer."

Steffi Kinkead joined the Z97-3 midday lineup a few weeks later. Pete was retained as program director.

Besides fearing for his job, Gary had something else on his mind.

***

"What a nice surprise! Come in." Michael motioned toward the couch with a manila folder. "Sit down." He gathered the rest of the files strewn across his coffee table, then sat across from the young man.

"You're busy. I don't want to disturb you."

"Nonsense, Gary. To what do I owe the pleasure?"

"I won't take up a lot of your time," he began, "but I kinda need to talk to you."

"Sounds important. What's up?"

"Well, Mr. Conwaye, there's something I need to ask you."

Michael leaned forward. "I hope nothing's wrong."

"Oh – no! Actually, sir, I think—"

He held up a hand. "Hold it. It took me *months* to get you to call me Michael. Now you're back to not only Mr. Conwaye, but *sir*? Am I not going to like this? You didn't break up with Kayla, did you?"

"No, sir, I didn't. I – um… Let's just say I'd like to start calling you something else."

The older man's jaw set sternly. "It had *better* not be 'Grandpa.'"

Gary lurched backward as though struck. "No! Nothing like that."

His heart pounded as he produced a velvet box. "I was thinking more along the lines of… *Dad.*" He opened it, revealing a dazzling emerald-and-diamond ring. "I'd like your permission to marry your daughter."

Michael remained silent for a long time. "You would, huh?" He leaned back. "Honestly, Gary, I'm far too young to be *anybody's* father-in-law. And Kayla *is* only twenty." Gary's heart plunged into his sneakers. "Still, I can't think of anyone I'd rather have call me that. Have you asked her?"

"Not yet. I'm planning to. Tonight. That is," he stammered, "I mean… with your permission."

Michael nodded. "Valentine's Day. Nice touch. You have my permission, Gary. And my blessing."

Relieved, Gary stood. "Thank you, sir – I mean, *Michael.*"

"Don't you mean *Dad?*" Michael embraced his future son-in-law. "Welcome to the family, Gary."


Michaela sat on her bed, fastening a decorative clip at the end tuft of her French-braided hair.

Mom stopped at the open door. "Going out with Gary?"

"Mm-hmm." She twirled in her green-and-black birthday dress. "How do I look?" It swirled to a stop around her slim calves. Black ribbing accentuated her trim waist. Green satin bow clips adorned her sleek black pumps.

"Very nice. Where're you going?"

"Out to dinner and from there" – she applied wineberry lipstick. Glancing at Mom in the mirror, she shrugged – "I dunno." She put on the emerald-and-diamond earrings Gary gave her last Christmas.

"Aren't you getting a little serious?"

She arched one eyebrow. "I hope so."

"But you're so young." Susan twirled a finger around a tendril of hair at the nape of Michaela's neck.

"I'm getting older all the time." She sighed, took a final look in the mirror and dabbed concealer on a blemish. "It's not like we're getting married. Well, not yet, anyway."

"He asked you to *marry* him?" she squawked.

Mom's expression was one Michaela wouldn't soon forget.

***

At Wong Lee's, the owner greeted the young couple and seated them personally.

Gary reached across the table for Michaela's hand.

A self-conscious smile played about her lips. "What?"

He said nothing, just kept looking at her.

A wisp of hair drifted across her face; she pushed it back, behind her ear. "What's the matter?"

"Nothing. I was just thinking about how much I love you."

She blushed. "I love you, too, sweetheart." Her delicate fingers curled around Gary's hand.

Noticing their menus lying closed on the table, their waiter approached. "Are you ready to order?"

They glanced up, their reverie broken. "Not yet." Gary drew his hand back. "Could you give us another few minutes, please?"

He nodded – more like bowed. "Yes. Few more minutes. Yes, sir. Thank you." He backed away.

Gary winked at Micki. "Guess we'd better decide, then, huh?"

She consulted her menu, then looked at Gary and saw his still lying, closed, on the table. "Aren't you gonna look at the menu?"

"I already know what I want," he told her, reaching discreetly into his jacket pocket.

"Oh." Returning her gaze to the menu, Micki didn't see Gary slip out of his chair. Lowering her menu to tell him about her mother's reaction to her marriage comment, she was bewildered to see him on one knee before her. For an instant, she figured he'd dropped his napkin.

Taking her hand, he looked into her eyes. "Michaela, I love you. And when I said I already know what I want, I wasn't talking about mu shu pork." He slid the ring onto her finger. "Will you marry me?"


Staring at the ring, Mom frowned. "But you said just tonight you weren't that serious."

Michaela shrugged. "So I was wrong."

A pink flush pricked at Susan's cheeks; she disguised it as indignation. "You're too young! What about college? If you marry him, you're his responsibility. He can pay for your education."

In an instant, Michaela's delight was sucked away. "Can't you just be happy for me?"

"I *am*. But who's to say you'll have anything in common a year from now? And what if he gets bored? Or the novelty wears off? Did you consider that?"

Churning inside, she kicked off her shoes. "You're jealous! You want to destroy my happiness because *you're* miserable. Well it won't work!" Snatching up her shoes, she stomped up to her room.


The engagement tested Gary and Michaela's vow to remain chaste until the wedding night. Suddenly it seemed they couldn't be in the same room without being practically all over each other.

After a particularly nasty fight with her mother, Micki retreated to Gary's place; he made up the spare room but she begged him to let her sleep with him. "I don't want to sleep alone tonight. Please, Gary?"

"Alright," he told her. "But just this once."

Once turned into twice… and then every time. But, they kept their promise. Which meant, more often than not, one or both of them went to sleep edgy and frustrated.

And "edgy" Gary did not need.

# *Chapter 22*

March came and went; rumors continued to fly about who would be next to go. The tension mounted daily. Through it all, Gary did his work and kept his mouth shut. His closed-mouthed approach spilled over into his personal relationships. He grew withdrawn and bit back his feelings. Most of the time.

(2 April, 1988 – Saturday)

Michaela buried her face in her pillow, tears stinging her eyes. All couples argued occasionally; and they'd had their share of doozies! But never like this. The crazy thing was, she couldn't recall how it started. All she remembered was he'd unleashed a venomous tirade.

The blowup was as much a surprise to Gary as it was to her. Her remark was neither provocative nor needling; it just struck him wrong. Angry words tore from his mouth before he had the sense or ability to stop them.

As soon as the words flew out of his mouth, Gary was deeply and terribly sorry; they were horrible words to say to anyone – much less his tenderhearted fiancée! It was like hearing two people arguing in another room. Their voices had spiraled upward in their fury, louder and louder.

"In fact," Michaela shouted, white-knuckling the phone, "don't even call me. I don't want to talk to you!" She slammed down the phone. The fury in his voice terrified her; she feared if they'd fought in person, he might have struck her.

In the car the next morning, Dad asked why she'd dodged Gary after Mass. She explained about their fight and her concerns about Gary's temper.

As soon as he dropped Michaela off after lunch, Michael got his daughter's fiancé on the phone, dispensing with the niceties.

"When you and Kay started dating, I laid down some ground

rules; but, otherwise, I've kept out of your relationship. But this is where it ends, Gary. I don't know what's gotten into you. But let me tell you this right now, mister: If you ever lay a hand on Kayla, it'll be the last thing you do. I swear to God, I'll kill you myself. And don't think for a minute I won't!"

Gary nearly dropped the receiver. He had never struck Michaela! "Wh-what?" he stammered.

"At the very least, you need a good lesson in the proper way to address a young lady."

If he spoke his mind, it would kill any chance of fixing things. Gary fully understood the considerable power his future father-in-law wielded. He bit his tongue as Micki's dad ripped into him.

The young man's only response was an occasional "Yes, sir," "No, sir" or "I'm sorry, sir."

Michael concluded his lecture with a strident warning. "Until you can show her the level of respect she deserves, I want you to stay the hell away from my daughter!"

Gary's final "Yes, sir" was a rough whisper as Michael hung up.


While driving to Milford, Gary mulled over his predicament: He longed to call Micki to apologize for making her believe – even for an instant – he posed any danger. Yet he dared not defy Michael.

"Gary!" On impulse, Joey hugged his brother when he answered the knock at his door.

"Happy birthday, kiddo."

Leaning in the doorway, Joey played it cool now, in front of his roommate. "What brings you here?"

Gary gave him a gentle punch in the arm. "Taking you to dinner; and… this."

Joey tore open the flat package Gary handed him. Taped to the new Van Halen CD was a card with "IOU" printed on it.

"IOU what?" he asked.

"Tickets; I'm taking you and two of your friends when they play Hartford."

Over dinner, the teen chattered almost nonstop: about friends, the promised concert tickets, school. Everything except Mom.

While he tried to relax and enjoy his kid brother's company, Gary felt stuck: He couldn't make things right with Micki, and he couldn't talk things over with Michael. All he could do was wait.

Late Thursday afternoon, Michaela broke the awful silence. "We need to talk."

"Micki! I've missed you so much." His voice sounded desperate and full of longing.

Chewing her lip, Michaela tried not to notice the warmth in his tone. "We need to talk," she repeated. "Tonight. Seven thirty. Meet me at the diner."

"Okay. Micki… I'm so sorry for those things I said."

Micki hung up; she doubled over on her bed, wishing away the hurt. She twisted her ring around and around on her finger. This was the hardest thing she ever had to do!

At their usual booth in an otherwise-empty diner, Michaela scuffed the toe of her sneaker against the table leg. Out of habit, her right hand went to fiddle with her engagement ring.

Gary parked beside Susan's blue Toyota and hurried inside. Laying a hand on Micki's shoulder, he kissed her on the cheek. "Hi, baby."

She recoiled as if his kiss burned.

He sat beside her, held out a white rose. "I'm sorry for those things I said the other day. Please forgive me." Taking her hand, he entwined their fingers. It felt different.

Micki's blood froze as Gary held up her ringless hand.

"What happened?"

Angry tears navigated her cheeks.

He misread them. "Did you lose it? Honey" – he hugged her – "is that why you wanted to see me? Have you thought where you might've left it?"

*Damn! Don't be like this! How can I do this when you're being so sweet?* Reaching into her jeans pocket, Micki took out the ring and, with a shaky indrawn breath, pressed it into his hand.

Gary looked from his weeping fiancée to the ring in the hollow of his hand… and back.

Aware that a cook and two waitresses were watching, Micki took a deep breath and pulled away, as if putting physical distance between them could make telling him easier. She fidgeted with the rose. "I don't think this is such a good idea."

"Don't think what's such a good idea?"

She looked into his eyes. Suddenly she wanted to hurt him. The one word she uttered cut him deeply and viciously. It was exactly what she wanted. "Us."

He glanced at the ring sparkling in his hand, then at Micki. "Does this mean…?"

Looking into his grey eyes, Michaela saw horror. And disbelief. She nodded.

"But, Micki" – he blinked back tears – "I was upset. I said things I didn't mean. Things I *never* should have said to you." Gary laid a hand on her arm.

She yanked it away. Her eyes narrowed as she glared at the man she loved and hated. "How dare you speak that way to me!"

"I'm *sorry*, Mick. I've been under so much pressure lately." He gestured urgently. "I dunno what I was thinking. I – I *wasn't* thinking. Please forgive me."

"I don't know if I can do that."

"Don't you love me?"

Michaela exhaled shakily. "I don't know anymore," she admitted plaintively.

"I can't believe you wanted to do this here," Gary muttered. Devastating silence enveloped them. He grasped her hand. "I love you, Micki. And I'm *sorry*," he said earnestly. "Please don't do this. Not now. I *need* you! I'm begging you, Michaela: Marry me," he implored, trying to slip the ring back onto her finger. "I *love* you."

Head bowed, Micki pulled her hand away. Tugging the ring off, she laid it on the table, shaking her head. "I'm sorry."

Brushing away a tear, she stared out the window. She ached for Gary to hold her, but she couldn't ask him. Crumbling, she turned away, leaned against the booth and cried.

His voice quavered. "Then I guess this is goodbye?" he asked, dispirited.

Michaela sniffled; her lower lip trembled. "Guess so."

He slipped the rejected ring into his pocket. "Alright, if that's how you want it."

Eyes brimming, she turned to him, needing to set him straight. "No, Gary, that's not how I *want* it; that's how it *is*. Now let me out." Pushing past him, she trudged toward the door, leaving the rose.

"Wait." His voice cut through the tense air. Following her, he tugged at her jacketed arm. "Please – let's don't do this, Mick," he urged in a desperate whisper. "Not like this. Please? Can't we talk about it?"

"Take your hands off me!"

He released her. "Please, come sit down, Micki. Let's talk it over, okay?"

Michaela let him lead her back. Sitting stiffly at the booth's outer edge – so he couldn't sit beside her – she stared him down and won. "You *frightened* me, Gary," she accused, "the way you yelled, and swore at me. I don't know if I can get past that."

He stared at her. "I could understand you wanting to call it quits if I'd hit you. But you're breaking up with me over a few ill-chosen words, said in anger?"

Her voice sounded steadier than she felt. "No, Gary. I'm breaking up with you because that's where it starts. It starts with words, then turns into hitting" – Michaela faltered – "and then worse," she whispered, toying with her spoon. Her eyes met his. "I don't wanna end up like my parents. *Or yours.*"

"It'll never get to that. It stops here. I *swear* it!" Gary paused. "Look, I've had a lot on my mind lately. I know I can't just explain it away, but" – he sighed – "c'mon, Micki. I'm *trying* here!" He took her hand.

She drew it away. "I can't afford to take chances. Don't you see? It's already started. I can't wait around to see if a pattern develops."

His tone was contrite. "Don't you think I've been beating myself up over this? Yes, what I said was horrible, Micki. But I promise you, sweetheart, it'll never happen again."

She studied him intently. "How can I be sure? How do I know I can believe you?"

After a long silence, Gary shrugged. "I can't answer that. I guess you'll just have to trust me."

*That's not good enough.* "How do I know I can believe you?" Michaela repeated slowly.

"I don't know," he whispered. "You tell me: What do I have to do?" He held out the ring again.

She closed her hand around the ring. A moment later, she laid it on the table. Lifting her hand, she waved him away. "Just go," she whispered. "Just… please – go."

"Do you hate me that much?"

"I don't hate you," she insisted. "I just don't know if I can trust you not to – not to hurt me." She met his gaze. "I need to know I can trust you. I'm sorry, Gary. "

Something snapped. "You trash my heart and all you can say is

*I'm sorry?*" Gary spoke evenly. "That's perfect."

Michaela was about to say he didn't need to be sarcastic, but his glare silenced her.

"You have *no* idea what's been going on in my life."

She shook her head, wondering why that would matter.

"Things have been a little tense lately. Since November, actually. The station's been sold; our jobs are hanging by a thread." His icy tone softened to deep remorse. "I've tried not to take it out on you, but last week it got to me and I unloaded on you. No, it wasn't fair. And I'm *sorry*. But all that's kept me sane these last few months is knowing you're there and you love me. Now you're saying I was *wrong?* Thanks a lot." Eyes glinting fiercely, Gary thrust the ring back. "This is yours. Take it."

Micki got to her feet, swaying slightly. She'd had no idea; but still… She clutched her arms about her middle. "Not 'til I can be sure where I stand." She hoped her words sounded sufficiently convincing to Gary, because they sure didn't sound like it to her.

Gary shook his head. "If you give back this ring, you can forget about where you stand. Give it back and it's over. I can't have you playing with my heart. So decide: You want to be with me, fine. Accept my apology and we'll get on with our lives. If not" – he searched for words – "just get out of my world, and don't look back. Not now. Not ever."

The coffee cups rattled in their saucers as he slammed down the twice-rejected ring. A spoon clattered on the tabletop. Gary stared at her for a long moment, then stalked out.

Withering into her seat, Michaela stared at the ring. She'd had no clue he was that upset; he never seemed ruffled or agitated. But then he blew up and said those horrible things.

Pulling a napkin from the spring-loaded chrome dispenser, she dabbed at her eyes. Blowing her nose, she wadded the napkin in her fist as Gary got into his car. *He looked awful – like his whole world collapsed.* She hated that she'd made him look that way. *Well, he never should've said those things! It's his own fault for not telling me sooner.*

Pushing aside her coffee, Michaela reached for another napkin, mopped at the tears that fell fast and hard. Whenever things went wrong, she always depended on Gary to make it better. But now she'd just turned her back on him when he needed her to be there for him.

Perhaps he was right: Maybe it *was* just angry words; maybe he'd never be that angry again. Still, his father had been abusive… and she'd heard that kind of thing ran in families. Or maybe that was alcoholism. She couldn't think straight.

Micki slipped the ring onto her finger. It felt wrong. Putting it back in her pocket was no better. Her coffee cup trembled in her hand.

Gary's words echoed through her heart: *Forget about where you stand… playing with my heart… Accept my apology… don't look back. Not now. Not ever… Over.*

Her knees shook as she returned to the car. She ached to go find Gary, but she was afraid. *What if he won't listen? What then?* Besides, she didn't know what to say. She pulled out of the parking lot, not wanting to go home.

Regan was washing his car. Grinning, he waved. "Hi! Patty's in the house; you can go on in."

She walked toward him, realizing suddenly she'd hoped more for him to be home than Trish. "Could I talk to you for a sec, Regan?"

"Sure." He dropped the hose and shut off the faucet, wiping his hands on his jeans as the spray died on the pavement. "What's up?"

"I think I just broke up with my fiancé. Or, at least, *he* thinks I did."

"C'mon. Let's sit." Putting an arm around her, Regan guided her to the porch. He sat on the steps; she sat a step down from him. "What happened?"

She told him, then added, "I love Gary. And I want to marry him; but I'm afraid. There's a history of abuse in his family, and I don't want to tempt fate."

"Did you tell him that?"

"I tried." Weeping, she was startled to feel Regan's hand patting her shoulder. He scooched down a step to sit with her. He smelled of car wax and damp earth… in a nice way, she noticed – which made her stop crying. Michaela tried to block it out of her head.

"And what did he say?" Regan asked, she realized, for a second time.

"He told me I wasn't being fair; he accused me of playing with his heart. I didn't know *what* to say; it happened so fast. And after… he just left." Tears rolled down her cheeks.

"Wish I knew what to tell you. Why don't you give him time to cool off? Then talk to him."

Sniffling, Michaela nodded. She wiped her eyes and looked gratefully at him. "Sounds like a good idea. Thanks, Regan. I wish I had a big brother like you."

Giving her a cockeyed grin, Regan patted her knee. "If it was up to Patty, you could have me." He motioned toward the car. "I'd better finish up here." He opened the door. "Patty's in her room; go on up."

Michaela hesitated. "Nah, I'll see her tomorrow. You won't tell her what I—"

Regan shook his head. "It'll be our secret."

***

Thoughts of Micki filled every moment, every corner of Gary's apartment. He recalled the waver in her voice as she pressed the ring into his hand, the river of tears coursing down her cheeks.

That image haunted him until he fell into a fitful sleep on the couch. When he awakened, he ached all over and felt like he hadn't had a moment's rest. The pain hadn't dulled, and all that had changed was now it was daylight.

He pulled on jeans and an OMD concert t-shirt. He devoured a slice of toast, then grabbed his wallet and keys. Despite the early-April chill, Gary craved the peace and solitude of the beach.

He tugged some early-sprouting weeds from the flower beds and tackled some of the indoor chores he'd been avoiding; then he wandered the shore. When he checked his watch, it was after 1.

After a last look over the water, he plodded to the car. Stopping for lunch on the way, he arrived barely 10 minutes before his shift. Rob's car was in the parking lot.

"You were supposed to meet me for lunch with a client, Elf-boy! What the hell happened to you?"

"I'm sorry," Gary told Charlie, trying to remember whom he was supposed to have met. "It must've slipped my mind. I hope it didn't make you—"

"Lose the account?" he puffed his cigar furiously. "If we had, you'd have been *dead meat!*" He jabbed a finger into Gary's chest to emphasize his final words; he tromped back to his office. Gary leaned against the wall and rubbed away the sharp pain inflicted by Charlie's stubby finger.

Debbie, the temporary receptionist, handed Gary a stack of messages and mail. "Mr. Donovan needs to see you," she informed him. "Right away. He's in his office."

"What *else* can go wrong?" Gary took the small paper mountain. "Thanks." His production schedule showed he was supposed to have three spots finished already. "Shit!" he hissed, grabbing the copy and tearing down the hall, only to find both studios occupied. 2:55. Gary let out a growl of frustration.

Pete's head poked out of his office. "Gary? Is that you making that ruckus? Could you step in here a minute, please?"

His heart lurched, then plummeted into his stomach, where it lay like a possum. He tried to act casual. "Sure. Debbie said you're looking for me. Guess ya found me."

The program director shut the door and invited Gary to sit.

Perching at the edge of a chair, Gary gripped its arms and braced for the worst. After what felt like years, Pete spoke.

"I know this is short notice and, believe me, Gar', I wouldn't do this to you now… except, I didn't have any choice. Tom wanted to have this talk with you, but noon rolled around and you hadn't shown up; and he had another meeting."

Gary's hands ached from their death grip.

"He, Jim and I met this morning; we discussed this at length and I've got to agree with their decision to let you go; it was either you or Marc, but we all felt you were really the logical choice."

He stared at his boss – his friend! – wondering how he could sit there so calmly and tell him he was being fired. *That's why Rob's here…* "During a ratings period?"

"Yeah, I was concerned about that. Tom said it can't be helped. Besides, it won't be for long." Pete reached into his desk drawer, producing a long envelope. "You'll be needing this."

Gary's heart sank; he laid the envelope on the desk. "I suppose you'll want me to leave today?"

"Well, naturally."

Gary's chest tightened. He had been expelled from school, given the ol' heave-ho by his fiancée. Disowned, even. But fired? Never. At least 'til now. *So now I'm a professional fuck-up, too.*

"We tried to call you this noon, save you a trip in. I apologize for the short notice; they didn't decide 'til today which of you it was gonna be. And they ran it by me strictly as a courtesy."

His voice sounded small, strangled. "Wasn't anything you could do about that." He hesitated. "I'll still be able to maintain my insurance, though, right?"

Pete's brow furrowed. "What do you mean?"

"I mean, I'm going to need medical coverage 'til I can find something else."

"Gary, you're not making sense. What're you getting at?"

"Insurance, Pete; I'm talking about keeping my benefits 'til I get another job." He bristled. "That *is* the law in this state."

"I thought you liked it here. Why are you looking for another job?"

"Isn't that what you generally do when you get fired?"

"*Fired?* Jesus, Gary – what're you talking about?"

"What am *I* talking about? Isn't that what–?" Gary eyed his boss suspiciously. "Wait a minute: You said you're letting me go. If you didn't just fire me, would you mind telling me what's going on?"

Pete laughed. Laughed!

Gary wondered what was so damn funny.

"Oh, Spike! Didn't Debbie tell you what I wanted to see you about? You're not being fired. You did so well as interim music director, Tom decided to make it permanent. As your first official duty, we're sending you to the national convention in San Diego."

Dumbstruck, Gary only half heard as Peter continued.

"Registration and an informal reception are tomorrow; and the convention runs from Monday to Thursday. Your reservations and tickets are in there." Pete indicated the envelope.

Gary's muscles all went weak at once; he stumbled backward into his chair.

"Just out of curiosity: What'd you think was in there?"

"Severance pay?"

His boss roared with laughter. "I'm sorry, Gar'. I should've said what it was, right off. I never thought you'd misunderstand."

Gary tried to shake off his jangled nerves. "Well, after that scare you gave me, I'm gonna *need* a week off – ratings or no ratings."

After finishing his production work, Gary went home to pack – and call Greg to have someone cover his CCD class that weekend. Then he dropped Attila at The Cathouse, a local kennel.

Just before 5, Pete picked up his new music director to drive him to JFK. "So, Spike, what's wrong? That is, aside from getting fired." He switched on the windshield wipers. "I don't think I've ever seen you like this. What's the matter?"

"Everything," he lamented, staring out the window and wishing he'd brought an umbrella.

Pete shut off the radio. "Define 'everything,'" he prompted.

"For starters, my dad's in the hospital. We don't exactly get along; haven't really talked in years." Gary hesitated. "He left me a message a few days ago; he sounded awful. Weak. It may be my last chance to…" He trailed off to regretful silence, recalling Dad's pleading tone on the machine and how he'd pressed "Erase" after listening to it.

"Is he local?" Pete asked.

"Jersey," Gary mumbled.

"Geez… and we're sending you clear across the country. I'm sorry, kid. That's gotta be tough."

A mile slipped past. Uneasy from the quiet, Gary went on. "But wait, it wouldn't seem quite like my life if there weren't half a dozen things going wrong all at once."

Pete looked stricken. "What could be worse than that?"

"Michaela gave back the ring. We had a fight last week and I said some things" – Gary shook his head – "stupid things. I thought it'd blow over. Guess I was wrong."

"Must've been a hell of a fight."

"It was pretty ugly," he admitted soberly, avoiding revealing any details.

***

During a free period Friday, Micki phoned Gary's apartment. No answer. She tried again after lunch. Still no answer. Later in the afternoon, she called the station.

"I'm sorry, Mr. Sheldon is out of the office today," Debbie informed her crisply.

"Do you know where he is?"

Denise or Brenda would have recognized her voice and told her. "I don't," the temp-agency receptionist replied in her most coolly professional manner. For all she knew, this was a rabid groupie. In her first week, she'd proven fiercely protective of the DJs. "Would you care to leave a message?"

Michaela sighed. "No, that's okay. Thanks anyway."

Still no answer at home that night.

She left a message Saturday. "Hi, it's me. I just wanted to say I love you, and I'm sorry about how we left things."

And another on Sunday afternoon. "Me again. Please don't hate me, Gary. I love you and I *do* want to marry you – *believe* me, I do. I just need to know I can trust you."

(14 April – Thursday)

The convention wrapped up late in the afternoon. Gary and four companions met for drinks and dinner at the airport. When the conversation turned to women, Gary grew suspiciously quiet.

The others badgered him into talking; they insisted on playing a modified version of 20 Questions, one that involved downing shots for each question asked in the right direction – while still drinking beers. Hitting upon the correct series of questions, they wore down Gary's resistance. And his sobriety.

Weary of their pestering – and really smashed – he finally caved and told them what they wanted to know.

His flight home was due to take off at 2:17. Against his better judgment, Gary had spent much of the night drinking in the airport bar with his new pals. By the time the boarding call came, he was wrecked.

The combination of whiskey and turbulence left him startlingly wide eyed, nauseated and wakeful. When the jet landed, he felt like it had taxied over him and rolled to a stop on his chest.

And by the time the cabbie left him in front of his apartment, Gary was praying for death.

***

Friday, Micki skipped school. In a dream, Gary's car screeched to a halt inches from her. Leaping out, he flung tomatoes at her. Looking down she saw, amid the splattered tomatoes, his heart, spurting blood and still beating weakly.

Michaela screamed, awakening with a gasp. Her heart clattered as she rubbed away sleep and tears, but the panicked feeling would not leave.

Sunlight streamed into her room, filtered by lacy curtains. Her phone's message light flashed. One message: the school office, asking why she was absent. She glanced at the clock: 1:49.

Reaching for the phone, she punched in Gary's number.

On the third ring, she heard a click and a muffled, "Hello?"

"Hi, Gary, it's me—"

"Not now." He hung up.

She stared at the receiver, then pressed "redial."

The line clicked and went dead.

Micki dropped the receiver in its cradle; clutching her pillow, she cried herself to sleep.

She awakened after 9 and tried again. Busy. A knot tied itself in her insides. She retreated under the covers, sobbing, and fell back to sleep.

In another disturbing dream, Gary handed her a hula hoop, an emperor penguin on a red leash, her toothbrush and a plastic bag filled with half a dozen bright-blue goldfish; he told her to take all her stuff back and not to call him anymore. Awakening in distress, she clasped her hands around her knees, reminding herself it was just a dream, and willed her body to stop shaking.

Finally, Michaela got up and went for a run. Looking east to the azure sky shot through with pink, she took a deep breath; the cool air helped clear the cobwebs and erase her dream. The only sound was the rhythmic thump of her feet. Over and over she replayed their last encounter in the diner.

Finally, as she headed home, reason won out. "I'm just being paranoid." Her voice startled her. "Gary would never hurt me."

Her step took on renewed lightness, her heart new hope. Back home, she slipped the ring back onto her finger. Turning her hand, she watched as the stones caught the light, shimmering with cool green and fiery white brilliance.

Over breakfast, she argued with her mother about her continued drinking. "I thought you stopped," Micki said around a mouthful of oatmeal.

"Sometimes I just need something to get me through the day."

She thumped her juice glass on the table. "That's just an excuse and you know it."

"It is not! I just have one now and then to relax me. And don't you take that tone with me, Michaela Rose. I'm fine."

"You're not fine, Mother. You're impossible!" Exasperated, she ran upstairs.

Donning her favorite sweatshirt, Michaela yanked her hair into a ponytail. A vein throbbed in her neck. Jamming her running shoes on her feet, she double-knotted the laces.

It was just before 10:15 when she thundered downstairs. "Going for a run," she called out as she sailed past Mom. "And I'm staying at Dad's this week."

Heading out into the April sunshine, Michaela looked down at her ring, its gems dazzling in the sunlight, then up into the broccoli trees just starting to bud. She decided to cut through Wickham Park on the way to Gary's. As she turned up Oak Street, the road fairly flew past.

# *Chapter 23*

Sunlight glistened on the surface of the pond. Little children played on the slide and the swings; older kids climbed around on the jungle gym. Michaela slowed, intending to take a few laps around the trail. Entering the arched wrought-iron gates, she waved to Dana and Joey Brickman and their mom. *How big they got since last time I sat for them! Dana's almost as tall as Joey.* And Elise looked about five months pregnant.

By the gazebo, a tallish man in faded jeans and a brown jacket waved her down. "Excuse me." He rubbed his nose with the side of one grimy hand. "My car broke down" – gesturing over his shoulder – "d'you have a dime I can use to call for a tow?"

She backed up a step, wary of this stranger, then chided herself for her suspicion. "Sure."

As she reached to open the zippered pouch on her wrist, a glint of steel caught her eye; she heard a *click-whoosh*.

Suddenly the stranded motorist wasn't so well meaning.

He twisted her arm behind her back. Holding the switchblade to her throat, he propelled her through the gracefully arched opening in the surrounding hedge enclosure, and into the gazebo.

Michaela tried to scream. No sound came out. She scratched at his face and hands.

His dirty fingers dug cruelly into her upper arm. He jerked the blade hard against her throat. "One scream and I'll slash your pretty throat, Pamela. Don't think I won't." His thick, guttural laugh sickened her. "Thought you could get away with it, huh? Thought you' outsmart me. That won't happen, Pamela!"

"I'm not Pamela," Michaela protested in a strangled whisper, tripping as he shoved her to her knees.

A hand came down across her face, knocking her, sprawling, to the floor. "Shut up!" he hissed.

She winced and shut up, panic in her eyes. *Oh, no! Please, God, this can't be happening!*

Reaching beneath her sweatshirt, he groped at her breasts. "Take it off!"

"What? No!" She slapped his hands away.

His open palm struck the side of her face. "Shut up, bitch! And do what I say. Take it off!"

With trembling hands and terror in her eyes, she complied.

Displeased with Michaela's slowness, the assailant yanked off the sweatshirt. Shoving her onto her back, he straddled her. Holding the edge of her t-shirt taut in his teeth, he slashed through it, from bottom to top, laying her chest bare.

"Please don't hurt me," Michaela begged, panic stricken. "I'll do anything – just don't hurt me."

"You better believe it, Pamela. You'll do anything I tell you… or I'll kill you." Again his sickening laugh filled the gazebo.

Michaela fought the urge to cry out as his teeth sank into her left breast. When he lifted his head and stared at her, wild eyed, she saw blood around his mouth. Her blood.

He grabbed at her crotch. "You love it, Pamela. You know you do. I see it in your eyes. You're aching for it. But I wanna *hear* you beg me for it. Go on. Beg!"

"Please don't do this," she whispered, shaking her head. "Please, don't."

"I said beg for it, bitch!" Another vicious slap punctuated his demand.

"Please… please," her lips formed the words. No sound came out.

"I didn't hear you, Pamela; maybe you need some coaxing." He slit her cheek with the knife.

Michaela winced but did not cry out.

"Go on, tell me what you want me to do to you," he demanded again.

Tears streamed down her face. "I can't."

"Sure you can. C'mon say it. *Fuck me!* Say it, Pamela! Say it or I'll slash your throat."

Through her tears, Michaela said it.

"Why you crying?" he taunted her, wiping a tear away with one finger. It was rough, calloused. "You're gonna enjoy this, Pamela." His gravelly voice filled her ears as he lifted her quivering chin with the knife. "You always do." He kissed her mouth; this only made Michaela cry harder.

He cut away the crotch of her sweats and laughed darkly. "Well, looky here! You knew I love you in lace, huh, Pamela? You must've *really* wanted it bad today to dress like this, didn't you, Pamela?"

Crazy with fear, she sobbed as he sliced through her panties. His erect penis lurched into view.

"Now beg me for it, you little whore!"

When Michaela shook her head, he grabbed her by the hair and slammed her head to the floor.

"I wanna hear you beg me to fuck you, Pamela."

Sobbing so hard she could barely speak, Michaela whispered the words.

He laughed sadistically; her stomach turned.

Smacking his lips, he yanked his dirty jeans down and penetrated her roughly.

She winced at the sharp and sudden pain.

"Today's your lucky day," he muttered as he pounded inside her.

His hot, putrid breath in her face made Michaela gag at his every word.

"You're number twelve. Next one ain't gonna be so lucky," he warned. "Thirteen's an awfully unlucky number, isn't it, Pamela?" He made eye contact with the terrorized girl. "Isn't it?" he hissed.

"Yes," she whispered, nodding. "Yes. It's very unlucky."

*Stay alert. Watch for a chance to escape. Then go. Don't look back. Just get to safety!*

"Tell me you love it, bitch!" He spat in her face. "Tell me you want more."

Gagging, she told him.

His coarse laughter filled her ears again as he brutalized her. It reminded Michaela of a dump truck spilling gravel onto pavement.

Then, abruptly, he pulled out.

She shut her eyes, resting her head against the floor; she exhaled quietly. *Thank God it's over!*

But when she opened her eyes again, his still-erect penis bobbed before her.

Forcing Michaela's mouth open, he shoved his way inside and thrust brutally until she nearly vomited from the smell and taste of the warm, seepy fluid in her mouth.

"Swallow it!" he ordered, holding the knife to her throat.

Sobbing and gagging, she obeyed.

"That's a good girl," her assailant mocked, zipping his pants. "Now get on all fours. Or you die."

Splinters jabbed into Michaela's palms as he shoved her down to her elbows. *Oh, God, what now?*

He yanked away the remains of her panties. Producing a leather-sheathed knife, he slid its long slender handle inside her, savaging her and babbling filthy dirty talk. Not daring to move, she silently pleaded for an end to this assault. Her tears dripped to the floor in tiny pools of terror.

After an agonizing eternity, Michaela heard him undo his zipper again; she glanced back as he pulled the knife handle out of her and dropped it to the gazebo floor.

Making disgusting little grunting noises, he coaxed the offensive organ to attention a second time.

As he forced himself inside her again, she assessed her situation: The switchblade lay beside her. The exit was a little over 100 yards away; fortunately, she still had her running shoes on. Lowering her head, Michaela glanced behind her. As his grunts told her he was finished, she drew a knee in to her chest and let it fly.

Knocked backward, he howled in agony and surprise. "Bitch! I'll get you for this! I'll get you, Pamela!"

Scrambling to her feet, Michaela pulled up her shredded sweats and grabbed the switchblade with her sweatshirt; then she snatched the second knife. Knowing his blood on the weapon could identify him as her attacker, she unsheathed it and cut a jagged slash down her assailant's face.

Blood spurted from the gash, mingling with hers on the floor.

"Not so much fun on that side of the knife, huh?" she jeered.

Roaring in fury, he lunged and fell, spattering blood across her face and her clothing.

Wrapping both knives in her sweatshirt, she stomped a foot into her rapist's crotch. Pulling her torn clothing around her, Michaela clutched the sweatshirt to her chest and fled to safety. Nearly three years' experience had taught her "safety" meant one thing.

Taking the stairs two at a time, she pounded at the door. *Please be home! Please be home!*

Annoyed at whoever was banging so insistently, Gary tugged the door open. "What the hel—"

Still clutching the sweatshirt, Michaela crumpled into his arms. Sobbing, she flailed with her free hand. "Help! The park… knife… said car… raped me!"

"Micki! Are you alright?"

"Had to" – she gasped for breath – "had to get away." The knives thudded to the floor.

"What the–!" Gary bent to reach for the switchblade.

"Don't!" She tugged at his arm, still panting. "His fingerprints – and blood."

Gary dialed 911.

Michaela gave the dispatcher as complete a description of her assailant as she could, right down to the color of his eyes, and the just-inflicted gash down his left cheek.

The dispatcher gave her the number for the rape-crisis center. Her hand shook as she jotted it down.

Micki handed the receiver and number to Gary, who rubbed her back as he spoke with Lisa at the crisis center.

Lisa told him to bring Michaela to the hospital with a change of clothes, cautioning him against letting her shower, change or even wash her face or hands. She would meet them there.

Micki shivered in her shredded t-shirt and sweats; her face was bruised and bleeding, her eyes swollen nearly shut. A woman in a denim dress approached, her light-brown hair in a loose bun. Micki guessed she was in her late 20s. Her emerald eyes looked piercing, yet kind. Her mouth formed a worried frown.

"Michaela?" Calm green eyes met terrified blue eyes, establishing a tenuous relationship. "I'm Lisa Barrows; let's go inside – they're expecting you." Her warmth eased Michaela's distrust.

She led them to a private examination room and asked to speak with Michaela alone.

"You do what you need to do," Gary said. "I'll start filling out paperwork."

"Don't be alarmed," Lisa cautioned. "There's a detective here to speak with you. She'll be in shortly."

Michaela followed the crisis counselor and a nurse into the exam room. Lisa shut the door. Nurse Caroline Froemer busied herself at a cabinet, assembling swabs, tubes and test kits. Setting them on the counter, she left.

Lisa told Michaela what to expect from the exam, keeping her tone as soothing as possible.

She bit her swollen lower lip. "What if… what if I'm pregnant?"

"They can't tell just yet. They'll do a test to determine if you were pregnant already."

Michaela shook her head. "I wasn't pregnant. I'm – I mean, I *was* – a virgin," she murmured, twisting her hands in her lap.

Lisa looked like she wanted to give Michaela a hug. She told her what she could expect the police to ask: where and when the rape occurred; the sequence of events; what, if anything, she could recall: distinguishing features, scars or marks; whether she'd ever seen her attacker before. "I know this is frightening, but you don't have to go through it alone."

Michaela's eyes widened when Caroline returned with a camera. "What's that for?"

"If you want to press charges, you'll need physical evidence. Assuming they catch this guy, by the time you get to trial, you won't have bruises anymore," she replied. "And photos provide solid evidence. I can't take them without your permission; but remember: If I don't, it's your word against his."

A new fear rose inside Michaela; her eyes swiveled toward Lisa.

"It's up to you," the nurse said kindly. "You'll need to sign a form allowing me to take pictures."

Micki looked around at the shelves of medical supplies. Despair consumed her. "I can't do this; it's just too much!" She began to cry. "I'm scared," she admitted.

"Of course you're scared," the nurse said. "What you've been through is terrifying; no one's denying that. I don't blame you for feeling angry and confused. What happened to you should never happen. To anyone. But don't let it defeat you." Caroline met her gaze. "You're going to get through this. Okay?"

Michaela swallowed hard and took Lisa's hand; its warmth bolstered her. "Okay," she whispered. Her nails were ragged, with blood and dirt caked beneath them. In her nervousness, she'd picked off almost all the light-blue polish. She signed the form, then gripped her copy in one trembling fist.

Looking around at the cold sterility of the room, Micki shivered as Caroline took photos of her sullied clothing, black eye, swollen mouth and cuts and bruises on her face, throat and arms. The nurse applied little stickers with ruler markings alongside each mark and laceration; when the photos were introduced as evidence, she explained, jurors could gauge the injuries' size and scope. Patterned bruises on her arms and legs would be photographed, measured and identified as handprints.

There were skin swabs and oral swabs to be done, plus hair and environmental samples to be collected – bits of leaves in her hair; wood splinters stuck in her sweatpants. Caroline scraped skin and dirt from beneath Micki's fingernails, and cut them all off, down to the quick. These were collected directly into little evidence bags, labeled "left hand" and "right hand."

It was a terrible indignity. But not as humiliating as having to stand in the center of what looked like a paper tablecloth and strip off all her clothes. Michaela wept as she peeled away the remaining tatters, yet another embarrassment added to the degradation she'd suffered. She was given a blue paper hospital gown.

She was so traumatized, they let Gary come in while they took samples and drew blood. He held her hand, comforting Michaela when she became agitated at the *click-click-whirr* of the camera. After the initial exam, she grew hysterical and insisted he leave.

Lisa drew in her breath when she saw what Micki hadn't wanted Gary to see: brutal bites that tore flesh from way up along her inner thighs, leaving raw, bloody gashes.

Despite years spent working with rape victims, Caroline found herself almost unable to peer through her camera's viewfinder as she pointed it toward the swollen, blood-encrusted bites.

The evidence-collection process took several hours. Every test, tissue and sample collection had to be done in a particular order, according to prescribed guidelines, and meticulously labeled.

All that remained was the internal exam. Caroline asked Micki to lie back; she adjusted the stirrups at the end of the table.

"What I'm going to do now," the nurse explained, warming a speculum in her hand, "is a quick swab for semen, collect samples and check for any internal injury. Normally, it doesn't hurt; but depending on your injuries, it might be uncomfortable. Just bear with me, alright?" The nurse, with short dirty-blonde hair and hazel eyes, leaned toward the terrified young woman as she spoke.

Michaela jolted upward; feet stuck in the stirrups, she struggled to free herself. "No!" she shrieked. "Don't hurt me! No, please don't hurt me—"

Amid her screams, she heard Lisa's soothing voice. "Michaela, it's okay. You're safe; Caroline's here to help you."

Micki stopped thrashing and screaming to listen, perceiving her as a voice of reason. She reached for the counselor's hands.

Lisa repeated the information. Helping Michaela lie down again, Lisa re-adjusted the young woman's feet in the stirrups. "It's alright, Michaela; you're in the hospital. You're safe here."

She looked at the nurse; their eyes locked. Seeing her attacker's eyes, Micki seized Lisa's hand; again her screams pierced the quiet.

Lisa remained calm. "It's okay, Michaela. Caroline's here to help you. It's going to be alright."

Stepping back, Caroline jotted notations in the file. Michaela searched the counselor's face.

"It's alright," Lisa reassured her again. "Nothing bad can happen to you here; I won't let anyone hurt you." She entwined her fingers with Michaela's. "You're safe now."

Hot tears slid down Micki's face; they dripped into her ears as she lay on the table, feet askew. "Don't let him hurt me," she pleaded through swollen lips. "Please don't let him hurt me again."

"No one's going to hurt you here," Lisa promised. "Is it okay for Caroline to do the exam?"

Michaela trembled fiercely. Gripping Lisa's hand, she tried hard to be brave. "Okay."

Caroline readjusted Michaela's feet in the stirrups.

Michaela repeatedly resisted the nurse's efforts to open her legs. She whimpered as the nurse adjusted the speculum.

Caroline collected samples under the detective's careful gaze. "There. All done. Let me suture and dress those wounds and you'll be all set."

When the nurse was finished, she helped Michaela sit up and get dressed.

Before they left, the ER doctor scribbled three prescriptions and handed them to Michaela with a tube of antiseptic cream. "Warm baths with Epsom salts should help ease the soreness," he told her.


Detective Genevieve Dickerson took copious notes as the girl related her ordeal in excruciating detail. Partway through, Michaela hesitated. Some details were too embarrassing to say aloud. When the detective asked whether Michaela wanted to write them into the police record herself, Micki looked to Lisa for direction.

"It's up to you," the counselor replied.

Squirming in her seat, Michaela reached for the pen and paper.

Detective Dickerson read the statement back, then called Gary in. "I'd like to speak to you both." She handed Micki her card. "If you remember anything else, call me. Something he said or did; what he was wearing; distinctive features, an accent or lisp – no matter how insignificant it seems. And Gary, be alert: If you notice anything unusual, call me immediately. She could be subconsciously reacting to something."

Micki fidgeted with her hands. She gasped. "My ring; it's gone! I put it on this morning; I was on my way over to tell you wh—" She broke off, staring at her ringless hand. "I don't even remember him taking it!" She looked at Gary, teary eyed. "What am I gonna do?"

"That's okay, honey" he reassured her. "It's just rocks and metal. It's not important. What matters is that you're okay."

Back at Gary's apartment, Michaela hobbled as far as the porch. She winced as she climbed the first two stairs. "I can't." She shook her head. "I can't make it."

"Take your time."

She sat. "I can't!" she wailed, defeated.

"Let me help." Crouching, he lifted her gingerly. "Hang on."

Wrapping her arms around his neck, she held on tight as Gary navigated the stairs.

Once inside, he ran a hot bath for her.

"Want me to help you into the tub?"

Panic struck. He would see the wounds she wanted so badly to conceal. "N-no, that's okay," she stammered. "I can manage."

The doctor had cautioned it'd sting some, but the baths would aid the healing process. The pain was less intense than she feared; but, no matter how long she soaked, Michaela didn't feel clean.

Lathering a washcloth, she scrubbed her skin practically raw. She scrubbed and scrubbed and still felt filthy dirty. Michaela flung the washcloth into the water and burst into tears. She jammed the heel of her hand against her mouth so her cries wouldn't bring Gary running; he was like that. And she loved him for it.

By the time her tears abated, the water had gone cold. Michaela drained and refilled the tub, hot as she could stand it. Adding three handfuls of Epsom salts, she let the heat and salts work their magic on her battered body.

When she finally emerged, Micki felt almost human again; some color had returned to her pallid cheeks. Hair wrapped in a towel, she came out of the steam-filled bathroom cocooned in Gary's green-plaid flannel robe. She found him in the kitchen.

"How d'you feel?"

She shied away from his embrace. "Better."

"Are you hungry? I made you some soup."

The towel wobbled as she shook her head. "I just wanna sleep. Can I go lie down?"

"Of course." Gary followed as Micki padded toward the spare room. He turned down the covers and fluffed the pillows; he drew the drapes against the moonlight.

She waited until he was safely out of the room before taking off the robe and climbing painfully into bed. Curling up into a ball, she drew the covers around her chin.

Despite her exhaustion, sleep eluded her. Finally, the narcotics won. In a fitful sleep, she thrashed about as frightening dreams tormented her. More than once she awakened, weeping, only to fall back into a drugged slumber.

In her most realistic nightmare, the attacker slashed her throat and watched her flail on the ground, dying. Piercing shrieks and icy terror tore her from sleep, her bare arms and legs tangled in the sheets.

Gary snapped on the overhead light to dispel the demon dreams and rushed to comfort Michaela. Hesitant to lay hands on her, he spoke gently to get her attention. "It was only a dream, honey. It's okay, baby; you're safe now. No one's gonna hurt you." He laid his hands on her shoulders.

She thrashed wildly. "No!" she screeched. "Oh, please, no!"

"Baby, it's me; it's Gary," he said, trying to calm her.

Working frantically to free herself from her linen entanglement, Michaela scrambled away from his touch. Her left foot caught in the blanket and she tumbled off the bed. She sprawled on the floor, clad only in panties. Crying out, she clutched her twisted ankle.

"Are you alright?" His voice startled her.

She looked up to see Gary – aghast – staring at her. In panic and shame, Michaela tried to cover herself up but she couldn't quickly enough hide the vicious bites on her breasts and inner thighs.

Picking up the robe from the bedside chair, he draped it around her.

She clutched it about herself, then buried her face in her hands, ashamed and weeping.

Sitting behind her on the floor, Gary cradled her in his arms and rocked her back and forth. "It's okay, baby. It's okay. Shh… shh."

Taking great gulps of air, Micki fought for composure. "I didn't want you to see," she sobbed into her hands. "Didn't want you to see."

Gary laid his cheek against her shoulder and drew close to her. When her sobs quieted, he helped her stand. She limped to the chair while he straightened the bedclothes; he helped her back into bed.

Micki rubbed her eyes with her fists. "I'm so sorry, Gary," she mumbled through swollen lips.

He sat beside her and stroked her hair. "For what?"

She pulled back the robe, exposing the savage bite on her left breast. "For letting him do these awful things." Tears spilled onto her bruised cheeks.

Gary kissed her forehead. "None of this was your fault. You did the smartest thing you could do: You stayed alert. And got away alive." He drew the robe back around Michaela, held her close and stroked her hair. "That's what's important: You're safe."

She clung to him and whimpered. At last, drawing back from the safety of his arms, Micki twisted her hands together. "I need to tell you something. There're things…" She hid her face in her hands; words poured out in an unstoppable torrent. "Things I did. If they catch him and he goes on trial and they make me tell what I did" – she took a jagged breath – "in front of everybody… you'll think I'm a whore and you'll send me away. You'll hate me!" She flung herself across the bed, sobbing.

Gary laid a hand on Micki's shoulder. "Nothing that happened could ever make me think that," he assured her. "You've been through a terrible ordeal; if something's too upsetting to talk about, that's okay. Whatever happened, I love you; and yes, I still want you to be my wife."

"No!" She shook her head, weeping into the covers. "If you knew what I did, you wouldn't say that!"

Gary rubbed slow, comforting circles on her back. "Trust me on this, okay?"

She lifted her head, swiping at tears. Sitting up, she glared at him. "How can you say that? I'm—" she stopped abruptly.

"You're what?" he prompted gently.

"Damaged goods!"

Gary's reaction was explosive. "What?"

Michaela rubbed her eyes with her fists. "Damaged goods," she repeated, looking morosely into the front of the robe.

"Christ! Where'd you ever get *that* idea?" His surprised and unintentionally sharp tone brought on a new barrage of tears.

"*Look* at me!" she screamed, standing and pulling the robe open, exposing the raw and oozing wounds. "Just look at me and tell me I'm not!"

Gary wrapped it gently around her again. "You're not," he said steadfastly, tying the belt at her waist. "You're not." He kissed her forehead and drew her tenderly into his arms.

"I am," Micki insisted, sobbing. Her knees felt ready to give way. "It's all my fault. If I hadn't cut through the park, it never would have happened."

"Yeah, and if I had a lamp and three wishes it wouldn't have happened, either."

"But you don't understand! I'm *horrible*… I let him do the most awful things."

Gary regarded Micki at arm's length. "Listen to me," he said, his tone bordering on firm. "None of this was your fault, sweetheart. You're no more responsible for what happened today than you are for your blue eyes and freckles. What happened to you is horrible, yes; but don't beat yourself up over it."

After another reassuring hug, he smoothed her hair away from her face and helped her back into bed.

# *Chapter 24*

Retreating to the living room, Gary slouched onto the couch and did the only thing he could do. He prayed for peace for Michaela; he prayed for his young fiancée to gain the wisdom to know she wasn't to blame – and for the strength to endure this ordeal. Gary also prayed to vanquish the dark hatred seeping into his soul, the venom he longed to unleash against the beast who'd done this to the woman he loved.

As he prayed, Gary swore he felt a gentle hand on his shoulder; in his head he heard, *Forgive, my child. The only way to heal is to forgive.*

By now he was well used to Grandpa's voice in his head; but this wasn't Edward. He whipped around, but saw no one.

"I can't," he murmured.

*You must,* the voice insisted calmly. *Example is the best teacher. Do as you've instructed the children.*

Just that morning, he'd gathered his first graders for a lesson on forgiveness: "It's normal to get angry. But holding grudges is never a good idea. We need to forgive each other. Even if we don't feel like it. Otherwise, you hurt yourself and the other person. Jesus said, 'Forgive us our trespasses *as we forgive* those who trespass against us.' If we don't forgive people who hurt us, how can we ask God to forgive us when we hurt someone else?" But – voices in his head? It was his imagination. That was the only logical explanation. "How can I forgive what that rat bastard did?" Gary challenged.

*Because I forgave,* it reminded him. *Forgiveness is the only way to overcome evil.*

Now he was shown an image of two hands reaching toward him in love and forgiveness. Hands with nail marks. At this, he broke down and wept. Mentally exhausted, it wasn't long before Gary fell into a troubled sleep on the couch.

Hours later, he woke when he heard Michaela calling his name.

He opened a drowsy eye. "Hmm? Oh, you're awake." Sitting up, he yawned and gave her a quick once-over. "How do you feel?"

She shrugged. "A little better, I guess."

"If you're hungry, I can warm up that soup… if you want." He headed toward the kitchen.

"Okay. Um… Gar? Please don't tell my parents."

Gary hugged her. "You have nothing to be ashamed of, honey. It wasn't your fault."

Her words were muffled against him. "I just don't want them to know; this is too personal."

He pulled back a little. "They're bound to notice the bruises on your face."

"Not if I don't go home. Please, can't I stay here?" She clung to him. "I'm s'posed to stay at my dad's this week. Don't make me leave, Gary. I don't feel safe. If I tell him, he won't understand. But he'll listen to you. Can't you just tell him I'm staying here?"

Gary couldn't tell Michael that. Especially after their last phone call. But if he sent her to her dad's, Michael would assume *he'd* hurt her. That would spell trouble. "I know you feel safe here; but I don't know if that's such a good idea."

"Why not?" Micki wailed.

"You'd be alone while I'm at work; I'd feel bad leaving you alone." He had no idea where his next words came from. "Maybe you'd feel safer at the cottage. It'll do you good to get away. And you can visit with Martha. She'd love to see you."

Michaela considered this. "Yeah… I'd like that."

"Why don't you call your dad?"

"Could you ask him?"

"It's really not my place to do that."

As she reached for the phone, Gary headed into the kitchen; he could just imagine what the other end of the conversation would sound like.

"Daddy?" Micki's voice had a little-girl quality to it. "What? No, I'm fine. I was wondering: Is it okay if I don't stay there this week? Nothing's wrong. I just wanted to go to the beach with Gary."

Gary saw fear in her eyes when she shuffled into the kitchen.

"He wants to talk to you; he sounds pissed."

Gary felt like somebody had stuffed an old, fraying sock into his mouth. He gave the soup a stir, dreading the showdown. To his dismay, Micki followed.

He tried to sound like he wasn't terrified. "Hi, Michael."

"Don't you 'Hi, Michael' me! I told you to stay the hell away from Kayla!"

"Y-yes. You did, sir." He turned away, kept his voice low. "But you see… I di—"

"I'm not interested in your justifications! What are you doing there?"

*For starters, I live here.* Gary swallowed the fraying sock. At least it felt that way. "May I explain, sir?"

He envisioned the determined set of Michael's jaw. "You'd *better* explain."

Curled up on the couch, Micki watched her fiancé. She looked worried.

Gary thought quickly; he couldn't say what had happened; she'd never forgive him! But he had to tell Michael *something.* "Micki came to see me." Which was true. "We had a long talk." Also true. "She said she knows I'd never hurt her. And she said she feels safer with me than" – he stole a glance at her – "just about anyone." Even if she hadn't actually said that, it's what she would've said.

A horrible silence followed.

"I swear to God, Gary: You'd better be telling me the truth!"

Gary's control slipped; still, he managed to keep his voice steady. "I have no reason not to."

"Wrong. You have *every* reason not to. But if you *are* lying to me and I find out abou—"

"Listen," he hissed. "I'm telling you for the last time: I pose no threat to Michaela. Now if she doesn't have a problem with me, I dunno why it's any of your damn business!"

"I see why she has concerns about your temper. You watch your tone – and your mouth – mister!"

Gary ignored the comment. "She'll be home next Sunday." He thumped the phone down.

Michaela watched him in silent worry, her eyes questioning his words, his anger.

"C'mon," he said more gruffly than he intended. "Let's go check on that soup." He steered her into the kitchen.

"Smells delicious. I thought you said you were a lousy cook."

"I lied," he teased, his tone a little too sharp.

The promise of homemade soup was wonderful. But, more exhausted than hungry, Micki begged off. Gary helped her back to bed, then brought a bowl of steaming soup on a tray, along with her next dose of medication. He sat beside her as she spooned up rich broth, hunks of chicken and tasty veggies.

As she ate, Michaela motioned toward the living room. "Um, Gar'? What was that all about?"

"What was what all about?"

"What you said to my dad. What did you mean, you have 'no reason not to'? Not to what?"

"Oh, that? It was nothing." He dabbed at her mouth with the napkin.

She snatched it. "Don't patronize me, Gary. No reason not to what?"

He couldn't say her father had threatened him with bodily harm. He opted for veiled truth, as he had with Michael. "Tell the truth. No reason not to tell him the truth."

"About what? And what was all that about you posing a threat? Does he really think that?"

"Of course not. Look, do we have to discuss it now? Get some rest. We can talk later."

"You promise?"

"I promise. Later. Alright?"

She took her pills, crawled into Gary's arms for a hug, then snuggled under the covers. Attila, who'd been idling at the door, jumped onto the bed. Walking its length, he curled up beside Micki, his face near her hand, and purred.

Smiling at his cat's sense of hospitality, Gary kissed Michaela on the cheek. Whisking the tray away, he turned out the light and shut the door.

Twice more she awakened screaming. Both times, Gary rushed to comfort her.

"I'm sorry," Micki wept the second time. "I don't mean to keep doing this to you."

Drying her tears, he held her until she was nearly asleep. Easing her back against her pillow, he turned on the bedside lamp.

Fetching his pillow and a blanket, Gary slept on the floor beside her, praying she would sleep through the night.

Next morning, Michaela awakened achy and sore. Gary ran a bath, throwing in handfuls of Epsom salts. While she soaked, he made breakfast.

Over scrambled eggs and bacon, she worried aloud what folks at church would say about her bruised face and awkward gait. "Can we go somewhere else today?" she asked. "I can't go where anyone knows me… not looking hideous."

"You're not hideous. But ya know what, sweetheart? Under the circumstances, I don't think God will mind if you skip Mass today. Why don't you go back to bed and get some sleep?"

She flung down her fork in frustration. It bounced off her plate and clattered to the floor. "I don't need sleep! I'm not sick, Gary. I was raped!"

"I know; but emotionally, you could probably use some rest."

She tensed at his touch. "I thought that's why we're going to the beach house."


Gary slid Cyndi Lauper's *She's So Unusual* into the tape deck. He glanced at Michaela, drowsing to the plaintive, yet oddly soothing, wail of "Time After Time." Attila purred in her lap. Gary knew she loved this tape. He recalled how thrilled she was to meet Cyndi last year. Michaela had been disappointed when he said he had to work that night. What he didn't tell her was the extent of his "work" was introducing the singer on stage.

Backstage before the concert, he'd been met with a yelp from the tiny redhead. "Gary! It's so good to see you!" Suddenly the singer was in his arms and had planted a loud kiss on his cheek.

He hugged her joyously. "Same here, sweetie!"

Cyndi wiped a lipstick smear off his face. "Oops! Don't wanna get'cha in trouble," she kidded, patting his cheek affectionately. Micki had watched, scarcely able to believe her boyfriend was on a first-name basis with her favorite singer. "Speaking of trouble," Gary said with a grin, one arm around Cyndi, "there's somebody I want you to meet."

"Ooh!" Her eyes went wide. "The fiancée?"

"Shh. Not yet. Soon."

Cyndi winked conspiratorially. "Got'cha. Mum's the word."

When Gary introduced them, Micki squeaked, "I can't believe I'm actually meeting you!"

The singer giggled and hugged her. "Hi, sweetie; happy birthday! So glad you could come. Gary's told me so much about you. I feel like I know you already!"

Michaela had been so excited! That was one of his favorite memories of his life with her. But this had to be the worst! The ugly purple-green bruises on her swollen face made Gary cringe; his eyes brimmed with tears.

When they got to the cottage, Gary nudged Michaela. "Baby, wake up. We're home."

She stirred with a little "Mmm," then she stretched, turned her head to look at Gary and smiled.

Despite her earlier insistence to the contrary, once they were inside, all she wanted to do was sleep. It was chilly, so Gary started a fire; laying a quilt over Micki on the couch, he tucked it around her and kissed her nose. "Get some rest."

He sat nearby, with a book from the study. Watching him, Attila didn't even purr. For nearly an hour, all that broke the silence was the sound of pages turning, crackles and pops from the fire and sleep sounds from Michaela.

She awakened in distress; another bad dream left her disoriented and sobbing, kicking the quilt to the floor.

There in an instant, Gary knelt to comfort her. "Bad dream?" Tearful, Micki let him take her into his arms. She nodded. "D'you want to tell me about it?" She shook her head against his shoulder.

"How about a soak in the tub? Maybe that'll help you relax."

Nodding, Micki got slowly to her feet. Seeing her wince, Gary carried her upstairs and started the bath; he poured in the Epsom salts and laid out towels.

Grateful for his attentive ministrations, she hugged him. "Thank you… for everything."

Tears dripped into the bath as Michaela studied her hands. *They look horrid!* Not only did that jerk steal the gift she promised Gary, but he took her ring and left her bruised, mangled and God-knows-what else! Diseased, for all she knew.

She hobbled downstairs in an old pair of sweats and one of Gary's "Team Z97-3" softball jerseys.

He smiled at her. "Feel better?"

Michaela sank onto on the couch beside him, tucking her feet beneath her. "Mm-hmm."

"Think you can go back to sleep now?"

"I'm afraid. Every time I close my eyes, I see his face… and it frightens me."

Laying Micki's head against his chest, Gary pulled the quilt over them and smoothed her wet hair; rivulets of water soaked his shirt.

She whimpered a bit at his nearness, struggling internally to keep from tearing away from his embrace. He caressed her cheek. "Shh, it's okay, honey. Settle down. Close your eyes. That's it."

Michaela found Gary's voice as comforting as the touch of his fingers over her skin. Her tension ebbed and she went limp; he stroked her hair until her fluttering eyelids closed and stayed shut.

Monday morning, as they walked along the beach, they met up with Martha, out walking Amber. "Oh, my goodness," she gasped. "What happened?"

Gary looked at Micki, seeking permission to reply. She nodded cautiously. He put an arm around her. "She was attacked over the weekend. Back home. We figured she should get away for a while."

Martha's eyes teared up. "Oh, my dear girl! I'm so sorry!"

Unable to speak, Micki just let Martha hug her. Amber whined, nosing her way into their embrace.

"Oh, you!" Martha scolded gently. "You can't stand to be left out of a hug, can you?"

Glad for the diversion, Micki bent to fondle Amber's ears. "Hi there." She forced a grin. "No one's paying attention to you, huh? Aww, you poor thing!" She hugged the dog. "You're a good girl; yes you are!" Her strained expression relaxed into a genuine smile as Amber, tail in full wag, licked her face.

Gary watched his fiancée, relieved to see her face devoid of the pain that had overtaken it the past two days. At least momentarily.

Later, on his way to work, he stopped at the Johnsons'. "I was hoping you could check on Micki during the day… just to be sure she's alright. But don't let her think she's being watched."

Martha patted Gary's arm. "Don't you fret, love. I can think up a whole slew of reasons to look in on her." She squeezed his hand. "It'll give us a chance to get better acquainted."

Most days, Micki slept late; when she awakened, she found notes from Gary in out-of-the-way places: in her teacup; under magazines on the coffee table; taped to her toothbrush; pinned to couch cushions. Even rolled into the toilet paper. His notes were seldom more than a scrawled "I love you" or "I miss you already" and a smiley face beside his name. But some were longer – a page or more – and filled with the sweetest words of love and affection she'd ever read.

In the mornings, she would walk the beach or sit on the porch.

In the afternoons, Martha visited. Grateful for the older woman's attention, Michaela enjoyed having a mother figure to care for her.

Gary called each afternoon to see how her day was going. Most days she was upbeat and positive; other days, she sounded tearful and frightened.

On Tuesday, he returned home to a delicious meal of pork chops, fresh asparagus and sweet potatoes. With chocolate cake for dessert. As antsy as Michaela was about going out, she wanted to do something to show her gratitude to Gary; so she asked Martha to take her grocery shopping.

Thursday was such a bad day, Michaela didn't even answer the phone.

Pleading 'personal emergency,' Gary left work at 6 and stopped at the florist on his way home. When he finally coaxed Micki out of bed, he ran a bath so she could soak while he made supper. Getting her out of bed took patience and finesse.

Sobbing, she trembled and clung to him. Gary ended up sitting on the bed with her in his lap, rocking her until she stopped crying. Nearest he could tell, she'd had another horrifying nightmare; but she refused to discuss it. It was after 8 before he got her out of bed.

By the time she'd finished her bath, it was nearly 9 and she was exhausted; but Gary insisted she eat; she needed nutrition to aid the healing process. Reluctantly, Micki ventured downstairs, cocooned in a long nightshirt and Gary's flannel robe.

Supper smelled wonderful. Cheesy and peppery… and delicious!

He wrapped her in a hug as she came into the kitchen, partly to comfort her, but mostly so she wouldn't see his tears. Seeing her like this devastated him; he couldn't bear that she had to endure this horrendous trauma, especially at such a tender age.

Micki brightened slightly at seeing the soft pink roses and white freesias on the table. But when they sat down to eat, she looked appalled. "What is it?" she asked, unable to disguise her alarm.

"That's exactly what I said the first time my grandfather made it for me. Trust me: It tastes a hundred times better than it looks."

Michaela looked skeptical. "I dunno if a hundred times is gonna be enough."

She laughed as Gary detailed his first encounter with "Eggs and Asparagus à la Grandpa."

He was just gratified to hear her laugh.

Her facial bruises had faded to a dusky mauve; the bites and slashes had begun to heal. But she had to go back on Sunday. Gary had tussled with this eventuality all week and still hadn't devised a suitable plan to fix his strained relationship with Michaela's dad.

Noticing the lingering bruises on his daughter's face, Michael grabbed Gary by his shirt collar. "You sonofabitch! I told you I'd kill you if you ever laid a hand on her!"

"Daddy! No!" Michaela wedged herself between them, her eyes flashing with fire and confusion. "Gary didn't touch me!"

"If he didn't do it, then how'd you get those bruises?" Michael demanded.

Her hurried glance at Gary urged him to back her up. "I was – mugged… i-in the park."

"Mugged! When? You weren't out at night were you? Are you okay? What'd they take?"

Michaela slumped onto the couch. "Just my ring." She looked at Gary, who clasped her hand.

"When was this?" Michael asked again. "Are you okay?"

"Last Saturday. In broad daylight." She gulped back a sob. "I'm *fine*, Daddy… thanks to Gary."

Michael scowled at the young man seated beside his daughter. He sat as Kayla continued.

"He took me to the hospital and the police. And let me stay at the cottage 'cause I was scared to go home" – tears slid down her cheeks – "only, I didn't want you to know I got hurt. But Gary took care of me… even af—" She laid her face against Gary's shoulder and wept. He stroked her hair, tenderly comforting her.

"Gary, I misjudged you," Michael admitted after Michaela went to the kitchen. "Thank you for taking care of Kayla. I should never have doubted you. I'm sorry."

Gary felt as if an unseen hand were nodding his head; he heard himself say it was just a misunderstanding; no harm done.

"No, Gary; it's not alright," Michael admitted. "It was wrong. *I* was wrong. After those phone calls… I was afraid you had hurt Kayla to spite me."

"I'd never do that, sir," Gary assured him.

Micki returned, setting a tray on the table. "Tea, anyone?"

# *Chapter 25*

Aside from some odd stares from other students, Micki's first week back at school passed uneventfully. Anyone who asked was told she'd been mugged in the park. The following week was easier; her bruises were gone, the strange looks abated and she could breathe easier. But her nightmares worsened. She'd awaken several times a night in a cold sweat. Sobbing.

They'd been best friends forever and Michaela felt bad deceiving her, but she wasn't exactly sure Trish was tightlipped about secrets. And this was one she *really* didn't want getting broadcast all over school.

(14 May – Saturday)
The phone rang. "Did you see the paper?"
"No. I'll go look at it now. Why?"
"No!" Gary's expression of alarm startled her.
"Why not?"
"Just don't. Come over here, quick. And don't go through the park."
She wondered what his cryptic commands meant.
Fifteen minutes later, he pulled her inside his apartment. "You'd better sit down."
"What's wrong?" Michaela kept asking questions as Gary led her into the living room; a newspaper lay, folded, on the coffee table "Gary, what? Why didn't you want me to see the paper?" Worried, she sat.
Across the front marched the bold headline: MURDER IN MIDDLEBURY; below it: *Local Woman Slain in Park.* She looked at him, puzzled. "Is it someone we know?" She scanned the article for a familiar name.
"Worse." Gary showed her the photo below the fold: A woman

with long hair and scads of freckles. He pointed. "She's the woman who was killed." Micki looked blankly at Gary. He slapped at the image with one hand. "Don't you see the resemblance?"

"To who?"

"You!" he exclaimed. "Look at her. Pretty face, dark hair, blue eyes…"

An evil laugh filled her head. Her stomach clenched. "Oh God!" She clasped her hands to her mouth and fled. Tripping over Attila, she sprawled to the kitchen floor. Gagging, she landed facedown on the linoleum, hands in her own vomit.

Paralyzed by an icy grip, Michaela heard the guttural laugh again, louder and more sinister. His sickening voice accompanied it.

"You're number twelve. Next one ain't gonna be so lucky." She vomited again. "Thirteen's an *awfully* unlucky number, isn't it, Pamela?" A deeper wave of nausea swept through Michaela, leaving her gasping for breath between the awful surges of puke. Her throat burned. She tried to push herself up to her knees; her hands slid in the mucky puddle and she fell with a dull splash, smacking her face against the floor.

Appearing at her shoulder, Gary lifted her hair out of the gooey mess. Holding it back, he helped her back up and wiped her face. She was still sobbing and shaking.

"Careful," he said, guiding her around the oozing pool. He held fast to her squishy hand, keeping an arm about her waist as he led her to the bathroom. Wiping a hand on his jeans, he reached in to turn on the shower.

While the water heated, he hugged Micki close and shushed her as she wailed that it was all her fault. Why hadn't she remembered his warning? She should've told the police. Ignoring her seemingly incoherent talk, Gary tried to strip off her swampy clothes.

Michaela fought him, splattering puke against the walls, all over him. "No! We gotta go to the police. He did it. I know he did. He told me he would! He told me. And I didn't tell them."

He wiped a dry bit of his shirt sleeve across his face. "What?"

"He *told* me! He said he would kill the next one. And I didn't tell them. It's all my fault she died!"

Gary grasped her arms, held them in place. Looking her straight in the eyes, he spoke firmly. "Wait. Slow down. What do you mean, *he told you*? He told you *what*, exactly?"

Taking several gasping breaths, Micki repeated what her attacker said. She tried gesturing, but Gary slid his hands to her wrists and was holding them fast. "And I didn't tell the police," she finished.

"Why not?"

"I don't know!" Michaela howled, thinking he was accusing her of something. "I musta blocked it out." She began to panic. "Am I gonna get in trouble?"

"Of course not." He looked at her face, still flecked with bits of her breakfast. "C'mon, let's get you out of these clothes and into the shower. Then we'll go to the police. No one'll be angry. They'll be glad you remembered. I'm sure it'll help them. They probably don't even know who they're looking for yet."

"You think?"

"Yes; now c'mon." He lifted her arms over her head and peeled off her sweatshirt. Tossing it onto the floor, he helped her off with her t-shirt, adding it to the pile of clothes to throw into the wash; then he bent to remove her sneakers and socks. "Okay, that's it for the messy stuff," he declared, helping her out of her jeans. "Water's hot… but maybe you wanna brush your teeth first?"

"I don't have my toothbrush here," she fretted.

"No problem." Gary turned off the shower, then reached into a cabinet beneath the sink and produced a new toothbrush, still in its box. He handed it to her. "Just went to the dentist last week."

Oblivious to her scanty dress, she protested. "I can't take this; it's *yours*."

"Don't worry. Lorraine's wildly generous with toothbrushes. She gave me three of 'em this time. Said I'd never know when I might be traveling – or need a spare at home. Guess she was right."

That did it. Michaela offered him a flicker of a smile.

Gary seized the opportunity to keep her focused on something pleasant. "Yeah, she must be psychic. Funky, too. She always has the best-colored toothbrushes! Open it. I can't wait to see what color this one is; the others were this wild turquoise with blue swirls and something like watermelon."

Micki opened the box. Gary looked at her hand gripping the purple toothbrush with silver glitter. Just starting to grow back, her nails were lilac this morning. "Hmm… purple fingernails, purple toothbrush. Coincidence?" He winked. "I think not."

Her smile was involuntary; her eyes even held a bit of a twinkle. "Kismet."

He tweaked her nose. "That's just what Lorraine would've said."

"Yeah? You seem pretty taken with this Lorraine chick. What else does she have to say?"

He thought for a moment. "Well, she did say I've got the perfect teeth for radio."

Michaela smiled. Gary had a gift for diverting her attention from the horrible to the ordinary. She gave him a hug. "Thank you."

"For what?"

"You know darn well what, Mister Perfect Radio Teeth." She grinned. "I love you."

Gary cleaned the kitchen floor while Micki showered. She put on the clean underwear and jeans she kept here. Pairing the jeans with one of his Team Z97-3 softball jerseys, she was dressed by the time he finished wiping down the bathroom walls.

He was feeding towels into the washer when she emerged from the bedroom. "You keep wearing my shirts and I'll sign you up for the team," he warned.

"You wouldn't want me; I throw like a girl."

"Yeah, but then you'd have your own shirts, and you could stop stealing mine."

"What're you complaining about? I always give 'em back."

"Yeah, with boobs! I'm the laughingstock of the team!"

She couldn't resist. "Honey, that's *not* why you're the laughingstock of the team."


"How can I help you?" Detective Dickerson asked. "Sergeant Lewis said it was urgent."

"I remembered something. Something he said."

She looked on with interest, pen poised over her pad. "Go on."

Words tumbled from Michaela's mouth; she was barely aware of Gary's hand grasping hers. "I must've blocked it out, 'cause I didn't remember it at all 'til I saw the paper; but I heard his voice in my head. And that laugh." She told the detective what she'd recalled. "That's another thing: He kept calling me Pamela."

Detective Dickerson scribbled notes. "Anything else you can remember? Anything at all?"

Micki thought hard, shook her head. "No, I'm sorry. That's it."

The detective capped her pen. "Thanks for coming in. Another woman came forward this morning, someone else who was raped in the park. She related something very close to what you said. Two other women in recent weeks reported incidents, too, involving a similar assailant."

"So this could be helpful?"

"It's quite a big help. It may help us catch the guy who did this."

"I just wish I'd remembered it sooner, 'cause now that lady's dead and it's all my fault!"

"It's not your fault, Micki," Gary assured her, laying a hand atop hers.

"Why would it be your fault?" Detective Dickerson asked at the same time.

"Because if I told you about this in the first place, you coulda had someone looking for this guy, and he wouldn'ta killed her..."

"You were in shock. Something this disturbing" – the detective shook her head – "I'm surprised you remembered it at all. Don't blame yourself. The important thing is, you did remember. It'll help. A lot."

(16 May – Monday)
All the talk at lunch centered on the Karen Burnham murder. Michaela said nothing – especially when the subject turned to the identity of the 20-year-old previous rape victim.

"She's local, so we probably know her," Trish observed at one end of the long cafeteria table. "She'd have been a senior when we were sophomores. So she's probably in college now."

"Or working," Linda Jamieson suggested.

"Maybe she stayed back – you know, and is still in high school," Jennie Falmouth postulated through her tuna sandwich at the other end of the table. "She could even be here at this table. Isn't that right, Michaela?"

Suddenly, all eyes were on Michaela. Her sandwich fell from her hand; she fled the cafeteria. The others gaped at Jennie, who stared back coldly. One by one, her friends followed Micki, leaving Jennie complacently munching her potato chips.

After school, Trish drove her friend to Gary's apartment. Micki asked her to stay awhile, to talk.

"I wanted so bad to tell you," she told Trish, wiping at her eyes, "but I couldn't. I felt like everyone was watching me, ya know? 'Cause of the bruises and all. I'm actually surprised it took Jennie so long to say anything. Of course, by now, the whole school knows."

"Well, it doesn't matter; at least, it shouldn't." She hugged Micki, who wept into a crumpled tissue. "Okay?" Plucking a fresh tissue, Trish dabbed at her friend's tears.

Gary came home to jackets and books piled atop the kitchen table. "Trish? What's wrong?" he asked, making his way toward the living room.

She gestured over her shoulder at her sleeping friend. "She's had a really bad day."

He steered the redhead toward the kitchen. "What happened?"

"It was awful, Gary. You want some tea? Water's already hot."

"I'll get it." He refilled her mug too. "What happened?"

Trish explained what happened at lunch. "KayCee told me what that guy did. God, I feel so awful for her."

Hearing voices, Michaela stirred. Shuffling into the kitchen, she rubbed her eyes woozily. "Oh, Gary. You're home." She went to him for a hug.

"Trish tells me you've had a beast of a day." Settling her on his lap, Gary kissed her nose. Sniffling, she cuddled close, whimpering.

"I should go." Trish patted her friend's shoulder. "Take it easy, Kayse. See ya tomorrow, huh?" Catching Gary's eye, she nodded a goodbye.

"Thank you," Gary mouthed over his fiancée's shoulder.

Embarrassed, Micki swiped at her tear-filled eyes. "I'm sorry," she mumbled, trying to pull herself together.

"It's alright." He held her close. "I'm sorry you had a bad day."

After her tears subsided, he thawed a quart of soup; when it was hot, he ladled up bowls for each of them, fishing out hunks of chicken to add to Attila's dinner.

While they ate, Michaela mulled Jennie's actions. "Maybe it's not so bad," she mused. "I mean, now that it's out in the open" – she shrugged – "maybe some of the pressure's off."

Late the next day, the police called; they had a suspect in custody and wanted Michaela to identify him from a lineup.

As soon as she saw her assailant's face, she gripped Gary's hand, turning toward his embrace. "It's him," she choked out, trembling. "That's him! Third one from the left."

"You're sure?" the detective asked. "Do you want to have them say something?"

"No. I never want to hear that voice again!"

"But you're sure that's him?"

Still in Gary's arms, she nodded vigorously. "It's him. I'd know that face anywhere. And that scar."

Earlier, three other victims had identified the same man as the one who abducted and raped them in the park. His blood sample matched those on the knives Micki had; tissue and semen samples from all four rape kits matched his. And the evidence taken from Karen Burnham was identical.

Timothy James Dunworthy was charged with one count of first-degree murder, five counts of first-degree aggravated sexual assault with a deadly weapon and five counts of first-degree kidnapping. When a search of area pawn shops traced a diamond-and-emerald ring to him, one count of first-degree armed robbery was tacked on to the existing charges.

For the first time since her attack, Michaela slept well.


(1:17 p.m., 19 May – Thursday)

Making her way up the single flight to the municipal courthouse, Micki stopped at her father's office door. She grasped the knob and turned it; the coolness of the air-conditioned office rushed against her arm. Pushing the door open, she stepped inside.

"Kayla, how nice to see you! How are you, dear?"

She smiled. "Hi, Mrs. Larabie. I'm fine, thanks; how are you?"

"Oh, couldn't be better" – she nodded toward the window – "on a day like this?"

"I couldn't agree more." Michaela leaned against a filing cabinet beside the desk. "Is my dad in?"

"Yes. And you're in luck. His one thirty cancelled. Go ahead in, dear."

State's Attorney Michael Conwaye was reviewing a file when the door opened. "Kayla! What a nice surprise." He motioned toward a plush armchair. "Sit down. Is this a social visit? Or are you seeking legal advice?" he teased.

Struggling for the right words, she looked around nervously. On his desk lay a manila folder with *Karen Burnham* in red ink across the tab. "Oh! You're prosecuting the Burnham case? Musta just gotten it." She tried to sound conversational. "Otherwise, you'd know why I'm here."

He sank into his chair. "This *isn't* a social visit. What do you know about it, Kayla?"

She let out a shaky breath. "The suspect's from Naugatuck. He's twenty-eight, has dirty-blond hair, muddy eyes and an ugly scar, right here" – she traced a finger along her left cheek. "He's been positively identified by at least four of his twelve surviving victims and—"

"Wait. Kayla, I've barely had a chance to open this file. How could you know all that?"

She took a deep breath. "I'm one of the four who identified him. In fact, I'm the one who gave him that scar." She wiped at her eyes. "Remember a few weeks back I told you I was mugged? I didn't get mugged, Daddy. I was raped."

Michael gaped at his daughter. "Why didn't you tell me?"

"I didn't want you to know. It's not exactly something I wanted to talk about. Anyway" – she tried to sound casual – "you'da found out when you read the file."

"You should have told me, Kayla. Besides, that's not the kind of thing you want to read in a file like this, under any circumstances. Why'd you wait so long?"

She gripped the arms of her chair. "I went to the police when it happened, alright? I don't need a guilt trip over not having told you sooner!" Cupping a hand to her mouth, she ran to the bathroom.

Kneeling on the tiled floor, Michaela rested her forehead against the toilet's cool porcelain surface.

When she returned, she sat, rocking back and forth, and spoke as though she'd never left. "I know I should have told you sooner; but I just couldn't."

Michael sat beside her. "Can you tell me what happened in the park that morning?"

He sounded like he was questioning a witness.

Michaela was struck by the likelihood she would have to do this, so she better get used to telling the story without breaking down.

Speaking carefully, she watched the scene unfold, sniffling as she related the story. "I tried to fight him off, but he was too strong for me. He beat me up and said awful, awful things, like 'You're lucky you're number twelve; number thirteen's really gonna get it.' He kept saying thirteen would really be unlucky."

Michael hugged his daughter, just like he used to when she was little and she'd had a bad dream, or when schoolyard bullies pushed her – the littlest kindergartner – down in the playground.

# *Chapter 26*

Michaela jolted awake, uncertain of her whereabouts. Falling back against the pillow, she rubbed her eyes and looked around Gary's darkened bedroom. "Oh! You startled me."

He stooped by the bed. "I went to get you, but Trish said you'd bugged out early. What happened?"

"Went to see my dad," Micki mumbled thickly, reaching out for a hug. "I told him."

"Was it awful?"

She nodded. "He was s'posed to prosecute the murder case; he just got the file today. But he's gonna have to get out of it. *Recuse* himself, I think he said."

Over dinner, Gary asked Michaela what she wanted to do for her birthday that weekend.

She said she didn't feel like celebrating, but promised to think it over. "Maybe dinner and a movie? I could really use a comedy. No dead people." She thought for a moment. "Surprise me."

Next morning, she awakened from her first good dream in ages. All she recalled was Gary holding her and saying, no matter what, he'd always love her. Those words in particular gave her great comfort: *No matter what.* It seemed so real she swore she could still feel his embrace.

Micki sat up in bed, clutching her arms around herself. A sudden wave of nausea swelled inside; instantly, the dream's pleasantness vanished amid her haste to reach the bathroom.

She brushed her teeth and took a hot shower. As she dressed, Micki tried to recall more of her dream, but it was gone. She could barely hear Gary's tenderly spoken words. She felt all empty inside.

She didn't trust her stomach enough to eat breakfast. Not even a banana.

Grabbing her backpack, she made sure she had enough cash to

get something in the cafeteria, in case she felt better by lunchtime.

No such luck. After English class, still feeling ill, she went to the nurse's office. And promptly threw up.

Mrs. Stone, a 50ish woman with kind eyes, handed her a tissue. "Was it something you ate?"

The girl shook her head. "I haven't eaten today; I didn't feel well."

"That's not healthy, missy," she reproved gently. "And it could explain why you feel dizzy. Opening a drawer, she handed Michaela a box of Saltines. "Here, eat these and sit awhile."

Another wave of nausea assailed Micki and she ran back to the bathroom.

When she returned, Mrs. Stone asked her delicately, "When was your last period, Michaela?"

"Sometime in March, I think."

"Is there any chance you could be pregnant?"

Micki turned away from the nurse and nodded.

"Would you like to take a pregnancy test?"

A single tear landed on her cheek. "I'm afraid to."

Mrs. Stone patted her hand. "Not knowing won't make it go away."

Her words and compassionate touch cracked Micki's defensive shell.

The nurse shushed away her tears. "It's alright, dear; no need to be afraid. Why don't we go ahead and do a test?"

Micki stared at the two lines on the test stick. Just the thought sickened her. "Oh, God, please! No, this can't be happening," she moaned. *I can't have a baby. Not _this_ baby.* She only half-heard Mrs. Stone outlining her options.

Numb, Michaela left the nurse's office with a women's center flyer tucked into her purse.

At home, she called and made an appointment for Monday at 9.


(21 May – Saturday)

"I need your help," Michaela said tearfully. "Can you ditch with me Monday? I need a ride somewhere, and I need you to wait for me."

"Can't Gary take you?"

"No." *He's so pro-life he won't even kill a spider!* Michaela felt like the world's worst sinner. A lump of something awful lodged itself in her throat. It felt like a blob of damp cornstarch. "Please, Trish?"

"Okay… I guess," she agreed hesitantly. "But where? Why?"

"I can't say right now."

Almost as soon as she put down the phone, it rang; she figured it was Trish, changing her mind.

Gary could tell she'd been crying. He asked what was wrong.

She said she'd fought with her mother.

"You wanna talk about it?"

Michaela sniffled. "No." Then, wanting to change the subject, she asked, "What's up?"

"Just wanted to know what you decided about tomorrow."

"What's tomorrow?" she asked, still sniffling.

"Your birthday, silly. Geez, she really *has* got you rattled."

"Umm, I don't think so, Gary. I'm really not in any mood to celebrate." Tears blurred her vision.

"Okay, but if you change your mind…"

"I'll think about it." She knew nothing would change her mind.


(23 May – Monday)

Trish turned in at the parking lot of a two-story brick building. "Why'd you wanna come here?"

Micki, who'd been sniffling into a wadded-up tissue most of the way, wept openly now. "Because I'm pregnant. I gotta get" – she couldn't say the word – "I hafta get rid of it. It's the only thing I can do."

"Oh, Kayse! Does Gary know?"

She shook her head. "No! And he can't know. If he finds out, he'll hate me!"

"Isn't it his?"

"*No!* We've never slept together," she sobbed. "I got pregnant when I was raped."

Trish hugged her. "How awful!" She squelched her feelings of distaste and prayed for forgiveness for what she was about to do. "Want me to go in with you?"


A coldly efficient young woman at the reception desk handed Michaela a clipboard with paperwork to fill out. Trish sat beside her friend, an arm around her shoulder.

She completed the forms, signed everything and handed it back. Pulling a crumpled wad of bills from her pocket – money she had earned at the camp last summer – she counted out the required payment. She was given a receipt and instructed to sit and wait.

Micki had promised herself she'd do something special with that money – get something she really wanted; she told herself she was buying peace. Fifteen minutes later, she was escorted into a tiny room at the end of a long corridor.

In the stark grey room, the staff had her put on a hospital-style gown that opened in the back. She lay, shivering, on a threadbare blue towel covering a cold metal gurney and waited.

A thin-lipped fellow with bushy eyebrows, cleft chin and a cold demeanor, the abortionist refused to let Trish stay in the room with her. Micki sobbed and pleaded, but he told her brusquely, "Rules are rules." Then he excused himself and left.

Frightened and alone, Michaela looked around at the unfamiliar surroundings. A set of stirrups hung from the ceiling; large flat lamps on movable arms were affixed to the wall. Surrounding her were several machines, with all manner of tubes, knobs and dials. Something was making a sucking sound in the next room. Micki heard the muffled sounds of running water and crying through the wall. She tried to shut them out and focus instead on something – anything – else.

Lying on the gurney, Michaela stared at the dingy, water-stained ceiling tiles. It looked like there'd been a leak in the office above or someone had left an upstairs window open during a rainstorm.

The abortionist returned with a dark-eyed woman in surgical scrubs.

"Prep this one for a D and C," he ordered curtly and left again.

Tears squeezed out from between Micki's tightly closed eyelids and began to drip into her ears.

The young woman slipped a mask over Micki's nose and mouth. "Breathe," she said softly, laying a hand on her shoulder. "You'll be fine. Just relax." A few minutes later, she gave Michaela a Walkman and a selection of cassettes to choose from. "It'll help you relax."

She picked *She's So Unusual.*

Music filled her head as the nitrous oxide did its work. Notes danced blue and green inside her brain; she smelled faint aromas of pink and yellow.

As the assistant positioned her feet in the stirrups, Micki vaguely recalled her exam at the hospital. Hazy fear built up within her, quickly scattered by her concentration on the brightly scented notes that swirled before her.

The door opened again and the abortionist reappeared. All she could see above his mask was his overgrown eyebrows. He pulled up a low, wheeled stool and sat at the end of the gurney. Switching on the lamps, he adjusted them. Donning gloves and goggles, he set to work. Michaela became aware of him inserting and opening a speculum. She tried to relax and refocus her attention on the music: *"Money… money changes everything… I said money…"*

He reached for a shiny metal tool on a nearby tray. Its blade glinted in the harsh light. Micki wondered what it was for. As he worked, she tried not to think about what was going on inside her.

She was aware of slight pressure and, now and then, a twinge of pain as he scraped the rapist's baby from her womb. *It's just a blob of tissue; not like a baby or anything. Not like a real baby.* In the silences between songs, she could hear the sucking, gurgling sound she had heard from the other room earlier. Now it sounded louder, more distinct; it felt like she was being wobbled and sucked inside out.

Afterward, the assistant helped her sit up. She was told to expect cramping and bleeding, like during her period, for a few days.

Michaela was given a maxi pad and told to dress and wait in the recovery area until she was no longer woozy. She obeyed, her tears just a foggy memory and two streaks on her face.

The recovery area was a dismal corner room, with a table and six metal folding chairs. They gave her some cookies, and a paper cup of cola to settle her stomach. To her relief, Trish was there.

She gripped Michaela's hand. "How d'you feel?"

"Awful," she whispered, thick lipped and squeamish. "But I'm glad it's over."

Micki skipped school the next day. On Wednesday, she felt like everyone was staring at her, like they could tell what she'd done.

***

The trial started the last week of July. The third day, Micki was called as a witness. Gary and Lisa went with her; their presence gave her the confidence she needed to, as Lisa put it, "put that monster behind bars."

When the questions grew difficult, and her responses gruesome, Micki's eyes welled with tears; but a glance in Gary's direction was enough to calm her.

Late in the afternoon on its first day of deliberation, the jury returned a verdict. Guilty on all counts.

(16 August – Tuesday)

Michaela's ring gouged into his finger, but Gary kept a firm grip on her hand during the sentencing.

Timothy James Dunworthy was led into the courtroom in leg irons, his wrists bound. He approached the judge's bench, clanking and mumbling incoherently, until the uniformed court officers told him to be quiet.

After listing the charges of which he'd been convicted, the judge sentenced him to 43 years and seven months in maximum security.

As Dunworthy was led away, his eyes bored through Michaela. Sneering, he spat at her, laughing the sickening, guttural laugh that had haunted her dreams for months.


"I changed my mind. About what I wanna do with my life," Michaela told Gary over dinner that night.

He put down his salad fork and feigned shock. "You mean you *don't* want to marry me and have my eleven children?"

She giggled. "Of course I do, silly! Hey, wait. Eleven?"

He shrugged. "Nine?"

"Sure. Whatever. I've been thinking. You know how Lisa stuck with me through, well… everything?" Micki waited for Gary's nod. "I want to help people – like *that*. I'm going to find out what I have to do to become a counselor."


Three nights later, she called Gary at home. "Can I see you?"

He heard the little waver in her voice, the one she got when she was agitated.

"Tonight?" It was poker night. He had lost so many months in a row: first to Charlie, then Rob. Even Brenda! The most he'd ever lost was 18 bucks. But it sure was nice to be able to mouth off to Pete one night a month without fear of reprisal. "Well… I kinda have plans tonight, but that's not 'til later. I'll be right over."

Waiting for Gary out front, she snuggled into his arms. "Thanks for coming."

"You sounded upset. But I have it on good authority ice cream fixes everything."

Gary tried to banish a long-ago image of eating misery sundaes with Mom. He missed those talks… missed Mom.

At the ice-cream shop, both ordered hot-fudge sundaes – with rocky road, extra fudge and chopped almonds. Michaela had been uncharacteristically quiet in the car; now, armed with ice cream, she related the conversation with her mom over her choice of college and career path.

"She said I'd never make any money; then she asked if I was still planning to marry 'Mr. Sports Car,' who'd likely 'never amount to much.'"

"So" – Gary licked a hot-fudge smear off his thumb – "what'd you tell her?"

"I told her of course I was. And to refer to you by name in the future."

"Well now." He smiled at her indignation on his behalf. "What'd she have to say to that?"

"She said she didn't know how *a counselor and a two-bit disc jockey* could ever afford to have kids. I told her we might not have money, but at least we'd raise our kids in a loving family." Michaela smiled through the threat of tears. "She didn't have anything to say after that."

"You could tell her I'm independently wealthy, and being a two-bit DJ is what I do for fun."

"Yeah, right. She'd believe that. Doesn't it bother you she's so hung up on money?"

"Honestly? No. But, well… I kinda have a confession to make."

Gary's use of the word 'confession' troubled Michaela. "Oh?"

"But I never quite knew how to bring it up," he added, discreetly checking the time.

"Bring *what* up?" Scrunching up her napkin, she eyed Gary with suspicion.

Poking at his sundae with his spoon, Gary chose his words carefully. "I'm not just, as your mom said, a 'two-bit disc jockey.'"

He explained about the trust fund.

"So, as of next January" – he lowered his voice and his gaze – "money's officially not a problem." Just the idea of all that money made Gary uneasy; he hadn't even told Michaela how much it was.

"So you weren't making that up, about being independently wealthy."

Gary shook his head. "No. And if she hassles you again about UMass, you tell her I've got it covered."

"I can't ask you to pay for my education."

"Who said you're asking?" He remembered Grandpa telling him that not so long ago.

(3 September – Saturday)

Outside her dad's car, Micki hugged her fiancé. "I'm gonna miss you."

"You'll be so busy you won't have time to miss me. I'll call some night and you're gonna say, 'Gary who?' Plus, you'll be home for weekends and semester breaks." He pulled a small gift from his pocket and handed it to her.

Nestled within the velvet-lined box was a heart-shaped sterling locket on a delicate chain. Inside was a tiny photo of them from her birthday weekend. Whatever she said was lost amid her weeping.

Gary fastened the locket around her neck. Michaela clung to him until he peeled her away. "C'mon, your dad's waiting for you." He reassured her he was just a phone call away and, if she really needed him, he could be there in two hours.

"I hate it here," Michaela wailed into the hallway pay phone that night. "I don't know anybody. And my roommate never showed up! I wanna come home!"

"It's only been six hours," Gary chided gently. He remembered how lonesome he'd been for Grandpa when he first moved out. "I know it's hard, but I'm sure there are people even more homesick than you; reach out to them, like any good counselor would."

She promised to give it a try.

On her way back from lunch the next day, Michaela noticed a bewildered girl staring by a stack of boxes, luggage and what looked to be an immensely heavy trunk. "Need some help?"

"I need to find Sanibel Hall."

Michaela pointed over her shoulder. "You found it. Let me help you with those."

"Thanks. Are you one of those, um, orientation people?"

"No, I'm a freshman. I felt out of place, too. And I even had my dad here to help carry stuff." Grabbing a suitcase and a carton, she headed for the door. "What floor are you on?"

The girl pulled a paper from her pocket. "Third." She said she'd flown from Telluride, Colorado alone. All the taxi driver had done was dump her stuff at the curb before roaring off.

"Didn't anyone come out here with you?"

She shook her head. "My ticket was expensive enough. No way my folks could afford another ticket."

They trooped up the stairs, grateful it wasn't as hot as had been forecast. Exiting the stairwell, Michaela put down the carton and flipped her hair back. "What room?"

The girl consulted her paper again. "Three twelve."

"We're roommates!" Unlocking the door, Micki nudged it open. "I hope you don't mind this side. I waited as long as I could before I had to pick one."

"That's okay. By the way, I'm Angela Martin; you can call me Angie."

"I'm Michaela Conwaye – Micki for short."

Angie, her four brothers and two sisters were all homeschooled; this was her first time being away from her close-knit family. As the youngest Martin, she was childlike in many respects, so she relied on Micki a lot, looking to her as sort of a big sister.

The next week, Gary could scarcely believe Micki was the same girl who'd sobbed plaintively that first night she wanted to come home. She chattered about classes, her roommate and her professors. She told him about people she'd met, places they'd explored, even a planned ski trip to nearby Mt. Tom.

"You don't ski," he reminded her.

"Angie's from Colorado; she said she'll teach me."

"Don't break anything," he said, smiling at her spunkiness.

"I'll be careful," Michaela assured him. "Oh, and I'm planning to come home for Columbus Day."

"Will you have time to see *me* when you're home? Or will you have forgotten all about me by then?"

"Of course I'll have time to see you," she said, twirling her ring on her finger. "What was your name again?"

He laughed. He needn't have worried; Micki was settling in fine.

Whenever Gary called the phone in their room, it just rang and rang. He wondered whether he'd written the number down wrong. Then, once, he got Angie. She seemed nice.

No, she said, Micki wasn't there; she was at the library. Or was it the pub? She couldn't remember whether it was free-photocopies-of-*Playgirl*-centerfolds night at the library or free-beer night at the pub. Either way, she'd be home late; did he want her to call? "Say, this isn't her father, is it?"

He laughed. "No. Could you just tell her Gary called?"

"Oh! You're the guy she was s'posed to have forgotten by now."

# Chapter 27

The girls talked nonstop on the 2:15 Greyhound. Angie was eager to meet Gary; and Micki, who'd last seen him seven weeks earlier, ached for his embrace.

Michael met the girls' bus and brought them home to freshen up. When he said he was taking them to Wong Lee's for supper, Angie grinned.

"Now I can practice my chopstick technique."

After lugging their bags to her room, Michaela phoned Gary. She returned dejected. "He's got plans." She slumped onto her bed. "*And* he'll be in Milford all weekend. He said he'll try to see me on Sunday. It's been like two months; you'd think he'd make more of an effort."

Michael ordered shrimp lo mein, and two orders of dim sum for the table; Angie chose General Tso's chicken. Michaela was torn between tangerine beef and mu shu pork. Consulting the menu a third time, she felt a touch on her left shoulder.

A voice behind her right ear murmured, "Get the mu shu."

Micki whipped around. Squealing, she leapt up, tipping her chair backward. "Gary!"

"Oof!" he exclaimed as she hugged him tight. Too tight. "You trying to kill me?"

She let go. "Sorry. I'm just so glad to see you!"

"I can see that." He righted her chair. "I wonder what I'd be in for if we'd been apart any longer."

"We'd be visiting you in the hospital," Michael joked.

Saturday morning, Gary brought the girls to the beach. Attila purred madly in Michaela's lap.

"See? I'm not the only one who missed you."

Micki hugged Attila, who continued to purr, drool and knead at her denim-clad lap.

"Me-you?" It was more a statement than the question it sounded like.

She giggled and put her face close to the little tabby's. "Me-you," she replied.

Angie, who'd only ever had barn cats, couldn't understand how a cat could be so glad to see a person. Or vice versa. She'd also never seen the ocean, so the jaunt to the beach was a real treat.

"It's not the real ocean; it's just Long Island Sound," Gary said. "Still, if you've never been, this'll do fine."

Angie was mesmerized by the waves' repetitive crashing onto shore. "It's so cool! All this water… and it keeps coming!"

She collected beach glass, amazed at the power of water and rocks to turn jagged shards into the smooth, opaque treasures that lay in her hand.

Leaving the girls meandering along the shore, Gary told them to come home when they felt hungry. When they returned, he was draining macaroni for pasta salad. He'd chopped peppers, tomatoes and hard-cooked eggs and whipped up an herb dressing with fresh parsley and basil. Grandpa had taught him to cover the herbs with burlap, to protect the delicate plants from frosts. That way, there'd be fresh herbs 'til well on past Thanksgiving, when Grandpa would close up the cottage for the winter and head back to Westville… until they renovated it for year-round living.

Over lunch, Gary suggested they stop in to see Martha. "She can't wait to see you. She's been dying to bake you some chocolate-chip cookies."

"Who's Martha?" Angela asked, a forkful of pasta poised at her mouth.

"My grandmother's best friend."

"Oh. Do your grandparents live nearby?"

"They used to live here. I inherited the place after they died. Martha and her husband, Sam, live four houses up" – Gary inclined his head toward the Johnsons' house – "that way."

After lunch, the trio trooped across the sand to pay the Johnsons a visit.

"Michaela, sweetheart! How are you, dear?" Martha drew the young woman into a massive hug.

"I'm fine, Martha. I've missed you," Michaela said, meaning it.

"How're you and Sam?"

Bolting to the door, Amber nosed her way between them.

"Amber!" Martha laughingly scolded the golden retriever. "You know better than that."

When Michaela introduced Martha to Angie, Martha motioned toward the door.

"Won't you come inside? I'll put tea on." She went inside, calling out, "Sam! Sam, come see who it is!"


(14 October, 1988 – Friday)

Joey knew Gary would keep his promise, but third-row floor seats were way better than he expected. "That was so awesome!" the teen exclaimed for what his brother was sure was the 50th time.

"It's kind of a rite of passage: your first rock concert" – Gary shrugged – "the kind of thing you do for your sixteenth birthday."

"Who'd you see?"

Bitterness rose like bile in Gary's throat. He shook his head. "I didn't."

"I thought you said it was the thing to do…?"

"I didn't have a big brother to spirit me off to concerts. I had Dad. Remember?"

At Gary's prickly tone, Joey fell silent. Their conversation had turned too dangerous for his liking: He didn't care to be reminded of Dad any more than Gary wanted to discuss Mom.

"That concert was so awesome!" he repeated after an awkward pause.

Joey carried his stuff up to the blue room. After playing with Attila for a few minutes, Gary joined him upstairs; they talked most of the night. For the rest of the weekend, neither mentioned the folks again. It felt unnatural, like ignoring a cow in the bathroom.


"How was the concert, honey?" Mom asked Saturday afternoon, when Joey called home.

"Awesome! Gary got us floor seats. Third row!"

"Wow! That's close." Her voice caught in her throat. "I-is your brother there?"

Joey glanced at Gary, slouched in a chair. "Uh… no," he lied. "I think he's over at Mr. Johnson's."

Gary looked up. His throat tightened. He went back to reading *Radio & Records.*

(23 October, 1989 – Monday)

The intercom buzzed. "Spike, I know you didn't want to be bothered; but Joey's on the phone."

"Thanks, Bren. Put him through."

Joey's voice sounded small, frightened. "I need you to come get me. At school…. the dean's office."

Tapping a pen against his desk, he checked the time: 11:10. *Crap!* He was swamped, and a big chunk out of his day was just what he didn't need. The memory of Dad's reaction when he got expelled stung like a swarm of hornets. *He needs you,* Gary chided himself.

"I'll be there in an hour," he told Joey.

Grabbing his keys, he stalked from his office. "My little brother's in trouble. I gotta go meet with his dean. In Milford. I'm sorry."

Pete waved off the apology. "Go. Do what you gotta do, Spike. Family comes first. If you're not back here by three, I'll cover your show." He reached into his desk drawer. "You might need this."


The polished-brass nameplate on the wall read, Dean Charles W. Littleton. Gary rapped at the open door.

The man behind the desk eyed him balefully. "Mr. Sheldon?" His tone was brittle and demanding.

"Yes; I'm Joe's brother, Gary. What seems to be the problem, Dean Littleton?" On a couch by a bank of windows sat a terrified Joey. He looked small for 17; he reminded Gary of himself – as an even younger teen.

"I asked Joseph to call his mother. I don't know why we ended up with you."

"Mom's out of town," Gary lied evenly. "How can I help?"

Keenly aware of his faded jeans and beat-up sneakers, he wished he'd remembered to put on the loafers he kept under his desk. At least his shirt was clean and pressed; and Pete had lent him that spare tie.

"Joseph was caught cheating on a midterm," the dean intoned crisply. "He'll be—"

"I didn't!" Joey blurted, leaping to his feet. "I wasn't! Gary, he's *lying!*"

Both men glared at him.

"That's enough out of you, Joseph," Gary barked. "We'll discuss it at home." Joey looked as if Gary had slapped him. "Now you sit yourself back down. And enjoy sitting while you still can."

Joey gaped at his brother. And, not wanting to take chances, sat.

The dean looked approvingly at Gary. "As I was saying, he'll be suspended. He's supposed to receive a failing grade for the term. But, as it was a first offense, the teacher agreed to factor the zero on this exam into his other grades."

Gary nodded. "I appreciate his leniency. And" – addressing Joey sternly – "I hope you appreciate what he's done on your behalf as well, young man. By the way, which class was it?"

"Anatomy & Physiology." Dean Littleton couldn't keep the dark amusement out of his voice. "Care to tell your brother what you were caught cheating on?"

Joey's fidgeting intensified; he stared at his shoes.

"Joseph" – the dean drummed his fingers against the polished top of his black-walnut desk – "we're waiting."

The teen squirmed. "Human reproduction," he mumbled.

"I'm sorry, I didn't hear you," Gary said, unwittingly adding to Joey's embarrassment.

He repeated it, barely audibly.

Gary shook his head. "You'll have to speak up, Joey. I can't hear you when you mumble."

"Sex! Alright?" Joey shouted, his cheeks scarlet. "It was about sex!"

Gary bit his lip to stifle laughter. "I see."

"Mr. Wells found answer sheets among the papers on Joseph's desk during the exam."

Gary glared disapprovingly at Joey, then addressed the dean. "Dean Littleton, be assured when I speak to our mother, she'll hear about this." Gary knew his meaning was not lost on Joey.

Gary followed Joey to his dorm. Several classmates, relaxing in a common area, hailed their friend.

"Hey, Joe – get some unscheduled vacation time?"

"Hey, maybe I shoulda thought of doing that."

Their laughter filled the room.

A scalding look from his brother silenced Joey's intended reply. Hanging his head, he trudged past.

Gary propelled him onward. "I suppose you think that's funny."

He shrugged, his bravado returning. "Well… yeah."

"It's not!" He spoke again inside Joey's room. "Pack your things. And get your books." Joey started to protest, but Gary was in no mood to be challenged. "I said, Get your books."

The earlier threat still in mind, Joey obeyed.

As they turned to leave, Gary spied something peeking out from behind the wastebasket. "What is this?"

Joey gulped. "It – it's… not mine."

Unsatisfied with his answer, Gary repeated the question. Slowly. Deliberately.

"Oh, c'mon, Gary. Don't tell me you never—"

"*What's it doing here?*" he roared, brandishing the half-empty Jack Daniel's bottle.

"I told you: It's not mine," Joey protested in a little voice.

"Don't lie to me, Joey. What's it doing here?"

"I don't know! It – it's not mine. That's just where Neil keeps it."

Gary grabbed Joey's collar. "If you don't start giving me straight answers – and I mean now – you're gonna wish you'd called Mom! Are you drinking?"

"Sometimes – we, um… it, uh – helps us… you know, um… relax. After a – a long day."

*Dear God, Joey's just a kid. Please don't let him be hooked on this crap already!* Gary masked fear with anger. "Do you know what the legal drinking age is in Connecticut?"

Joey shook his head.

"It's twenty-one. And unless my math is way off, Joey, you're nowhere near that!"

The teen's blank stare fueled Gary's ire.

"So help me, Joey, I'm warning you: If I ask you a question and you don't answer the first time, I'll put you over my knee. And don't you challenge me, 'cause I don't care if the whole *dorm* hears!"

Joey gulped, certain Gary's threat in the dean's office wasn't an idle one. And he was *really* gonna get it when they got home.

"Before we leave, I have one question. Your answer determines whether I pour this down the drain or go to the house master. Is it Neil's?"

The teen hesitated for half a second. "It – it's mine."

"You're sure about that?"

Joey nodded. "It's mine."

"Fine. I'll pour it out. And we'll deal with your lying at home. Understood?"

"Yeah," he mumbled, shouldering his bag of clothes. He knew

'dealing with his lying' probably meant a whipping. A huge one! He had distant, terrifying memories of hearing Gary getting it from Dad. And *he* always used the belt. Joey swiped away his tears so Gary wouldn't think him a baby.

The teen pointed over his shoulder as Gary turned toward the highway. "The cottage is that way."

"You're not on vacation, Joey. And neither am I."

Twice on the ride back to the station, Joey tried to tell his side of the story; both times, Gary silenced him with a sharp, "I said we'll discuss it at home!"

Pulling into his parking space just after 2:15, Gary issued a final warning: "You better be on your best behavior. You hear me?"

Joey nodded. He was beginning to wish he *had* called Mom.

"Omigod! Spike, is that your brother?" Brenda squealed as he entered, Joey trailing miserably behind him. "What a cutie! Denise, doesn't he look *exactly* like Gary?"

"Spike!" Denise exclaimed. "I didn't know you had a brother."

Brenda ran to find Lauren, so she could see the incredible look-alike Sheldon brothers for herself.

Gary tolerated the women's fawning for a few minutes. Then he retrieved his phone messages and hauled Joey into his office.

"Sit down. Don't touch anything," he warned, before heading to his boss' office.

"Hey, chief," Gary called from the open door. "Thanks."

Pete looked up as the borrowed tie sailed in and landed on his desk. "How'd it go?"

Gary scowled. "Suspended for a week. He's in my office now. I don't know what to do the rest of the week. I can't take all that time off to babysit."

Pete shrugged. "So bring him in. It's only four more days."

"That's not exactly professional."

"Well, we're pretty flexible around here; and anyway, he's not a toddler. He's not going to run around swallowing paper clips."

Despite his irritation, Gary smiled. "True."

"We can put him to work; he might even turn out to have some of your production talent."

"No. He's being punished for cheating. Turning him loose in production would be a reward. One he doesn't deserve. I'm not gonna send that message."

"Ease up, Gar'," Pete cajoled. "I thought you were more family friendly."

"Family friendly doesn't mean permissive. He called me instead of our mom; he'll have to deal with how I choose to discipline him. Which is, frankly, probably worse than anything she'd come up with." Slumping into a chair, Gary dropped his head into his hands, rubbing his throbbing temples.

"You're not gonna hurt him…?" Pete worried.

He shook his head, still resting in his hands. "Nah. I'm just too good at mental torture."

During the 4:00 news, the door to Gary's office opened. Joey looked up from copying chapter seven of his world-history text; Gary had told him to start on page 97. "How's it goin'?"

Joey pointed to the middle of the first column on page 99. "I'm up to here."

Gary perched on his desk; he flipped the book shut. "You can stop now." His earlier fury seemed to have evaporated. "C'mon."

Joey put down his pen, stretching his cramped fingers. "Where we going?"

"Thought you'd wanna see what I do around here, besides cause trouble."

His brother's smile meant everything to Joey.

Gary led him to the on-air studio. He plugged a headset into the control board so Joey could hear what went over the air. Putting on his own headphones, he signaled for silence. "After this break I can give you the nickel tour. Hang on."

Joey slid the headphones over his ears, enjoying being included in Gary's world. Admiration filled him with a warmth he hadn't felt in years. Beneath the newswoman's voice, music pulsed in his ears.

Gary spoke. "Thanks Lauren. It's five minutes past four on a gorgeous Monday. Good afternoon, I'm Gary Sheldon; thanks for letting me be part of your day. We're smack in the middle of New Music Monday. This hour, we've got Art of Noise, the Cure, a flashback to '84 from Bronski Beat… and your request, if you ask nicely." Joey heard the smile in his brother's voice. "Give me a call at 264-Z97-3 or 264-WZBX. Let's kick off hour two with Scritti Politti. 'Wood Beez' on Z97-3." Gary shut off the mic and took off his headphones. "C'mon, I'll show you around."

Just after 7, Gary steered Joey back to his office. He had three calls to return from West Coast record-company reps. And a fourth message: *Micki – confirming weekend plans.*

"Crap!" Crumpling the message, he shot it across the room, into the wastebasket. Gary phoned the record execs and shmoozed with two; he left a detailed message for the third. It was nearly 8 and he was frazzled.

"Come on," he said more gruffly than he intended. "Let's go."

The drive home was filled with the same icy silence that had marked the ride to the station. No sign of the affable Gary who'd been on the air an hour earlier.

Tossing Joey's satchel onto the bed in the guest room, Gary laid the bookbag on the desk. "I don't feel like cooking; whaddaya like on your pizza?"

Joey wouldn't meet his gaze. "I don't care," he muttered.

Gary leaned against the doorjamb. "What don't you like?"

Now Joey slumped onto the bed. "Nothin'."

"So if I order a squirrel and onion pizza, you'll eat it?"

Joey stared at his brother in horror. Did he really mean it? His tone sounded serious; some rural places probably *did* serve squirrel.

As kids, he could never tell when Gary was teasing. He might've been joking now, but there was no amusement in his voice. And he didn't want to eat *that!* Joey couldn't think straight. He'd been anxious and stressed all day; and even a decision about pizza toppings was too much to make.

Agitated and frightened, remorseful and ashamed all at the same time, he couldn't give proper voice to his pent-up emotions. Joey rocked back and forth on the bed, trembling.

Gary sat beside his brother and laid a hand on his shoulder. "You alright?"

The more the teenager fought for composure, the less control he had; he clutched his arms around himself. Gary's kindness now, his teasing before and his irritation and disappointment earlier left Joey at a loss. He couldn't relate to this brother who seemed at once angry and jovial.

Gary's hands worked the tightened muscles in Joey's shoulders.

Gradually the physical tension eased; but Joey's inner turmoil remained. Fury and compassion wasn't an easy combination to process. He took deep breaths, tried to calm himself.

"We need to talk, kiddo." Gary's tone was calm now; but if the anger returned, there'd be big trouble.

Gary's comforting touch made Joey feel all the more vulnerable.

Today was easily his worst day ever! He'd been suspended; Gary was gonna make him eat a horrible redneck pizza; and before the night was over, he'd get a whipping for lying about the liquor.

Joey flung himself into his brother's arms and sobbed. He tried to voice the fears that had plagued him all afternoon; incoherent babble spilled from his lips.

And that was okay. Gary held him close and let him cry it all out.

When Joey finally managed to find words, they left Gary cold. "I just don't want you to hate me!"

"Joey! Of course I don't hate you!"

"But I – I let you down, and I lied to you." Joey's face streamed with tears. "Please don't hit me, Gary. I know it was… and you said… about lying… but" – now hiccupping sobs took the place of words – "*please!*"

Gary had been right when he told Pete he excelled at mental torture; more so than he realized. He wiped away the overwrought teen's tears. "Joey, listen to me," he murmured.

Joey fell silent.

"You're my brother, and I love you. But about that cheating…"

The teen looked away.

Gary waited until Joey's eyes met his. "I meant what I said about being disappointed, and expecting better from you."

His gaze dropped. "I'm sorry."

"I know. And I think a week's suspension and a zero on the exam is plenty enough. For cheating. But," he continued, "there's still the matter of your drinking we need to discuss. And the lying."

Inching away, the teen shook his head; his tears began again in earnest. "Please, Gary. I won't do it again. I swear! Just please don't hit me."

Grandpa's voice filled Gary's head. *Need I remind you, boy: I caught _you_ smoking pot and never so much as laid a hand on you?*

*Yeah, but…* Gary shot back silently – until he realized he had no basis on which to argue.

*And you were _years_ younger than he is, so don't you start with me about Joseph's being underage.*

Gary considered that. *I suppose you're right,* he acquiesced.

He met his brother's gaze. "Promise me something."

Joey gulped. "Anything."

His eyes were kind, yet determined. "I want you to promise you won't drink any more alcohol 'til your twenty-first birthday."

Joey's gaze locked on his. "No more drinking. I *promise*."

"Okay. As long as you keep that promise, we're cool. Now, I'm gonna go order that pizza. What d'you want on it?"

Joey managed a little grin through what was left of his tears. "Anything but squirrel."

"I just don't want to see you screw up," Gary said over dinner. "Like I did."

Joey looked astonished. "How'd *you* screw up?"

He felt deeply ashamed to admit this, but there was a lesson to be learned. "Don't tell *anybody*; not even Mom. God, *especially* not Mom! You're the only one who knows – except Micki. Six weeks before graduation, I got kicked out of school."

"Wh-why?" the teen stammered, his eyes wide as basketballs. "What happened?"

Gary's cheeks reddened; he told Joey about how their drinking had led to monumentally bad decisions and – ultimately – Ellen's pregnancy and their subsequent expulsion. "Look, you've only got a few months left before you go off to college. Don't mess it up by drinking. Trust me on this."

"And what if I totally screw up at college? I mean, Grandpa paid for me to go to Milford Academy. And college afterward. If I flunk out, it's like I'm letting him down."

*The only way I'd feel let down is if he never gave it a try,* Gary heard the old man say. *I just wanted to make sure he had a chance.*

"Believe me," Gary told his brother gently, "nothing could be further from the truth."

After Joey went to sleep, Gary returned Michaela's call. She was disappointed he couldn't come up that weekend; but, knowing how important family was to him, she didn't fuss.

By Thursday, Gary felt justified in requesting Friday off. Confident Joey had learned his lesson, he saw no need to belabor the point; besides, they both needed a break. Their week together had been valuable; they'd bonded again. It felt almost like old times.

"I didn't wanna bring this up again," Gary told his little brother Friday morning as they walked along the beach, "but I need you to understand why I was so upset about your drinking."

"Okay." Nodding, Joey studied Gary's face; his eyes were dark.

Intense. And the little vertical lines between his eyebrows deepened when he got serious. They were little trenches now, like a miniature farmer had come by and dug tiny furrows.

"Dad's an alcoholic. And alcoholism runs in families, so seeing that bottle in your room *really* freaked me out. I love you, Joe; and I don't wanna see you go down that road."

"But Gary, just 'cause he's a drunk doesn't mean I'm gonna be. I mean, *you're* not…"

"I've had my difficulties with alcohol," he admitted. "I wouldn't necessarily call it a drinking problem. But maybe my refusal to call it that *is* a problem. There were times – and I'm not proud of it – times I turned to alcohol as a way out. Generally, knowing there's real potential for a problem frightens me into not drinking. But it's an ugly thing, alcohol is. And I'd hate to see you get caught in its web."

Joey nodded again. He felt safe here with his brother – so safe, he almost told him why he and Mom left all those years ago. But he didn't want to ruin how good he was feeling by getting Gary upset with him.

# Chapter 28

(20 December – Wednesday)

The stack of unopened cards on the table had grown too tempting to ignore.

"I love Christmas cards," Michaela said, bubbling with childlike enthusiasm; she reached for the teetering pile. "Can I open 'em?"

"Knock yourself out," Gary replied tersely. They reminded him of the innocent days of youth, before Mom left and destroyed him. Retrieving a letter opener, he laid it on the table.

Ignoring it, Michaela picked up the first envelope. No return address. Tearing open the flap with gusto, she gazed in delight at the scene on the front, silently read its inside message, then read the name aloud.

He looked up at the sound of her voice. "Huh? Oh, that's nice." Same with the next card: a glance, a nod, a disinterested, "That's nice." And on to the next one.

About halfway through the pile, Michaela asked, "Who's David St. Pierre?"

"I don't know David St. Pierre," Gary replied curtly. "Maybe it's addressed wrong."

Michaela checked. *Gary J. Sheldon, 17 Maxwell Road, Middlebury.* "It's right; even your middle initial."

"What's the return address?"

"Sparta, Tennessee."

"Lemme see." Taking the envelope, he studied it. *Mr. and Mrs. David St. Pierre.*

"Hmm." He handed it back with a shrug. "Open it."

Inside was a striking stained-glass image of the Holy Family; she stared at it, entranced. The printed greeting wished Gary blessings throughout this holy season and peace in the coming year. A photo landed, facedown, on the table. "Ooh – a picture."

Laying aside the card, Micki picked up the picture of a young family in holiday-motif sweaters, gathered around a professional studio's backdrop: a fireplace, with bulging stockings hung from the mantel. The blond man had one arm around his wife. In his other he cradled an infant; the auburn-haired lady also held a baby. Twins. A tow-headed boy of about three stood in front, holding a gift.

"What a cute family!" She handed Gary the photo, then read the signature. "Dave, Tanya, Danny, Spencer and Jessica."

As she read the names, his gaze landed on the mother; his heart skipped a beat. "No wonder I didn't recognize his name. I don't know *him*; I know *her!*"

"Who is she?"

Gary hesitated. "College girlfriend." He studied the photo, then smiled. "Haven't seen her in ages. Last time we talked was" – he paused – "years ago."

"She wrote you a novel in *here*." Michaela flipped the card across the table.

Seeing the hurt in her eyes, Gary captured her hand as it hovered in mid-air. "You have nothing to worry about. We dated for a year; she graduated and that was it. Only other time I saw her was my graduation party; my grandfather invited her. And I called her when he died. But I lost track of her years ago."

Michaela pouted. "I don't recall you ever mentioning her. You obviously meant something to each other."

"We stayed friends; but dating was geographically inconvenient. I didn't want a long-distance relationship, and she was dating some of Philly's most-eligible bachelors. Let's face it" – he flashed a self-deprecating smile – "I couldn't compete with that."

"Ah, but you *wanted* to," she hissed.

Gary wished he'd opened those damn cards himself! Or, better yet, burned them. He didn't want to get into a protracted argument over a non-issue.

"You have no reason to be jealous," he told Michaela curtly. "If I wanted to be with her, it would've been me in that picture, not Dave St. Pierre."

Gary reached for Tanya's card.

*Gary,*
*As you can see from the picture, a <u>lot</u> has changed in the last five years! Sorry I haven't been in touch sooner... and I feel just*

*awful about being such a lousy correspondent - but I lost your address when Dave and I moved, and I only just now came across it again… while packing to move again. I hope you're still living in the same place and this finds its way to you.*

*I trust Attila's taking good care of you. Please tell him I said "Me-you," okay?*

*It'd be great to hear from you again (hint, hint).*

*As of January 15, we'll be in Nashua, New Hamster (that's how Danny - our eldest - says it). I'd love to see you; it would be quite a road-trip… but less of a trek than traveling from Sparta (which, in case you were wondering, is a thriving metropolis almost 2/3 as exciting as Waterbury… YAWN!).*

*I think Dave's sick of hearing me tell Gary stories… especially since I can scarcely get through one of them without giggling irrepressibly (is that even a word?! I figured you'd know 'cause you're the word guy.). But I seem to have an endless supply of them - Gary stories, that is… we sure did have some fun, huh? Come to think of it, I seem to have an endless supply of words, too.*

*I hope I haven't rambled too terribly and you're not bored silly reading this (yep, I still have my remarkable self-esteem! I can just see you rolling your eyes and shaking your head). Have a wonderful Christmas! I know it's not your most-favorite holiday, but please know I've been thinking of you… and I miss you - and, as always, I love you.*

*Hugs and kisses (and a pat on the head to Attila),*
*Tanya & Co. :)*

Gary could practically hear Tanya speaking, in that endearing Midwestern twang. "She's a hoot!" He passed the card to Michaela, who sneered and tossed the card aside.

Next night, Gary was up to his elbows in dishwater when the phone rang. "Can you get that, please, honey?"

As she did, Michaela was greeted by an unfamiliar voice.

"Um, hello. Have I reached Gary Sheldon's home?"

"Yes," she replied guardedly.

"Oh good! Might I speak with him, please? This is Tanya St. Pierre; he'll know me as Tanya Jackson. I'm an old friend."

Without responding, Micki clunked the receiver onto the table and stalked into the kitchen. "It's *her.* Miss *Southern Accent,*" she mocked, mimicking Tanya.

Gary looked at her oddly for a moment. "Oh – Tanya!" Drying

his hands, he hurried into the living room. "Thanks, hon."

Micki slunk off to the bedroom, where, for the next half hour, she endured his laughter from the next room. Ordinarily, she loved that sound; tonight she felt betrayed by it.


When Gary came to find his fiancée, she was sulking. Stretching out beside Micki on the bed, he kissed her elbow.

She pulled as far away as she could without falling off.

"Leave me alone," she grumped.

He drew her close. "She's not so awfully bad once you get to know her."

"I don't want to get to know her." Resistant at first, she settled into his arms.

"I'm not saying I expect you to be best pals; but, come to think of it, you'd get along great. Just know this, Mick: I chose you. Not Tanya. *You.*" He gathered her hair into a ponytail. Nosing aside the collar of her shirt, he kissed the nape of her neck. "And there's no one I'd rather spend forever with."


The following weekend, Michaela and Marie scoured several bridal boutiques in New York. Nothing struck her fancy, until they were ready to give up. Then she spotted it. All the air rushed out of her lungs.

Marie, heading out the door, felt herself being yanked backward. "What?"

Michaela pointed toward a mannequin. "This is it." Her tone was hushed, almost reverent.

Plucking her size gown from its rack, she swept into the dressing room. Swiftly shedding her clothes – as if it could lose its magical quality the longer she took – she waited as Marie guided her arms into the pouf sleeves and allowed the satin to glide down over her body to her feet.

Only after it had settled into place with a luxurious swoosh did Micki dare to glance in the mirror. It felt as if it had been specially made for her.

"It looks *gorgeous* on you! Look at the train." Marie directed her attention to its intricately beaded lace insets.

Micki caught her future sister-in-law's eye in the mirror. "This is it," she murmured, hesitant to say it aloud, lest it not be real. "This is the dress!"

(9 February, 1990 – Friday)

Greg, now *Deacon* Greg Andrews, whom they had asked to officiate at the wedding, agreed to see Gary and Micki at his home for pre-Cana counseling instead of the parish center, so they could meet at night. While her husband met with the couple in his study, Kim busied herself in the kitchen, preparing supper for the four of them.

The young couple not only learned about themselves and their faith; they learned from Greg and Kim how to behave toward one another as a loving couple building a marriage centered in Christ.

Michaela loved watching them together, marveling at how they listened to each other – really listened – with their whole being, not just with their ears. And Greg's considerate manner in interacting with Kim made Gary realize even more his obligation to treat his bride-to-be tenderly, with respect and affection.

***

Meeting with a realtor was also on their to-do list while Michaela was home that weekend. Katie Gilchrist's bangle bracelets jingled as she shook their hands outside the first house.

"What an exciting time: buying your first house! Have you been married long?"

"We're not yet," Gary replied. "Not 'til August; but we're hoping to buy before then. Provided we find something we like."

That house was a no go. Same with the next: hardwood floors, big yard, front porch. But much smaller than they wanted, and on a busy street. The last three were no better. Micki's disappointment surged.

(9 April – Monday)

With Micki busy studying, Gary began doing the initial legwork on his own, weeding out houses that didn't meet their basic criteria; this way, all she had to do was look at actual prospects. That would save them the frustration of trudging through house after disappointing house. He leafed through a stack of printouts. Everything was either too small, on a busy street, had too few bedrooms or baths or had water in the basement. Or they just didn't "feel" right.

He flopped onto the bed to review printouts. He was sure he'd specified more than 1,600 square feet. The next listing was 1,212 square feet. Crumpling it, he sent it flying across the room.

Gary scanned the next sheet. It was a restored 1909 Victorian in

258

Southbury; gingerbread trim; 3,800 square feet; 11 rooms; five beds; three and a half baths; large, sunny eat-in kitchen; pantry; formal dining room; fireplaces in the living room, dining room and master suite; hardwood floors throughout; walk-up attic; newer roof and furnace; updated electrical system; finished basement; an acre-plus lot; wraparound porch; beautifully landscaped, park-like setting; paved driveway; two-car garage. It had everything on their wish list. And then some.

He scribbled a note at the bottom of the page.

Not even bothering to check the asking price, he flipped to the next listing. Seven rooms; three beds; two baths; easy-to-maintain yard. *It's probably about the size of a postage stamp.* He knew, from the description, Michaela would fall in love with that Victorian. He probably would, too; he was a sucker for a wraparound porch and gingerbread trim!

He turned back to the listing. Now he checked the price. Gary silently thanked Grandpa, for the umpteenth time. It felt great to never have to say, "It really *is* a nice house… and I know you really want it, honey; but it's out of our price range."

His thoughts drifted to Michaela; it'd been nearly a month since he'd seen her. Resisting the impulse to drive up to Amherst, he settled for a phone call.

"I'm glad you called; I'm studying for midterms," Micki told him distastefully. "What're you doing?"

"Looking at house listings."

"Without me?"

"Well, you're not here," he teased. "If you were, we'd be looking at 'em together." *That's not true. We'd be making out… and those listings would be all over the floor.*

"Can't you wait 'til I get there? I'll be home this weekend."

"I know you will. And I'm counting the hours."

"But you're still doing house stuff without me."

Gary groaned. "Yeah, but it's all the boring stuff you wouldn't be interested in. Besides, the more of this I get out of the way now, the more time we'll have for looking at houses when you do get home."

"Oh. Alright." Michaela seemed satisfied with his explanation. "Find anything good?"

The corners of his mouth twitched. "Oh, a couple of things."

"Tell me about 'em."

"No. You'll never be able to concentrate; and when you fail your midterms, I don't want to hear that it's my fault 'cause I never should have told you about those houses," he teased, his accent surfacing just a bit. "You just keep your mind on your studies."

***

Gary tapped his pen against the countertop, pondering the guest list during the news. *Sam & Martha. Marc. Joey (usher). Marie. Pete. Charlie. Brenda. Molly.* Glancing at the log, he pulled next hour's commercials, stacking them beside the cart decks. He cued three discs in the top row of CD players, then returned to the list. By Marc's name he jotted *best man.*

Micki's list was longer than his, but short by anyone's standards: Parents, grandparents, other relatives; a few friends. Two questions at the end caught his eye: Guests for singles? Friends of parents?

"Why not?" he said aloud, in answer to both questions. At least he didn't have to worry about inviting his parents' friends. A twinge of something – regret? – fluttered inside Gary. Suddenly, he really missed Grandpa.

The phone rang; he glanced at the clock. Lauren was still doing the news. "Hi, 'ZBX."

"Hi, honey."

"Hey, when'd you get in?"

"Little after ten. I took an early bus. What'cha up to?"

"Going over the guest list. Counting us, we've got thirty-one. Spouses and dates brings it to" – he did the math – "forty-eight. And to answer your other question, go ahead and invite your folks' friends."

"Okay." Michaela counted the couples with whom her parents maintained relationships. That added 10 more. "Guess we won't have any trouble finding a hall big enough, huh?"

"We could rent a phone booth. Or clear out that broom closet in your mom's front hall," Gary teased. "Or… do something non-traditional. Maybe Wong Lee's? They could handle sixty people."

"Ooh! I like that idea. My mom's gonna be really disappointed, though."

"Why? She doesn't like Chinese?" he asked, half-serious.

"She always wanted me to have this big, splashy reception. At some hall with a sweeping staircase and tons of flowers. Lots of big, smelly lilies. Somehow, I don't think this'll measure up."

"It's our wedding. If she doesn't like it, she doesn't have to

260

come. More egg rolls for us. Right?"

"I suppose. Is that what you wanna do?"

"We're there so much we're practically family. Anyway, why rent a big hall for so few people? Hang on a sec." Gary put on his headphones. "Thanks, Lauren. Six minutes past four on Z97-3. Good afternoon, It's Gary Sheldon, keeping you company this afternoon. Thanks for joining me. This hour we'll hear from Crowded House, Billy Joel and maybe New Order. Something you want to hear? Call me at 264-Z97-3. Let's kick off the hour with OMD: 'If You Leave' on Z97-3, WZBX." He hated working Good Friday; but in the house-hunting and pre-wedding frenzies, he'd neglected to ask for it off. "Listen, speaking of Wong Lee's, why don't we meet there for dinner. Say, half past seven?"

An hour later, Michaela cast aside book and notes in favor of a bubble bath. She settled amid the froth of orange-scented bubbles. She missed the soothing rumble of Gary's laughter and the security of his arms around her. Michaela slipped beneath the citrusy foam. Submerging entirely, she slowly surfaced, her sopping hair clinging to her shoulders. Each outgoing breath released more tension. She soaked a washcloth and wrung it out, letting scented water cascade over her body. She was still soaking when Mom got home.

"Kayla? Where are you?" Mom tapped at the bathroom door. "Kay?"

Michaela pulled out the stop; the water began gurgling away. "Be out in a minute."

"Good, 'cause we've got plans."

The water swirled away around Micki's feet. "What?" Wrapping herself in a towel, she hurried after her mother, leaving a trail of wet footprints. "Wait a minute. What plans?"

"The Ventrillos' engagement party." She unclasped her earrings. "You remember Tom and Carol; they were a few years ahead of you in school. We're due there at seven."

"I can't go. I've got plans."

"I promised them," Mom said in her *I'm-in-no-mood-to-be-trifled-with* voice.

"You can just un-promise them, then. I'm seeing Gary."

She waved a hand. "Oh, you can see him anytime. This is an event."

"Not my problem, Mother."

"What will Bob and Alicia think when you don't show up?"

"I don't care what they think." Micki thumped down the hall to her room, leaving her mom sputtering.

"Michaela Rose, you come back here! Do you hear me? Come back here this instant!"

Micki clicked her bedroom door shut, muffling Mom's shouts.

But her voice grew louder, nearer and – if it was possible – even angrier. "I told them we'd be there. And I won't let you embarrass me!"

Michaela continued toweling her hair. "Mother, I told you: I'm seeing Gary tonight. We're—"

"But it's Tom and Carol's en*gage*ment party," Mom interrupted in the whiny, cajoling tone that always infuriated Dad.

"I don't *ca*-are," she mimicked. "In case you've forgotten, Gary and I are engaged, too. And we have wedding plans to make. That's what we're doing tonight."

"But I promised Alicia!"

"Oh, Mother, quit whining! If she'd wanted me there, she could have made an effort to contact me, instead of telling you at the last min—"

"She invited us weeks ago. I just didn't have a chance to tell you. I wa—"

Micki flung the door wide. "You knew *weeks ago* and you didn't have a chance? Forget how to use the phone, did you?"

"Don't you take that tone, Lady Jane! I just forgot to tel—"

"No you didn't; you meant to spring it on me, so I couldn't get out of it. Well, I've got news for you. I won't be dragged to parties simply because you've got no one to go with. You can't order me around like a child. I'm an adult, with plans of my own. If you'd told me sooner, Gary and I would have happily gone. But this is unacceptable!"

Mom stood in the doorway. "How dare you! You say you're not a child, but you're acting like one. As for being an adult: If that's what you are, then just pack your things and go!"

"Fine." Micki flung down her towel. "Enjoy your stupid party!" Resisting the urge to slam the door, she quietly shut out the image of Mom's face.

Struggling to stay calm, she told herself it would be fine; but no amount of convincing could stop her tears. She piled clothes into suitcases. On her bed sat the stuffed pooch Dad won for her at a carnival before she started chemo. Crumpling onto the bed in tears, Michaela hugged Smedley.

From her earliest memory, the click of high heels in the hallway meant Mommy was going out. The sound stopped. There was a rap on Michaela's door.

"Leave the key on the table."

The clicking resumed along the hall and downstairs, then faded as Mom left.

As she always had, Michaela went to the window seat. Mommy would invariably turn to see her face pressed to the glass, smile and blow a kiss, waving goodbye to the little girl in the window.

Without looking back, Mom got into her car and drove away. As her blue Toyota chugged up the street and rounded the corner, a piece of Michaela's childhood died.

Gary was alarmed at the urgency in Michaela's voice. She'd been fine, if a little bus-weary, when they'd spoken two hours earlier.

"My mom threw me out."

He knew that fluttery, displaced feeling. "It's gonna be okay. Sit tight 'til I get there."

When he arrived, he hugged Michaela, then carried her hastily packed things to the car.

Micki looked up at him, her tearful eyes begging. "I wanna take Ginger. Can we? Please?"

"Lease says only one pet," Gary replied, bringing on a storm of tears and pleading. "But it also says no wild parties, no nails in the walls and no two-bit disc jockeys. We'll smuggle her in."

She packed Ginger's things into a box; Gary lugged it out to the car. Coming back inside, he put an arm around Micki. "How about you leave your mom a note?"

Sniffling, Michaela pouted and hugged Ginger. "No." At Gary's raised-eyebrow response, she said, "Gary, this wasn't my idea."

"You should keep an avenue open for communication." He hated the idea of the two of them ending up like Dad and him. In spite of everything, he regretted their estrangement.

"Gary, please… can we just get outta here?"

"No." He shook his head. "Not like this. It's not what you want; you said so yourself."

Mewing in protest, Ginger clawed at Michaela's sweatered arms. "C'mon, Gary; Ginger's getting cranky."

*She's not the only one.* "Then put her down." Gary's words were staccato; his exasperation mounted.

"She'll hide."

"So put her in the car!" Dashing the keys onto the countertop, Gary reached for the wriggling cat.

The waterworks started. "Why're you being so *mean?*" Michaela demanded as Ginger scrambled to get free.

"I'm not. I just can't understand why you're being so stubborn." His impatience was directed as much at his own years of pighead-edness as hers. Gary carried Ginger to the car. Returning to the porch, he sat beside his pouting fiancée. Now she *really* reminded him of a 6-year-old. "I know this is hard. Can we talk about it?"

She shook her head.

"Why not?"

She clasped her arms about her knees and trembled; a tear slid down her cheek. "I don't wanna."

"Leave her a note. She'll feel better knowing you took the time to reach out. You will, too. Trust me."

In the end, she agreed. She left a brief note on the kitchen table, with the key taped to it.


(2:30 p.m., 14 April – Saturday)

Michaela cuddled close to Gary on the couch, tucking her feet beneath her. "Hey, Gar'?"

Slipping Grandpa's rosary beads back into his pocket, he kissed her nose. "Hmm?"

"About the wedding. I do like the idea of having it at Wong Lee's" – she picked at her nail polish – "but I think we should have a regular reception." Micki scrunched up her nose. "I'm sorry I'm so indecisive."

*Well, you excel at it.* "Whatever you want."

"One other thing?"

He smoothed a wisp of hair away from her face. "What's that?"

She chewed her lip. "I want you to invite Tanya and her family."

***

Easter at Michael's was awkward. It was the first holiday since the divorce was finalized. While he'd held out hope of reconciling, he had to accept the reality of his marriage's demise.

With great trepidation, Michaela told him about her new living arrangements.

"You know I don't approve." He looked from Micki to Gary. "And don't try to tell me she's sleeping in the other bedroom, Gary, 'cause I don't buy it."

Gary's candidness startled Michael. "No, she isn't. But, there'll be nothin' goin' on 'til we're married." He reached for Michaela's hand. "I promised Micki that three years ago, sir. And I intend to keep my word."

That afternoon, Gary asked to speak to Michael alone. "I've given this a lot of thought," he said as they stepped onto the porch. "I know it's a little unusual…"

Michaela awakened tearful and agitated on Monday – the second anniversary of her assault. Gary did his best to distract her. While out running errands, he took a circuitous route that avoided the park. After going to the bank and the pharmacy, he took her out to lunch.

Then they went to look at the yellow Victorian. As they pulled into the driveway, Michaela gripped his arm. Her eyes lit up for the first time all day.

"This is it," she murmured. "Gary, this is the house!"

He smiled. "Why don't we have a look inside before you start sending change-of-address cards?"

Micki gave him that look, the one that meant, *Why can't you just trust me?* and tried to make light of it. "Oh, al*right*. If you insist." She paused. "But mark my words: This one's it."

"From what I read, it sounds just about perfect; but they don't have to know that. So, play it cool, no matter how wonderful it is," he cautioned. "If you're not sure what to do or say, follow my lead. Okay?"

Michaela loved how Gary's eyes held her gaze when he spoke to her. She loved how he made her feel so loved, so secure – so cared for. And if he wanted her to act noncommittal, she would happily comply.

He kissed her. "Good. Now let's go check out our house."

Although she wanted to burst, Michaela remained dispassionate. Quietly elated, she squeezed Gary's hand during the walk-through, murmuring occasional comments. He'd nod or squeeze her hand in reply, doing his best to seem reserved. The sellers' realtor answered all their questions thoroughly and efficiently.

"It's perfect!" Michaela squealed as they drove away. "I told you that was the house!"

He smiled. "That you did."

She grabbed his arm; she couldn't believe his calmness. "Aren't you excited?"

"Not yet. We have to make an offer. Then get it accepted; that can take ages. We have to get a lawyer; do credit checks, get home inspections – all that stuff. Settle on a date, go through closing and *then* I'll be excited."

Micki pouted. "Do you always have to be such a grownup?"

Gary patted her hand. "Just don't get your hopes up, honey. I mean, what if someone swoops in and buys it first?"

She gnawed at her thumb nail. "I hadn't thought about that."

He loved her naïveté. "That's something we have to consider."

Her enthusiasm wasted, Micki rode the rest of the way in silence.

On Thursday, his office phone rang. Lifting the receiver, he tucked it between his shoulder and chin. "Music department; this is Gary."

The voice was crisp, businesslike. "Mr. Sheldon? This is Rebecca Deasy. From Sage-Bonham."

"Yes, Rebecca; what can I do for you?" Turning to a clean sheet of paper, Gary jotted notes as she spoke. "I see," he said at last. "Thanks very much, Rebecca. I appreciate your letting me know."

Graduation. Michaela's birthday. House hunting. The wedding. Car shopping. Glancing at his notes, he scratched one item off the list and smiled. "One down; four to go."

"I don't care. Just pick one," Micki had told him after their fifth test drive. "My brain's full of finals and wedding plans; there's not a scrap of grey matter left for cars."

*One of us should drive a sensible car.* Gary was secretly glad it wasn't him.

It was May 22 – Michaela's birthday – when Rebecca called back with the news: The contract was ready.

At graduation the following Sunday, Gary gave Michaela roses. Inside the card was a doodle of her in the driver's seat of her new car. "This'll have to suffice for now," he said, his eyes as mirthful as his tone.

Michaela, expecting the Honda, was speechless when she saw the dark-blue BMW out front.

# Chapter 29

Michaela didn't take the news well. "I *told* you we should've made an offer right away! Doesn't it bother you, losing that house?"

"Some. But it's not the end of the world. Besides," Gary said, "sometimes contracts fall through. If it does, I promise: We'll make an offer."

"What are the chances of that happening?" Micki grumbled.

She had more reason to be grouchy three weeks later, when a *Sold* sign replaced the *Under Contract* one.

(9 June – Saturday)

Gary had the top down in the Camaro and they were eager for a relaxing weekend at the cottage. Scraps of wedding chatter and stretches of easy silence intermingled with mews from the cats in their carriers.

Michaela had secured a small banquet hall at the Terrace Room in Southbury. Their guest list had swelled to 80, including Angie's family; Tanya, Dave and their brood; a handful of Gary's boyhood friends and relatives on his mom's side.

Micki bubbled about menu selections, seating plans and flowers.

As they approached Milford, Gary wondered aloud how Joey was doing.

"Why don't you call him?" Micki suggested. "Have him stay the weekend."

Joey had weekend plans, but suggested they meet for dinner. "I'll finally get to meet Michaela. About time, too; I've only been hearing about her forever."

They picked him up at 6:30 and went to Angie's Pizza Barn; the trio laughed and talked easily over a large sausage-and-mushroom pizza and a pitcher of Coke. But when he learned the all-night grad party at Pomperaug was the same night as his own graduation, Joey accused Gary of avoiding it because he didn't want to run into Mom.

"That's not true," he half lied. "You know I'd go if I could. But this has been scheduled for… well, ever since the last one."

"I thought family was important to you," Joey grumbled.

"It *is* important, Joey. You're important! If I could get out of it, I would. You know that."

*****

That Friday, they addressed wedding invitations. Micki struggled mightily over whether to invite Susan.

"Send it," Gary suggested. "If she ignores it, it's her loss. But if you don't invite her, you might end up regretting it the rest of your life."

Her smile mocked him. "Why don't we invite *your* mother, too?" She thrust an invitation at Gary. "No time like the present to re-establish contact."

He shoved it away, his old insecurity surfacing. "I'm not inviting that deserter to our wedding!"

Micki slapped her hand on the tabletop. "Now you know how I feel." Flinging the list at him, she retreated to the bedroom.

Five minutes later, Gary appeared in the doorway, half expecting a tirade. Getting none, he sat beside his fiancée.

"I know the past few months have been rough," he murmured. "It's hard to fix a relationship once it's damaged… or severed. I'm sorry."

"I'm sorry, too," Michaela said in a tiny voice. "I shouldn't have needled you about your mom." She snuggled into his arms, loving how they fit together so nicely.

Back in the kitchen, they resumed their task. Gary's hand shook as it grasped the invitation he just couldn't bring himself to address. "What if she doesn't come?"

Micki saw fear of rejection in his eyes. Deep inside her poised, caring fiancé was an angst-ridden teenager whose mother had left without saying why; his spirit was so withered, another rebuff could be disastrous. She put down her pen and reached for Gary's hand, the one still clutching the foil-lined envelope.

He dropped the envelope and stared at it. It felt like admitting defeat. Just beneath Gary's wounded pride swirled deep-seated, immobilizing fear. What if he invited her? What if she came? It had been so long, he had no idea what he would do if he saw her again.

It was easier not to have to think about it.

Michaela slid her arms around Gary. "It's okay; we don't have to invite her." She stroked his hair. "Maybe we can go visit her some day. The two of us together. How would that be?"

His breath was a strangled rush. Trembling, he began to nod… shook his head… then shrugged. "I dunno," he whispered, clinging to her.


(10 a.m., 11 August – Saturday)

In the vestibule of St. John of the Cross Church, Michaela waited with the rest of the wedding party; when their cue came, Marie and Joey began the procession, with Angie right behind. Trish followed.

The women were resplendent in tea-length, royal-blue silk. The rich color accented Angie and Marie's auburn hair and Trish's classic red Irish tresses. Short, slim and fine featured, the trio could have passed for sisters. Their bouquets of ivory roses sported shiny, triangular-leaved ivy trailing over the sides.

The men wore grey tuxedos; their boutonnières were ivory roses with sprigs of ivy.

Micki's bouquet of ivory roses trembled in her hands; her throat tightened. The moment she'd waited for – waited years for! – was finally here. A few minutes from now, she'd be Michaela Sheldon. She looked down the aisle and saw Gary standing with Marc at the side of the sanctuary.

*He's so handsome!* Michaela took Dad's arm, just as she had during the rehearsal, and began the long trek up the aisle toward marriage.

On each side were the smiling faces of everyone they loved. The satin swoosh of her gown sounded to her like crashing waves; she was sure it was drowning out the string quartet. And still, there was Gary. He smiled and, as their eyes met, her butterflies vanished.

Michaela's ivory-satin gown was edged with lace; a full skirt accentuated the intricately beaded bodice. The neckline was a modest vee; her flowing tulle-and-lace veil featured the same iridescent-beaded lace as the cathedral train.

She'd been so old-fashioned about not wanting Gary to see it. Not just conventional; she was almost frantic. And he'd teased her mercilessly the entire time it hung in the spare bedroom.

"I'm just gonna take a look at your dress," he'd say casually, sauntering toward the closet door.

"Don't!" she would screech, flying across the room to block the door with her body. Gary would laugh and hug her; while her arms were around him, he'd reach behind her to jiggle the doorknob, setting her off again.

But now he was glad he'd indulged her. He smiled; she caught his eye. Her return smile lit her face.

At the sanctuary, Michael kissed Michaela, greeted his imminent son-in-law and extended his best wishes. He took his place beside Joey as Gary took Michaela's hand to escort her to the altar. Trish and Marc stood alongside.

Gary's CCD students all sat together; nobody giggled, whispered or caused any disruption during the ceremony. But when Deacon Greg pronounced Gary and Michaela husband and wife, the children cheered wildly.

Just before the final blessing, a teen in the last row of students came forward. Gary and Micki looked at one another, then at the boy, curious. Nearly rivaling Gary in height, the teen stepped up to the lectern, adjusting the microphone.

"Would Gary's CCD students please stand?"

At the great rustling of clothing and programs, Gary glanced back; he was greeted by a grinning wall of children, aglow with a collective secret. Some of them waved excitedly. He gave a small wave back.

They'd bugged him all year about the wedding date; he figured a handful might show up for the ceremony. He never expected this.

"For those of you who don't know me, I'm Ryan Campbell; I was in Gary's first CCD class."

The wedding guests looked back at the teenager, politely mute.

"Gary, over the course of the past eight years, you've taught nearly every student in the CCD program. Now, in case you've lost count, that's a hundred sixty-two of us. You've been a teacher and a friend. You were there whenever we needed a grownup to talk to, someone to listen and care about us." An appreciative murmur ran among the rows of students. "We wanted to do something special, to thank you for everything that you've done, and been, for us." He fidgeted as nervousness took hold. "But we weren't sure what to do."

Still focused intently on Ryan, Gary took his bride's hand.

"We wanted you to know how much we love you – and we wish you both all the best. So we'd like to invite everyone down to the parish hall, for punch and cookies."

Gary swallowed hard. Looking over at Michaela, he saw love and admiration in her eyes.

Micki squeezed Gary's hand and, smiling, whispered, "Well? Say something."

His eyes misting, Gary stepped around her train and approached Ryan. Giving him a heartfelt hug, he patted the teen on the back.

"Thanks, Ry." Gripping the sides of the lectern, he looked out at the sea of expectant faces. "What can I say? I'm *deeply* touched" — smiling, he motioned to Michaela — "We both are. This means so much to us. On behalf of my wife, our families and friends, we'd be honored to join you. Thank you all."

Gary returned to his place beside Michaela to hoorays from the children. Once his back was safely turned, he flicked away a tear.

Fr. Dave invited everyone to stand. Issuing the final blessing, he sent the newlyweds forth amid a fanfare of trumpets and spirited organ music.

As shouts of "They're coming!" rang out, older students poured punch and set out cookies while the littlest ones stood ready.

Whooping with glee, they showered the Sheldons with confetti, which Kim had heaped into baskets. The kids tossed handful upon gaily hued handful in the air. The fluttering rainbow blizzard settled in their hair, on their clothes, in Michaela's veil.

As the newlyweds made the rounds, chatting with everyone and thanking them for the lovely reception, Kim made an announcement. The children were excited about seeing their teacher and his bride exchange vows, but disappointed they wouldn't see their first dance. Moving to an old piano they'd wheeled in, she beckoned Ryan, Sara McKeon and Jessica Donahue forward.

"I know you considered having this as your first dance; and we hoped to persuade you to have an unofficial first dance here."

"How sweet," Michaela cooed, taking Gary's hand.

The trio, about to start high school, had all been in his first class; they waited expectantly.

"No. Absolutely not," Gary replied flatly, his expression somber. "No unofficial first dance."

Kim stared in dismay. Gary had never denied a student anything; she couldn't believe he'd start now.

Michaela turned to her husband, astounded.

Gary squeezed her hand. "No *unofficial* first dance," he repeated, breaking the awful silence. "But we'd love to have our *official* first dance here."

The children cheered; the youngest among them leapt up and down, hooraying. Kim sat at the piano and began the opening bars of "When I Fall in Love."

Joining her husband at the center of the circle of guests, Micki felt like a princess; what's more, she felt safe. She loved the security of being in Gary's arms as he danced her around the room. And she felt a surge of gratitude to Gary's students for helping to make their wedding day so special.

Afterward, the wedding couple breezed over to thank the trio of singers. And Kim.

Kim hugged them both. "I love you guys. When they said they wanted to do this, I was happy to help."

At the Terrace Room, Trish, Angie and Marie whisked Micki into the bridal room to bustle her gown and fix her hair while Gary, Marc, Joey and Michael hung out in the groom's lounge.

Gary checked his watch again. "Women! Is this what I've got to look forward to the next fifty years?"

Michael's smile was wistful. "If you're lucky."

It was then Gary realized Susan was absent.

After Deacon Greg gave the blessing, Pete asked the guests to remain standing and raise their champagne glasses. He handed the microphone to Marc to make the toast.

"I gotta tell you a story," Marc began. "When Gary said he asked Michaela to marry him, I asked him, *Do you have a date?* He got this strange look on his face and said, *I get to bring a date?*" When the laughter died down, he continued. "When he asked me to be best man, I was almost speechless. *Almost*," he repeated over a twitter of laughter from the station staff. "All kidding aside, Spike: I'm truly honored. We've been friends, what, forever? I can't tell you how happy I am you've found such a wonderful lady to share your life. Michaela is a treasure. And I'm not just saying that 'cause her dad's" – he pointed – "right there. I really mean it. I wish you both a lifetime of companionship, lasting friendship, true happiness and the blessings of many children. I don't have to wish you love, because you already have that. To Gary and Michaela… cheers!"

Pete reclaimed the microphone. "Marc, that was lovely. Truly. But you forgot to mention a lifetime of hot, guilt-free sex! Gary, you get two minutes for rebuttal."

Ooh, rebuttal; I like this," he said with a chuckle as Pete handed him the microphone. "Whatever we're paying you, double it. Now, unaccustomed as I am to using one of these," he quipped, wielding the microphone, "thank you, Marc, for that beautiful, touching and, may I add, surprisingly clean toast. You had me worried there for a minute. Fortunately, we have Pete to make the base comments you so kindly omitted." Grinning, Gary took Micki's hand. "And Marc, you're right: She is a treasure and I am truly blessed to call this woman my wife."

Amid "awww"'s from the guests, Michaela blushed deeply and kissed her husband.

"But, there's more to that story Marc was telling. What he didn't say is that when Michaela found out he was best man, she asked, *So, why should I marry _you?_*" Gary leaned to kiss his bride; she drew away, eyes dancing. He grinned. "Ooh, I'll be payin' for *that* later. But before I end up permanently in the doghouse, let me say this: Thank you all, for your love and support – and for being here to celebrate with us today."

Between courses, Pete summoned Gary and Michaela to the dance floor for their "second first dance." Their guests applauded enthusiastically; a few shrill whistles punctuated the air.

"That's our cue," Gary whispered. "Ready, Mrs. Sheldon?"

Michaela's fingers curled around his; her lips turned upward in a blushing smile as they swept out onto the dance floor. She smiled demurely as Gary took her in his arms amid the opening notes of "Follow You, Follow Me."

Now and then, they murmured the sweet things newlyweds whisper; mostly, though, they gazed at one another adoringly.

All afternoon, they danced and laughed and visited with friends and family. As Gary had predicted, Michaela and Tanya got along famously; before the day was over, they'd already made plans to spend Thanksgiving in New Hampshire.

Gary was thrilled to see so many of his cousins; he watched in amusement and alarm the mannerisms that mirrored those of their parents. Tim's voice had the same cadence as Uncle Jonathan's; so did Josh's. And Liz and Marnie looked just like Aunt Joanna. That threw Gary because, being sisters, she and Mom had always looked alike. And now the girls even sounded like her!

Naturally, his cousins asked where his folks were.

"Oh, they couldn't make it," he replied glibly. He didn't care that none of them believed him.

Gary watched as Micki danced with her dad. He recalled going over music with Pete after work one evening.

"Okay, she's gonna dance with her father; you dancing with your mom?"

He'd shaken his head. "No."

"Lousy dancer?" Pete kidded.

"She's not invited." And he'd left it at that. Now he felt a twinge of regret. Pushing it aside, he looked around the room.

Everyone seemed to be having fun. But one detail still needed attention.

Joey pocketed the keys Gary gave him and clapped him on the shoulder. "It's all under control. I feed the cats once a week, return your tuxedo Thursday after next and plan to be out of town on Friday."

Gary socked Joey's arm playfully. "You missed the part about spilling grape juice on Michaela's gown."

Joey snapped his fingers, blue eyes gleaming. "I *knew* I forgot something!" He paused. "And thanks, Gary, for letting me crash at the cottage while you're gone. It's been awful at home lately… like Mom's losin' it or something."

For once, thinking about her didn't hurt. He shrugged. "You're her last kid; you're about to leave the nest. That's gotta be hard on her. You're *always* welcome there, Joey. It's your home too," Gary said, not even realizing how much he sounded like Grandpa at that moment.

# Chapter 30

Outside the cottage, Gary grinned at Michaela. "We're home, Mrs. Sheldon."

"Yes, we certainly seem to be, Mr. Sheldon."

He carried his bride over the threshold, then chased her up to the rose room. Upon opening the door, Micki noticed hundreds of pale-pink rose petals scattered across the bedspread; she turned to Gary. His fingers grazed her cheek.

"I wanted tonight to be special for you," he murmured, nuzzling her throat.

She pulled him close, enjoying the warmth of his body. "You mean, for *us*." She tilted her head up for a long, slow kiss.

After changing, they headed out for a romp in the surf, laughing and splashing – and kissing. Plenty of kissing. When they tired of playing, they ran back toward the cottage, tracking sand inside.

Stripping off each other's swimsuits, they kissed in the kitchen. His mouth descended on hers with a need surpassing mere sexual desire. He'd longed for this woman fiercely – longed for her for years! And now, at last, she was his wife.

Micki's heart thumped; her mouth felt dry. The buzzing in her ears grew louder as they made their way up to the bedroom. Their bedroom. Her hands roamed lightly over Gary's skin, reveling in its smoothness over nicely toned muscles; she sighed in anticipation.

He caressed her body, smelling now of sweat and salt water. Nuzzling her throat, he kissed his way to her ear and nibbled it.

"You know," he suggested, "we might enjoy this more after a shower."

After turning off the water, Gary licked at the droplets clinging to her skin. Starting at her cheek, he kissed a path down her throat to one breast. His erection pressed insistently against her hip.

Warm waves of pleasure surged through Michaela as Gary awakened passions she'd locked away after her assault. Amid the swirls of vapor mist, she moaned softly and dropped her head backward, arching her back. "Mmm! Oh, Gary, that feels so good."

Scampering back down the hall, they climbed onto the marital bed; Gary coaxed Micki toward him, drinking in the smoothness and the fresh, clean scent of her golden-tanned skin. Moving as one, they caressed and loved each other, kissing, touching and whispering sweetly together amid fresh, crisp sheets.

All night, they slept and awakened, satisfying their passions as the mood struck. Just after 4, Gary slipped away, returning with champagne and strawberries, to entice his beloved.

Kissing Michaela awake, he chose a berry and held the succulent morsel to her lips. Micki savored the sweet juiciness of the plump fruit. They kissed, softly at first, then with mounting desire. She tasted of strawberries and champagne. Setting their crystal flutes aside, he slid his arms around her and pulled her atop him again.

In the morning, Michaela watched Gary sleeping; he looked so peaceful she hated to wake him. But she'd waited a long time to make love with this man; now they were married, she wasn't about to wait any longer. Pulling back the sheet a bit, she drew it down to the middle of his chest. He had a beautiful chest. Nicely defined, just muscular enough, with a few stray hairs. Her fingers danced, feathery soft, over his deeply tanned skin.

Gary let out a little "mmm" and kept on sleeping.

Tugging the sheet back, Michaela was gratified to see he wasn't entirely unresponsive; her hand crept downward. A Mona Lisa smile played about her mouth as her caresses were duly rewarded. Licking her lips, she purred aloud in anticipation.

His eyes fluttered. Watching his wife's face in profile, he smiled. As her mouth engulfed him, Gary reached out a hand and stroked her hair. His "Good morning" was a whispered sigh.

Startled, she turned to face him, her cheeks flaming.

"C'mere."

At his invitation, Micki moved into his arms.

"Hello there, Mrs. Sheldon," he whispered, nuzzling her earlobe.

Ticklish, the young Mrs. Sheldon giggled. "Why, hello there, Mr. Sheldon," she murmured, smiling as Gary raised himself onto one elbow. Her mouth yielded to the pressure of his.

Michaela still tasted like strawberries. Gary maneuvered over her, nudging her legs apart.

Quivering at his touch, she groaned with delight and wrapped herself around her husband's firm body as he slid inside her.

"Is this what you were looking for under those sheets?" he teased gently.

Micki sighed in breathless pleasure, laying her head back against the pillows.

His smile was slow, tempting. "I'll take that as a yes."

***

Charlie and Janice Burns had celebrated their 30th anniversary at the Red Thistle Inn last fall. He called it "one of the most romantic places in New England."

He'd been right: David and Elaine Burroughs had mastered the art of romantic hospitality in their charming New Hampshire farmhouse.

At work in the flower beds when the Connecticut vehicle pulled in, Elaine wiped her hands on her jeans and greeted the couple by name. She poured them lemonade and pointed out the common areas before showing them to their room.

The innkeepers left a "honeymooners' basket" in the Sheldons' room. It held a selection of fresh fruit, six of Elaine's raspberry scones (perfect for snacking on after lovemaking) and jars of her locally famous strawberry-plum jam. Tucked into the basket were scented candles, chocolates, a certificate for dinner at a local eatery, a bottle of champagne and etched crystal flutes. The attached card offered "Best wishes for a lifetime of happiness" and, as a gift from the proprietors, half off their first night's stay.

Their week flew by, amid sightseeing, antiquing and prowling through little out-of-the-way shops – and, as Micki's cousin Joannie put it, "some really hot honeymoon sex."

The days were sunny, the nights crisp as fresh apples; but Thursday was damp and chilly – unusual for August in New Hampshire. At least, that's what the locals said.

Driving back after dinner, Gary squinted past the frantically flapping windshield wipers. "This weather is just awful."

"No it's not," Michaela replied, patting his thigh. "It's perfect for snuggling by the fire."

When they got back, Gary built a fire in the parlor; they claimed a loveseat by the hearth. Two other couples, drawn by the inviting crackling of the fire, settled in the parlor, too.

Tim and Cindy, also honeymooning, were from Texas.

"Tim's been up here on business," the pert redhead twanged. "He said it was lovely; I couldn't wait to see for myself. He's right! It's plum gorgeous!"

Jack and Marjorie, in their 60s, were living out a lifelong dream: a full year of traveling, spending a week in each of the 50 states. "Enjoying our golden years," Marjorie said, patting her hubby's cheek.

Gary asked what they planned to do the remaining two weeks of the year.

Jack chuckled. "We figured we should probably take two weeks' vacation."

After awhile, Micki quietly related her cousin's honeymoon-sex comment.

Gary snickered. "We'll have to see about that, won't we?"

Excusing themselves, they scurried upstairs.

***

The Sheldons checked out right after breakfast Sunday. They wanted to get an early start, beginning with Mass at St. Thérèse of Lisieux, a quaint stone church by the town green.

Mid-afternoon, they arrived at Shepard Seaside Cottage, a rustic getaway in Freeport, Maine. Almost before the car pulled to a stop, Michaela had torn off her seatbelt. She scampered up the steps, turning to survey the surroundings. "Gary, this is fabulous!"

He carried their bags. "C'mon, let's go see what the rest of the place is like."

The days were idyllic, the nights filled with passion. They strolled along wooded trails from the birch-treed grounds to nearby parks; snuggled in the hammock-for-two; enjoyed quiet moments watching the water from a large rock overlooking the craggy shoreline. They meandered along the streets of Freeport with hundreds of other late-summer tourists and took the obligatory prowl through L.L. Bean.

Michaela wondered what had gotten into Gary when he insisted on buying a heavy brass door knocker in one of the little antique shops in Yarmouth. "We don't even have a proper door to put it on," she complained bitterly.

"You never know when one'll come in handy."

She stalked off, muttering that she'd never figure men out.

That night they feasted on lobster and wine at the Haraseeket Inn, the door knocker and her hostility forgotten. For the moment.

Later, curled up on the loveseat, Micki looked up from her fat novel. Spurred on by his frivolous purchase, she asked when they would resume house hunting.

"I dunno," Gary replied absently, glancing up scanning a map. "We'll find something when the time's right." He patted the bed. "C'mere. Let's see if I can't help you forget about real estate for a while."

"I thought you wanted to find a house before we got married," she grumbled.

He shrugged. "Well, we didn't. And I'm sorry, but no amount of pouting can change that."

Grouchy because her period was due, she wasn't sure what she'd wanted to hear – but that wasn't it. Besides, she felt all bloated, and nowhere near amorous. Cursing, she flung her paperback.

Gary ducked; the book bounced off the headboard, thumped to the floor. He peered over the side of the bed at the unlikely missile, then at his scowling wife.

"I thought you liked Rosamunde Pilcher," he mused, unruffled.

His tranquility annoyed Michaela even more. "Oh, shut up," she snarled, stomping out of the bedroom.

Gary let her go. After several minutes, he went to the kitchen to make tea.

Bringing the hot brew outside, he found his grumping bride on the porch, gnawing at an aqua thumbnail.

Standing over her, he removed the hand from her mouth.

"Hey." His voice was as soft as the breeze that stirred the leaves overhead.

Michaela stopped rocking and met his gaze; her anger dissipated.

Bending, Gary kissed his wife on the forehead, then offered the steaming mug. "It's orange spice."

Her favorite. He was also holding her book. Beset by hormones, she began to bawl.

Setting the mug and the book on the floor, Gary gathered Micki into his arms. She resisted at first, then settled against him.

"I'm sorry," she sobbed, ashamed. "I'm so sorry!"

He stroked Micki's hair, dried her tears and kissed the tip of her nose. "It's okay, sweetheart. No harm done. Look, I know you're disappointed. I promise, we'll start looking the minute we get back. Alright?"

***

Michaela was dozing before they left Maine. She awakened as Gary pulled off at a rest stop on the Mass Pike to find a bathroom and grab some shut-eye. Finally, they reached the Exit 9 toll plaza, the start of I-84, which would bring them home. And still she slept.

From time to time, Gary would steal a glance at her. Her long lashes cast shadows across her cheeks as the late-day sun bathed her face in a ruddy glow.

At last Micki stretched, gave a big yawn and opened her eyes sleepily. "Where are we?"

He patted her leg. "Outside Manchester. 'Bout an hour to go."

"You must be exhausted. Want me to drive for a while?"

Gary stroked her cheek with the back of his hand. "That's okay, baby; you rest."

A sly smile crossed her lips. "You planning on wearing me out again tonight?"

"Perhaps."

"Mmm." Laying her head back, she shut her eyes and smiled.

Gary recalled that morning's spirited lovemaking. Odd how the dynamic sex that so invigorated him had left her completely wiped out. He grinned. *Whatever works.* Come to think of it, he'd probably need to rest up, too. A shiver of delight or anticipation – he wasn't sure which – shot up his spine. *Man, it's gonna be a hell of a long hour!* Besides being awkward, the throb in his jeans was distracting.

*Think of something to make it go away. But what?* Gary snapped his fingers: the bane of husbands everywhere. The throbbing ceased. It left so quickly at the thought of his mother-in-law, he was afraid it just might be permanent.

His sudden burst of laughter at the ridiculous, albeit horrifying, notion startled Micki.

"What?" she asked, rubbing her eyes. "What's wrong?"

"Nothing; sorry, hon." The corners of his mouth twitched. "Go back to sleep."

It was nearly 4:30 when Gary stopped at the traffic light off exit 15. He was sure the braking would awaken Michaela again; but she was sound asleep. It wouldn't be long now.

"Honey, wake up," he cooed a few minutes later, nudging her arm. "We're home."

Her eyelids fluttered open; her blue eyes still looked sleepy. She yawned hugely and stretched, rubbing the sleep from her eyes.

"Have a nice nap?" he asked.

"Mm-hmm." Half asleep, she nodded and kissed her husband.

Eyes bright with anticipation, Gary watched as Michaela realized they were outside the yellow Victorian. The *sold* sign was gone.

Micki opened her mouth, but no words came out. The freshly painted house looked more beautiful than ever. New dark-green shutters graced the windows; the gingerbread trim adorning the wraparound porch and peaked roof was the same hue. The porch had received a fresh coat of yellow paint, its turned-wood posts boasting light- and dark-green accents.

A banner across the porch read, *Welcome Home, Michaela & Gary!* Clusters of gaily colored balloons swayed in the late-August breeze.

"Gary!" she breathed, putting a trembling hand to her mouth.

"Welcome home," he whispered, leaning to kiss her. He guided her up the walk. On the porch, they embraced enthusiastically.

"Do you like it?"

"Are you kidding? I love it!" She was shaking. "And I love you!"

"Then it's okay I went ahead and bought it without asking you? I know we agreed we wouldn't make any major purchases without consulting each other."

A broad smile spread across her face. She squealed with delight and hugged him. "I guess I'll let it slide just this once."

Gary found the keys where Joey had left them. "Ready?"

The Sheldons swept into their home. Lifting Micki off her feet, Gary whirled his wife around in the open entryway; they whooped and rejoiced, their excitement ringing throughout the house.

But their glee was short lived.

# *Chapter 31*

After walking through the new house, Gary and Michaela checked messages. There were several: mostly friends calling to say what a lovely time they had at the wedding, or welcoming them home; and one from Lisa at the crisis center, offering Michaela a full-time job. The most unsettling message was from Lucy Desmond.

"I know you're on your honeymoon, but when you get back, it's urgent I speak with you." The parish secretary left both work and home numbers, reiterating her need to speak with Gary as soon as possible.

Micki went upstairs to unpack while Gary returned Lucy's call. Ten minutes later, he appeared at the bedroom door. Before she could ask what was wrong, he'd crossed the room and enveloped her in a hug.

"Gary? What're you doing?"

He just held her tight.

"Honey, what's wrong?" she asked, concerned.

Gary pulled away, his face a mask of devastation. "Sit down," he said dully, slumping onto the bed.

Apprehension gnawed at Michaela as she sat beside him. "Gary, what's the matter? You're frightening me."

Gary drooped forward, elbows on knees and head in his hands. "Kim's dead," he intoned sluggishly.

Micki's gasp tore through the room. "Kim *Andrews?* How?" She laid a hand on his shoulder. "Honey?" she prompted gently. "What happened?"

"She was hit head-on. By a drunk driver. Tuesday before last."

"Oh my God! Gary, how awful! Poor Greg!" She shook her head, unable to grasp the enormity – the permanence – of it. *What would I do if Gary was taken from me?* Michaela couldn't even console herself by thinking it couldn't happen; no one was guaranteed anything… not even a couple as in love as Greg and Kim. In an instant, their future was snuffed out. Shattered.

Right away the Sheldons went to be with their friend.

When Grandpa died, Greg and Kim had given Gary such comfort; they afforded him a safe space to grieve. And when he and Michaela began pre-marital counseling, long talks with Kim allayed his apprehensions. "You'll be a wonderful husband," she'd said as they sat in her 4th-grade classroom one Saturday last May, "a terrific dad. I see so much good in you, Gary. I wish you'd recognize it in yourself."

"I hope you're right," he'd fretted. "I mean, we're both so young. I don't feel ready."

Kim had soothed his nerves with a smile. "That's what these sessions are for, silly. Look, when you got your first radio job, they didn't sit you at a microphone and say, 'Here ya go, kid – knock 'em dead!'… did they?"

"Of course not."

"So, why would you think we'd let you jump into something as life changing as marriage without the necessary preparation?" Her smile had reassured him more than her words.

He'd shared other concerns, too: about their ability to grow together in faith; fears over his being able to make Michaela happy; and his mounting insecurities about fatherhood, in light of his own upbringing.

"I've seen you in the classroom," Kim reassured him. "The kids adore you; you're so good with them. As for your faith: Stay close to your beliefs – and your wife. God will give you the grace you need to face all these things. And more." It was then she confided her struggle with infertility. "It's taken a toll on our marriage. But our faith in God, and each other, keeps us strong." She shrugged. "Who knows? I might never have babies of my own; but Greg and I both know whatever happens is in God's hands. It's all part of His plan for us."

*How could this be part of Your plan?* Indignant, Gary railed at God on Kim's behalf. *What possible reason could You have had for letting her die like this – and so young? How dare You!*

He gripped the wheel so tightly his fingers hurt. She'd been so trusting in God's plan; and this is what He did to her! Gary reached over and clasped his wife's hand. When she sniffled, he turned to look at Micki, who turned big, sad eyes toward him; tears slid down her bronzed cheeks.

Gary squeezed her hand. "I know," he murmured. He held tight to it the rest of the way there.

The Sheldons encouraged Greg to share his story and his pain.

He didn't want to; rather, he tried to get them to tell him about the honeymoon. At last, over coffee, he relented, without dredging up any of the awful details. He admitted it did help to talk about it; and he thanked them for listening.

When the conversation dwindled to uneasy silence, Michaela went to rinse the cups.

Gary stood. "We won't keep you, Greg. We just wanted to say how sorry we are, and how awful we feel that we couldn't be here for you." He enfolded his friend in a comforting embrace.

When Micki returned, she hugged him, too.

"Oh, and I didn't tell you the worst part," Greg said, meeting Gary's gaze again.

Gary steeled himself for the news. "What's that?"

"Kim was eight weeks pregnant. She'd just found out. That's why she'd gone to the doctor. She called from his office to tell me. That was the last time I ever heard her voice – last time I ever spoke to…" His words trailed off to muted cries as he crumpled onto the couch.

Micki went to get him some water.

Gary sat beside Greg. "I'm so sorry. I know how long you and Kim prayed for that news." He clasped his friend's hand.

When Michaela returned, the two men's heads were bent close together; they were deep in prayer. She set the glass on the coffee table and retreated to the kitchen. Presently, she rejoined them.

Little by little, Greg was borne up on their prayers, filled with a sense of momentary comfort.

The late-August sun had begun to set when Gary and Michaela returned home.


(25 November – Sunday)

Traffic wasn't too bad. Micki smiled drowsily at Gary. "That was fun," she said, recalling her chat with Tanya while the guys and the kids watched the Macy's parade.

He smiled. "Yeah, it really was. I'm glad you enjoyed yourself." Impatient with the distant radio stations' signals fading in and out, he slid *She's So Unusual* into the tape deck.

"*...well yeah, I know but when we did, there was one thing we weren't thinkin' of and that's money...*"

Michaela whimpered; her face contorted. She looked like she was having a seizure.

"Micki? Are you alright?" When she didn't reply, Gary called her name again.

"*...we'll be your friends, we'll stick with you 'til the end; ah, but everybody's only looking out for themselves...*"

Tears began to squeeze out from beneath Michaela's clenched-shut eyelids; her shuddering intensified. And she couldn't stop that awful gurgling sound!

Gary pulled out of traffic, onto the shoulder. "Micki? Honey... What's the matter?"

"Make it stop – please... make it stop," she begged, clamping her hands over her ears as the gurgle persisted, louder now.

"I thought you liked Cyndi Lauper..."

"*...we don't pull the strings. It's all in the past now—*"

"*Please* – make it stop," Micki moaned, huddling into a ball. "Just make it stop!"

He pressed "eject." The singing stopped. After several moments, so did her strange twitching. And the gurgling, rushing noise.

Micki's whimpering subsided; her tightly scrunched body went limp. Her head drooped. She clutched her arms around herself. Rocking forward and back, she wept softly.

Shaken by her odd behavior, Gary pressed her for an answer. "Baby, what's wrong?"

At first, she didn't reply. Just sat there rocking. After he repeated the question twice more, she seemed to acknowledge his presence. She swiveled her head, studying him fixedly. Her intensely blue eyes grew larger as she tried to take in what he was asking.

"Micki, what's the matter?" His eyes were the color of rained-on slate.

She shook her head. "I dunno. I couldn't stand that noise."

Searching her memory, she struggled for answers. Her favorite singer shouldn't evoke such a reaction. *And what was that horrible gurgling?*

After an uneasy silence, she asked, "Do we have any OMD?"

***

Michaela wanted to spend Christmas at the cottage. Gary tried to beg off, but she was persistent. She wanted their first married

Christmas to be special, she told him.

"*Please*," he begged Marie the next night. "It'll feel more like Christmas if you're there."

"I can't. I already have plans. Besides, shouldn't you two start some new traditions all your own?"

Gary sighed. She was right. "It won't be the same without you."

Next he called Sam and Martha. Surely *they'd* be around. It was a tradition.

"Thank you, dear. But we'll be spending the holidays with our grandkids in Arizona. It won't be like Christmas Eve here… and certainly not a white Christmas. But we'll be thinking of you."

Gary felt empty inside, and sad. Not as sad as that first Christmas without Grandpa, but still sad. *Was it five Christmases ago already?*

***

(3 December – Monday)

"What're you doing for Christmas?" Pete asked over lunch. "Aside from hosting the Holiday Bash?"

Gary contemplated his wonton soup. "Micki wants to spend it at the cottage."

"You don't sound very enthusiastic. Santa bring you too much coal as a kid?"

Gary smirked. "Yeah. You found me out. Anyway, we celebrate Christmas Eve; it's an Italian thing."

"Since when is Sheldon an Italian name?"

"It's not," he admitted. "But Arena, Sciocco and Annunziata sure are." Gary hadn't given a thought to his wise, caring Nonna Annunziata in ages. His maternal grandmother was a short, round woman with twinkling eyes and a smile that could light up Milan for a month! She smelled of basil and fresh-baked bread, and her comforting arms were always ready to offer a hug.

Nonna had never approved of Dad; she was ahead of her time in thinking Mom should have given her children her own surname instead of their father's. "He'sa no good, that one. He gonna end uppa hurta you family," she warned.

When Gary landed his first job, Nonna had patted her teenage grandson's cheek. "Ah! The announcer. You live uppa you name… Annunziata," she'd told him in proud but broken English, her mouth drawn upward in a gap-toothed smile.

Almost 15, he hadn't given her words more than a passing thought; now he did. "Annunciation" – when the Angel Gabriel appeared to Mary to announce she would bear the Christ Child. *The announcer. Fitting,* he realized with a wan smile. For that matter, Sciocco meant silly. *Silly announcer. Now, that's <u>really</u> appropriate!* Gary pondered his soup again.

***

Arriving home on Christmas Eve, Gary kissed Michaela beneath the mistletoe in the doorway. He took a whiff of the mulled cider she handed him. "Mmm. Thanks."

The warm, spiced brew felt soothing all the way down his throat. As he entered the living room, sudden movement in the kitchen caught Gary's eye.

"Merry Christmas," Marie, Sam and Martha greeted him with one voice. A moment later, he was being embraced by six arms all at once.

"How did you know to do this?" he asked Michaela when the others broke their affectionate huddle.

She shrugged. "I wanted to know what traditions you loved. So I went to the experts."

Marie grinned conspiratorially. "You married a very wise, very clever woman, little brother."

Gary framed his very wise and very clever wife's face. His voice was rough with emotion. "Thank you. This is the nicest gift I could have hoped for."

In the middle of the night, Michaela awoke, hungering for Gary. When she nudged him, he didn't stir. She tried again. No luck. She began nuzzling his neck, stroking his chest.

"Mmm," he purred at her touch.

Okay, that was a start; but he was still asleep. She slid one hand down beneath the sheet to awaken the important – and, frankly, easiest – parts first. As she fondled him, he stirred. She was kissing his nipples when he opened his eyes and smiled. Reaching out a hand, he caressed her shoulder, smoothed her hair. Michaela turned to Gary in the dark, folding her hands over his chest and laying her chin atop them.

"What're you doing?" he whispered.

He could hear her smile and feel the seductive throatiness of her voice vibrating against his chest. "Just wanted to see if you were awake."

"So what's the verdict?" he asked as Michaela continued where she'd left off.

She looked up from kissing him; she squeezed a hand around his erection. "You are down here."

Awake was an understatement. Even in the darkened room, he could tell she had that wicked grin on her face, the one that usually meant he was about to get really lucky.

Michaela nestled against her husband; she wanted him badly. Gary pulled her on top of him; she let her breath out in a slow sigh of longing. She was wet and ready; he slid easily inside her, rocking slowly, gently, beneath her. She met his upward movements with her own downward thrusts. Michaela had always delighted in his exquisite tenderness in making love.

But tonight she churned with passionate urgency; she needed his strength, his power. She wanted – no, *needed* – to feel the weight of Gary's body against hers.

Whispering her desire, she slid off him. Rolling onto her back, she drew her knees in to her chest, opening herself to him fully.

But Gary murmured a craving of his own; he knelt before his wife and kissed her. She was on fire where his lips nuzzled and sucked.

Her insides burned for wanting him; spasms of pleasure coursed through her body as his mouth took in her warm sweetness. When he'd taken his fill of her this way, he gave Michaela what her body begged for. Her knees trembled as he penetrated her – deeply but gently.

She wanted it harder and told him so.

He obliged and was gratified when she let out a purr of delight. Her moans intensified as her desire surged. Clenching her legs around his hips, Micki bucked furiously. She raked her nails across his back. Passion surged through her as she stretched up to kiss him. Twining her fingers in his hair, she pulled him close. Their mouths met with breathless passion. His kisses left her giddy; and ohh, he tasted wonderful! – warm and strong – and just slightly of her sweetness. She kissed him again, wondering if her kisses tasted like him after she'd gone down on him. The mingled scents of sex, sweat and salty air excited her. Gary slowed his pace. The frenzied buildup intoxicated Micki as much as the release, and it was heaven to feel his body moving with hers, without that sense of urgency.

She touched Gary's face with gentle fingers. "I love you."

His reply was a smile and another kiss.

By the time he rocked with the staggering orgasm that exploded deep within Michaela, she'd rushed headlong into a second climax, pulsating and sweetly satisfying.

Sweating and spent, Michaela wrapped herself around Gary and held him close, not letting him pull out. The heat of their bodies intensified. "That was amazing," she sighed, breathless.

Gary was drenched with sweat; his scent intoxicated her. His tongue coaxed her lips apart, his mouth kissing hers languidly as he lay atop her. "Merry Christmas, baby," he murmured.

"Mmm. Merry Christmas." Micki loved feeling his body against hers. "Ohh… you feel so good."

Gary lay inside her, stroking her still-quivering body. She smelled all warm and sexy. He kissed her throat. His mouth ran along her throat, the back of her neck and down her shoulder.

Easing himself off her at last, Gary snuggled behind his wife and wrapped his arms around her, kissing her tenderly.

Sleepy and sated, Micki drifted off to sleep. Gary continued to nuzzle her neck, breathing the musky, intoxicating aroma of warm, sexually satisfied female.

# *Chapter 32*

(26 January, 1991 – Saturday)
Almost asleep, Gary considered letting the machine answer, but that ringing was making his head throb. Reaching over, he grabbed the receiver.

"May I speak with Gary Sheldon, please?"

He didn't recognize the voice; a glance at the clock told him it better not be a telemarketer! He tried to keep the irritation out of his voice. "This is he."

"Mr. Sheldon, I'm Garrison Hathaway, your father's attorney."

Listening to the surf crashing outside, Gary sat up and blinked the sleep from his eyes. "Go on."

The Garden State Parkway was 50 miles of slush; and, as if that weren't bad enough, Gary groused about the roads the whole way.

By the time they reached Pine Cove, his nerves were shot and Micki was ready to slap him because he was wearing on hers, too. At least they'd taken her car; the Camaro was useless in snow.

They met Marie and Joey at a coffee shop in town. Just back at NYU after semester break, Joey was annoyed when Marie called to say she was picking him up – and to bring a dark suit.

"She doesn't get it," Joey grumbled. "Skirt-chasing old buzzard meant less than shit to me." He turned to his sister again. "Why should I even be here, after what he did?"

"Just play along for three days," she chided. Before Gary could speak, she poked a preemptive finger into his shoulder. "Same goes for you."

***

Marie looked sophisticated in a dark-blue tailored dress with gleaming gold buttons. Her hair framed her face like an auburn halo.

Gary shifted in his seat, staring at the sleek wooden coffin. "I hate these things," he muttered.

Michaela laid a hand on his other arm. "Won't be much longer."

He rubbed his throbbing temples. "It's already been too long."

Marie nudged Gary, nodding discreetly toward the door. "Get a load of this one."

A bleached blonde wearing a black jacket and leather miniskirt teetered in on four-inch heels; her hair looked like it had been styled by a tornado. She approached, clutching a wadded-up tissue in one red-lacquered hand. Dabbing at her eyes behind oversized dark glasses, she knelt at the coffin and began wailing loudly.

"Girlfriend," Joey whispered to his sister-in-law. "I counted at least three already. I predict a catfight before the night's over."

The siblings and Michaela stood to greet the squalling blonde; she embraced them, blubbering damply against their respective shoulders before wobbling to the back of the room. She collapsed onto a couch to moan.

A surge of people entered. Some were lawyers from Jeremy's firm, all in pricey three-piece suits. Gary recognized a frail elderly couple from their old neighborhood. He spoke quietly with Dad's law partners, accepting their condolences; he shook others' hands, thanking them for coming. The old couple he hugged.

Pete never spoke, just hugged him. As they parted, he squeezed Gary's shoulder.

Gary appreciated his making the three-hour trek, but hoped he didn't realize it was a wasted trip; his own presence was a farce. He was glad Dad was dead, and secretly hoped his demise had been long and painful.

Gary hugged Marc. "Thanks for coming. It means a lot to me." Suddenly he realized it did.

Sometime later, an attractive dark-haired lady approached, her dark shoulder-length tresses secured by a tortoise-shell hairclip.

Hands raised, Gary drew away from her intended hug. "Don't," he warned.

"Gary…" She reached a hand toward him.

His response was an icy glare.

"I'm so sorry," the woman whispered before moving on.

Gary turned his attention to another former neighbor. "Oh, Mr. Brenner, how good of you to come…"

The funeral director glided in to say the priest had arrived to conduct a prayer service.

Afterward, Gary introduced his wife to the former dean of St. Joseph Academy.

Michaela accepted the priest's outstretched hand. "Bet he spent an awful lot of time in your office."

Fr. Maynard laughed. "That he did. Still in the radio biz, Gary? Or have you got a real job now?"

"No honest work for me, padre. Still doing radio. In Connecticut. What're you up to?"

Fr. Maynard indicated his brown robes. "I'm still a priest."

"And still a smart aleck."

"Much to my provincial's dismay," he acknowledged with a grin.

Later, when only the family remained, the shunned woman approached.

"Get out," Gary commanded. "You know how: Just walk away. No need to say goodbye. I mean, why start now?"

This wasn't the reunion she'd envisioned. "Sweetheart, please." Her voice cracked. "Let me explain."

He scowled, then grudgingly relented. "I'll give you two minutes. Which is more than you deserve."

She looked from Gary to the woman beside him.

Gary drew a protective arm around his wife. "This is Michaela. Micki, this is" – his pause was long and deliberate – "Diane."

"Pleased to meet you, Michaela." Her eyes rested on Michaela's ruby-accented Claddagh ring. She patted the younger woman's arm. "Would you excuse us a moment?"

"Uh, y-yeah, sure." With an uneasy glance at Gary, Micki drifted toward Marie.

"I see you like them young. Just like your dad."

Gary bristled. "What's that supposed to mean?"

"Don't tell me you never knew about your father's… pastime."

He'd never felt any particular allegiance to Dad; but she didn't have to know that. He folded his arms. "Don't turn this into a Dad bashing."

She held up her hands. "I'm not. I just want to clarify—"

"Clarify *what*? You walk out without even *goodbye*; and now you dance back into the picture and expect a warm welcome? Well, *fuck you!*"

"I wrote you—"

"Yeah, a note. You left me a fucking note. That's how you said goodbye!"

"No, Gary. I wrote to you every week."

"*Bullshit!*" he hissed, mindful to keep his voice down. "I never got anythi—"

"Your father intercepted my letters," she said softly. "He never let me talk to you, either. And we called every week. That's why he changed the number."

Gary recalled the locking mailbox, the abrupt switch to that unpublished number. Tears stung his eyes. Angrily, he smeared them away. "I don't believe you."

"Ask Joey. He wrote to you, too." She clamped a hand to her mouth, stifling a cry. "You think I'd keep my sons apart if I could help it?"

Gary's insides seared with rage and longing. He felt nauseated. "Then why did you leave?"

"Because, sweetheart, I *had* to."

"*Why* did you have to?" he demanded. Now he was crying, too.

"He threatened to kill Joey." She wiped away tears. "I'm sorry I didn't take you, too. I've regretted it every day. I figured you could defend yourself, or at least stand up to him." She blew her nose. "I was sick with worry over Joey; he was just eight, and your father threatened his life. Gary, he would have killed him! I put up with him beating me for years, for you kids' sake, but when he threa—"

"That's a lie! I never saw—" He stopped. He *had* seen evidence of Dad's brutality against her. Twice. The first was when he was 12. Mom said she banged into the stove while cleaning the kitchen; he believed her. The second was three years later, after Dad's temper had become more volatile. She was due to meet a friend for lunch, but they were in the midst of a long talk. Mom brushed her hair, keeping eye contact with her teenage son in the mirror. As she raised her arms to secure her hair, her sleeve slid back.

Gary had gasped at the hideous blue-green discoloration, but she waved off his concern. "I hit it on the car door the other day. Right on the corner, too!" The bruise was too big for that. It looked like she'd been grabbed – by someone who meant her harm. He didn't contradict her outright; but he'd heard the late-night arguments, even what sounded like slaps. Still, he never wanted to acknowledge what he knew was going on. But now she'd admitted it.

Gary felt ill. He waited to hear what she had to say about his challenge. His denial. His lie.

Lifting her chin, Diane met her son's gaze for the first time in 10 years. "Of course you didn't. He was shrewd, seldom left marks where you kids would see; if he did, I covered them."

Gary inhaled sharply. "If you knew what he was capable of, why'd you leave me there?"

The pain in his eyes flooded her with guilt. "I hated to do it, Gary. But you were settled at St. Joe's. I knew you'd never forgive me if I made you leave Ellen. Besides, I didn't expect he'd hurt *you*; Grandpa said he'd cut him out of his will – and you know how money driven your father was."

Gary looked away, then into Diane's sad grey eyes. She opened her arms to him, beseeching. He didn't back away.

"Mom," he whispered, choking back tears. "I'm sorry."

"I'm sorry, too, honey. I'm so sorry about all those years we lost. I love you, Gary." Night after night – year after year – she dreamed of this moment; at last she held her son in her arms again. She had agonized over her decision to leave, and ached with his loss. But now he was here; everything was alright again.

Gary wept. Mom was here, and she loved him! Nothing else mattered. All those years of hurt and rejection were gone in an instant. Wiping away her tears, he kissed her on the forehead and said the words she'd longed to hear for years. "I love you, Mom."

The following night, they met Diane for dinner at Franco's.

Her favorite bistro hadn't changed in the dozen years since she'd last been there. She swirled the wine in her glass. "Guess who I ran into yesterday."

Gary reached for his water goblet. "Who?"

She took a sip, set the glass down. "Ellen."

He nearly choked. "Yeah?" He tried to sound casually interested. "How is she?"

"Great. She's got a little girl now… Erin; she's eight," Mom said, without doing the math.

"Really?" He stared at his roast duckling, hearing only fragments of Mom's words amid the whoosh of blood in his ears. "…darling little girl… so sad… not married." Gary still couldn't respond.

"I'm really surprised you didn't know," Mom said again.

"We lost touch after high school," he intoned.

"That surprises me. You were so close, I always thought you

would've—" She smiled apologetically at Michaela. "Sorry, dear; I didn't mean – well, they just always seemed so perfect together. She asked me to tell you she's sorry… about Dad." Mom pulled a piece of paper from her purse. "Give her a call; she wanted to know what you're up to."

Gary let it drop onto the table.

Diane excused herself to use the ladies' room. As she left, Gary's shoulders sagged. "That was brutal." He crumpled the paper and tossed it into the ashtray.

Michaela touched his wrist. "Aren't you gonna call her?"

"Are you kidding? After that colossal lie? How could you think I'd want to talk to her?"

"But, honey… What about Erin?" she implored. "Don't you want to see your daughter?"

*My daughter.* He struggled for air. "You can't even imagine."

She squeezed his hand. "Then do it." Plucking the paper from the ashtray, she smoothed it against the table and handed it to Gary. "Erin deserves to know she's got a daddy who loves her."


The siblings had agreed someone should stay at the house. Marie and Joey both refused, so Gary and Micki reluctantly agreed. That night, they sat up late, talking. Before kissing goodnight, Michaela convinced Gary to confront Ellen about her lie and get to know Erin. He promised to call the next day.

Late at night, something nudged Gary from sleep. It felt strange, being here as an autonomous adult, no longer fearing Dad.

He wandered the house. It felt like trespassing when he opened the door to the study; it was Dad's refuge, his sanctuary from his family. Not sure what he was searching for, Gary walked to the massive cherry desk and sat in the matching chair. He had a sudden flashback to a scene in here when he was four. Daddy had spun him silly in this creaky old chair. In his head, he heard his gleeful giggles; but the memory saddened him. *Why didn't I recall these times while he was alive? Why didn't he? Why couldn't he remember we were happy once? Why couldn't he remember he loved me?*

Leaning back, Gary propped his feet on the desk, like Dad used to; it made his spine feel weird. He sat up. Tugging open the center drawer, he peered inside. Black pens. All facing the same way in their niches. In the paper-clip well lay a silver key, probably to the drawers at the right side of the desk. Gary turned the key, heard the works rearrange themselves. It felt like an unseen hand was guiding him through his late-night scavenger hunt, like Dad wanted him to find something. The drawer slid open. Inside were file folders. All neatly labeled. Mostly work related. Or home-maintenance stuff.

He removed a folder at the front: *St. Joseph Academy*. Tuition bills, report cards, every memo and letter sent home, including one from late 1980 citing concern for his *deteriorating emotional state* and *faltering academic performance*. Subsequent letters reflected increasing concern, even alarm. He noted words here and there: *melancholy, despondent, sad*. And disturbing phrases: *consider professional counseling; so unlike Gary* and *concern about possible self-destructive ideation*. The next item was on Carey Sheldon Paige letterhead: a letter to St. Joseph Academy, promising swift, devastating legal action if information about Gary was divulged to anyone but him. Another letter threatened similar action against WTRR. *He was bullying <u>them</u>, too!*

Gary continued paging through the file. The final item was a handwritten letter from Msgr. Streng. He hadn't seen that scrawl in years! It looked like a simple thank-you note. As he scanned the page, key words caught his eye. To be sure he understood, he read it through. The words chilled him. It *couldn't* be. Yet there it was, on St. Joseph Academy letterhead. Gary checked the date. He had to investigate. But Msgr. Streng died years ago; and now Dad was dead. Gary's insides clenched; he hated conflict, especially when he was so fond of the person he had to confront!

Carefully replacing the folder, Gary discovered a second key, hanging from a chain on a magnetized hook inside the file drawer. *Strange place for a key*. He took it out, wondering what it unlocked. It was after 4; too tired to give it much thought, he promised himself he'd look into it tomorrow.

Turning to leave, he spotted a framed photo. Dad and Ellen. With a child who could only be Erin. She looked eerily like the two of them. Gary's stomach flip-flopped: They all looked so happy.

Surging with jealousy, he flung the frame as hard as he could against the wall. It hit with a satisfying wooden thunk and shattering of glass. Leaving the ruined photo where it lay, Gary stalked from the room and back to bed. In the morning, he felt as though the garbage truck gobbling trash outside his window had taken an unscheduled detour across his chest on its way up Beach Avenue.

Gary's heart thumped louder than the Tears for Fears song that blared from the radio; his hands gripped the wheel as he struggled to contain his fury. He'd planned to storm in and demand answers. But, greeted warmly, his anger dissipated, leaving him with pain-filled questions.

"I understand your pain and, given your history, the anger you're feeling," the priest said. "But I have to tell you: Your dad had many regrets; the one that cut most deeply was that he'd treated you so badly… and he never fixed things." When Gary scoffed, he added, "It's true. And while he enjoyed a wonderful relationship with Erin, he died brokenhearted. Because he'd lost you."

"It was his own fault. He's the one who severed ties, not me."

"He said he tried to reach out; and you spurned him every time."

"So now it's my fault."

"I'm not saying that, Gary. I'm just relaying his words. Your dad loved you; and he truly regrette—"

"I don't care what he regretted," he interrupted, trying to banish any affection for Jeremy. "He can rot in hell, wallowing in regret!"

"You hadn't spoken in years; yet your anger seems as fresh as if you'd just now argued. Why're you still so bitter?"

Fr. Maynard was the only adult Gary had ever told about the beatings and only when the priest was bound morally to keep silent.

"You want to know why I'm bitter?" Gary parroted. "Don't you remember how I used to come in limping? Or with a black eye? And always avoided talking about what happened? He was beating the shit outta me. And you knew. So you got a lotta freakin' nerve asking me that!"

The priest recalled the day Gary mentioned it. He'd sat across from him during Confession and added, at the very end, "And I've been lying."

Justin had leaned forward slightly. "To whom?"

"Everybody, really." That's when he admitted he'd lied about his injuries: He wasn't as clumsy as he'd led them all to believe; his dad was beating him. Then, defiantly, he said he wasn't sorry for lying, he'd do it again if he had to.

Even now, Justin recalled the determined set of Gary's jaw, as if daring him to do something about it. He'd tried to get the teen to discuss the abuse in conversation. "How're things at home?" he'd ask casually. But, evasive as he was clever, Gary dodged all attempts to get him to say anything the priest could tell the authorities, or even the school counselors. Or he lied outright. Justin didn't want to jeopardize his trust; too much was invested in that relationship. He kept pursuing, gently. But Gary never let his guard down.

Now those defensive walls were back up. And higher than ever. The room prickled with hatred.

"I have every reason to be bitter. I'm glad he's dead. In fact, I'm going to the cemetery now, to dance on his fucking grave!"

"For what it's worth, he asked me to tell you he was sorry."

Gary scowled. "Why didn't he tell me himself? Damn coward!"

"He figured you'd react that way, but he asked me to try." Justin paused. "And he quit drinking."

"Big deal," he muttered, staring across the room at nothing in particular.

"It was a big deal. He quit – cold turkey – the day your daughter was born."

Those words again: *your daughter.*

"And that's supposed to make up for years of abuse?"

"Your dad realized the mistakes he made with his kids; he didn't want to repeat them with Erin. I thought it might give you a new perspective."

"I like the one I've got now: separated by six feet of dirt."

When Gary's fury ebbed, they talked for a while, like old times.

In a gesture of familiarity, the priest said he could drop the title *Father* and simply call him Justin.

Before long Gary's ire flared again. "Okay, tell me something: Why all of a sudden did Monsignor Streng let us graduate? Why the turnaround, Father? Answer me that."

Justin shifted in his seat. "I don't know. Perhaps a change of heart?"

"Bullshit!" He glared at the priest. "A change of financial situation is what he had."

"What're you saying?"

"Don't tell me you didn't know why he suddenly agreed to let us have our precious diplomas from St. Joseph fucking Academy!" he hissed. "How much was it for?"

"How much was what for?"

"The check! How much did it take to pay off Monsignor Streng?"

"Gary… I'm not at all sure I like what you're hinting at."

"Oh, come off it, *Justin!* You were privy to all the goings-on there. Don't tell me you didn't know."

The priest bristled. Interesting Gary would use his first name in a challenge situation. "I don't know about any check and I resent the allegation." He tugged open the door. "I'll gladly help you work through your hostility. But this, Gary – this is not the way to go about it. Nor will I tolerate it in my office."

Gary spent the evening rummaging through boxes of old check registers until he found what he needed; then he pawed through bundles of cancelled checks. Dad was a packrat.

Michaela appeared at the door twice, offering refreshment or respite. Both times, obsessed and driven, he'd sent her away.

*You really should be nicer,* he chided himself the second time he snarled at her. *She's trying to be supportive.* Getting slowly to his feet – he ached from kneeling over boxes – Gary found Michaela at the island, nursing hurt feelings and a cup of tea.

It felt odd, sitting here, where he and Mom used to talk. He reached for Micki's hand; she pulled away.

"I'm sorry I've been such a beast. I've gotta figure something out, and I'm so close. There's just one last thing I have to find." Gary reached for her hand again; this time she didn't pull away. "Please forgive me." Smiling, he coaxed his wife to her feet, nuzzled her neck. "C'mon, let's go upstairs."

Michaela tensed. "So when you want sex, what you're looking for can wait. But when I interrupt, I get my head bit off." Shaking him off, she gulped her tea in stony silence.

Her rejection confounded Gary. She'd never refused him. It wasn't even sex he wanted; he hoped to smooth things out, make amends for his behavior. Laying hold of her arm, he yanked her off the stool and pulled her powerfully to him. Before Michaela could protest, his mouth invaded hers.

Her eyes widened. "No!" she yelled, wrenching free. "How dare you! I said no!"

Startled as much by her strength as the force of her slap, Gary's hand flew to his cheek. His grey eyes blazed; he lunged again.

Michaela's fear instinct kicked in. Scrambling to the other side of the island, she eyed him warily, ready to bolt.

Heart pounding, Gary held her gaze. He was furious beyond words – and highly aroused. Turning at last in rage and frustration, he stalked to the study and slammed the door. Moving woodenly to the couch, he slouched onto it. Staring at the carpet, Gary saw only the terror in Micki's eyes; he came to a frightening realization: She'd been right to break off the engagement; he'd followed in the worst of Dad's footsteps. How often had Dad exploded, then skulked off here? And how many times had Gary sworn to treat his own family better? Yet, here he was, guilty of what he vowed never to do.

"I'm as bad as he was," he whispered. "Dear Jesus, forgive me." Yet, as desperately as he prayed, he felt no peace. Just emptiness, longing and deep-rooted, ugly guilt.

On the other side of the door, there was no peace, either. Micki hunched against the island, facing the direction toward which he'd disappeared, ready to run. Feeling ill, she trembled, icy cold all of a sudden. What's worse, far worse, she felt violated by the man she'd trusted with her safety. The thought nauseated her. Michaela felt out of control – as if her life was being directed from somewhere outside her and she was powerless against it. She clasped her arms about herself, still eyeing the closed door.

Gary remained in the study the rest of the night. Pulling the crumpled paper from his jeans pocket, he stared at it for a long time.

"Ellen?" he croaked. It felt awkward, speaking her name aloud after all this time.

The voice that used to make his heart flutter out of control now made it lurch. "Yes?"

"It's Gary."

"Gary! It's so good to hear your voice," she gushed. "Where are you?"

"At my dad's. Going through his things."

"Oh, that's right." She sobered instantly. "Honey, I'm so sorry."

"Save it," Gary snapped, angry with himself for the tugging ache at his insides. "Spare me the fake sincerity."

But he'd seen that picture in the study. *She probably _is_ sorry.* And he felt bad for Erin's having lost her grandpa.

He realized she'd asked a question.

"Excuse me?" It seemed odd to speak so reservedly. Yet part of him felt like he didn't know who she was anymore.

"I said, How long are you in town? When can I see you?"

"You can't. I want to see Erin." Silence filled the phone line. "Why did you lie to me?" he demanded.

"I didn't want you to feel obligated. Besides, I was angry."

"Angry!" The word exploded from his mouth. "You destroyed my world 'cause you were angry? What the hell were you angry about?"

"I thought you didn't love me."

"Jesus, Ellen! I begged you to marry me. Didn't that tell you something?"

"For someone who supposedly loved me, you sure took off in a hurry. I thought you'da been more persistent. You never seemed the leaving type, especially after what your mother did. Or" – she baited him – "maybe that runs in the family."

"You leave her out of this. You told me you aborted our baby. What was left to be persistent about?"

"Us!" Ellen flung the word. "You said you loved me."

"I did. But you told me to get lost. And how was I s'posed to forgive what you'd done?"

"I didn't *do anything*."

"I had no reason to think you were lying. How did you know I left?"

"I called," Ellen murmured. "Just before the baby came. I was afraid. I needed you. Your dad said you'd left, and he couldn't reach you."

Gary couldn't speak. His heart felt like it was collapsing.

"I still love you, Gary. We could start over: You, me and Erin."

He ached for what he'd lost: the woman he'd loved, his child. "It's too late, Ellen. I'm married to a terrific woman" – *who isn't even speaking to you now* – "I won't jeopardize that by chasing after some fantasy."

"Alright. If that's how you want it…"

Awkward silence stretched across the phone line. "When can I see Erin?"


It was after 9 when Gary found what he was looking for: check #4782; dated 21 April, 1982; payable to St. Joseph Academy. The amount was staggering.


Michaela never expected to fear Gary. Right now, all she wanted was for him to stay on the other side of that door. For the first time since the wedding, they slept apart: him on the living-room couch and her upstairs in Gary's old bedroom.

During the night, Gary crept back to the study and unlocked the file drawer. He didn't know why he felt a need to act in stealth; no one would question his actions. He was sorting through his father's things, like any good son. Was he a good son? Snooping through stuff with Dad in the ground barely 36 hours? Maybe Justin was right. *He __had__ tried to patch things up.* Gary decided he'd been a rotten son, and he couldn't fix it. Time for that was past. Dad was gone. He'd never get a chance to make it better.

He took the key from its hook. *He went to plenty of trouble to hide this.* Gary stared at the key he jiggled in the hollow of his hand. He cast about the room, looking for anything that might lock.

Gary noticed another picture of Dad with Erin. On the desk. He laid it facedown so he wouldn't have to feel guilty looking into their beaming faces. Sighing in frustration, he opened the closet. Behind Dad's black trench coat was a filing cabinet.

Biting his lower lip, Gary slid the key in the lock and turned it.

*Once you know what's inside, you can't ever un-know it,* Grandpa's voice cautioned. *Is this really what you want?*

Did he really want to know? Did it mean that much to him?

*There's a __reason__ some things are secrets,* the voice reminded him.

He paused, hand poised above the drawer pull. Yes. He needed to know. And dammit, he *deserved* to know!

Gripping the handle, Gary pulled; the drawer was empty, save for two files. Curiosity gnawing at him, he carried the *Diane* file to the desk. It was enormously thick, jammed with sealed envelopes addressed to *him*. Hundreds — most in Mom's writing, others in a child's scrawl. Written over a period of years, judging from the printing, which grew steadily neater and more fluid. *Joey must've been crushed when I never replied!*

A slip of paper bore a North Madison address in Dad's script.

Replacing the folder, Gary opened the one marked *Erin*. It was filled with photos, and something else. He studied a small, official-looking yellow paper: his daughter's birth certificate. Name: Erin Elizabeth Farricelli. Date of Birth: October 8, 1982. Mother: Ellen Katharine Farricelli. Father: Gary Joseph Sheldon.

It looked so strange to see his name typed on the document. But there it was. *Father.* It was official: He was a father. Gary felt cold and alone. *This isn't what fatherhood should feel like. It's s'posed to feel loving and warm! Not frightening and shaming. But I abandoned my daughter — just like Mom abandoned me.*

Suddenly, he felt ashamed of himself for revisiting the notion he had harbored all these years. He silently apologized – *to whom? Erin? Mom? The Orwellian Thought Police?* – for thinking it.

Shaking free of his thoughts, he returned his attention to the file. Next was her birth record. Full-term female; 7 pounds, 2 ounces; 20½ inches. At the bottom were the tiniest footprints he'd ever seen. Erin's photo was rubber-cemented to the page. She had big brown eyes with long lashes, a teensy pink mouth and a headful of dark hair.

He stared at the photo, scarcely believing he was seeing his baby, the one he'd mourned all this time. His heart soared. His baby was alive! Beautiful and, as far as he knew, healthy. And perfect! But no longer a baby. Dozens of photos documented each stage of her life. Newborn pictures; first Christmas; three-, six- and nine-month shots. Professional one-, two- and three-year photos. Others in between: Erin with Mommy; with Ellen's family; with Jeremy.

Gary spread them out on the desk. There were lots of pictures of Erin with Jeremy: digging in the sand at the beach; sliding into his arms at the playground; at Christmas; photos of grandpa and granddaughter enjoying ordinary, everyday activities: fishing, picnics in the park, playing. Gary's insides knotted and churned. *Things he never made time for with us.* Ellen's writing on the back listed the date, occasion, Erin's age and everyone's names.

It irked Gary to see Jeremy identified as Grandpa Sheldon. One thing was certain, though: Jeremy had been greatly involved in Erin's life. Almost as if trying to make up for his absence from his own children's lives. Or Gary's absence from *her* life. Guilt tugged at his heart. *This is insane! I'm jealous of my own daughter!*

Gary rifled through a packet of photos in a small envelope. In flowing gown, the Kindergarten graduate stood demurely, clutching her diploma, holding Grandpa's hand. An impish smile peeked out from beneath the tiny mortarboard cocked jauntily atop her head.

His heart crashed to a painful stop. That smile. It was identical to his in that Popsicle picture with Gamma Jo! He couldn't get over that sweet little face – with that smile and those eyes that were his!

As he put the pictures back, he noticed a wide-ruled paper filled with a child's writing. Dated January 30, 1990. Exactly a year ago. At the top was "My Hero," crayoned in careful second-grade print. "My Hero is my Grandpa Sheldon. He is fun and good to me. He comes over when Mommy has to work. And he plays with me. Even when I want to play Barbies. My Grandpa Sheldon always has time for me. We go to the park and feed the ducks. I love him. He is sort of like a Daddy to me. My Daddy was bad. He left me."

It was the worst sort of condemnation. His own daughter had decried his abandonment – and she had done so in a classroom assignment. She'd gotten an A.

Tears of remorse and humiliation coursed down Gary's face as he reread her words – words that cut him swift and deep.


Neither Gary nor Michaela slept well. From separate rooms, they grunted and snarled over breakfast and the morning paper. Finally, about 11, unable to stand the brewing hostility, Gary found Micki on the couch, thumbing through his yearbook. He spoke her name.

She looked up, ready to flee.

"Wait. Please," he said. "I was way wrong yesterday. I want to apologize."

Michaela eyed him, fearful. "Okay." She laid the book aside.

Gary sat. "I'm sorry for how I treated you yesterday. I need you, Michaela." His eyes glistened with tears. "I need you so bad. I can't begin to tell you ho—" he stopped, his words choked off by a rush of emotion.

Micki put her arms around him. "I know," she soothed. "You've been through the wringer. I don't blame you for being upset." *I just wish you hadn't taken it out on me.*

Gary listened to the calming sound of her voice. When his breathing slowed to normal, he spoke – as much a peace offering as an imparting of information: "I'm meeting Erin today. And I'm terrified."

She'd never known Gary to be afraid of *anything*. Much less a child. He was great with kids! Still, Erin wasn't just any kid; she was his kid. "It'll be fine," she whispered. "I have faith in you."


But first, Gary had one other stop to make. Standing on the porch, he rang the bell. Faint footsteps sounded from within; his heart clattered as the friary's wooden door creaked open.

"Can I help you?" the secretary asked, one hand on the door, the other shoved in her sweater pocket.

"Is—" His voice faltered. "Is Justin in?"

"Was *Father Maynard* expecting you?" she corrected indelicately.

"Not exactly… I – um—"

"He's very busy," fussed the middle-aged woman, "and if you haven't got an appoi—"

Just then the priest passed by. He smiled. "It's okay, Janet. I've got a few minutes. C'mon in, Gary."

Standing aside, Janet watched the pastor lead the presumptuous young man into his private office.

"I'm surprised to see you," he admitted. "I thought for sure I'd scared you off yesterday." Gathering his robes, Justin sat in a chair in the corner of the room. "I only have twenty minutes; but, please, sit."

Gary sat beside his – his what? Was he a friend? An adversary? His confessor? He wasn't sure how to classify the priest anymore.

He met Justin's gaze. "This won't take long. I came to apologize. I was acting crazy. If the offer still stands, I would like help dealing with my anger. I need to do something before it destroys me. And my marriage," he ended in a whisper.

The priest nodded, his elbows resting on the arms of his chair, fingertips touching, as if encircling a grapefruit. "Of course, Gary. We can set something up."

Gary pulled a paper from his shirt pocket. "I found the check." Unfolding it, he handed it to Justin.

The priest whistled as he read the amount. "Wow. How did you learn about this?"

"I found a letter among his papers, from Monsignor Streng; I'm thinking, maybe he meant for me to find it. It was dated April '82, thanking him for his *generous donation*. There's no other reason he would've given twenty-five grand. It *had* to be a payoff."

He nodded in acknowledgment. "I can see that. But Gary, please believe me: I knew nothing about it." His tone gentled. "And I still don't understand: Why does it upset you so badly?"

"Justin, he paid an enormous amount of money to ensure we'd graduate. It couldn't have been to save face; we weren't allowed at graduation. Why couldn't he say, '*I know you screwed up, but I love you and I think you deserve a second chance*'? What would've been so hard about that?"

Now the priest understood. "Sometimes it's easier to act angry than to express love or concern. Especially to those closest to us. And sometimes, the people toward whom we should act the most tenderly are the ones we unleash our greatest hostilities on. The converse is also true: Those we have legitimate reason to be angry with are often the ones we seem least willing to offend."

Gary nodded. "That makes sense." Then, fidgeting, he said, "I'm meeting Erin this afternoon."

Justin looked astonished. "You've never seen your daughter?"

"Ellen told me she got an abortion. I had no reason to believe she lied."

"I can see how you'd feel betrayed. And anxious. But don't look so worried; she's delightful. What a spitfire! Takes after her father."

Gary looked slightly reassured. "Does Ellen ever mention me?" he asked after a long pause.

"She did at first. But after a while, she basically gave up hope of ever seeing you again. She wanted to get in touch with you after the accident, but your fa—"

"What accident?"

"Erin was, oh, two and a half. She was thrown from the car and hospitalized for six weeks."

"Six weeks! Jesus! – Oh, sorry, Father. What happened to her?"

"Lots of internal injuries. First few weeks, didn't look like she'd make it. The next day, your dad got word your grandfather died." The news sank in slowly. Then Justin added a new layer of pain. "Jeremy had called him the night before; he said he promised he'd tell you. Guess he never got a chance."

Emptiness filled Gary as realization settled into his brain. Dad's calls began in late '82. *That's why he tried to contact me!* After Grandpa died, he purged messages from the machine at the cottage every week: "Gary, it's Dad. *Please* call me."

Regret stabbed at his heart. He could have patched things up and married Ellen. They could have been the happy family he had mourned for all those Junes ago. Dad had tried to tell him. And when he wouldn't listen, Dad did the only right thing: He stepped in and took over Gary's responsibility.

Suddenly he regretted shunning Dad at Grandpa's wake. How hard would it have been to listen to what Dad had to say? But he'd let pride and anger get in the way. At the reading of the will – when Dad probably didn't know if Erin would live – he again endured Gary's hostility when he would have rather been at his granddaughter's side.

Stubbornness had been Gary's undoing more than once: first his refusal to have anything to do with Mom… and now this. He'd squandered a chance to repair his relationship with Dad and missed his daughter's childhood. How much richer his life would be if only he'd met them both halfway!

The touch of Justin's hand on his arm startled Gary from his self loathing. "He may have wanted to tell you in person. Hearing that on the phone would have devastated you. From what you've said, your grandfather would never have done anything to hurt you. I can't see him withholding that on purpose."

"I guess you're right." His voice was hesitant. "Justin?" – it felt so weird, calling him that – "Thanks. For taking the time to talk."

"I'm glad we did; I hope this has brought you some peace. Call me; we'll set up a time to meet again."

"Okay." Gary tried to sound upbeat. "Any last words of advice before I go meet my daughter?"

Justin smiled. "Yeah: Stop beating yourself up."

Promptly at 3:30, Ellen answered the door to see Gary, in khakis and a brown leather bomber jacket. Snowflakes clung tenuously to his hair and jacket collar. "Gary, c'mon in. How are you?"

"Fine. You?" Setting his shoes in the boot tray, he assessed her. She'd hardly changed, except she was all grown up. Her dark hair fell to the middle of her back; her chocolate eyes were as enchanting as ever.

Ellen bobbed her head. "Terrific! It's so good to see you!" Impulsively, she hugged him. "I can't tell you how much I've missed you!" Taken aback, he pulled away. "Sooo?" She tugged his sleeve. "What've you been up to?" She draped his jacket over the sofa.

"Like I said, I'm married. Her name's Michaela."

"D'you have a picture?" she asked. As Ellen studied the wedding photo in Gary's wallet, he realized how similar the two women's appearances were. "You make a lovely couple." Her voice sounded strained; her hand brushed against his as she gave back the wallet. "Then again, so did we."

Gary's eyes locked on hers. "Where's Erin?"

"I thought it'd be best if we talked first… to get reacquainted. Please, Gary, give me another chance."

"To what? Lie to me? No, Ellen. I want to see my daughter. You'll be hearing from my lawyer."

"Gary, wait." He turned back toward the woman he once loved. Ellen closed the space between them. Backing him to the wall, she kissed him. "I've missed you so much, Gary. Can't we start over? We could make it work this time. I know we can. And Erin needs a daddy…"

"No!" He pushed back. "Damn it, Ellen, I'm married."

"You still want me though, *don't* you?" Her mouth found his hungrily, its tantalizing warmth driving him mad. Ellen traced the curve of his ear. "You know you do. I want it, too. Don't fight it, Gary. Please don't make me beg…"

"Stop it," he commanded, his voice wavering.

Hands planted on the wall on either side of him, Ellen pressed her body against his. "You know you want me," she tempted him throatily. "C'mon… doggie-style, like we used to." Blowing a slow stream of hot breath in his ear, she nipped at Gary's earlobe.

Her hair smelled of lily of the valley. Almost instinctively, Gary inhaled its scent.

She slid Gary's hands beneath her skirt and guided them up her shapely legs. Then, twining her fingers in his hair, she held him fast. "Remember this?" Ellen ground her pelvis against his. "You want it, don't you?" She unleashed a smoldering kiss.

He kissed back. Giving in to desire, Gary's hands gripped her ass cheeks and pulled her to him. A loud buzz filled his head; passion took over as reason failed. In one fluid motion, Ellen peeled off her top, arching her back and revealing luscious breasts as warm and succulent as a decade ago.

She moaned as he flicked his tongue over her rosy nipples. She reached to undo his fly; groping at his pants, Ellen yanked them down. Dropping to her knees, she was gratified to hear Gary's pleasured groans as she engulfed him. She raked her nails across his ass, making him clench and squirm.

Consumed with passion, he kicked free of his pants and laid her on the carpet. Shoving her skirt aside, he mounted her from behind and took her vigorously.

Minutes later, they lay on the carpet, spent and sweating. Gary gathered Ellen's hair out of the way and began kissing her neck — just the way Michaela always liked him to do.

"Mmm, nice." She stroked the arm that held her. "Ohh, Gary, you always were an amazing lover."

Ellen's voice jolted through his brain. Shocked into the reality of what he'd done, and remorse stricken over it, Gary recoiled from the half-naked woman beside him, her skirt still bunched at her waist. "Oh, God!" he exclaimed. "What have I done?"

Aghast and deeply ashamed, he dressed hurriedly and left — amid

# *Chapter 33*

"How'd it go?" Michaela chirped, tipping her head back for a kiss. "Is she as wonderful as her dad?"

Shaky, he peeled her away, unkissed. "Baby… sit down. I need to talk to you."

She settled onto the couch. "Is everything okay?"

Besieged by guilt, he sank to his knees. "I don't know how to tell you this," he began mournfully. "When I went to meet Erin, I—" *Sweet Jesus, forgive me!* Laying his head in his wife's lap, Gary wept.

Stroking his hair, Micki tried to comfort him, which only made his news harder to deliver.

"I had sex with Ellen," he confessed. "I'm sorry, Michaela – *so sorry!* I never meant for this to happen! Please forgive me."

Tenderness yielded to anger. Michaela felt sickened. Trembling, fighting the urge to vomit, she smacked his face. "You bastard! Gary, how *could* you?" She leapt up and stalked away, a loud buzz in her ears.

Scrambling to his feet, he followed, grasping at her arm. "If I could go back and undo it, I would – in an instant. I swear! I'm so, *so* sorry."

"Get away from me," Micki hissed, yanking her arm away. "Just get away – you disgust me, Gary! I can't stand the sight of you."

"Micki, please," he begged. "I know what I did was wrong – way wrong! And I take full responsibility. I won't insult you by saying it just happened. But please, *please*, you've got to believe me—"

"What? It was the first time? It'll never happen again?" Michaela choked back a sob. "Well, it never should've happened at all!" Her right hand shot out, connecting with his face in an oddly satisfying smack. "You sonofabitch!"

"Please, honey," he wept. "I know I don't deserve your forgiveness. But please, I'm begging you: *Please* forgive me. I love you…"

Michaela pummeled Gary with upraised fists. He backed away. The irony that Jeremy had beaten him in this very room, over the consequences of his union with Ellen, was not lost on him.

"If this is your idea of love" – she gestured futilely – "You broke our wedding vows! I *loved* you, you asshole! And you betrayed me!" She smeared away tears. "I hate you for this, Gary! I hate you!" Her stomach clenched. Convulsing, Michaela vomited. She ran upstairs, sobbing, one hand covering her mouth.

She returned clutching a hastily packed suitcase, her purse and the car keys.

Gary intercepted her at the bottom of the stairs. "Where are you going?"

The acrid sting of bile still burned her throat. "I'm leaving. Don't come home. I don't want to see your face anymore."

"Micki, I'm *sorry!*" He ground away tears with both fists. "Wait! Can't we talk about this?"

"What's to talk about? You fucked your old girlfriend. What's left to say?" She pushed past him.

"Michaela, please!" Gary grasped at logistics. "Look, if you take the car, how'm I gonna get back?"

"Let Ellen give you a ride. I bet she gave you quite a ride this afternoon!"

The slippery roads gave Michaela five nerve-wracking hours to think. To brood. To sob. It was after 10 when she pulled into the driveway. Her eyes ached from driving in oncoming snow and from crying. Her hands throbbed from gripping the steering wheel.

She shoved her bag into a corner; flinging herself onto the bed, she wept bitterly. Anger and humiliation churned within her. Her stomach was in tangles. *Damn this indigestion! And damn Gary… Damn him!* As worn out as she was, sleep eluded her.

Finally, sometime after 2, Michaela drifted into a fitful slumber.

***

Gary awakened after noon on the couch, disoriented. Yesterday flooded back. It felt like a nightmare. He kept hoping it *had* been a dream. But no, it was real: He'd cheated on Michaela. And she had left him. The bruise on his shoulder reminded him where she punched him. And not even Lysol could erase the odor from the carpet; the lingering puke stench assailed his nostrils.

310

Achy from another restless night on the couch, he dragged himself upstairs to shower. The shower encompassed the only things Gary missed about this house: endless hot water and terrific water pressure!

As he dressed, he wondered how to right this. Then something hit him: *I'm s'posed to call Justin. But I can't go to him now — not after this!* Shame tore through Gary. Now the priest would *really* see what a failure he was.

***

Micki awakened feeling ill; her chest ached. Around 3, she got up to make soup. Seeing Gary's car, her heart leapt and fluttered; then she remembered. Her eyes welled with tears; her stomach flopped and she ran to the bathroom.

Miserable and queasy, she ate her soup and went to bed. She drowsed and awoke several times that night, listening to the sleet slashing at the windows. In spite of herself, her thoughts turned to Gary: where he was now, what he was doing. Images of him locked in passionate embrace with Ellen tormented her.

Micki roamed the house, searching for traces of the man she loved, before he became the man who'd betrayed her. In the study, she opened one of his books, saw his neat script on the bookplate. Replacing it, she picked up another. Then another. This one, she'd given him. She read the inscription. A piece of her heart tore.

At the front door, she stared out at the street. Sleet and snow danced like dervishes past the streetlamps. Flipping the porch light on, she chided herself for holding to the quaint tradition despite Gary's disloyalty.

In the family room, Michaela crumpled onto the too-big couch. Empty and alone, she flipped through all the TV channels, then put on the radio. A love song left her stifling anguished sobs.

Her throat burned; she felt dizzy and feverish. In the morning, she called her doctor, certain it was food poisoning.

"What was the date of your last period?" Dr. Quill asked.

She counted. It was late.

"Sounds like you may be pregnant," he told Micki with a kind, almost paternal, smile.

The test confirmed it. "Congratulations, Michaela. You're going to be a mom."

She stared at the doctor in unblinking shock. *Pregnant.*

The news crashed through Micki's protective wall. It crumbled, leaving her raw. She hadn't wanted to admit what she aborted was a baby. But she felt the same way now as she had then: nausea; that fluttery feeling. It was, undeniably, the same. And if *this* was a baby, this tiny being growing inside of her, then *that* had to have been a baby, too.

Michaela wept the whole way home, then crawled into bed. At 6 she forced down a frozen dinner. Minutes later, she hunched over the toilet, cursing herself for wasting the dinner. She cursed herself for not keeping ginger ale in the house; she cursed Gary for putting her in this jam: alone and pregnant. Crumpled against the toilet's porcelain coolness, she sobbed out her misery.

She sagged onto the couch to watch a movie. A commercial for baby wipes sent her into another crying jag. She sobbed herself to sleep on the couch a second straight night.

Micki awoke depressingly early. Her neck was stiff; everything ached. Nauseated and dizzy, she didn't quite reach the bathroom. After cleaning the kitchen floor, she went upstairs to shower.

As the warm water poured down, so did her tears. "I'm sorry, baby. I'm so sorry!" she wept, a hand over her belly. She scrunched to a sitting position. Hugging her arms around herself, she rocked back and forth as the water rained down; but nothing could wash away her sorrow. She felt evil. She was bad. And she was guilty.

She knew she should probably try to eat something, for the baby. But she couldn't stand the thought of puking again. She tried to focus on anything but her gnawing hunger. *I killed one baby. What's one more? I'm an awful mother anyway; if I starve this one to death now, no one'll ever know; and I won't have to worry about being called a lousy mother.* But something inside – *Is it the baby?* – told her to fight for her baby's life. A tiny voice convinced her this time was different. *This* child was conceived in love. As angry and betrayed as she felt now, Michaela knew in her heart she wanted nothing more than to have Gary's baby.

That night, she left the porch light on again. *Just in case.* Wanting to be strong for the life within her, Michaela prayed for strength to face whatever she decided to do, wherever this road led.

Climbing into bed, she whispered another prayer. "I love him so much, God! But I feel so betrayed. Please help me figure out what to do."

She fell into a dismal, dream-haunted sleep, tormented by a

shadowy specter of Ellen, her enemy and rival. In one dream, Gary told her she shouldn't hate Ellen; she wasn't so bad. As he said this, Ellen's eyes glowed red and her face transfigured into pure evil. In another, he told her he'd gotten Ellen pregnant, and he was leaving her to marry Ellen. *But <u>I'm</u> pregnant, too,* Michaela protested. She heard Ellen's cruel laugh as she gripped Gary's arm with long, cold fingers and dragged him away. In a third dream, Gary said he was sorry he'd slept with Ellen; the bouquet of roses he gave her turned into snakes. Hissing, they lunged and bit at her with gleaming fangs.

Micki startled herself awake; telling herself it was just a dream, she clutched Gary's pillow in the too-big bed.

Again he came to her. Said he was sorry. No roses, no snakes, no fangs.

In her sleep, Micki smiled as the dream Gary caressed her cheek. She stirred. *It's almost like I could feel him; but it's only a dream.*

The dream continued.

Bending over the bed, Gary whispered tenderly, "I just wanted to say I'm sorry, sweetheart. And I love you." He kissed the tip of her nose.

Smiling in her sleep, Micki rolled over and drifted deeper. She dreamt no more that night.

In the morning, Michaela yawned, stretched. "Good morning, baby" – she laid a hand on her tummy, rubbing it in circles – "I love you."

Downstairs, she surveyed last night's snowfall; footprints and tire tracks lined the now-empty driveway. Gary's keys were gone from the hook by the door. On the kitchen table lay an envelope with her name in the same neat script as on the bookplates.

Emptiness tore at her. Gary was here. He'd stood right here… holding that envelope in his hands – those hands whose touch she missed so terribly! He'd been so close, and she'd missed him. A sob of misery and longing bubbled up from Michaela's gut.

A moment later, she trembled with fury: *How dare he sneak in here! Like a thief! Like a sneaking, cheating—* Her hand flew to her mouth, stifling a sob. Iron bands constricted around her chest. She picked up the envelope. For an instant, Michaela was tempted to rip it, unopened, to shreds. Instead, she tore open one edge. Hands shaking, she removed a single sheet of paper filled with line after line of his smooth, precise writing.

*My dearest Michaela,*

*I wanted so much to wake you, to tell you in person… but I was afraid you'd throw me out - and I don't think I could stand that. Not that you wouldn't have had ample reason. Besides, you looked so peaceful sleeping, and I know you haven't had much peace these past few days.*

*I often wondered, 'What kind of man cheats on his wife?' I always reached this conclusion: a weak, pathetic, foolish man. I _am_ that man: weak, pathetic and foolish. And I am sorry.*

*Looking at the words I just wrote - "I am sorry" - I realize how hollow and meaningless they are. How could I use such unsuitable words - words that fall so far short - to convince you how much I regret cheating on you? There aren't words to say how sorry I am for my infidelity and betrayal. I could tell you "I'm sorry" every hour of every day for the rest of my life - and it still wouldn't be enough. I know I don't deserve a second chance, but I'm asking you - no, I'm begging you, Michaela - to forgive me and take me back.*

*I can't imagine what you must be going through - and I can't begin to express how terrible I feel that I've caused you so much anguish.*

*Michaela, I can't undo my actions. And I won't try to make excuses, because there is no excuse. All I can do is admit what I did was wrong - it's beyond wrong, it's reprehensible - and offer my deepest apologies.*

*As horribly inadequate as that is, it's all I can offer you - along with my solemn promise that it will _never_ happen again. I know right now my promises don't mean anything… but I swear to you I'll do whatever it takes to win back your trust and your love. Whatever it takes.*

*Please, Michaela: Give me another chance to prove to you how sorry I am… and how much I love you.*

*In love and sorrow,*

*Gary*

*P.S. - Thank you for leaving the light on.*

Dropping the letter, Michaela covered her face with her hands. Torn between anger and pity, her emotions struggled for position.

"I don't know. I just don't know," she said, as if to the feelings themselves. She reread the letter, trying to imagine Gary saying the words. *He's right… they _are_ meaningless and hollow.*

Michaela flipped through the phone book. A minute later, she listened to the phone ring against her ear.

Gary awoke to waves crashing. High tide. It was 10:32; he hadn't meant to sleep so late. Shivering, he leapt out of bed and pulled on his robe. The hardwood floor felt like ice against his feet.

He crossed the room to shut the window. He'd needed fresh air last night; but, mired in his own personal fog, he'd forgotten it was February. Reaching for the phone, he punched in the number. A large woodchuck fell into the pit of his stomach and began gnawing there as he heard a click and her "Hello."

"Hi. It's Gary. Did I wake you?"

"No, of course not, honey."

Relief inched its way into his tormented soul. "Can I see you?"

His insides were a knotted jumble; every nerve screamed at him as he jabbed at the doorbell; he took a deep breath, then another… and still another, before he heard the deadbolt slide.

Her smile eased the chill surrounding his heart. "C'mon in."

It was hard to decide if her voice or smile was more welcoming. What was most welcoming was her hug. The moment he stepped inside, he was in her arms.

"I'm so glad to see you, sweetheart!"

"Oh, Mom," he murmured. "I didn't know where else to go. I really screwed up this time!"

Taking his coat, Diane ushered her son inside. She led him into the kitchen, where a pot of coffee burbled. She nodded toward a chair. "Sit down, honey. Tell me what's wrong."

Guilt-ridden, he poured out his heart. As awful as he felt, it was so freeing to confide in her! He told her how his relationship with Ellen soured after they learned she was pregnant; that they'd been expelled from St. Joe's… and that Erin was his daughter.

"Gary, I'm surprised at you," Mom scolded. "How could you have left that darling child?"

Tears pricked at his eyes. "I *didn't* leave Erin. Ellen told me she had an abortion." He shook his head, hating the memory. "Then, that same night, Dad threw me out. I went to Grandpa's. I never went back. It hurt too much!" He told her Erin was as much of a surprise to him as she was to Diane.

"You're telling me, all this time, you never knew you had a daughter?"

"Never. Not a clue."

She slapped a hand on the table. "That's not right! She should've told you the truth." Head bowed, she took his hand. "Like I should have," she added regretfully. "Gary, I'm so sorry for all the time we lost. I should have listened when Grandpa told me to tell you why we left."

Gary went numb inside. "He knew?"

She gripped her son's hand, afraid he wouldn't let her explain. "Yes. It was his idea. He found us this house, put Joey in school, even helped us move out. Don't be angry, honey. He wanted to tell you; it almost killed him not to. I made him swear he wouldn't."

Yanking free, he stood and turned away; he ran a hand through his hair. His chest tightened as he struggled with the enormity of this new, awful reality. "He *lied* to me? Like *you* lied to me!" Gary whipped around to face her. "Jesus! What *else* did you lie about?"

Mom took a tremulous breath. "I love you, Gary. I never lied about that. I always loved you. And I regretted leaving you… every minute."

"How can you expect me to believe that?"

"It's the truth." Her voice quieted. "The letters. You said you found my letters. Would I have bothered to write if I didn't love you?"

He stared at her. Grandpa – the one person he expected *never* to hurt him – had lied to him! Lied right to his face. For years!

"Sweetheart, haven't you ever done something you've regretted? And wished every moment you could take it back? Well that's how *I* feel!"

Gary's eyes filled with tears. *Of course I have regrets! I wanna take back dozens of things.* But none more than his infidelity. "There *is* something. That's what I need to talk to you about," he murmured. "I've done… something awful."

Diane watched him in silence. "Oh?"

Gary laid his hands palms-down on the table, unsure where to begin. "I love my wife," he said mournfully. "But I think I've just destroyed my marriage."

"Why's that?"

He wrapped his hands around the mug she set before him; even its heat couldn't chase the lingering chill. This was so hard to say, especially in light of Dad's infidelities. His words were shaming and terrible. "I cheated on Micki. With Ellen."

Diane couldn't disguise her shock and disgust. "Oh, Gary."

Gary told her about his caving in to Ellen's seduction.

Leaning his elbows on the table, he rested his chin in his hands; his tear-filled eyes sought hers.

Her tone was sharp, disapproving. "And you don't know whether to tell Michaela?"

"No. I told her right away. I'll never forget the hurt in her eyes — that awful, betrayed look. I told her how sorry I was, and I begged her to forgive me."

Diane looked at Gary and, for an instant, saw Jeremy's loveless eyes staring back. "What'd she say?"

"She left me. And I don't blame her." He rested his head in his hands. "I'm such a failure. I didn't even honor our wedding vows for six months. I'm no better than Dad," he whispered.

Diane never imagined she would hear Gary confessing infidelity. "That's not true, Gary. At least *you've* got the decency to regret what you've done, and admit it was wrong. Which is more than I could ever say for him."

***

"I appreciate your coming on such short notice."

"No problem, ma'am. I know how upsetting it is to feel unsafe in your own home."

Half an hour later, the workman pocketed her check. "Now, be sure to keep those in a safe place."

As he left, Micki dissolved into tears, the shiny new keys digging into her palm.

Next morning, she called the cottage. Gary answered on the first ring. She ignored the flutter in her stomach at the sound of his voice. "Gary, it's me."

"Micki!" he exclaimed. "Oh, sweetheart, I'm so glad to hear your voi—"

"Shut up," she told him curtly. "I want to see you tomorrow afternoon. Be here at two."


Anxious but filled with hope, Gary rang the doorbell at 18 Mayfair Lane.

Michaela dodged him as he tried to kiss her. "Don't touch me."

"Micki, please," he begged. "I love you so much. And I'm so sorry for hur—"

"We need some time apart." She indicated the three bags by the fireplace. "I packed your things."

"N-no!" he sputtered, feeling as if he'd been struck. "Don't do this. *Please*. Let's talk about it…"

"I can't talk to you right now. Just get out." She hoped he didn't see the tears glistening in her eyes; biting her lip, Michaela tried to force them to stop.

"Can't we talk about this?"

"No." She advanced toward her husband. "And how *dare* you" – she smacked his face for emphasis – "sneak in here in the dead of night! What'd you think? You'd just waltz in, win me over with a few sweet words and everything would be alright? It's not gonna happen that way!"

Gary reached for her hand. "Don't do this, baby. *Please!* Give me another chance…"

Hearing the word *baby*, Micki's heart lurched. She pulled free, folded her arms and turned away. "Don't make me call the police, Gary. I want you out. Now!"

Michaela wept openly at the door as Gary struggled along the icy sidewalk with his suitcases. Twice he fell; each time she had to stop herself from running to help him.

The next day, anguished and desperate for comfort, Michaela drove to church. Choking back sobs, she tried the door; her tug was rewarded by a yielding as the wooden behemoth opened. She glanced about in the chilly semi-darkness. Pulling open an inside door, she stepped inside. The flickering light of dozens of votive candles in wrought-iron holders danced up the walls at either side of the altar. Pew after empty pew met her. Relief nudged away her anxiety; tears slid down her cheeks as she knelt to pray.

Her cries rang through the church where, not six months earlier, she vowed to love Gary forever and he promised to be true to her. Her chest heaved with gasping sobs. He'd broken his promise, but she wasn't sure whether she'd broken hers.

When a hand rested on her shoulder, Michaela leapt.

"Sorry. I didn't mean to startle you." Deacon Greg crouched beside her. "Do you want to talk?"

She slid over to let him sit; kicking at the kneeler, she wept. He honored her silence. When she spoke, the deacon had to strain to hear her.

"I'm angry."

"That's okay. And it's okay to bring that anger to God. I was angry with Him for a long time."

Wiping her eyes, Michaela sniffled. "About Kim?"

"Yeah. And I found if you bring your anger to God, it's easier to let go of."

She considered this. Anger simmered beneath her pain. "What if I don't *want* to let go of it?"

Greg responded with a question of his own. "Why're you so angry?"

Michaela dug her nails into her palms. Her face burned with fury as she spoke the words she never expected to say: "Gary cheated on me."

The young deacon couldn't mask his shock. "How do you know?"

Her face crumpled. "He admitted it," she whispered, anguished. "And I dunno what to do."

Greg put an arm around her. "What do you want to do?"

"I threw him out; and I changed the locks. But I don't know if I did the right thing." Michaela thumped a hand against her chest. "It hurts so much… in here."

He nodded. "I can understand that."

Fear gripped her. "D'you think I did the right thing?"

"Only you can decide that."

Leaning weakly against him, she shook her head. "I don't think I can."

"No one said you have to decide right now. But you said he confessed, so it must be weighing on him. That ought to count for something. Take some time; pray about it, okay?"

Sniffling, she wiped away the last of her tears and nodded.

The rest of the week, Micki called in sick to work. She stumbled through her days, sobbed away her nights.

The littlest things started her crying, especially thoughts of Gary or the mention of his name. Or anything that reminded her of him: his voice on a commercial, his name on the electric bill in Friday's mail – even the cozy blue-flannel bathrobe he'd given her last year for Christmas. Michaela couldn't escape him. No matter how hard she tried. Everywhere she turned, she was surrounded by memories of Gary.

# Chapter 34

(11 February – Monday)

Greg offered Michaela a cup of tea. "How are you feeling today?"

"Awful." She sank into the armchair opposite the deacon's desk. "Today we've been married six months. And I feel like such a failure!" Tears drizzled onto her cheeks.

"Milestones can be difficult." Greg sat beside Michaela and set a box of tissues next to her. "Why do you feel like a failure?"

She dabbed at her eyes. "Because I can't even keep my husband faithful for six months."

"That's hardly your fault."

She wept into her tissue, twisted her wedding ring. "I still feel bad about kicking him out."

Greg sat forward. "Of course you do. That must've been a tough decision."

She gestured with the hand that gripped the tissue. "It hurts, but I think I did the right thing. On the other hand, I might be making the biggest mistake of my life."

"Did you talk to him about it at all?"

"I *can't*. Could you? If Kim had cheated on— oh, geez! I'm sorry, Greg…" Her face reddened.

He smiled gently. "That's alright. It's hard to discuss marital problems with someone in my situation."

Michaela studied the young widower. "How do you go on after what you've been through?"

"I ask myself that every day. It always comes back to faith. It's as simple as that. Just faith."

"Is it enough?"

"Sometimes it has to be."

Shifting, she tucked her feet beneath her. "I haven't even told Gary this yet. I'm pregnant."

Greg sucked in his breath. "How do you feel about that?"

She wiped at her eyes, wadded the tissue in her fist. "I dunno. But it sure explains all the vomiting."

*What a pretty smile*, he thought, unbidden. "You and Gary talked about having children."

Her head bobbed in assent. "We talked about lots of things; all kinds of plans. Serious and goofy. But yeah, one thing we were sure about was wanting kids."

Greg cocked his head. "And now? Now that you're pregnant?"

"Now that I'm pregnant," she echoed, gnawing at a thumbnail, "that man I married… I don't know who he is anymore," Michaela lamented. "I want this baby. I just don't know if I want her calling *him* 'Daddy.'" She scrunched into a ball and wept.

Stooping to console her, Greg stroked her hair. "It's okay," he murmured. "Don't cry."

Looking up, Micki found their mouths inches apart; their eyes locked. Inhaling sharply, she trembled. After several seconds, she straightened up, wiping at her eyes. "I should go."

Relieved, the young deacon returned to his chair.


(13 February – Ash Wednesday)

Gary felt little need to receive ashes, the outward reminder of man's sinful nature; every time he looked in the mirror, guilt stared back. Feeling the weight of his adultery, he hadn't been to Mass since Dad's funeral. And he felt undeserving to seek solace in the confessional; he could hardly ask God's pardon until Micki forgave him.

With a despairing heart, he slipped into church after noon Mass. To the left of the sanctuary stood his longtime friend; on the right, Fr. Williams. Joining Greg's queue, he shuffled to the front.

When he reached the head of the line, Gary thought he'd gotten a particularly steely glare from Greg. But he hadn't imagined the angry pressure of the deacon's thumb grinding dampened ashes against his forehead.

"Remember, man, that thou art dust and unto dust you shall return," he intoned, his normally friendly brown eyes glinting angrily. *Or did he say, "thou art dirt"?*

Gary couldn't be certain. But dirt was what he felt like.

The next day, Greg phoned Michaela. "I don't want to seem too forward, but would you like to go to dinner?" Startled by his offer, she smiled as she heard herself accept.

Greg looked dapper in a grey suit. "You clean up pretty nice," she teased, fingering his red tie; that's when she realized what day it was. *Gary wore a red tie on Valentine's Day when he proposed.*

He grinned. "Thanks. Want to go to Wong Lee's?"

"Not toni—" She wrinkled her nose. "How 'bout Italian?"

"It's been kind of a bad day," Greg admitted over cold antipasto at Sorrento in Woodbury.

"Valentine's Day. I know; same here."

"Not that. It's six months since I lost Kim. And the baby." He paused, wiped his eyes. "Sometimes it feels like that was a hundred years ago. And other times – like now – it's still so close, so raw."

"Must be awful, seeing all these couples. Do you wanna leave?"

"No. Actually, it helps, being out. Plus, I feel like I can really talk to you." Then Greg blurted, "Let me ask you something. When I suggested Wong Lee's, you started to say 'Not tonight.' Why?"

Micki set down her water goblet. "That's where Gary proposed to me, three years ago tonight." Tears stung her eyes. "Since I was eighteen, I've only loved him. I can't understand how can that turn so quickly into, I dunno, disdain? I don't get it. I mean, I don't hate Gary, but I'm not sure I love him anymore. Besides, *he* cheated on *me*; so why do *I* feel like the bad guy here?"

A light snow was falling when Greg invited Michaela back to his house. He built a fire; they sat on the couch to talk. He shared his pain at losing Kim so young, destroying their dreams for the future.

She let Greg talk, comforting him when he wept.

He urged her again to forgive Gary. "It's a shame to lose time. Who knows how long you have left?"

They talked until it grew late. Micki fell asleep, her head on his shoulder. They awakened after 2; the fire had dwindled to embers.

Going to start the car, Greg was met by sleet pelting his face; the sidewalk was slick, the grass crunchy. Frozen roads glittered in the streetlights' glare; ice-laden branches clicked in a bitter arctic wind.

"Roads look bad. I'd rather not chance it," he said, rubbing his hands together. "If you want to go, I'll take you; but you're welcome to stay." He slid his arms around her. "Besides, I don't think I can stand being alone. C'mon, stay… bed's plenty big," he murmured, kissing her temple. "Nothing will happen. You can wear something of Kim's – if that won't creep you out."

Keenly aware of the deep ache within her, she agreed sleepily. When he kissed her, Michaela's eyes flew open; she almost pulled away. Reconsidering, she settled into his arms.

Greg kissed her lips, eyes and throat with a hungry yearning. Pulling away, she changed in the bathroom, climbed into bed and burrowed under the covers. After they murmured their goodnights, she curled into a ball, her back to him; but his pillow-muffled cries made sleep unlikely. She rolled over, slid her arms around Greg.

"Oh, Kimmy… Kimmy," he sobbed against her shoulder. His mouth found hers again.

Alarms sounded in her head. She ignored them and kissed back.

In the morning, Michaela helped Greg clear off the car.

On the way home, he held her hand; it felt cold. "Thank you for last night," he told her. "It meant so much, having you there."

She didn't know what to say.

***

Life without Michaela was an endless cycle of work, sleep and missing her like hell. When he awoke, it startled Gary not to find her beside him. As the shock dissipated, lingering emptiness took its place. That morphed into profound, oppressive guilt. Nothing followed the guilt; it deepened as the hours dragged. But he had to deal with record-company reps all day and be spirited and genial on air. Every day, Gary summoned a cheerful façade and disguised despair as effervescence.

(15 February – Friday)
When Pete lowered the monitor's volume, Gary whirled about to see him shaking his head. "You'll never change. At seventy-five, you'll still be dancin' around with the volume cranked. 'Course, *then* it'll be 'cause you're too stubborn to wear your hearing aid."

Gary forced a grin. "Probably."

The program director wasted no more time on chatter. "Come see me when you're off." He offered no explanation.

Suspicion settled in Gary's gut; it'd be another hour 'til he'd learn whether it was warranted. Just past 7, he slouched into a chair in the program director's office. "What's wrong?"

"Why's something gotta be wrong?"

"If nothing's wrong, why're you being so fucking cryptic?"

Some sales reps were still milling about. Pete nodded toward the

323

door. "Shut the door, Gar'."

Gary suddenly rued his use of 'fucking.' Masking his unease, he reached back and gave the door a cavalier shove. It clicked shut.

When he had Gary's attention, Pete spoke. "What's going on?"

He acted like the question surprised him. "What d'you mean?"

"Don't do this, Gary." He tried again. "What's wrong?"

Gary eyed his boss. Challenged him, was more like it. "I don't know what you're getting at."

"Something's bothering you."

The tilt of Gary's chin was defiant. "What makes you say that?" If Pete could dance around the subject, he could, too. Hell, dancing was practically what he did best!

"For starters, you're – I dunno – almost too *perky* on air lately."

Gary toyed with Pete like Attila with a moth. "Since when's that a bad thing?"

"I've played enough poker with you to recognize your tell. I just want to help. But I can't do that if you won't tell me what's wrong. I'm asking as a friend."

"So why are we having this conversation in your *office?*" he shot back.

It was cards-on-the-table time. "I called your house yesterday. Micki said you don't live there anymore."

That tore it. "Damn it, Pete! Why didn't you just *say* that, instead of playing fucking mind games?" Fury ripped through him. "Why'd you call me in under false pretenses and… and" – seething and lost for words, Gary stared at Pete, who was shaking his head – "*What?*"

"I didn't want to presume; but I figured something was up when you got talkative last week. At first I thought it was about your dad; but then I talked to Michaela and…" he gestured; his voice trailed off.

Sinking back into his chair, he clenched and unclenched his fists.

"Okay, I went about it wrong," Pete admitted. "But I'm worried about you, Gary. Talk to me."

His fist clenching stopped. As he met Pete's gaze, a lump caught in his throat. "She threw me out," he whispered. "Packed my bags and told me to get lost."

Speaking the words brought a new dimension of shame. Head in his hands, Gary sighed. "I screwed up big-time, Pete. And now I'm payin' for it."

# *Chapter 35*

(16 February – Saturday)

A touch on her arm made Michaela look up. "Oh! Hi, Greg. How are you?"

"Today's a good day," he acknowledged. "How're you doing?"

She shook her head. "Not so good."

"Want to talk about it?"

"Not in the grocery store. Come for supper." When she saw he was about to protest, she added, "I'm cooking anyway. Besides, I'm tired of talking to the plants."

As Greg left, she headed back to the produce aisle. For broccoli.

Greg arrived just after 5 with white roses and a quart of milk. "I would've brought wine, but I thought this was more appropriate."

"Thank you." She gave him a peck on the cheek and plated up the chicken Divan.

***

Right after work on Monday, Gary drove to Pine Cove. Next morning, he attended early Mass.

Fr. Maynard had never known Gary to shun the Eucharist.

After breakfast, they went to Justin's office. An ornately carved olivewood crucifix hung opposite his desk.

"Have a seat," the priest invited. "Perhaps we should begin with what's troubling you this morning."

Gary felt like Justin had struck him. Wanting to flee his piercing gaze, Gary eyed the priest's Siena and St. Bonaventure diplomas, and his state certifications as a psychologist and family counselor. On the walls hung comforting images: the resurrected Christ; Jesus consoling others.

"I uh" – Gary crunched into a little ball and whispered – "I did something terrible."

"Is there something you need to confess?" The priest's tone was

325

non-intrusive.

Ashamed, Gary looked away. He nodded.

"Whatever it is, Gary, He's already forgiven you," Justin said. "He's just waiting for you to accept that forgiveness, and that grace. Won't you say *Yes* to Him?"

Gary stared at the ornate crucifix, feeling as though his sin were solely responsible for sending Christ to hang there. Repentant tears slid down his face. Confessing his failings, he admitted how shameful he'd felt since his infidelity.

This wasn't the first time he'd confessed sexual sins with Ellen; although, granted, adultery was significantly different from a couple of kids having sex. There were other things, minor things, none so shaming as what he'd done with Ellen against his wife.

Gary knew Justin had let him off easy; he expected his penance to be far greater than Scripture meditations and prayer.

He wept openly as the priest pronounced the words freeing him from his sins.

With that burden lifted, they set to work. Justin opened a gentle dialogue: "Now, about your dad… Is there a good memory of him you can hold onto?" He admitted that it was a tough question, and reflecting on it would be, quite frankly, painful.

Gary said nothing.

"There must be something," Justin prompted.

"Why do I even want a good memory of him?"

He'd expected resistance. "I thought it'd be a good place to start. Take your time."

Gary described the chair-spinning scene he recalled in the study.

"That's good, Gary. I knew you'd find something. Now think back: What was Dad like then?"

His voice sounded soft, almost childlike. "He was my daddy. I loved him."

"Can you recall anything else positive from that same time?"

Gary's "No" was almost automatic.

"Don't shut down, Gary; you're doing great. I realize your recent memories were painful. You said just the touch of his hand caused you anxiety – even when he meant no harm – like at the reading of your grandfather's will."

Justin watched Gary nod.

"Now, this'll be difficult, but I need you to focus on an image of his hands. Really focus. And tell me a positive memory of them."

"No." Gary backed away slightly; his mouth twitched like a child under duress.

"If we're going to continue, Gary, I need you to work with me." Justin's voice sounded like it came through a cardboard tube. "And 'No' isn't an option."

Gary recalled the times Dad had beaten him, when he'd raised his fists or used his hands to wield a belt.

Suddenly, a long-buried image shimmered into view.

"Daddy – help! Help!" His voice. Young. Screaming. Panicked.

Fully clothed, Dad dove into the swift-moving river and pulled his young son to safety.

"You gotta be more careful, little one," Jeremy had cooed as he set his 4-year-old boy on dry land. No scolding; no cross words or punishment. Just hugs, soothing words and kisses from his daddy. Who loved him.

Tears filled Gary's eyes as he described the scene. He finally had a tender memory of his father to form the basis for the rest of their work; it brought him peace and let the healing begin.

When he left Justin's office late that afternoon, he felt drained. But strangely calm. He'd spent hours unfolding his life, unpacking the past in excruciating detail. Justin made him discuss things he'd buried so deep it hurt to recall them. It was hard work. But he'd gotten through the worst of it.

He returned to the Star-Lite Motor Inn and slept. It was dark when he awoke. Maybe the diner was still open.

A bowl of soup and a tuna melt later, Gary began his journaling exercise for tomorrow.

"Just sit down and write," Justin had said, giving him a spiral-bound notebook and this caution: "Don't try to make sense of it – and don't censor. Write whatever comes. But do it now. Don't go to sleep." He'd protested, but Justin silenced him. "I know you're tired. I *want* you tired; it breaks down your defenses."

It was a new intensive-therapy technique he'd begun using. Then tomorrow they'd assess his progress, figuring out where, and how, to take the next session.

When Gary stopped writing, he had filled 15 pages. Most of it – long, rambling portions – was a letter to his dad. Alternately the one he loved and the one he'd feared and hated. There were other things, too: threads of pain running amid the pages; and frequent references to his wife. *Michaela.*

Gary ached at the thought of her. Opening the notebook again, he turned to a fresh sheet. He poured out page after wrenching page in apology to the woman he loved and betrayed. It was after 2 when he fell asleep, his pen skidding across page 17 of the tear-splotched letter he never finished.

Justin reached for the notebook. "Did you do your homework?"

Gary didn't relinquish it. "Yeah… but not right away," he admitted sheepishly. "I had to take a nap."

Waggling a chiding finger at Gary, Justin swiped the notebook and whapped him in the arm with it. He flipped through the 30-plus filled pages. "My goodness, you don't even shut up on paper."

He handed it back.

"Will you read it for me? It's part of the process. Writing is one thing; but to speak the words aloud gives them a whole new dimension. Validates them. Makes them almost more *real*."

Gary had never intended for these words to be spoken aloud; he thought he had spilled out his feelings in the silent safety of the notebook's pages.

***

All the next week, Michaela's days were filled with work, fretting over Gary… and increasingly fond thoughts of Greg. They spent evenings together: dinner at her place Monday; Wong Lee's takeout and *Casablanca* at his house on Tuesday; skiing and hot cocoa in Woodbury on Wednesday; and dinner and a second-run show at the Bantam Cinema on Thursday. Friday, they hopped a train to New York. Last July, Greg had given Kim tickets to *Cats* for her birthday; it'd be a shame to let them go to waste, he reasoned.

They held hands throughout the show, then they stopped for cappuccino and biscotti. When Greg kissed a smidgen of frothed milk from a corner of her mouth, Micki twittered like a schoolgirl.

They strolled the city streets, hand in hand; then caught a taxi back to the hotel. By the time the cabbie dropped them off, Greg and Michaela could scarcely keep their hands to themselves.

While she showered, he called room service. Two bacon cheeseburgers and champagne showed up as she emerged in a cloud of steam and a Waldorf-Astoria robe. Greeting her in a matching robe, Greg kissed her.

After they devoured the burgers and giddily toasted everything from the view to the cozy robes to the king-size bed, Greg nudged aside Michaela's robe and kissed a meandering line down to the valley between her breasts. She undid the knot at her waist; the robe slid to the floor.

Tracing a path to her navel with his lips and tongue, he put his mouth to her belly. "Hello in there!"

Ticklish, Michaela giggled, pulling him to her breast. Her nimble fingers untied his robe and cast it off. They clambered onto the bed, naked and unashamed. Greg kissed his way up and down her body. She quivered with anticipation.

His erection throbbed. Greg clamped his mouth onto Michaela's breast, sucking first at one rock-hard nipple then the other. At last, opening her legs wide, he penetrated her deeply and energetically.

He was bigger than Gary, she noticed immediately. Groaning with pleasure as he filled her, Micki raked his back with her nails, crying out as he sent her into a pulsing orgasm.

In the morning, she awakened Greg by taking advantage of his morning hard-on. Pulling back the covers, she slipped him inside her. Rocking atop him, Micki pressed her breasts against his bare chest. He opened his eyes and saw her blue eyes looking back.

After bagels and lox at Roxie's Broadway Deli, they wandered through the local art galleries. Then they caught an early train back and went home to their separate houses and empty beds.

***

"I've got warm scones from the bakery. How 'bout you bring the OJ and we do the *Times* crossword?"

Michaela's insides fluttered. "Mmm. Sounds wonderful. I'll be right over."

Greeting her 20 minutes later with a kiss that promised more than breakfast, Greg herded Micki into the living room. A napkin-draped basket sat by the coffeepot, near a bowl of whipped cream. On the table sat a crystal vase full of tulips, and the *Times*, folded out to the crossword puzzle. Throw pillows surrounded the table; a fire crackled in the hearth.

"If I didn't know better, Greg, I'd say you were trying to seduce me."

He kissed her. "Anything's possible."

While she poured juice, he settled beside her and poured coffee; Greg spooned in a dollop of cream, then deliberately left a dab at the tip of her nose. "Oops!"

Michaela was about to wipe it off when he leaned in to kiss it away. Leaning against the couch, he patted his leg. "C'mere."

She sat, resting her arms against Greg's muscular thighs; they worked the puzzle in cozy silence.

"Mmm. These smell like heaven," Michaela murmured at last, lifting the napkin that covered the scones.

"Cream for your scone, madam?"

"What do you think?"

"You definitely need cream. I think you need some here." Greg dropped a soft drift onto her scone. "Here" – smearing a bit on her right cheek – "and here." He touched the spoon to her lips, then licked the cream off her cheek.

Micki's mouth met his hungrily; she quivered and burned at his touch. Running her hands through his hair, she kissed him… softly at first, then urgently.

"Anything else you can think of that needs cream?"

Cheeks flushed, Micki undid her shirt; she shivered as Greg daubed the chilled cream onto her breasts. She arched her back as he licked it off. "Good?" she asked in a breathless sigh.

"Mmm," he responded, amid a mouthful of breast. "Tasty."

"Save some for me. I'm sure there are some bits on you that'll taste nummy with cream." She undid his bathrobe, pushed it open. Smearing the cream on his nipples, Michaela descended on them. Then she snapped the elastic waistband of his boxers. "Bet I can find something else to amuse me."

"Think so, eh?" He reclaimed the spoon and anointed her breasts again.

Licking her lips in anticipation, she wrestled with Greg to free him of his shorts. Her efforts were rewarded with his formidable hard-on. "I *told* you there was something else to play with." Taking back the spoon, she plunged it into the bowl. Slathering cream over him, she pushed him against the pillows and proceeded to lick it off slowly, tormenting him.

Greg helped Micki out of her jeans, laid her down and entered her. Waves of pleasure swept through her as he brought her swiftly and skillfully to orgasm.

Afterward, she rested in his arms. He kissed her shoulder. "I think your coffee's cold."

Wrinkling her nose, Micki smiled. "Must've been that cream."

They drowsed in each other's arms.

They awakened after 2, chilled and sticky. After scurrying to the bathroom for a shower, they tumbled into bed to make love again.

After their second nap, Greg called a little Italian deli around the corner. He paid the delivery boy and returned to bed.

As they feasted on meatball and eggplant grinders, he told Micki about his brother-in-law, a divorce lawyer. "I'm sure he could help you out… if you're ready to make a move."

His words nauseated her. Or was it the eggplant? She dashed from the bed.

Greg stood at the bathroom door. "Are you okay?"

Micki looked up, wishing it was Gary. *It's _his_ baby making me puke; it should be _him_ asking me that.* Wiping her mouth with a wad of toilet paper, she hunched over the toilet bowl; her throat burned.

"Can I get you anything?" he asked solicitously.

*Go away. Just please go away. I don't want you. I want Gary.* She lifted her head. "Ginger ale?"

"I'll see if we have any."

*Thought he'd never leave.* Her head drooped. *It's so comfortable here – so cool… so cool.*

Greg returned with the golden liquid. Micki sipped it, then held the glass to her forehead, her cheeks.

"Ohh," she moaned, grateful for its coolness against her flushed skin. She wobbled back to bed and lay down, as far from Greg's side of the bed as she could get. She fell asleep. If she dreamed, she didn't recall.


(25 February – Monday)

Gary stepped onto the back porch. High tide. The shore was shrouded in a fog that looked as dismal as he felt. It was three weeks since Michaela threw him out; he'd never felt so miserable.

He called in sick and crawled back into bed. Burrowing under the covers, he wondered how he had made such a mess of his life. Married scarcely six months, he was hurtling toward divorce. He'd had everything. And now, because of one lousy decision, it'd all been stripped away. Well, all that *mattered.* He had a career he loved, a terrific old Victorian home and, after more years than he cared to think about, a solid relationship with his mom. But none of that mattered. His wife, whom he adored, was gone. Maybe forever; and it was all his fault. His heart cried out for Michaela. He longed to see her face, hear her voice, feel the smoothness of her cheek beneath his fingers and inhale the scent that was hers alone. He wanted to go home. For all the comfort the cottage ever offered, now he hated the lonely hours, rooms filled only with memories and longing. Mostly, Gary hated himself for how he'd betrayed his wife. *Michaela.* Her name was a sigh on his lips.

***

Michaela awakened late. She dressed, feeling wicked: a married woman leaving another man's home at noon – in the same clothes she'd arrived in the day before. Greg had scrawled a note on the kitchen memo board: "Wong Lee's 2nite at 7? Call me. Love you. G."

Guilt gnawed at Michaela, but her feelings were too strong to ignore. Or deny. *I'm falling in love with him,* she admitted hesitantly, as if trying it on for size. But what to do about Gary? *I want a divorce.*

She rolled the words around in her mouth, tried saying them aloud. They wouldn't come out. She forced them. Still no good. *I don't want a divorce,* Michaela realized as wind-driven snow flew into her windshield. *I still love him.*

***

Around 1, Gary dragged himself out of bed and called back to say he was coming in to work after all. He couldn't withdraw from life. New Music Monday nearly killed him. It took all his patience to answer the request lines.

After work, he stopped at Wong Lee's for takeout.

"Ahh, Meester Gary! Meeses Gary is here already with the other gentleman," the owner greeted him.

He feigned enthusiasm. "Oh, good. I was afraid I was early."

In the back room, he spotted the booth beneath the rose painting. Blood froze in his veins. Sickened, he watched them laughing and chatting cozily. *Like we used to.* When Greg kissed Micki's hand, Gary fought the urge to strangle him.

"Well now." He choked back the shattered remains of his heart. "Isn't this cozy?"

Michaela pulled her hand back. "Gary! What're you doing here?"

"I could ask you the same thing," he replied icily. "But I can see you're on a date."

Greg raised a hand in protest. "Gary, it's not what it looks like."

"Please, don't you start!" Gary scowled. "One self-righteous, holier-than-thou liar is all I can stand."

"I think you'd better leave," Michaela warned indignantly. Her cheeks flushed.

"You're right. Three's a crowd." He turned to go, then said, intentionally loudly: "She's pretty hot in the sack, especially after the mu shu. 'Course, you gotta get her drunk first. Guess I don't have to tell you that."

Reaching for his wife's glass, he swirled the wine, took a swig, then dashed the rest over her.

Michaela gasped, her face as red as the spill.

He banged the glass onto the table, watching in evil amusement as the claret liquid cascaded down the front of his wife's ivory sweater.

Standing to confront him, Greg clenched a fist. "The lady said to get lost!"

"She's no lady; she's a whore," Gary jeered.

Greg's fist shot out, striking him squarely on the jaw.

Gary put a hand to his face. "You'll regret that," he promised darkly.

Micki scrambled to her feet, trying to sop up the wine with her napkin. "I hate you," she yelled, flinging a spoon at her husband's head. It missed and struck the wall.

"Meester Gary – aren't you staying?"

"I'm afraid not," he replied tersely. "I've lost my appetite."

In her fury and humiliation, Michaela's memories of her love for Gary scattered. "What'd you say your brother-in-law's name was?"

She couldn't help noticing a trace of a victorious smile on Greg's face.

He pulled an ecru business card from his pocket. "Your initial consultation's free."

*Robert W. Goodley, Attorney At Law.* Slipping it into her purse, Micki felt like more of a failure than ever.


Gary couldn't tell whether it was emptiness, fury or hunger gnawing at him; he didn't care. He just knew he hurt worse than before, and he couldn't make it go away. "Bastard!" he growled, rubbing his throbbing jaw. "It better not be broken!"

Preoccupied with images of Micki and Greg, he screeched onto Route 8. Gary didn't notice the cruiser until its flashing lights in his rearview mirror caught his attention. Cursing, he pulled over. He'd never been stopped for speeding, never even had a parking ticket.

But now he'd just been clocked at 83 mph; that meant a hefty fine, along with a gruff lecture from the cocky young 'statey' who reminded him far too much of that shithead who was banging his wife. Half an hour later, he tucked the $378 ticket into the visor and pulled back into traffic.

He stopped at Angie's Pizza Barn for a couple slices with mushroom and sausage and a beer; then another beer. And another. He hit the local watering hole for something stronger, something to blot out the image of his wife with Greg. *Good thing I'm only a few blocks from home,* he told himself fuzzily at closing time.

Their run-in with Gary left Michaela anything but amorous. At her insistence, Greg drove her home. In the family room, she took their wedding photo from the entertainment center. She and Gary gazed dreamily into each other's eyes. *What happened to that love?*

Sighing, she put it back. She lifted another wedding photo from the mantel; within its lead-crystal frame, she and Gary had their arms around Greg and Kim. *How happy we all look!* Her hand shook as she reached to replace it; misjudging the edge, she dropped the frame. Jagged crystal shards flew everywhere.

Micki fell to her knees, lamenting the broken frame, her broken marriage and the broken lives of everyone in the picture. Studying the ruined photo, her eyes kept getting drawn to Greg and, guiltily, to Kim. *Who could have predicted that three days later, one of these four people would be dead? And six months later, the others' lives would be turned upside-down?* "I'm sorry, Kim," she heard herself say. "I'm so sorry."

That night, Gary heard a little voice. "Daddy."

Looking around, he saw no one.

A miniature fist gripped his finger. "Daddy," the voice called again. "Please come home. I love you."

Startled awake, his breathing was rapid and shallow. Emptiness tore at him. He checked the time: 3:37. Drawn inexplicably to the study, Gary sat in Grandpa's chair. Moonlight streamed through the wooden-slat blinds. Shivering, he drew a quilt around himself.

They'd sat here and talked every night the year they renovated this place, and after he told him Ellen aborted the baby. Grandpa's words soothed him now. *If there's anything in your life that needs fixing, best to do that.*

"Yeah, but *how?*" he asked desperately. "How do I fix *this?* I'm afraid it's too late."

Gary could almost see smoke rising as Grandpa waved his pipe around. Echoes of long-ago advice filled his head. *It's never too late if the love is real. And when you screw up — and you will, because we all do — be man enough to admit it and do whatever it takes to fix it.*

Gary blinked back tears. "I've tried, Grandpa. But she threw me out… and now she's—"

*I didn't say it'd be easy,* his voice interrupted gently. *But if you still love her — and I know you do — make amends. If not for you or Michaela, then for your unborn baby.*

A sudden chill shot through Gary. His eyes flew open; his nose twitched. He was *sure* he'd caught a whiff of cherry tobacco. He cast about the room, looking for Grandpa. But he was dismally alone. Gary returned upstairs, his heart aching with desolation.

"I miss you so much," he whispered to the lonely darkness. "I wanna come home."

Nothing whispered back. Tears slid down his cheeks and soaked his pillow. At last, tortured sleep won.

With that sleep came unsettling dreams of Michaela and Greg: her laughing, clinging to Greg's arm. *I want a divorce.*

Greg's evil leer. *You were right about that mu shu.*

And another dream — a dream of a tiny fist gripping his finger. "Mama's crying, Daddy. Please come home."

This time, he was prepared with a reply: "Your mama's cheating, baby. How do I know you're mine?"

"You don't have to. I know you're mine. Please, Daddy, I love you. Please come home."

In the morning, Gary inspected his jaw in the bathroom. It was a dreadful shade of purple. He could forget about shaving. Just *thinking* about touching it hurt. Tuesday. He had a ton of work. But he called in sick and spent the day sulking. Walking the beach, Gary fingered the onyx rosary in his pocket; but his prayers were empty today and offered no comfort. He got in his car and drove, ending up at a dealership on Route 1. He left there with a receipt in hand. For a brand-new BMW. Bright, screaming red.

The dealer had plenty of cars left over from Presidents' Day — including the convertible he wanted.

"Good. I hate waiting." He wrote a check for payment in full and said he'd pick it up the next day.

***

"Something smells wonderful," Micki enthused, heading toward the kitchen.

"Roast pork with apples, onions and sage; roasted asparagus, sweet potatoes and braised fennel."

"Mmm," she purred. "Where'd you learn to cook like this?"

"Kim was studying to be a chef," he replied wistfully. "I learned from the best." He nuzzled her neck. "Mmm… forget dinner. Think I'll snack on you instead."

Shoving her mittens into her pockets, Michaela unbuttoned her coat. When he slid the navy-blue overcoat off her shoulders, Greg realized his lover was wearing only a negligee.

"I brought the appetizers," she announced, kissing his throat.

"My favorite kind. Oh, what a thoughtful guest!" Cupping her breasts, he kissed her nipples through the lacy material. "Dinner'll be ready in half an hour. Any ideas how to amuse ourselves 'til then?" He led her to the bedroom.

Too soon, the timer summoned them. Wearing one of his white oxford shirts, Micki finished setting the table while Greg lit candles and sliced the roast.

"So, did you call Rob?" he asked during dinner.

"Not yet." She didn't tell him she was having second thoughts.

Afterward, they retired to the bedroom. Micki stretched across the bed. Greg's mouth meandered over her body. "And now, for dessert…" He explored and kissed every freckle and birth mark.

"Mmm," Michaela purred, running her fingers through his hair. "Gary, that feels so good…"

He flinched but kept kissing. "I think I saw a freckle somewhere near here." Licking his lips, he coaxed her knees apart. "Ah, here it is. Here… and here… and I think there's another one right… about…"

Twining her fingers in his hair, she moaned aloud. "Ohh, Gary!" Thunderstruck, she gasped. Her eyes flew open. "Oh, my God!"

Stroking her thigh, Greg shrugged, unconcerned. "So you called me by his name. No harm done."

Recoiling, Micki wrapped the sheet around herself. "No, Greg — there *is* harm done! This is *wrong*! I shouldn't be here — we shouldn't be doing this."

Caressing her arm, he told her it wasn't all that bad. "We're just helping each other through a rough time."

"No! It's way more than that. I threw Gary out for less than this. He stumbled – once! We're having an affair. We're *involved*, Greg. And it's *wrong*!"

"Look, you can't say you didn't need me as much as I needed you."

"It started innocently. But Greg, it got way out of hand." Micki pulled on her negligee. "I have to go."

"Please don't. I haven't felt this complete in months…"

Ashamed, she shook her head as she slid into her coat. "Don't say that. Goodbye, Greg."

Averting her eyes, Michaela pulled the door shut behind her.

***

Gary called Lucy Desmond the next morning to schedule an appointment.

Promptly at 10 on Thursday, Deacon Andrews saw Gary into his office and shut the door.

"Can I get you some coffee?" He motioned toward a chair.

Gary ignored it. "Spare me the cozy shit, Deacon. I want you transferred."

Greg's knees threatened to give way; he sat. "I really don't think that's necessary."

"*I* don't care *what* you think!"

"It's *over*, Gary. Michaela broke it off. I *swear* to you, this won't be a problem."

"It's already a problem. You've trashed my marriage and I want you out of here."

"No, Gary. *You* trashed your marriage! I was helping Michaela pick up the bits of her heart."

Gary clenched his teeth; his jaw still throbbed. "I want you out, Greg. I'll go to the archbishop if I have to."

Panic filled Greg's eyes. "Please, don't do that. We can resolve this quietly, between us. C'mon, Gary, I *work* here. If this gets out, I don't just get transferred; I'm out of a *job*."

"You should've thought of that before you fucked my wife."

"*Please*, Gary… we're talking about my *livelihood* here! Isn't there some way we can wor—?"

Gary slammed his fist down on the desk. "*No!* I don't want any reminders of you in our lives." Yanking the door open, he issued a final warning. "If I were you, I'd start packing."

(7 March – Thursday)

Gathering her courage, Michaela called Fr. Williams; she said she and Gary were on the verge of divorce and asked for his help. "I'm afraid if we go it alone, we'll break up for good."

Saturday morning, the pastor waited until the students left, then tapped at the door. "Can we talk?"

Gary looked up. "Sure, Father. C'mon in." He carried a stack of bibles to the bookcase; kneeling, he slid them in. "I'm listening; I just want to get these put away."

Fr. Williams asked him to sit. "Please. It's important."

Gary sat, figuring it had to do with the CCD curriculum, or the impending DRE vacancy.

"Michaela told me you two are having" – he gestured vaguely – "problems. She asked me to intervene."

Abruptly Gary stood, grabbing the remaining bibles. He shook his head. "You're wasting your time, Father."

"I don't think saving a marriage is ever a waste of time." Their eyes met with a fierceness the priest had never seen from Gary.

"Then save someone else's!" Gary shoved the books into place. "My marriage is over."

"Please don't say that, Gary. I can tell you're hurt, and angry; but I know how much Michaela means to you. And I know how much your marriage means to you. To *both* of you."

"Yeah?" he scoffed. "Last time I saw her – out with her lover – it didn't seem that way."

"It does. Otherwise, why would she have asked for help? Don't let it die here. Not without trying to fix it."

Before he could protest, Fr. Dave suggested a meeting at the rectory.

*Do whatever it takes to fix it,* Gary heard his grandfather's voice say.


(7:15 p.m., 11 March – Monday)

"Thank you for coming, Gary. C'mon in."

Fr. Dave led him to a parlor at the end of the hall.

Gary saw Michaela seated on one couch. His throat constricted; he couldn't face her – not after what he'd done with Ellen. And certainly not after what she'd done with Greg. "I can't do this." He trembled with shame and fury.

The pastor laid a steadying hand on Gary's arm. "Yes, you can. Please. Come in and sit down."

He faced his wife for the first time in what felt like ages. They sat on different couches, a coffee table separating them.

Gary had last seen Michaela two weeks earlier. He ached to hold her, but he steamrollered over his tender feelings with animosity.

Fr. Dave sat to one side, struggling in the angry silence to find words to open a dialogue between the troubled pair.

Gary's calm tone defied his fury. "Is this how you decided to punish me? Sleeping with Greg?"

Ashamed at his having named her offense aloud, she averted her eyes. "I'm sorry."

He eyed her with loathing. "What – sorry you got caught?"

Not wanting to escalate hostilities further, Micki ignored the bait he dangled. "No, Gary," she said, filled with anguish and remorse. "I'm sorry I cheated on you."

Gary stared Michaela down, his anger boiling over. "Why should I accept your apology? I begged you to forgive me. I *begged* you! But you went and changed the locks on the house *that I pay for!*"

His thunderous voice filled the room. He leapt to his feet, pointing across the divide, intimidating Micki. "Is *that* how you want it? 'Cause – God damn it! – if it is, lady, I can do a whole lot better than that!"

The priest motioned for him to sit. Ignoring him, Gary loomed over his wife, fists clenching.

"Gary, please… let's don't do this," she begged, starting to cry. "Please. We both hurt each other. Badly. And we both know what we did was wrong. So how do we get past this?"

Still fuming, Gary folded his arms. "I don't know if I even want to." It was a lie. That was all he wanted!

"Can't we at least *try?*" Michaela beseeched, salty rivers pouring down her cheeks. A paralyzing ache surged through her. Crumpling forward, she jammed the heel of a hand against her mouth to stifle her sobs.

Gary ached. Here was the woman he loved most in the world – whom he promised to love and care for forever – hurting. Begging for help. His help. And his forgiveness.

Taking a deep breath, he released it slowly. With that exhale, all his venom, all his rage, drained away.

Michaela swiped at her tears. Her voice quavered. "Please, Gary? I love you so much… Please?"

After an agonizing silence, he stepped around the table, crossing to the other couch.

Trying not to let on how frightened she was, Michaela wondered what he would do next. His own eyes misting, and Justin's words about speaking tenderly to those closest to us pressing on his heart, Gary sat beside his wife.

He took her hand and looked into her eyes. "We got a long road ahead, baby; if we're gonna make it, we've got to do it together." Hot tears coursed down his cheeks as he lifted her hand to his lips.

Trembling, she embraced him for the first time in nearly two months. When they parted, both their faces streamed with tears.

Michaela turned to the pastor, who still hadn't spoken, and said there was something she needed to confess; she asked if he would hear her confession.

"Of course," he replied gently. "But, before you seek the Lord's pardon, perhaps you'll want to ask each other's forgiveness. Take whatever time you need. I'll be in my office; come in when you're ready."

When the door latched, Michaela wept. "Ohh, Gary…" She touched his face, as if to ensure he was really there. "I never meant for any of this to happen. I'm so ashamed. I felt hurt and I wanted revenge. I know how childish that was, and how much I hurt you — and our marriage. I'm so sorry! Gary, I love you so much; please forgive me. And please come home… it's so lonely without you."

Gary framed her face, kissing away her tears. Hurt twanged at his heart; he knew no healing could take place unless he forgave her, and accepted her pardon for his own wrongs. "I forgive you, Michaela," he whispered. The bands around his chest loosened; he could breathe again. He gazed into her watery eyes. Eyes bright with tears, he took her hands. "I know what I did was wrong. What I did, I did to both of us. I didn't think about how it would hurt you. And I've regretted it *every minute.*"

He touched Michaela's face, wanting desperately to dispel his wife's anguish. "It hurts, *so much*, knowing I caused you such terrible pain. I'm sorry I humiliated you in public. I'm so sorry, Micki. You're my world. I just want you to forgive me and let me come home. I miss you so much! Please forgive me."

Drawing him close, Micki murmured the words she longed to say as much as he ached to hear them: "I forgive you, Gary."

In turn, they confessed their infidelities to their pastor.

Even after confessing to Justin, Gary hadn't felt forgiven; if anything, he felt more heavily laden with guilt. When Fr. Dave gave him his penance, he shook his head. "It hardly seems like… *enough.* Isn't there something more you can…?" His voice trailed away.

The priest smiled. In his 22 years as a priest, he'd never had any-one request a stricter penance. "It isn't meant to be a punishment. It's more of a" – he sought words to touch Gary's heart – "gesture to show a desire to heal your relationship. When you and Michaela argue, maybe the next day you'll get her flowers, or she'll cook your favorite meal. You've made up, but you take extra steps to show you want to put things right."

Fr. Dave absolved Gary, then added words of comfort. "God doesn't want to punish us. He wants to forgive our sins. No matter what they are – or how awful we feel about them. Okay?"

Amid a rising swell of emotion, Gary could only nod.

"Go on back to Michaela; I'll be along soon. There's something I want to talk to you both about."

Back in the parlor, he said, "I'd like you to start praying together, regularly. Decide whether that's three times a week, twice a day or something in between. Find what works for you. But make that commitment to yourselves and your marriage. Will you do that?"

They agreed.

"Good. One other thing: I'd like you to renew your marriage vows. Right now." He smiled. "To give you kind of a fresh start."

Michaela's eyes shimmered with tears. "What a wonderful idea. Thank you, Father."

After they restated their vows, Fr. Williams pronounced a new blessing on the Sheldons' union. They left his office with their arms around each other, and their vows and their commitment intact.


At home, Gary laid a hand on Michaela's arm. "C'mere. I just want to hold you. I've missed you so much."

A cry caught in her throat. "I missed you, too, Gary. I'm so sor-ry," she whispered hoarsely.

He took her face in his hands. "Let's put this behind us and move forward. Okay?"

Micki sniffled and nodded. Settling into his arms, she savored the comfort of his embrace.

"Can I ask you something?" he asked. She looked up at him and nodded. "When's our baby due?"

Michaela's hand went immediately to her tummy. "How did you know?"

Gary placed his hand over hers and kissed her. "I dreamed about her."

"Her?"

"Her." Smiling, he held her close again.

Her eyes welled with tears. "I'm sorry… I should've told you."

"I know now; that's what matters. So, when're you due?"

"October second." She searched his face. "Are you happy?"

"You're carrying our baby; how could I be anything else?"

A queasy flutter twitched at her stomach. "Gary, there's, um — something I need to tell you."

The anxiety in her eyes worried him. "What is it?" He sat her down on the couch.

"I don't know how to say this." She put a hand to her mouth, struggled to stop shaking. "I never said anything before 'cause I was afraid you would leave me."

Gary tensed. "It's okay, honey. Whatever it is, we'll work it out."

The gentleness of his words nudged away her worry; Michaela decided to trust him. About to speak, a cry caught her off guard.

"I'm so sorry," she wailed. "I thought I could put it behind me and forget. But I can't. It hurts, Gary – it hurts so much!"

He held her close and tried to quell her tears. "It's okay, Micki. Whatever it is, it'll be okay. Tell me what happened."

"I'm a horrible person. And I'm going to hell! Because I—" she broke off, sobbing again. At last, summoning her courage, Michaela confessed the terrible secret she'd hidden for nearly three years.

Gary didn't mean to gape. "Wh-what?" he stammered.

Words tumbled like an avalanche from her lips. "I was afraid to tell you, 'cause I know how upset you were when El—" Michaela stopped. "I knew you'd be angry, but I had no choice! I couldn't have that baby. I know it was wrong; and I'm sorry. But I couldn't do it." She saw tears in his eyes. "I thought it'd be easy, ya know? Go to the clinic, get it done and go on with my life. I tried so hard to forget. But I can't. I keep hearing her calling at night, *Mommy, Mommy.* I can't make it stop!" Desperate, Michaela reached for him. "You hate me, don't you?" she moaned, searching Gary's face for the truth — and terrified of finding it.

"I don't hate you," he soothed, his embrace tender. "And you're not going to hell." He helped her to her feet. "C'mon."

"Where're we going?"

"Back to see Father Dave."

Michaela pulled back, her eyes filled with panic. She shook her head. "But, Gary, it's late—"

Gary put a finger to her lips. "I'll call him. It'll be alright, honey. I'm sure he'll understand."

When he learned it was urgent, the priest insisted they come right away. It was after 9:30 when their pastor greeted them again. Gary waited in the parlor while Micki went with the priest into his office.

"Sorry to bother you again, Father – and so late, too. But there's something else I need to confess."

He invited her to sit. Drawing a chair close, he donned his stole.

With trembling fingers, she made the sign of the cross. For the longest time, Michaela felt as though she couldn't cry hard enough. Her chest ached; her eyes stung; her mouth felt dry.

Fr. Dave got her a glass of water; she drank it amid choking sobs, wiped her tears and cried some more.

Weighed down with guilt and shame at the hideousness of her sin, she couldn't meet the priest's gaze. Finally, she'd spent most of her tears. And half of his box of tissues.

Haltingly, Michaela told him about her abortion, sobbing as she explained how awful it felt to carry that guilt. "I knew what I was doing was wrong, but I didn't see any other way out. I just couldn't have that baby. I'm so sorry, Father! I know it's one of the Big Ten," she added. "I'm not doin' so hot, huh? I'm only twenty-three and I've already knocked off two of 'em. And I made it worse by still going to Communion all this time, huh?" She sighed heavily. "Father, I feel like I'm on the express bus to hell!"

The priest weighed the gravity of Michaela's offense against the depth of her remorse. "No sin is too awful," he reassured her. "If you seek God with a repentant heart, He'll forgive you anything."

"Even this?"

He took her hands. "Even this, Michaela. Believe me when I tell you: There is great rejoicing in heaven. God has been wanting to forgive you, but He had to wait until you were ready to ask. He knows how sorry you are, and what a painful decision it must have been. He's waiting to embrace you with His forgiveness and infinite love. Are you ready to accept God's forgiving grace?"

Michaela dabbed at her eyes and nodded, sniffling. "I think so, Father. But how do I forgive *myself*?"

"That's a toughie," Fr. Dave admitted. "We're always hardest on ourselves. But once you accept that God has forgiven you, you'll begin to heal. I'm glad you came back, Michaela. Is there anything else you can think of that you need to confess?"

Michaela sniffled. "There is one thing: It's kinda about work. I counsel pregnant rape victims about their… options. Including abortion." She wiped away her tears. "And now that I'm pregnant again, well – I mean, *I* wouldn't do it again, so why would I advise someone else to do it?"

Fr. Dave shook his head. "You can't. If that's part of your job, you have to leave."

"But this is what I *do*. I counsel women who've been through trauma."

"Do you have to work *there*?" A trace of a smile lit his face.

Michaela wondered why. "What're you suggesting?"

"We can discuss that later. Is there anything else you need to confess?"

She shook her head.

"Okay. For your penance: Tomorrow and the next two days" – his gentle tone erased her fears – "I want you to say a little prayer, just from your heart, thanking God for forgiving you. Can you do that for me?"

She nodded, both surprised and relieved her penance for such a horrid offense was so light. "Yes," she replied quietly. "Thank you, Father."

Fr. Dave laid his hands on Michaela's bowed head; offering her absolution, he embraced her. "Go in the peace of Christ, Michaela. Your sins are forgiven." Then he said, "Come see me tomorrow; I may be able to help you out."

Back at home, Michaela wanted to discuss leaving her job with Gary; but more than that, she desperately wanted him to take her upstairs and make love to her.

Next morning, Micki gave her notice at the crisis center. "I feel bad leaving," she told Lisa, "but encouraging abortion goes against everything I believe. I know how much it messed me up."

That afternoon, Fr. Dave told her about a new post-abortive outreach ministry. "You can help women heal, help them through their trauma and beyond the guilt. If you'd like, I'll give you the director's name."

Michaela could scarcely hear her voice over the pounding of her heart. "That sounds like something I could do – and take pride in."

When she left his office, she was smiling. And there was a look of peace about her.

# *Chapter 36*

(31 March – Sunday – Easter)

Michaela and Gary met her father for breakfast after sunrise Mass; they were due at Gary's mom's house at 1.

By 3, Micki had begun feeling a strange gurgling and twitching. When the cramps started, she slipped into the bathroom.

Her panicked cries brought Gary running. He did his best to calm her as he settled her on the couch.

Back in the kitchen, his face lined with worry, he explained, "She's bleeding."

Diane sent him to the quiet of her bedroom to call Michaela's obstetrician. The on-call doctor told him Micki would be fine, but suggested she take it easy.

Apologizing for their abrupt departure, Gary told Mom he'd feel better with Micki resting at home.

Diane patted his cheek. "Oh hush, sweetheart. You look after your family." *You'll make a terrific dad.*

Joey begged off as Gary told him to get his things. "You don't need me getting in the way."

"Don't be silly," Michaela insisted. "I'm fine. C'mon, I've looked forward to your visit all week."

"Are you sure it won't be too much trouble, having him under-foot?" Mom fretted.

"What trouble? I'm putting him to work! The nursery's gotta be painted; the garage has to be cleared out; and the driveway needs to be paved. *Someone's* gotta help Micki do all that," Gary teased. "You can have him back for his birthday."

"Oh, keep him. I kinda like the quiet. Besides, I've already rented out his room."

Gary laughed. "You don't waste any time, do you?"

Diane hugged her older son. "Not a moment, my boy. Life's too short."

*Sounds like something Grandpa would have said.* He kissed her on the forehead. "I love you, Mom. And despite what you say, I know you want him back; I'll get him home Wednesday."

Next morning, Gary called to explain why Micki couldn't make it to her interview. The retreat-center director said she would look forward to meeting Michaela when she was better.

"I don't want you taking chances," he told her when he brought her breakfast in bed. "The doctor said to take it easy. And driving around half the morning doesn't sound like taking it easy."

Insisting she felt fine, Michaela was angry that he'd canceled her interview. "You had no right!"

"You're my wife. And this" – Gary laid a hand on her belly – "is our child. Your safety, yours and the baby's, is my responsibility. So, yes, Michaela, I had every right."

Micki hated being fussed over; but she couldn't fault Gary for thinking of their well being. Grateful for his take-charge attitude, even if a smidgen resentful at his bossiness, she snuggled beneath the covers after he cleared away her breakfast tray. *His assertiveness is kinda sexy.* She'd never seen Gary act that way; she rather liked it.

Micki smiled as she drifted off to sleep, both cats purring nearby.

(3 April – Wednesday)

When they returned from bringing Joey home, Micki voiced the question that had troubled her for weeks. "What're you going to do about Erin?"

Gary thought his heart would stop. "I don't know. Why?"

"You haven't said a word about her since—" she broke off.

*Since we got back together,* he finished silently. Steel bands wrapped around his chest.

"I was wondering if you'd decided whether to seek custody."

Tighter and tighter the bands grew. "I've thought about that," he admitted. She'd haunted his thoughts for months. "As much as I want custody, I won't do anything to jeopardize our marriage again. I don't want to risk" – he restarted in another direction – "I know I destroyed any trust you had in me. I regret that so much." He choked up as Michaela's hand squeezed his. "I want to restore that trust. And if letting Erin go is what I need to do to…" He paused to compose himself. "If that's what it takes, I'll do it."

She looked at her husband as if he'd offered to chew off his arm. "What kind of wife would I be if I did that?" She gathered him into her arms. "No, Gary. I *want* you to fight for her."

Pulling away, he shook his head uncertainly. "Even though…?"

Micki put a finger to his lips. "Shh. I know you won't put our love in harm's way." She recognized the shame in his eyes. "And I want you to seek custody. Erin deserves to have you in her life."


(21 June – Friday)

Gary was half an hour into his show when Brenda transferred the urgent call.

"Mr. Sheldon, this is Sandra Whitson from St. Raphael's in New Haven…"

His heart lurched. "I'll be right there." Rushing into Pete's office, he stammered the disturbing news.

"I'll drive you," Pete said. "Just give me a second." He pressed the intercom button. "Brenda? Where's Jeff?" Jeff Dorsey was the new production assistant. Her reply crackled over the intercom.

Pete bolted from the room; ignoring the glowing *Recording* light, he burst into Studio C. "Sorry to interrupt, Jeff, but I need you on the air – pronto. Gary's gotta leave," he said, giving Jeff the only explanation he'd get now.

Jeff gathered his things. In the on-air studio, he played the three commercials on the program log and then read the weather. "Yeah, I know: I'm not Gary Sheldon. I'm Jeff Dorsey, sitting in. I think Gary decided it was too nice a day to be indoors."


Michaela had been out with her mother-in-law, looking at baby furniture. They'd spent the morning browsing in department stores and she was beginning to tire. Diane suggested they get something to eat and go home so Michaela could rest.

Partway through lunch, she felt a surge of warm fluid. "Uh-oh," Micki whimpered, pale as the baked scrod on her plate.

Diane summoned the manager, who called for a paramedic.


Gary twirled knobs, poked the radio-preset buttons and adjusted the temperature controls in Pete's Acura the whole way down to the sprawling Chapel Street complex. Anything to keep at bay the fears seeping into his heart. By the time they arrived, Michaela had given birth and the baby was hurried off to Neonatal Intensive

Care. Meanwhile, complications had arisen and Micki was rushed to ICU. The doctors couldn't say why her water had broken at 26 weeks; nor were they certain what caused the 104.3° temperature spike that was making her delirious.

Diane hovered anxiously in the ICU anteroom. When Gary swept in, he raced over to her. Mother and son embraced, sharing worry and support. She tried not to let him see her tears. He did likewise.

Almost immediately, a nurse ushered Gary in. He held Micki's hand and talked to her, though his calm tone was more for his benefit than hers. When her blood pressure plunged and they lost her pulse, they herded him out.

He watched through the glass window as she lay, unconscious, connected to an array of blipping, whirring machines. After what seemed like weeks, one of the doctors stepped back and shook his head. Putting a hand to his mouth, Gary turned away in anguish.

Glancing up a scant instant before Gary turned away, and seeing the fear in his eyes, Amanda Petersen, one of Michaela's nurses, came out to talk to him. "It's not as bad as it looks, Mr. Sheldon," she assured Gary, steering him away from the window. "At the moment, she's comatose; but that's not necessarily bad. They're trying to stabilize her."

"What about the baby?" His voice was a strangled whisper.

"She's in NICU – Neonatal ICU. I'll take you to her." Amanda led him to a bank of elevators. "Just so you're prepared: She's tiny – less than two pounds – and only about thirteen inches long." She held her hands about an album-cover's width apart.

Fear ground Gary to a dead stop. "Is she gonna live?"

Her warm brown eyes met his frightened grey ones. "They're doing everything they can." She hoped she sounded sufficiently reassuring. "It's still too soon to say, but they're optimistic."

In the NICU, she introduced Gary to the head nurse, Lori Ann Staley. "Mom's in ICU," Amanda told her quietly. "And 'til she's stabilized, it might be best to keep Dad here."

Lori Ann tried to explain what they were doing for the baby, the extent of her development and the seriousness of her condition.

"Is she gonna live?" Gary asked, too numb to take in any of the information she'd offered.

"We're very hopeful," she replied, as upbeat as possible. "Even preemies this small have a good survival rate here. I'm optimistic."

"Would you be this optimistic if she was your baby?" he asked, neither convinced nor reassured.

"Every bit." She met his gaze. "My daughter *was* here. Now, she was a little farther along than yours, but it was six years ago." The nurse laid a comforting hand on his arm. "Our team is excellent, Mr. Sheldon; and we have one of the best NICUs in the state."

"Can I see her?"

Lori Ann brought him to a little room with a huge window and lots of machines: heart monitors, IVs, oxygen pumps, a respirator — even a neonatal crash-cart. Amid it all was a clear Lucite incubator.

Inside, hooked to all those machines, a doll-sized baby — his baby — struggled for breath.

Gary blanched. "It looks so… bleak," he moaned in dismay. But as he watched the little girl — surely the tiniest baby he'd ever seen — his heart melted with love. "Can I hold her?" When Lori Ann shook her head, he asked, "Can I at least touch her? Talk to her?"

"Yes; that you can do. But you'll have to wear a mask and gown. And gloves. Okay?"

If she said he had to wear a spacesuit crawling with spiders, he'd have suited up in an instant. Gary nodded in agreement, too overcome even to form the word "yes."

Lori Ann helped him into the protective garb, then opened the door. "I know you'll want to pick her up," she reminded him, "but you can't, because of the IVs and the monitors."

He nodded, shaky. He approached the Isolette, stooping to peer inside; his eyes filled with tears. Gary stared in wonder for a long time, then slipped a hand through an opening in the side of the box. With a trembling finger, he stroked her miniature arm, her tiny cheek. He felt delicate bones beneath her paper-fine skin. The baby turned toward his touch.

"Hey, little girl," he cooed. "I'm your daddy. I love you. Mommy can't come down right now, baby; but she can't wait to see you." Her eyelids fluttered. Pleasant warmth spread through his chest. Gary smiled. A cry caught in his throat. "You know my voice. I knew you would. That's my girl."

He spent a few minutes telling his daughter everything would be fine… and she chose the perfect day to be born: the first day of summer… warm and sunny, the kind of day she would come to appreciate as she grew. It made him feel better to offer something positive. Gary stroked her tiny arm; she turned toward him and his throat just about closed up. "I'm gonna go visit Mommy for awhile, but I'll be back. Meantime, the nurses'll take good care of you – and soon you can come home." He took a sharp breath. "See you later, baby. I love you." Giving her cheek a final caress, he backed away.

"Thank you," he told Lori Ann at the door. He felt less troubled now, more peaceful.

"Come back again," she invited. "Human touch is crucial. Too bad she's hooked up to those monitors. Holding gives the babies such security. Not to mention how it helps the parents!"


"She's beautiful! So tiny and perfect!" Gary told his mom.

Diane hugged him. She tried to get him to go to the cafeteria, but he wouldn't leave Michaela; he even refused the soup his mom brought back. "I don't think I could keep it down."

When visiting hours ended, Gary urged her to go. "No sense both of us pacing. I'll keep you posted." He hugged her. "Now please: Go home and get some rest, huh?"

After she left, he found a payphone.

"What's wrong?" Michael asked, alarmed by Gary's tone.

"The good news is: We can officially call you *Grandpa*."

Michael inundated him with questions. Gary related all he knew about Michaela's condition – and the baby's – and promised to call him when he knew more.


Half past 10. Gary's footsteps echoed in the silent corridor upon his return to ICU. No change. He kept vigil at Micki's side.

About 3, Nurse Petersen checked her vitals. At 6 she brought Gary some hot tea. "You've been here all night, Mr. Sheldon. Go on home and get some rest."

He stifled a yawn. Aching from leaning against the bed's safety bar half the night, he rubbed the back of his neck. Looking at Micki lying motionless, he felt guilty for even considering leaving.

After her shift, Nurse Petersen slipped into the chapel off the ICU; she saw someone kneeling before the crucifix. She recognized the slumped shoulders and the head bent in supplication. Sadness poking at her heart, Amanda slid into the pew beside Gary.

He didn't seem to notice.

The chapel's subdued lights illuminated the tear streaks on his unshaven face. Making the sign of the cross, Amanda murmured a prayer; then laid a hand on his arm. "I thought you'd gone home."

Gary gestured toward ICU. Fresh tears glistened in his eyes. "How could I leave her like that?"

"It could be some time before she's stabilized."

He shook his head. "I've got nothing but time. I'm not going anywhere." Besides, he realized, he had no car; Pete had driven him here.

She took his hands; they were cold. "As long as you're staying, okay if I pray with you?" When Gary nodded, she pulled a rosary from her pocket. Beginning with the Joyful Mysteries, the pair prayed their way through all 15 mysteries. When they finished, she patted his hand. "It's late, Mr. Sheldon. Please, get some rest."

He shook his head, squelched a yawn. "Not unless you do, too. You worked all night and you've been here with me half the morning. When're you back on, anyway?"

*He's stubborn, this young father.* "I work three to eleven today."

"Well then, you better take your own advice: Go to sleep."

Amanda couldn't tell whether he was trying to sound brave or stern. *He's neither. He's just sweet. And worried out of his mind.* "Okay." She pocketed her beads and hugged Gary. "I'll be praying for you. All three of you."

When she returned at 2, Amanda knew Gary had barely budged from his wife's side; he looked wilted. The circles under his eyes told her he hadn't slept. Periodically, he would duck into the chapel to pray or cry; sometimes both.

Late that night, he noticed a tall gentleman in clerical garb kneeling in one of the pews. "Sorry," Gary whispered. "I didn't mean to disturb you." He started to back away.

"Please – you don't need to leave." The man's serene voice was soothing.

Gary's jangled nerves welcomed that. "I – I don't wanna bother you…" he begged off.

"But you're not here to see *me.*" There was a peace about him that Gary envied and craved.

"I uh…" he faltered, then conceded, "Y-you're right."

"Please," the cleric insisted gently. His smile drew Gary in more readily than his hand motion. "I know you're here to talk to *Him*" – he inclined his head toward the crucifix – "but would you like to tell me what's troubling you?"

Something about his offer made Gary want to sit down and talk.

In a hushed and wavering voice, he told the tall priest his wife and preemie daughter were in ICU – and the doctors weren't sure yet how either of them would fare.

"I see. Then it's a good thing I asked you to come and talk; *you're* who I was about to go looking for. They said I would find you in ICU," he explained. "I just stopped in here to pray for you."

"Are you the chaplain?"

His smile melted away the fear that had encrusted Gary's soul the past two days. "Not exactly."

Uncertainty clouded Gary's face. "Well then, what, exactly?"

"I live nearby, and I stop in from time to time."

Still baffled, Gary shook his head. "So if you're not the chaplain, who are you? You're not a figment of my imagination, or an angel or" – fear, exhaustion and irrationality collided – "or a messenger sent to tell me they're gonna die, are you?"

"Ohh, no." He patted Gary's arm soothingly. "No. Nothing like that."

"Then what?" Gary's eyes fell on the man's silver ring, set with a huge garnet. Instinctively, almost fearfully, he backed away. Ten years of Catholic schooling vanished. "You're not just a priest, are you? You're a… a monsignor or – or something, right?"

The tall clergyman smiled gently. "Or something."

The two men sat in a shadow cast by the crucifix and talked for a long time. They discussed Gary's fears of losing both his wife and infant daughter; his hopes for their future; and his faith, which – surprisingly, Gary admitted – had stood firm thus far.

"Often, these rough patches reveal how strong our faith really is," the 'monsignor-or-something' observed. He took Gary's hands and prayed: He prayed for the young husband and father to have the strength of faith to endure this trial, trust in the answer God would provide and hope in the doctors' and nurses' abilities to care for his wife and daughter.

When the tall clergyman left, he took away with him much of Gary's fear.

Sometime later, Nurse Petersen slipped into the chapel to find Gary kneeling before the crucifix; his head was bowed, but his shoulders weren't quite so hunched.

Approaching on quiet feet, she laid a hand on his shoulder. "Mr. Sheldon? I take it Bishop DiCarlo found you?"

Gary's eyes widened. "That was a bishop I was talking to?"

"Yeah. You'd never know it, though. That's what I love about him; he's so easy to talk to."

He pointed over his shoulder. "He said he'd been looking for me; how did he…?"

Amanda held up a hand and wiggled her fingers. "I asked him to come. I hope it's okay. You just seemed like you could use a heavy hitter on your side."

Gary smiled – really smiled – for the first time in days. "You can say that again."

"I'm on my break now; may I pray with you?"

Just under two hours later, Amanda's shift was over – and Gary was back in the chapel. Sobbing. The infant had taken a bad turn; the neonatologist didn't expect her to survive the night.

At that news, Gary had collapsed – as much from exhaustion as from shock and fear. The doctor had to help him to a chair.

After learning Gary hadn't eaten anything in more than a day, a nurse brought him soup, crackers and apple juice, and stood over him while he ate. When he felt steady enough to walk, he returned to the chapel.

Having gone to check on Baby Girl Sheldon, Amanda knew where to find Gary. She slid into the pew beside the grief-stricken dad. He sobbed into her shoulder. "What if she doesn't make it?"

"Don't think about that," Amanda said, holding him close. "Just envision her getting well."

The only image that filled his mind was his newborn daughter hooked to all those machines; in his head he heard the heart monitor flatlining.

Gary tried to tell her about his looming fear, but the words got jumbled up in sobs. His insides hurt from crying, his eyes burned and he was sure he had no tears left. He and Amanda joined hands.

Four hands, clasped in a mixture of desperation and hope – one pair shaking and deeply tanned; the other long-fingered, dark-skinned and graceful – prayed for courage in the face of whatever came next. Two heads, bowed in fervent prayer, petitioned God for miracles. And two voices – one clear, soft and strong, the other wavering and hesitant – pleaded for Divine intervention and some glimmer of hope.

Somewhere in the quiet of the night, their earnest prayers were answered. Just after 3, a NICU nurse entered the chapel. "Looks like she's going to be okay."

Dazed from grief and exhaustion, Gary had to ask her to repeat herself twice before it sank in.

Amanda gripped his hand and whispered, "Praise Jesus! Thank you, Lord!"

Before racing out of the chapel, Gary sank to his knees and uttered a grateful prayer.

When he went to see his baby, he gazed in awe. Her pallid skin tone was replaced by a healthy pinkish tinge.

Gary laughed and cried at the same time. He hugged Amanda; tears of joy and relief streamed down his face.

Hearing the commotion, a doctor came running.

Gary hugged him, too.

Daybreak brought encouraging news from the ICU. Michaela's vital signs had stabilized, her breathing returned to normal and, best of all, she'd regained consciousness.

She blinked as her eyes tried to adjust to the lights. She looked around, confused. "Where am I?" she whispered. "Where's Gary?"

"Right here, baby." He bent down so she could see his face.

"I had the strangest dream," she murmured, reaching to touch her husband's stubbled cheek.

"Tell me." He stooped beside her bed to listen.

"I dreamed you were holding the baby and there was an angel behind you – with her wings folded around you – protecting you both. She had big brown eyes, and the kindest face I've ever seen."

Gary took her hand. "She was no dream," he whispered as his tears landed on his wife's hand. "Her name is Amanda, and she absolutely has been an angel."

Michaela smiled. "Amanda… what a pretty name."

Bishop DiCarlo baptized little Amanda Josephine in the NICU the next afternoon.

Four weeks later, the NICU doctors gave the Sheldons the okay to hold Amanda.

Michaela trembled as she held her baby for the first time. Tears spilled from her eyes. "But she's so early!" she whispered fearfully. "Why'd she come so early?"

Gary dried his wife's tears. "I've got a theory about that, honey: She loved you so much, she just couldn't wait 'til October to meet you." He kissed her on the temple. "And, frankly, who could blame her?"

He had spoken to Amanda from the other side of that incubator for so long – talked to her, stroked her skin, told her stories, prayed with her and for her. It was such a relief, finally, to hold her!

Gary gazed in wonder at the tiny infant in his arms. His arms had done plenty in the last 27 years, he mused; but never had they held something – someone! – so tiny, so delicate.

They'd curled around Grandma's neck in a child's earnest hugs; carried squirming puppies and mewing kittens; thrown and caught baseballs and held Ellen in a lover's clinch. His arms had grown achy, then tan and muscular, during a summer's worth of home renovation; and then hugged literally hundreds of Sunday-school students. They'd lugged groceries in a nasty June downpour; draped over Micki's shoulders on countless walks; protected her when she was afraid. They had encircled his bride as they danced on their wedding day; held Micki through the night as she slept; pulled his wife close in passionate embraces as they made love – creating new life. *This* life. And now… now they cradled his infant daughter.

The wee, wiggling fingers on the baby's perfect hands clutched at the air, and then grasped her father's finger.

In his head he heard, *I love you, Daddy. I'm glad you came home.*

Gary drew the miniature fingers to his lips. "Me too, baby," he whispered back. "Me too."


(2 October – Wednesday)

It was Amanda's due date, but she was already 14 weeks old.

Mommy, Daddy and baby sat on the beach, a blanket wrapped about them, enjoying the waning remnants of a glorious early-autumn day. They cooed over her as they watched the sunset's fiery brilliance. Then suddenly, just above the horizon, emerald light appeared and shot across the sea.

"Was that the green flash?" Micki gasped. "It's beautiful! It's like God winking a gigantic green eye! It's like He's saying, 'It's okay. Everything's fine. I've got it all under control.'"

Slipping an arm around Michaela, Gary kissed her and Amanda. "I was just thinking the same thing."